New Blood

CRITICAL APPROACHES TO CONTEMPORARY HORROR

HORROR STUDIES

Series Editor
Xavier Aldana Reyes, Manchester Metropolitan University

Editorial Board
Stacey Abbott, Roehampton University
Linnie Blake, Manchester Metropolitan University
Harry M. Benshoff, University of North Texas
Fred Botting, Kingston University
Steven Bruhm, Western University
Steffen Hantke, Sogang University
Joan Hawkins, Indiana University
Agnieszka Soltysik Monnet, University of Lausanne
Bernice M. Murphy, Trinity College Dublin
Johnny Walker, Northumbria University

Preface
Horror Studies is the first book series exclusively dedicated to the study of the genre in its various manifestations – from fiction to cinema and television, magazines to comics, and extending to other forms of narrative texts such as video games and music. Horror Studies aims to raise the profile of Horror and to further its academic institutionalisation by providing a pubishing home for cutting-edge research. As an exciting new venture within the established Cultural Studies and Literary Criticism programme, Horror Studies will expand the field in innovative and student-friendly ways.

CRITICAL APPROACHES TO CONTEMPORARY HORROR

EDITED BY EDDIE FALVEY, JOE HICKINBOTTOM
AND JONATHAN WROOT

UNIVERSITY OF WALES PRESS
2020

© The Contributors, 2020
Reprinted 2024

All rights reserved. No part of this book may be reproduced in any material form (including photocopying or storing it in any medium by electronic means and whether or not transiently or incidentally to some other use of this publication) without the written permission of the copyright owner except in accordance with the provisions of the Copyright, Designs and Patents Act. Applications for the copyright owner's written permission to reproduce any part of this publication should be addressed to the University of Wales Press, University Registry, King Edward VII Avenue, Cardiff, CF10 3NS.

www.uwp.co.uk

British Library Cataloguing-in-Publication Data

A catalogue record for this book is available from the British Library.

ISBN   978-1-78683-634-2
eISBN 978-1-78683-635-9

The rights of The Contributors to be identified as authors of this work have been asserted in accordance with sections 77 and 79 of the Copyright, Designs and Patents Act 1988.

Typeset by Chris Bell, cbdesign

Printed on demand by CPI Group (UK) Ltd, Croydon, CR0 4YY

Contents

Acknowledgements	vii
Figures and Tables	ix
Notes on Contributors	xi
Horror 2020: Introducing New Blood Eddie Falvey, Joe Hickinbottom, Jonathan Wroot	1

Part One: Framing Horror — 13

1. **Apprehension Engines:** The New Independent 'Prestige Horror'
   David Church — 15

2. **Hardcore Horror:** Challenging the Discourses of 'Extremity'
   Steve Jones — 35

3. **From Midnight Movies to Mainstream Excess:**
   Cult Horror Festivals and the Academy
   Xavier Mendik — 53

Part Two: Horror Reception — 81

4. **A Master of Horror?** The Making and Marketing of Takashi Miike's Horror Reputation
   Joe Hickinbottom — 83

5. **Bloody Muscles on VHS:** When Asia Extreme Met the Video Nasties
   Jonathan Wroot — 107

6. Streaming Netflix Original Horror: *Black Mirror*,
   Stranger Things and Datafied TV Horror   125
   Matt Hills

Part Three: Emerging Subgenres   145

7. The digital gothic and the Mainstream Horror Genre:
   Uncanny Vernacular Creativity and Adaptation   147
   Jessica Balanzategui

8. Nazi Horror, Reanimated: Rethinking Subgenres and Cycles   167
   Abigail Whittall

9. Digital Witness: Found Footage and Desktop Horror
   as Post-cinematic Experience   183
   Lindsay Hallam

Part Four: Horror in the World   201

10. Revisiting the Female Monster: Sex and Monstrosity
    in Contemporary Body Horror   203
    Eddie Falvey

11. The Kids are Alt-right: Hardcore Punk, Subcultural
    Violence and Contemporary American Politics
    in Jeremy Saulnier's *Green Room*   225
    Thomas Joseph Watson

12. Twenty-first-century Euro-snuff: *A Serbian Film* for
    the Family   247
    Neil Jackson

Bibliography   265

Index   295

Acknowledgements

The editors wish to thank the series editor, Xavier Aldana Reyes, for his enthusiasm and support for this book. They also wish to thank Sarah Lewis and her colleagues at the University of Wales Press for their support, advice and professionalism.

Eddie Falvey thanks his co-editors, Joe and Jon, for their help along the way. He wishes to dedicate his part in this volume to his father, Martin, who would watch all of these films, and to his mother, Jane, who would watch none of them.

Joe Hickinbottom thanks his fellow editors, Eddie and Jon, for working with him on this project, and offers his gratitude to Eddie for his unwavering support while writing his chapter. His contribution to this volume is dedicated to four people who, collectively, have inspired him and listened to him talk about Takashi Miike for more years than any of them would like to be reminded of: Rhiannon, Mum and Dad, and Song.

Jonathan Wroot wishes to thank Eddie and Joe for allowing him to assist in the publication of this volume. He also offers his thanks to the Cult Film Research Group at King's College London for some very useful feedback on his chapter.

Figures and Tables

Figures

Figure 1.1. Mark Korven's 'Apprehension Engine'.
Photograph, Kai Korven.   17

Figure 3.1. The image from the Nouveaux-Pictures *Cine-Excess* DVD release of *Suspiria* reproduced in this volume is courtesy of its present distributor CultFilms.co.uk. We wish to thank the company for providing the permission to reproduce the image in this volume.   56

Figure 3.2. Roger Corman receives his *Cine-Excess* Lifetime Achievement Award from actress Jane Asher at the festival in 2008.   66

Figure 3.3. Cult performer Franco Nero receives his *Cine-Excess* Lifetime Achievement Award at the festival in 2011.   68

Figure 3.4. Author Victoria Price receives a posthumous *Cine-Excess* Lifetime Achievement Award for her father, actor Vincent Price, in 2018.   69

Figure 5.1. Graham Humphreys's artwork for *Bloody Muscle Body Builder in Hell* © Stand Entertainment.   114

Tables

Table 9.1. A table of feature-length post-cinematic horror films.   185

Notes on Contributors

Jessica Balanzategui is Lecturer in Cinema and Screen Studies at Swinburne University of Technology. Jessica's research examines childhood, history and national identity in global film and television; the impact of technological and industrial change on cinema and entertainment cultures; and vernacular storytelling and aesthetics in digital cultures (particularly the digital gothic). Her book, *The Uncanny Child in Transnational Cinema: Ghosts of Futurity at the Turn of the Twenty-first Century*, was published in 2018 by Amsterdam University Press, and her work has been published in numerous edited collections and refereed journals.

David Church is a Postdoctoral Fellow in Gender Studies at Indiana University. His specialisms include genre studies, taste cultures, gender/sexuality studies and histories of film exhibition and distribution. He is the author of *Disposable Passions: Vintage Pornography and the Material Legacies of Adult Cinema* (2016), *Grindhouse Nostalgia: Memory, Home Video, and Exploitation Film Fandom* (2015) and a forthcoming monograph on the Mortal Kombat video game franchise. He is currently at work on a book titled *Post-Horror: Art, Genre, and Cultural Elevation* (forthcoming, Edinburgh University Press).

Eddie Falvey completed his AHRC-funded PhD project on the early films of New York at the University of Exeter, where he taught in the Department of English. Since finishing his PhD, Eddie has been Lecturer in the

School of Arts and Media at Plymouth College of Art. He is the author of an upcoming monograph on *Re-Animator* (2021) and is in the process of developing his thesis into a monograph for Amsterdam University Press.

Lindsay Hallam is Senior Lecturer in Film at the University of East London. She is the author of *Screening the Marquis de Sade: Pleasure, Pain and the Transgressive Body in Film* (2012) and *Twin Peaks: Fire Walk with Me* (2018). She has contributed to various collections, including *Trauma, Media, Art: New Perspectives* (M. Broderick and A. Traverso (eds), 2010), *Dracula's Daughters: The Female Vampire on Film* (D. Brode and L. Deyneka (eds), 2013) and *Transnational Horror Across Visual Media: Fragmented Bodies* (D. Och and K. Strayer (eds), 2014).

Joe Hickinbottom completed his AHRC-funded PhD project on the reception of Takashi Miike at the University of Exeter, where he also taught in the Department of English. His PhD thesis, 'Takashi Miike and the Dynamics of Cult Authorship' (2017), offers an extensive critical history of the reception of Miike and his cinema, which demonstrates the discursive currency of his established status as a cult auteur. Joe's research interests include questions of authorship, cult cinema, genre studies and Japanese cinema.

Matt Hills is Professor of Media and Film at the University of Huddersfield. He is the author of six monographs, including *Fan Cultures* (2002) and *The Pleasures of Horror* (2005), as well as being the editor of *New Dimensions of Doctor Who* (2013) and co-editor of *Transatlantic Television Drama* (2019). Matt has published more than a hundred book chapters/journal articles on fandom and cult media, including chapters in *Horror Zone: The Cultural Experience of Contemporary Horror Cinema* (I. Conrich (ed.), 2009) and Wiley-Blackwell's *A Companion to the Horror Film* (H. M. Benshoff (ed.), 2014).

Neil Jackson is Senior Lecturer in Film Studies at the University of Lincoln. Neil is the co-editor of *Snuff: Real Death and Screen Media* (2016). He recently contributed chapters on 'Exhausted: John C Holmes the Real Story' (1981) to *Grindhouse: Cultural Exchange on 42nd Street and Beyond* (A. Fisher and J. Walker (eds), 2016) and 'Forced Entry' (1972) to the *Porn Studies* journal. He is currently preparing a study of the representation of the Vietnam War in exploitation cinema for Bloomsbury.

Steve Jones is Senior Lecturer and Head of Media in the Department of Social Sciences at Northumbria University, as well as Adjunct Research Professor in Law and Legal Studies at Carleton University, Ottawa. His research principally focuses on sex, violence, ethics and selfhood within horror and pornography. He is the author of *Torture Porn: Popular Horror after Saw* (2013). His work has been published in *Feminist Media Studies*, *Sexuality & Culture*, *Sexualities* and *Film-Philosophy*. He is also on the editorial board of *Porn Studies*.

Xavier Mendik is Professor of Cult Cinema Studies at Birmingham City University, from where he runs the *Cine-Excess* International Film Festival. He is the author, editor and co-editor of nine volumes that explore cult and horror film traditions. Some of his publications in this area include *Bodies of Desire and Bodies in Distress: The Golden Age of Italian Cult Cinema* (2015), *Peep Shows: Cult Film and the Cine-Erotic* (2012) and *The Cult Film Reader* (with E. Mathijs, 2008). Xavier has also completed a number of documentaries on cult horror film traditions, most recently *The Quiet Revolution: State, Society and the Canadian Horror Film* (2019).

Thomas Joseph Watson is Lecturer in Transmedia Production at Teesside University. His research interests include popular genres, representations of violence in contemporary cinema, transgression and noise music. He has published on various topics, including pornography, horror cinema, real crime documentary and experimental video art.

Abigail Whittall recently completed her PhD at the University of Winchester with a study on contemporary Nazi horror films titled 'Horrors of the Second World War: Nazi Monsters on 21st Century Screens'. Abigail has presented papers at various national and international conferences. Her research interests include horror cinema, genre studies and psychoanalysis. This is her first publication.

Jonathan Wroot is Senior Lecturer and Programme Leader for Film Studies at the University of Greenwich. He has previously published book chapters on home media formats and Asian cinema distribution with Palgrave Macmillan, as well as journal articles in *Arts and the Market*, *The East Asian Journal of Popular Culture* and *Participations: Journal of Audience & Reception Studies*. Jonathan is currently writing a history of the *Zatoichi* media franchise for Lexington Books.

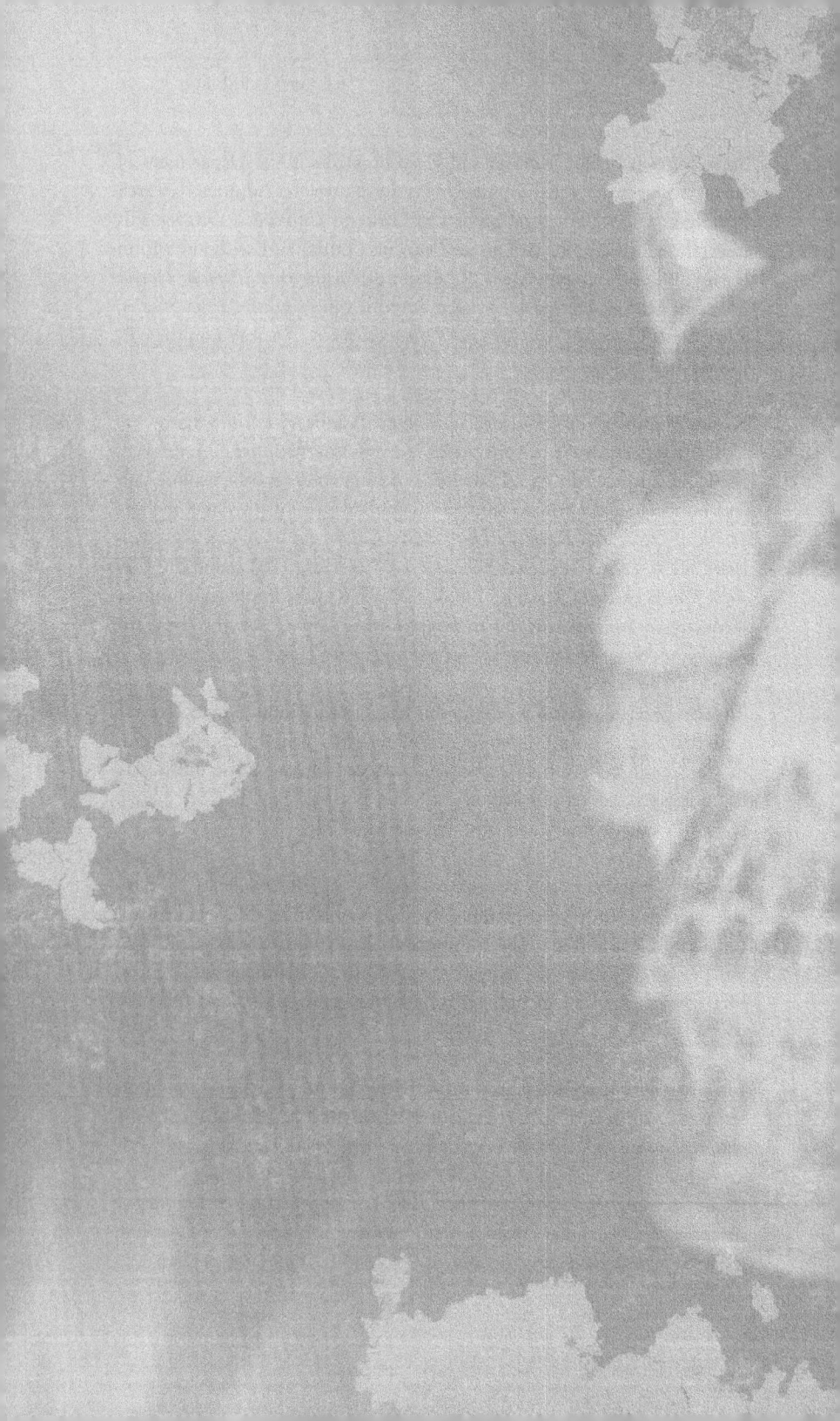

Horror 2020

Introducing New Blood

Eddie Falvey, Joe Hickinbottom and Jonathan Wroot

AS THE SECOND DECADE of the twenty-first century draws to a close, it is clear that horror cinema remains as prolific as it has ever been. A constant production of titles, emanating from a wide array of industries, has ensured that horror continues to possess a strong presence in wider film culture; moreover, the genre is currently enjoying unprecedented levels of commercial and critical success, as demonstrated by the box-office returns and reception of releases such as *Get Out* (Jordan Peele, 2017), *It* (Andy Muschietti, 2017) and *Halloween* (David Gordon Green, 2018). While the enduring interest in horror is perhaps unremarkable in isolation (the genre has been popular since the inception of film itself, and for even longer if one looks to its antecedents in art, literature and mythology), recent developments in horror cinema are more than worthy of attention, for they are marked by shifts in tastes, industry paradigms and distribution practices that call for fresh perspectives. It is high time for a new academic collection to take stock of horror during its current popularity and to offer original critical approaches to the genre that push forward existing debates and carve out pathways for new ones. *New Blood* is that collection.

To this end, some recent evolutions within this turbulent genre are worth documenting briefly here. The contemporary horror boom has yielded a diverse range of texts, from effects-laden blockbusters, such as *World War Z* (Marc Forster, 2013), *Godzilla* (Gareth Edwards, 2014) and the aforementioned *It*, to critically acclaimed independent horror films emerging from a variety of global contexts. Garnering levels of praise that it has arguably not reached since the 1970s, films such as *It Follows* (David Robert Mitchell, 2014), *Green Room* (Jeremy Saulnier, 2015), *The Witch* (Robert Eggers, 2015), *Raw* (Julia Ducournau, 2016), *Get Out* and *Hereditary* (Ari Aster, 2018) have ushered in an intensified critical engagement with horror cinema, prompting significant enquiries about generic distinctions.[1] Beyond such critical darlings, horror has somewhat unsurprisingly seen the continuation and resurrection of numerous franchises through a slew of sequels, reboots and remakes, with many fan favourites returning alongside the establishment of entirely new series, including *Saw* (2004–) and *The Conjuring* (2013–). Indeed, the antagonist of the *Saw* franchise, Jigsaw, joins the company of Leatherface, Freddy Krueger, Jason Voorhees and Michael Myers as one of the genre's most iconic villains, all of whom have made appearances in some form or another over the last two decades.

In keeping with historic practices, some horror franchises have proven so popular (and, thus, so rich for the mining of new productions) that they have been afforded multiple revivals in relatively quick succession. A recent example of this is the 2018 *Halloween* sequel/reboot from respected indie auteur David Gordon Green, following on from the two reimaginings Rob Zombie contributed to the franchise a decade prior (2007/2009). That same year, award-winning auteur Luca Guadagnino helmed a largely well-received remake/reimagining of Dario Argento's *giallo* masterpiece *Suspiria* (1977/Luca Guadagnino, 2018). All manner of classic horror films, from *The Crazies* (George A. Romero, 1973/Breck Eisner, 2010) to *The Evil Dead* (Sam Raimi, 1981/Fede Álvarez, 2013), have been subject to this treatment. The velocity with which such franchises have been revamped in recent years is demonstrative of the economic security of, and sustained cultural currency attached to, famous series and their signifying characters and tropes, which continue to inspire both established and new fan bases decades after their initial emergence.

Much of horror's continued success can be attributed to its popularity across a variety of exhibition formats, including theatre and home releases as well as dedicated festivals, such as *Cine-Excess* and Frightfest, and streaming services like Shudder, an on-demand subscription service supported by AMC that is dedicated to horror. In the current age of cinema, in which theatre attendance has steadily declined due to inflated ticket prices and an ever-increasing range of options for home media consumption, horror continues to thrive. To understand the genre's enduring popularity, it is important to observe the many lives of a horror release, which can be traced across physical media re-releases and the collecting cultures attributed to home formats, including merchandise and other associated memorabilia.[2] The chapters within *New Blood* examine many of these contexts, considering both continuing patterns of consumption and the emergence of new modalities. Indeed, the taste for horror and the energy of its consumers – invigorated by multiple media formats – is one of the key driving forces of this collection.

New Blood aims to complement other publications with shared intentions, while progressing the field with up-to-date research. Horror at the turn of the millennium has been documented in several noteworthy volumes. Ian Conrich's *Horror Zone: The Cultural Experience of Contemporary Horror Cinema* (2009), for example, brings together numerous writers to document shifts in the genre from the late twentieth century into the new millennium.[3] Steffen Hantke's similarly inclined edited volume, *Horror Film: Creating and Marketing Fear* (2004), posits key reasons as to why horror films have been prolific for so long, considering how horror has been promoted through a selection of case studies.[4] Following this exploration of historic and contemporary trends, in 2010 Hantke again assembled a team of scholars in *The American Horror Film: The Genre at the Turn of the Millennium*.[5] Of course, despite the significance of the American industry and its adjacent cultural contexts, horror films continue to emerge from around the world in an ever-increasing variety of forms. Much research has been conducted on these trends, such as Adam Lowenstein's 2005 overview of contemporary horror, *Shocking Representation: Historical Trauma, National Cinema, and the Modern Horror Film*.[6] Lowenstein's emphasis on the horror of other nations represents a turn towards thinking about horror globally, a move that has continued with Steven Jay Schneider and Tony Williams's volume, *Horror International* (2005), and Dana Och and Kirsten Strayer's book, *Transnational Horror Across Visual Media: Fragmented Bodies* (2014).[7] Yet, it should not be surprising that specific regions have been given more attention in regards to horror, particularly East Asian countries such as Hong Kong, Japan and South Korea, as examined in the work of Daniel Martin and several other scholars.[8]

New Blood takes cues from preceding works, such as those mentioned above, in its provision of a survey of fresh critical perspectives. Like such works, the rationale for this volume stems from a desire to link current trends in horror production to the commercial performance and business infrastructure of horror across media. Critical acclaim has been given in many cases – but whether praised or derided, horror has carried on regardless. Stephen Follows astutely illustrates this fact in his 2017 publication *The Horror Report*.[9] Follows provides data confirming that horror is the most profitable of all film genres, through both theatrical releases and TV broadcasting, as well as evidence that the most popular films include either paranormal elements, monsters or killers.[10] Horror continues to offer a wide range of antagonists, as zombies, vampires and other creatures, ghosts, murderers and evil spirits have remained popular mainstays of the genre. This can be seen in films ranging from *28 Days Later* (Danny Boyle, 2002) to *World War Z* and *Train to Busan* (Yeon Sang-ho, 2016); from *Twilight* (Catherine Hardwicke, 2008) to *What We Do in the Shadows* (Jermaine Clement and Taika Waititi, 2014) and *A Girl Walks Home Alone at Night* (Ana Lily Amirpour, 2014); and from *Ringu* (Hideo Nakata, 1998) and *Ju-on: The Grudge* (Takashi Shimizu, 2002) to *Crimson Peak* (Guillermo del Toro, 2015) and *Hereditary*.

Many larger studio horror films of recent years – including *The Wolfman* (Joe Johnston, 2010), *World War Z*, *Godzilla* and *The Mummy* (Alex Kurtzman, 2017) – have depended upon the resurrection of traditional screen monsters, illustrating the substantial ongoing appeal of staple characters. Despite the genre's current popularity, however, large studio horror titles are often inconsistent at the box office, with the likes of *The Wolfman* and *The Mummy* failing to match commercial expectations. Meanwhile, comparatively smaller films have gone on to return their budgets many times over. Indeed, as low-budget horrors such as *Saw* and *Paranormal Activity* (Oren Peli, 2007) have turned over astronomical box-office sums against miniscule budgets, moderate-sized horror releases such as *It* and *Halloween* have managed to haul in considerable profits at home and overseas, aided no doubt by extensive marketing campaigns and consumer familiarity with their source texts. As Murray Leeder writes, 'the cinema is full of ghosts [and] the ghost is a powerful, versatile metaphor. It can signify the ways in which memory and history, whether traumatic, nostalgic, or both, linger.'[11] Recurring tendencies in horror, demonstrated by the industrial and textual parallels between horror's earlier and later manifestations, operate in this ghostly manner, revealing tangible markers of cyclicity at work within the genre. As the producers of horror cinema consciously cash in on a lucrative subcultural rate of exchange (illustrated in revived monsters and/or franchises), they convey how horror's past is continually utilised to inform its present.

Accordingly, in recent years some contemporary film-makers have adopted a revisionist approach to horror's history and iconography, perhaps best demonstrated by the sprawling, radical *Halloween* canon. Green's *Halloween* finds Jamie Lee Curtis's Laurie unshackled from her status as the Scream Queen/Final Girl of the original film and reimagined as an action hero in a manner that recalls Sarah Connor's transformation in *Terminator 2: Judgement Day* (James Cameron, 1991). Following Wes Craven's seminal meta-slasher *Scream* in 1996, the Final Girl trope (in line with the concept established by Carol J. Clover[12]) has been referenced, revised and parodied in many subsequent titles. These include three *Scream* sequels, a spin-off TV series, a further MTV series called *Scream Queens* (starring Curtis and other famous horror actors) and a cycle of films consisting of, among others, Fede Álvarez's *Evil Dead*, *The Final Girls* (Todd Strauss-Schulson, 2015), *Final Girl* (Tyler Shields, 2015) and *Happy Death Day* and its sequel (Christopher Landon, 2017/2019). The *Halloween* reboot included, such revisionist horror films offering intriguing twists on familiar concepts have regularly found audiences amid other high-concept horror films and prolific franchise instalments, signalling the wide-reaching appeal of the genre's many permutations.

Revisionist horror does not end, however, with the self-conscious reinstatement of Clover's Final Girl. In the twenty-five years that have passed since Barbara Creed's work on the monstrous-feminine, or female Other, horror continues to offer fascinating avenues for exploring gender and its construction in popular media.[13] *Ginger Snaps* (John Fawcett, 2000) was celebrated for its alignment of werewolf mythology with teenage and menstrual angst, while *Teeth* (Mitchell Lichtenstein, 2007) directly addressed the sexual and bloody themes of the monstrous-feminine through its gory premise of the *vagina dentata*. A variety of female protagonists and antagonists can be found in horror globally, as seen in films as diverse as the Japanese splatter movies of Yoshihiro Nishimura, including *Tokyo Gore Police* (2008), and New French Extremity horrors, such as Alexander Bustillo and Julien Maury's *Inside* (2007) and Pascale Laugier's *Martyrs* (2008). Katharine Isabelle, star of *Ginger Snaps*, returned to horror under a different guise in *American Mary* (Jen and Sylvia Soska, 2012), a film which navigates both body modification subcultures and structures of oppression in the male-dominated neoliberal context of North America. *American Mary* announced the arrival of the Soska sisters, marking a much-needed turning point in the visibility of female directors within the genre, strengthened by the subsequent work of Jennifer Kent (*The Babadook* (2014)), Ana Lily Amirpour (*A Girl Walks Home Alone at Night*, *The Bad Batch* (2016)) and Julia Ducournau (*Raw*).

The popularity of revisionist horror arguably reached its apex with the simultaneous Oscar successes of Jordan Peele's *Get Out* and Guillermo del Toro's *The Shape of Water* in 2018. Both films relied heavily upon traditional horror iconography and employed the genre's dark thematic currency as a means of scrutinising prevailing social anxieties. Similarly, titles such as *It Follows*, *The Witch*, *It Comes at Night* (Trey Edward Shults, 2017) and *Hereditary* have all been praised for building an atmosphere of sustained dread and despair, as opposed to relying on 'cheap' jump scares and monstrous reveals. Although many horror scholars and fans could explain how the genre has been offering alternative scares for decades, it is for this supposed divergence from the 'traditional' characteristics of horror that such titles have revitalised debates surrounding the qualities of modern horror – a discussion that reflects a long-standing critical aversion to the supposedly inherent base nature of the genre.

Certain studios have profited considerably from horror's recent popularity. The most notable of these is Blumhouse Productions, founded by Jason Blum, which saw substantial financial returns with the release of *Paranormal Activity* in 2009, launching a franchise that now includes five sequels. Blumhouse's impressive commercial performance can be traced through a series of popular franchises, including *Insidious* (2011–), *Sinister* (2012–), *The Purge* (2013–) and the aforementioned *Happy Death Day* films. Following the success of *Get Out*, Blumhouse has even broadened its horizons beyond the horror genre, producing Spike Lee's *BlacKkKlansman* (2018). A24, meanwhile, has produced a number of horrors that have performed well both critically and commercially, with films such as *A Ghost Story* (David Lowery, 2017) and *Hereditary* quickly rising to become significant titles for the modern horror canon. While other horror production houses, like Twisted Pictures, Dark Castle Entertainment, Ghost House Pictures and Platinum Dunes, have found varying degrees of success across the last two decades, arguably none have matched Blumhouse's or A24's consistency or crossover potential.

It is not just in cinemas and with feature films that horror has continued to proliferate. Horror television series have also grown in number and popularity throughout the twenty-first century. *Supernatural* (2005–20) recently bowed out with its fifteenth and final season, while the similarly enormous success of *The Walking Dead* (2010–) and spin-off show *Fear the Walking Dead* (2015–) illustrates horror's abundant capital for home audiences. Television and streaming formats continue to expand, bringing to serialised horror media a wealth of talent (in front of and behind the camera) and higher production budgets. This is exemplified by *Masters of Horror* (2005–7), an anthology featuring key horror auteurs, as well as later shows such as *True Blood* (2008–14), *American Horror Story* (2011–), *Black Mirror* (2011–), *Hannibal* (2013–15), *Bates Motel* (2013–17), *Penny Dreadful* (2014–16), *The Strain* (2014–17), *Stranger Things* (2016–), *Castle Rock* (2018–) and *The Haunting of Hill House* (2018–). The large quantity of series produced for and/or distributed by online streaming services demonstrates that home-viewing culture lends itself well to the consumption of horror media. Indeed, Netflix and Amazon have both produced original content that caters to horror fans, while simultaneously expanding their libraries with older titles to bolster their status as leading distributors/exhibitors of horror. In terms of original content, Netflix's adaptation of Stephen King's *Gerald's Game* (Mike Flanagan, 2017), alongside Gareth Evan's *Apostle* (2018), were considerable successes for the studio, while Amazon produced Guadagnino's high-profile remake of *Suspiria*.

Meanwhile, other companies have made horror a key focus of their marketing and business strategies. For example, Shudder provides a wide selection of horror films and television shows to consumers in the USA, Canada, UK and Ireland. Similarly, Vinegar Syndrome, an independent American distributor of low-budget horror and sexploitation films from the 1970s and 1980s that mostly releases its titles on DVD and Blu-ray, has also made its catalogue available through Amazon Prime Video. In the UK, distributors such as Arrow Video and Eureka have targeted horror collectors with prestige limited-edition home releases as well as making their content available through pay-per-view and subscription services, such as Amazon's. Other distributors both in the UK and overseas (including, but not limited to, Indicator, Vestron, 88 Films, Diabolik, Severin Films, Turbine Media, Koch Media and Second Sight) have all repackaged and re-released various types of horror for specialist audiences, signalling – through the demand for, and value of, such products – a continuing and substantial subcultural capital pertaining to horror media.

New Blood does not claim to provide a comprehensive account of each and every advancement that might have been witnessed across the past two decades of horror production. Naturally, as is the case with all the collections that precede it, many key works, contexts and approaches will go without sufficient representation. What this collection does offer is a series of in-depth case studies that give new (or renewed) critical focus to some of the more noteworthy characteristics and trends of contemporary horror media.

Part one of the volume gathers together a series of fresh critical perspectives on contemporary horror media. Opening with a timely intervention in the debate surrounding so-called 'prestige' horror, David Church's chapter weighs in on current discussions of 'post-horror' and the issues raised by changing ideas about horror's central characteristics. Church's piece examines the industrial modalities, generic templates and aesthetic choices that coincide with shifting discourses, while also challenging the terminology with which such shifts are discussed. Following this, Steve Jones builds upon the topics of hardcore horror and discourses of extremity that have characterised much of his work. Jones's chapter takes to task the prevailing means by which horror scholars have approached the extreme, reframing the debate to take into account the ways in which external influences, such as popular journalism, have engineered the moral outrage that predicates extreme horror's discussion. In the final chapter of part one, Xavier Mendik recounts his personal experiences as the founder of the *Cine-Excess* International Film Festival as a platform for exploring the discursive impact cult- and horror-oriented festivals have had on spectatorship and scholarship. Mendik's chapter illustrates how festivals offer unique spaces within which academic and popular discourses are able to overlap and feed into one another.

In part two, the volume offers a series of frameworks for considering horror reception today. First, Joe Hickinbottom surveys the horror reputation of Takashi Miike. Despite a markedly protean approach to genre, Miike's prevailing reputation as a horror director following *Audition* (1999) presents a fascinating means of evaluating how authorship operates within horror discourses and how it is utilised as a key marketing strategy to reach certain target audiences. Continuing part two is Jonathan Wroot's chapter, which investigates how retro-formatted releases of new horror titles reveal the genre's substantial appeal to media collectors. Using Shinichi Fukazawa's *Bloody Muscle Body Builder in Hell* (2012) and its VHS release as a case study, Wroot considers how the viewing and collecting cultures generated by horror fans embody the genre's pre-eminence amid current forms of media consumption, which are sometimes found to be more nostalgic as time goes on.[14] Finally, Matt Hills considers how Netflix Original horror illustrates the ways in which emergent industrial contexts reflect new subcultural dynamics for horror fans. Hills's chapter offers an important insight into the formats presented by streaming services, observing how they have capitalised on existing fandoms while creating new ones.

Part three considers established and emerging subgenres, beginning with Jessica Balanzategui's exploration of the transmediality of contemporary horror in relation to an important context for the modern genre: internet folk horror. In this chapter, Balanzategui observes how horror has continued to find a home on diverse media platforms, carving out a position for the multimodal online narratives of the 'digital gothic' within mainstream horror media. Next, Abigail Whittall discusses the ongoing appeal of Nazi horror. Whittall examines how the subgenre has grown considerably in popularity over the last couple of decades, shifting from low-budget B-movies to large studio fare, as seen in 2018's *Overlord* (Julius Avery). With Nazi horror as a case study, Whittall explores distinctions between cycles and subgenres and accounts for the ways in which the revived exploitation format reflects current industrial paradigms that convey both the economies and textual resonances of contemporary horror. Finally in part three is Lindsay Hallam's chapter on desktop horror, a popular new mode of horror cinema that has emerged over the last decade. Hallam's piece ruminates on the horror genre's sustained interest in new (haunted) technologies. Not only do such developments exhibit contemporary horror film-makers' canny ability to find economic production models for simple yet effective horror films, they also signify how the genre continues to engage with mounting cultural anxieties, including new sources of horror emerging from digital spaces.

In part four, the book considers horror film-making in the world today, opening with Eddie Falvey's interrogation of female monstrosity in contemporary horror films. Falvey observes how monstrosity continues to be employed to convey a range of issues relating to sex and power (in particular, sexual trauma and its consequences), locating horror in the corporeal traumas experienced by many horror protagonists. With reference to texts such as *Teeth* and *Raw*, Falvey's chapter highlights how horror persistently finds currency in monstrosity's capacity to critique the world. Following this, Thomas Joseph Watson looks at how prominent political discourses have informed contemporary horror and its reception. Examining Jeremy Saulnier's *Green Room*, Watson's chapter investigates how violent political tribalism, here represented by the Nazism of the alt-right, offers a political economy for recent interrogations of the shifting American nightmare. The final chapter in the collection sees Neil Jackson writing on twenty-first-century Euro-snuff. Jackson's chapter challenges the prevalent reception of Srđan Spasojević's controversial horror film *A Serbian Film* (2010), situating the text in relation to long-standing realist horror traditions. The chapter brings a vital new textual focus to Spasojević's notorious film, which has become something of a scapegoat in the ongoing discussion of contemporary 'extreme' horror, its antecedents and complex textual resonances.

While by no means wholly illustrative of all the nuances held within this collection, the preceding overview maps out *New Blood*'s various interventions within the fertile ground of horror studies. Across a series of focused chapters offered by emerging and established scholarly voices in the field, *New Blood* provides a vital congregation of current critical approaches to a genre that continues to develop across varied national contexts, media platforms and modes of production.

Notes

1. S. Rose, 'How post-horror movies are taking over cinema', *The Guardian* (6 July 2017), https://www.theguardian.com/film/2017/jul/06/post-horror-films-scary-movies-ghost-story-it-comes-at-night (accessed 30 January 2020).
2. This is noted in publications such as: H. O'Hara, 'Is VHS making a comeback?', *The Telegraph* (23 April 2015), http://www.telegraph.co.uk/culture/film/film-news/11555663/Is-VHS-making-a-comeback.html (accessed 30 January 2020); J. Wroot and A. Willis (eds), *Cult Media: Re-packaged, Re-released and Restored* (Basingstoke: Palgrave Macmillan, 2017); and the documentary *Rewind This!* (Josh Johnson, 2013).
3. I. Conrich (ed.), *Horror Zone: The Cultural Experience of Contemporary Horror Cinema* (London: I. B. Tauris, 2009).
4. S. Hantke (ed.), *Horror Film: Creating and Marketing Fear* (Jackson, MS: University Press of Mississippi, 2004).
5. S. Hantke (ed.), *American Horror Film: The Genre at the Turn of the Millennium* (Jackson, MS: University Press of Mississippi, 2010).
6. Adam Lowenstein, *Shocking Representation: Historical Trauma, National Cinema, and the Modern Horror Film* (New York, NY: Columbia University Press, 2005).

7. S. J. Schneider and T. Williams (eds), *Horror International* (Detroit, MI: Wayne State University Press, 2005); D. Och and K. Strayer (eds), *Transnational Horror Across Visual Media: Fragmented Bodies* (London: Routledge, 2014).
8. G. Bettinson and D. Martin (eds), *Hong Kong Horror Cinema* (Edinburgh: Edinburgh University Press, 2018); Daniel Martin, *Extreme Asia: The Rise of Cult Cinema from the Far East* (Edinburgh: Edinburgh University Press, 2015); A. Peirse and D. Martin (eds), *Korean Horror Cinema* (Edinburgh: Edinburgh University Press, 2013).
9. Stephen Follows, *The Horror Report*, StephenFollows.com (2017), https://stephenfollows.com/horrorreport/ (accessed 29 August 2019).
10. Follows, *The Horror Report*, pp. 9, 12, 134, 140, 156.
11. M. Leeder, 'Introduction', in M. Leeder (ed.), *Cinematic Ghosts: Haunting and Spectrality from Silent Cinema to the Digital Era* (London: Bloomsbury, 2015), p. 1.
12. Carol J. Clover, *Men, Women, and Chain Saws: Gender in the Modern Horror Film* (Princeton, NJ: Princeton University Press, 1992).
13. Barbara Creed, *The Monstrous-Feminine: Film, Feminism, Psychoanalysis* (London: Routledge, 1993).
14. J. Squires, 'UK Store HMV Releasing "The Thing" Blu-ray in Exclusive VHS Packaging!', *Bloody Disgusting* (18 June 2018), https://bloody-disgusting.com/home-video/3504836/uk-store-hmv-releasing-thing-Blu-ray-exclusive-vhs-packaging/ (accessed 30 January 2020).

PART ONE

FRAMING HORROR

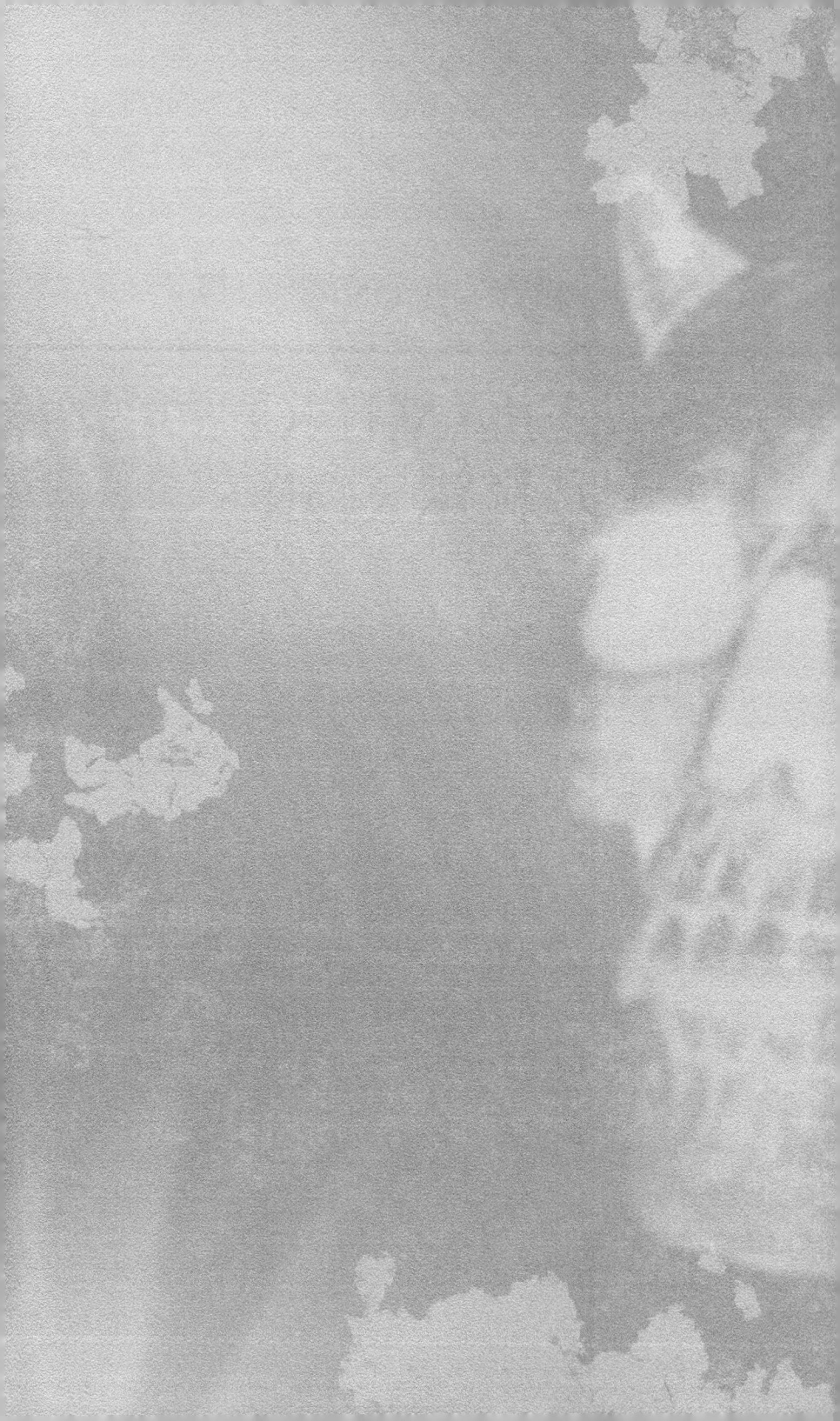

1

Apprehension Engines

The New Independent 'Prestige Horror'

David Church

UNEARTHLY DRONES, metallic whines and ominous clanks emanate from a contraption consisting of several wooden boxes with a guitar-like neck, onto which are affixed magnets, metal wires and coils, and a hurdy-gurdy crank (Figure 1.1). The 'Apprehension Engine' is the nickname for this unique musical instrument, commissioned by Mark Korven, composer of *The Witch* (Robert Eggers, 2015), and designed/built by guitar maker Tony Duggan-Smith. As its name suggests, the foreboding ambience created by this device is intended to instil anxiety and dread via eldritch sounds that cannot be easily associated with conventional musical instruments or arrangements. Inspired by his score for *The Witch*, Korven commissioned this experimental instrument to lend his film scores a more original sound than the overused digital samples previously at his disposal.[1] Both the ethos and the effects of this device provide a useful way to approach a new breed of independently produced horror films that merge art-cinema style with decentred genre tropes, privileging lingering dread and visual restraint over audio-visual shock and monstrous disgust. As 'apprehension engines' in their own right, these films represent 'a new-wave horror that diverges from the assembly line and strays from overpitched archetypes', sharing with Korven and Duggan-Smith's instrument a sense of handmade artistry, low-budget ingenuity and striking originality – all in the service of producing affective tones that unsettle both viewers and the genre itself.[2]

The recent rise to prominence of films such as *It Follows* (David Robert Mitchell, 2014), *The Witch*, *The Blackcoat's Daughter* (Osgood Perkins, 2015), *I Am the Pretty Thing That Lives in the House* (Osgood Perkins, 2016), *It Comes at Night* (Trey Edward Shults, 2017) and *Hereditary* (Ari Aster, 2018) is among the horror genre's most widely discussed recent developments. Variously dubbed 'prestige horror', 'indie horror', 'smart horror', 'quiet horror', 'elevated horror' and 'post-horror', all emerged from the crucible of major film festivals like Sundance and Toronto with significant critical buzz for supposedly transcending the horror genre's oft-presumed lowbrow status. Heralded for possessing an aesthetically higher tone than the average multiplex horror film, these films have received disproportionate critical acclaim for catering to more rarefied tastes, even as casual viewers and even some horror fans have proved more ambivalent towards these films' aesthetic strategies. In this chapter, however, I will engage most prominently with the films' critical nomination as 'prestige horror', since this particular nomenclature helps us not only to situate them within a longer history of horror texts that have seemingly risen above the genre's disrepute, but also marks them off as a different development due to so many of these films originating from the independent production/distribution market during a close cluster of years.

Film critics have deemed various productions 'prestige' in earlier periods of horror film history, usually based on some combination of high production values, the presence of an established auteur or major star, or an adaptation from middlebrow, often literary source material. Some of the more canonical horror films – including *Frankenstein* (James Whale, 1931), *Dracula* (Tod Browning, 1931), *Cat People* (Jacques Tourneur, 1942), *The Spiral Staircase* (Robert Siodmak, 1946), *Psycho* (Alfred Hitchcock, 1960), *The Haunting* (Robert Wise, 1963), *Rosemary's Baby* (Roman Polanski, 1968), *The Shining* (Stanley Kubrick, 1980), *The Silence of the Lambs* (Jonathan Demme, 1990), *Bram Stoker's Dracula* (Francis Ford Coppola, 1992) and *The Sixth Sense* (M. Night Shyamalan, 1999) – emerged from such industrial and publicity strategies. In many cases, critics claimed these films to be oriented more towards 'adult' viewers than the genre's dominant reputation as juvenilia, more attuned to the pleasures of female viewers or worthy of participation by above-the-line personnel

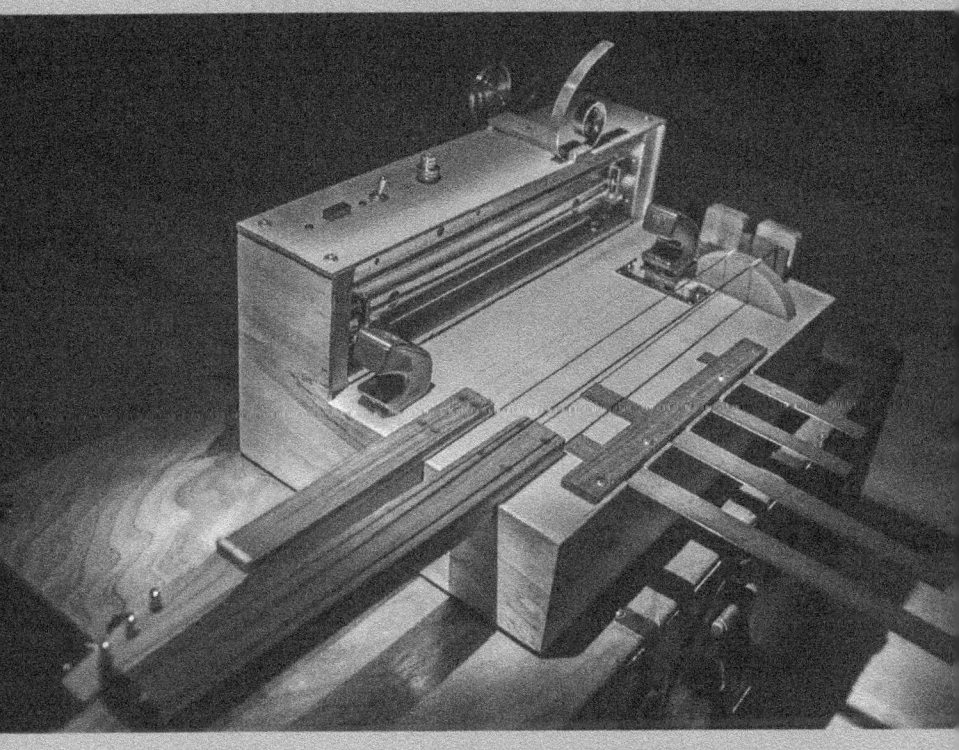

Figure 1.1. Mark Korven's 'Apprehension Engine'. Photograph, Kai Korven.

who might 'elevate' such an otherwise lowly genre.[3] Overall, the 'prestige-ness' of horror has generally been constructed against the monolithic image of relatively young, male, uncouth viewership. This is not to say, of course, that prestige horror films are bereft of shock value or have enjoyed unanimously positive critical reception – witness Michael Powell's career implosion for directing *Peeping Tom* (1960) or the various controversies about lewd and sacrilegious imagery in *The Exorcist* (William Friedkin, 1973), for instance – but that the above qualities of prestige-ness frequently serve as mitigating factors against negative criticism. And importantly, most of these earlier films predominantly obey classical narrative conventions, not the qualities of art cinema seen in the new wave of independent 'prestige horror'. By occupying a stylistic position closer to 'difficult' art cinema than populist genre cinema, yet being marketed and released to multiplexes as potential crossover films, the new prestige horror offers wider audiences an expanded view of what the horror film can feel like, but – as Rotten Tomatoes reviews and CinemaScore audience polls reveal – at the cost of potentially alienating many of the genre's quotidian viewers.

Minimalist art-horror

Horror cinema has long been a consistently popular but critically denigrated genre, often derided for its corporeal appeals, fantastical conceits and thematic focus on evil, monstrosity and death. Accordingly, it is a critical commonplace for reviewers to celebrate horror texts that privilege haunting atmospheres and indirect chills over shocking spectacles and visceral disgust. Joan Hawkins has argued that, despite the cultural stratification of tastes that privilege cognition over bodily sensations, art films trade in many of the same capacities to shock, disgust and offend as horror films – albeit framed for supposedly different purposes (e.g. symbolism over literalism). For Hawkins, then, 'art-horror' films represent a key site for levelling the taste hierarchies between so-called 'high' and 'low' culture.[4] Although Hawkins is primarily interested in comparing the shock effect of taboo spectacle and avant-garde distanciation, she also notes how an art-horror film's 'affective properties tend to be divorced from its "artistic" and "poetic" ones, so that it's difficult to find a critical language that allows us to speak about the film as a whole'.[5] Hence, even when horror films bear the more subtle qualities of art cinema, as outlined by David

Bordwell – including drifting and open-ended narratives, ambiguous and psychologically complex characters, and spatial/temporal manipulation (e.g. continuity violations, durational realism)[6] – critics often downplay such traits in order to preserve the hierarchies that keep the horror genre near the bottom of the ladder of cultural taste.

The new wave of prestige horror films exhibits many of the art-cinema traits noted by Bordwell, but without so many of the genre's critically countervailing traits like graphic violence/gore, unrealistic monsters and so on. Indeed, these films' difference from the mainstream horror film is primarily one of *tone*. As Douglas Pye argues, a film's tone resides in how its dramatic content is stylistically conveyed via the construction of an overall mood that shapes our affective horizon as viewers. For Pye, tone can register through a film's apparent generic or formal/stylistic distance from established norms – and is especially apparent when alternative uses of film form unsettle our conventional ways of approaching generic material.[7] Stylistically, these particular horror films favour minimalism over maximalism, eschewing jump scares, frenetic editing and energetic and/or handheld cinematography in favour of cold and distanced shot framing, longer-than-average shot durations, slow camera movements and unhurried narrative pacing. This tendency towards a 'vulnerable stillness' increases the viewer's dread that something might occur at any moment, affectively stretching out the temporal experience of the film.[8] In *It Follows*, for instance, David Robert Mitchell uses slow 360-degree pans, static long shots and slow zooms that allow the viewer to share the protagonist's paranoid searching of her visual field for a perpetually approaching monster that can take anyone's form, while *The Witch* presents interiors as chiaroscuro tableaux and exteriors as distanced vistas where even a waving tree branch conjures supernatural fears among its family of early American colonists. As critics observe, these films avoid 'the annoying modern tendency towards wobblicam and over-editing' and 'don't fit neatly into the "rising action, jump scare, rinse, repeat" model' of mainstream Hollywood horror.[9]

In many respects, these stylistic choices recall the American 'smart films' described by Jeffrey Sconce as an 'indie' aesthetic developed in the late 1990s that favours 'long-shots, static composition, and sparse editing' to suggest a hip, ironic distance from white, middle-class conformity and the 'horrors of life under advanced capitalism'.[10] Although film-makers like Todd Solondz, Paul Thomas Anderson and Alexander Payne used this style to produce a quirky or dark comedic tone, Todd Haynes's deadly serious

Safe (1995) perhaps comes closest to evoking the nebulously defined (and possibly imagined) threats, the overwhelming dread and the narrative ambiguity seen in the new prestige horror films. Their visual style and slow pace thus suggest a cool and ironic distance from conventional horror tropes themselves, as though the film-makers are visually signalling the space they wish to occupy between the art/indie film and the mainstream Hollywood horror film. After all, these are not 'smart' horror films in the winking sense of humorously oversaturated references to genre conventions – see the heavily allusive intertextuality of 'smart' meta-horror films like *Wes Craven's New Nightmare* (Wes Craven, 1994), *Scream* (Wes Craven, 1996), *The Cabin in the Woods* (Drew Goddard, 2012) or *The Final Girls* (Todd Strauss-Schulson, 2015) – and hence they seem less blatantly indebted to popular horror cinema for direct inspiration. That is, these latter films use self-reflexivity to 'smartly' play with the genre's more tired conventions. By contrast, *Get Out* (Jordan Peele, 2017) has been critically dubbed a 'smart' horror film less for playing with long-time conventions (though it does that as well) than for using the horror genre as a timely platform to 'smartly' intervene in American racial-equality debates during the Black Lives Matter era – albeit remaining a more populist intervention by evincing fewer of the art-film stylistics that mark the new prestige horror films under discussion here.

Confirming Hawkins's argument, critics often highlight the poetic and dream-like qualities of such films, while typically downplaying the more visceral moments. For instance, *I Am the Pretty Thing* is described as 'a tone poem', 'almost pornographic in its portent, every second of it seductive and ripe with tension, promising money shots that never come',[11] while a representative review of *The Blackcoat's Daughter* observes, 'To call the story a slow burn would be a mischaracterisation of the word *slow*. It's more like a meditation or a waking nightmare, the kind you're not actually sure is a dream at all until it's over and you're safe again.'[12] Of course, not all films critically ascribed to the new wave of prestige horror share all of these stylistic traits, nor are these traits wholly new or exclusive to the films clustered beneath that banner. Told from the perspective of a female-presenting extraterrestrial who seduces and consumes unsuspecting men, *Under the Skin* (Jonathan Glazer, 2013) shares the hypnotically languid pace, long shot durations and unsettling musical score of many of the new prestige horror films, albeit in a more science-fiction context. Meanwhile, *The Babadook* (Jennifer Kent, 2014) and *Get Out* bear a less minimalistic style than *It Follows* or *The Witch*, but close temporal proximity to the latter's critical and commercial success has sometimes caused the former to be retrospectively lumped in with them. By contrast, *The Invitation* (Karyn Kusama, 2015), *Don't Breathe* (Fede Álvarez, 2016) and *mother!* (Darren Aronofsky, 2017) initially share their claustrophobic ambience and shortage of jump scares, but eventually turn towards faster, action-oriented pacing in their final acts. Likewise, *House of the Devil* (Ti West, 2009) predated many of these films but foreshadows their atmospheric restraint, its frequent comparison to the films of John Carpenter another common motif in critical praise for the new prestige horror. Nevertheless, I would posit that the films most often identified as the core examples of new prestige horror bear a distinctly slow, austere and minimalist style for their duration.

Although these films occupy established horror subgenres (ghostly hauntings in *I Am the Pretty Thing*; supernatural curses in *It Follows*; post-apocalyptic survivalism in *It Comes at Night*; demonic possession in *The Blackcoat's Daughter* and *Hereditary*), familiar genre tropes are decentred, making space for characters and viewers alike to soak in contemplative or emotionally fraught moods, not to be shuffled along to the next abrupt scare. As Osgood Perkins, director of *I Am the Pretty Thing* and *The Blackcoat's Daughter*, notes,

> I find myself much more turned on by mood and colour and shadow and being observational . . . But I think I couch these movies enough in [genre] – 'oh, it's a demonic possession movie', 'oh, it's a ghost story' – so you can kind of feel the edges, and then be inside that with the character, and feel the human experience within that framework.[13]

Indeed, one of the major characteristics of these prestige horror films is a thematic exploration of other negative affects (such as grief, sadness, loss, guilt), with fear serving as a platform for shifting to affects that might be more closely associated with serious dramas. The alternate nomenclature for these films, 'elevated horror', speaks to this idea of 'elevating' the genre to the higher aesthetic plane that other genres are more likely to call home – hence, genre-mixing in these films can serve as an indicator of their apparent transcendence of 'pure' horror – much as Steve Rose's epithet 'post-horror' attempts to distance these films from their capacity to scare.[14] *I Am the Pretty Thing* and *A Ghost Story* (David Lowery, 2017), for instance, use the figure of the ghost for poetically meditating on mortality, memory and time, while other films have more worldly concerns. *It Follows* explores issues of sexual shame, the constraints of monogamy and the ethics of sexual communitarianism, sometimes hedging closer to a coming-of-age drama than a horror film, while *The Witch* uses its teenage protagonist's budding sexuality and growing defiance of her family patriarch as a quasi-feminist exploration of puritanical paranoia about unruly female bodies, as though contextualising the historical roots of the sexual shame and control depicted in *It Follows*.[15] *Hereditary*, meanwhile, reworks elements of *Rosemary's Baby* and other occult films via a dysfunctional family drama about a mother's resentment of her children as displaced resentment of her own mother, while *Under the Shadow* (Babak Anvari, 2016), like a more politicised version of *The Bababook*, uses its ghost story to explore the trauma of war and post-revolution life for Iranian women.

In these films, the appearance of the monster itself is frequently downplayed or presented only indirectly – whether turned into an invisible or abstract force (*It Follows*, *It Comes at Night*) or presented as a potential figment of a character's overwrought imagination (*The Witch*, *I Am the Pretty Thing*) or mental illness (*The Blackcoat's Daughter*, *Hereditary*). Even when the monster does appear, it often takes a recognisably human form, not that of a grotesquely inhuman creature. *A Ghost Story* takes this decentring of the conventional monster to an extreme, presenting its titular ghost as an actor under a white sheet with black eyeholes – thus replacing the horror genre's fear-inducing ghosts with a more comic image (à la *Scooby Doo*) that marks the film's closer generic resemblance to an existential drama, much as *Under the Skin* uses a seductive image in its generic border case with science fiction. Rather than the monster serving as the horror genre's conventional emotional locus of fear and disgust (as Noël Carroll has argued[16]), many of these films veer closer to Tzvetan Todorov's concept of 'the fantastic', as narratives rooted in epistemological hesitation over whether apparently supernatural occurrences can be explained away as mere 'uncanny' events with rational elucidation or whether something truly 'marvellous' is afoot.[17] *The Witch*, for example, creates considerable ambiguity about whether a witch has actually beset a colonial family (even when we see the witch early in the film, it is unclear whether these scenes are projections of the family's fears), whether the various travails (child disappearances, crop/livestock failures, etc.) of frontier life are mere projections of puritanical fears about Satan's invisible assaults, or even whether blame can be attributed to the rot on the family's corn (the hallucinogenic ergot fungus has been theorised as a possible scientific explanation for symptoms of bewitchment in early America). In classic art-cinema style, then, these films predominantly filter their diegetic visions through the vagaries of characters' distressed psychological states, often refusing to confirm or deny the truth of their seemingly supernatural happenings.

Matt Hills argues that horror cinema may be organised less around the object-directed emotions that Carroll privileges and instead 'immerses its audiences in an "anticipatory" mood or ambience that endures across the text', an overwhelming affect of 'objectless anxiety' that may especially linger beyond the text when a film ends without clear narrative resolution.[18] For Hills, horror should be defined more as 'event-based' than 'entity-based', with narrative circumstances and the details of mise-en-scène/cinematography capable of generating horror even in films like *The Haunting* and *The Blair Witch Project* (Daniel Myrick and Eduardo Sánchez, 1999), where a monster is never explicitly manifest.[19] This fits the new prestige horror's lessened focus on the terror-inducing monster as the clearly defined locus for horror than on more ambient states of fearful unease; hence, in a film like *It Comes at Night*, there is no 'it' revealed over the course of the film, beyond the literal nightmares among a family of plague survivors. Even in *The Blackcoat's Daughter*, a film with multiple (if indirect) sources of horror, critics emphasise its 'suffocating mood' and 'stillness, quiet, and isolation – the elements that . . . feel like lying alone and awake in a dark house, letting your mind play tricks on you'.[20] As Robert Spadoni argues, atmosphere in horror cinema is often considered secondary and subservient to narrative concerns, but affective moods like dread prove that atmosphere is functionally inseparable from narrative – operating less as accompaniment than *culmination* of certain scenes – and thus 'may have as special a relationship to the *absence* of narrative as it does to narrative'.[21] He suggests that atmosphere and narrative exist in tension with each other, with one side filling in when the other is used more sparsely.[22] In this regard, I would also highlight the ambient scores and claustrophobic sound design used in these films, from Rich Vreeland's eerie retro-synth vibes in *It Follows* to Korven's more abstract, quasi-medieval noisescapes for *The Witch*. If orchestral scores traditionally cater to object/character-based emotions, then these more affectively immersive, dread-inducing uses of music underscore the films' apt description as 'apprehension engines'.

Much as horror films may shift from narrative to atmosphere, it is precisely this ability for horror to shift fluidly from objectless affect to object-directed emotion (and vice versa)[23] that, I would argue, allows the genre's traditional emotion (fear) to be shifted towards other negative affects in these prestige horror films, as also illustrated by their open endings. Unlike the near-obligatory jump scares that abruptly punctuate the final frames of many recent Hollywood horror releases, the new prestige horror films extend their sense of fantastic hesitation and ambient affect by way of abrupt endings more akin to art-cinema ambiguity than delivering one last scare before the lights come up. In *It Follows*, Jay and her new boyfriend Paul walk hand-in-hand together thinking they have resolved the curse, but their 'happy' ending is ironically undercut by their ignorance that they are still likely being followed by the entity in the distant background, whereas *The Witch* ends with Thomasin, her family's sole survivor, joining a coven of witches in the woods and levitating into the trees (another ironically 'happy' ending?), but whether this is a fantasy sequence or an actual event is left unclear.

Indie credibility as alternative 'prestige'

What separates the new wave of prestige horror from earlier 'prestige' productions are stronger affinities with the lower-budget, quasi-generic category of 'indie' cinema than with major studio productions. The term 'indie', as applied to cinema, largely developed from the 1990s rise of film festivals like Sundance and was subsequently adopted by the short-lived 'Indiewood' specialty divisions which developed within the major studios in the early 2000s, whereas the new prestige horror films have emerged at a moment when the majors have again retracted from the independent film market.[24] Yet, Jamie Sexton argues that the idea of 'indie-horror' serves as a conceptual Other to American independent cinema, since the various qualities attributed to indie cinema (e.g. authorial originality, formal innovation and self-consciousness, inclusion of marginalised characters/ voices) are not often attributed to horror, particularly given the genre's popular association with well-trodden generic conventions, commercial motivations and lower bodily appeals. Indeed, apart from character-centred dramas, horror films constitute perhaps the most prolific genre within the annual output of American independent film-makers, but only certain types of films are discursively positioned as 'indie', regardless of whether truly produced independently from the major studios.[25] And yet, these films all managed to seemingly transcend their generic roots by evincing a contra-Hollywood style at the blurred borderline of art-cinema narration and indie distribution practices.

Whereas many of horror's earlier prestige films were promoted as singular, high-profile events transcending common generic mediocrity, often appearing years apart from each other, the new wave instead resembles an emergent trend, with multiple films largely following the same trajectory from festival to multiplex in close succession since 2014. Although some of these films also played at Fantastic Fest, Fantasia Film Festival and other genre film festivals populated by independent horror films, the fact that these particular films broke out at prominent non-genre festivals is noteworthy. Even as some of the major film festivals have sidebars dedicated to cultish genre films (e.g. Toronto's Midnight Madness series), many prestige horror films were screened in regular competition. This may stand as a testament to their inability to be qualitatively segregated based on genre alone, though former Midnight Madness programmer Colin Geddes deems this part of a longer pattern of cultural gatekeepers periodically flirting with the horror genre as a redeemable object.[26]

With more conventional generic appeal than the typical indie drama or comedy, these prestige horror films held more crossover potential than the average art-house offering and hence earned distribution deals for limited and expanded release into multiplexes. Genre-centric producer-distributors like Lionsgate and Blumhouse have been responsible for leveraging independently produced horror films into mainstream distribution deals, thereby helping shape several of the largest trends in twenty-first-century horror cinema (such as the 'torture porn' and found-footage cycles). By contrast, many of the new prestige horror films have instead used distributors with more cultural capital – such as rising indie distributor A24, which gained significant repute as the producer-distributor of best picture Oscar winner, *Moonlight* (Barry Jenkins, 2016).[27] In 2016, for instance, A24's *The Witch* was the seventh-highest-grossing horror film of the year at the US box office, earning over $25 million, well above more established properties like *Blair Witch* (Adam Wingard, 2016).[28] Hence, these independently produced, low-budget films clearly demonstrated their earning power (especially given their outsized budget-to-return ratios) by contending alongside major studio productions.

James Kendrick compares the American horror genre to a pendulum swinging periodically between spiritual/supernatural and materialist/graphic horror films, with the post-*Scream* neo-slasher cycle followed by an early 2000s trend towards ghost films (*The Sixth Sense*, *The Others* (Alejandro Amenebar, 2001)) that eventually yielded to the mid-2000s 'torture porn' cycle (*Saw* (James Wan, 2004), *Hostel* (Eli Roth, 2005)).[29] Focusing primarily on independent films that did not achieve wide crossover visibility (such as the early works of Mike Flanagan and Ti West), Hawkins uses the alternate sobriquet 'quiet horror' to describe the post-9/11 return to the gothic as an outgrowth of indie horror production that only became a wider market trend circa 2013.[30] Indeed, compared to the mainstream horror genre's most popular trends since the turn of the century, most of the new prestige horror films are considerably less violent and more supernaturally suggestive than the graphic gore of the post-9/11 torture porn (with some exceptions like *The Eyes of My Mother* (Nicolas Pesce, 2016) and *Hereditary*). Torture porn's divisively violent and nihilistic tone ultimately proved less popular (and thus less profitable) with general audiences than supernatural horror films whose visual restraint was more broadly palatable.[31]

Following Kendrick and Hawkins, we can likewise see a swing back towards supernatural topics in the post-torture-porn box-office popularity of films like *Insidious* (James Wan, 2011), *Sinister* (Scott Derrickson, 2012), *The Conjuring* (James Wan, 2013), *Oculus* (Mike Flanagan, 2013) and *Crimson Peak* (Guillermo del Toro, 2015). For my purposes, it is useful to see the new prestige horror films as an outgrowth of this supernatural revival, even as their austere style differentiates them from the more clichéd aspects of such mainstream horror films – especially the predominant use of jump scares as an accelerationist assault on the viewer's senses.[32] As *The Telegraph*'s Anne Billson suggests,

> Recent high-profile horror films such as *Annabelle* [John R. Leonetti, 2014], *Jessabelle* [Kevin Greutert, 2014] and *The Woman in Black 2: Angel of Death* [Tom Harper, 2014] founder on sloppy storytelling and an over-reliance on hoary old methods of making us jump, but are still a welcome sign of the decline of noughties torture-porn, an unremittingly grim ordeal not only for the unfortunate characters, but for audiences as well.[33]

Films like *Insidious* and *The Conjuring* actually received very positive reviews as gore-free throwbacks to old-fashioned haunted-house scares – including plaudits for *Saw* director James Wan finally 'making good' on his torture-porn roots with these two high-profile films – confirming the old pattern that horror films with higher budgets and less graphic violence tend to earn stronger critical acclaim. Yet, the fact that the overuse of jump scares quickly became target for criticism of these supernatural films suggests how even more reputable productions like *The Conjuring* can be negatively affected by subsequent imitators, and hence how fragile the horror genre's reputability ever truly is.

Prestige or pretension: critical vs popular reception

The art/auteur vs horror/genre divide is reflected most strongly in the notable disjunction between high praise from film-literate viewers (professional critics, genre fans) and disappointment expressed by more populist viewers as these prestige films crossed over to multiplexes. Whereas these films earned very strong reviews from most film critics on the basis of their distinction from more conventional Hollywood fare, broad-based websites like IMDb and Rotten Tomatoes, along with audience-polling services like CinemaScore, demonstrate far lower scores from general viewers: *It Comes at Night* and *Hereditary* respectively earned 'D' and 'D-' CinemaScore grades, for example, despite earning critical plaudits. According to reviewers, these are 'no jump-scare, teen-bait multiplex horror movie[s]', but instead 'make . . . the viewer work for gratification' and 'cherish . . . the intelligence of [their] audience'.[34] Negative reviews from casual viewers, meanwhile, criticise the films' slow pacing, ambiguous endings and lack of conventional monsters/thrills, deeming the films boring, confusing, not scary and utterly unsatisfying; indeed, the vast majority of audience criticism hinges precisely on the traits of art cinema that these films display. Misleadingly genre-centric trailers (especially by A24) have been suggested as one reason for this disappointment: 'One hallmark of the new wave of prestige horror is that the movies are often nothing like the trailers . . . Cutting together duplicitous trailers to bait a broader audience into seeing these very good movies seems like the best of a lot of bad options.'[35]

But even among the minority of professional critics who gave negative reviews of these films, the same traits that they might praise in an international art film – stylistic self-consciousness, mood over narrative, cryptic character motivations, depressive affect – are here deemed faults by virtue of their presence in a feature-length horror film. Hence, *The Witch* is a 'witches' brew of half-formed subplots, under-baked themes, a grating score and unlikable characters' that 'needs to be less proud of itself and yeah, it needs to be scarier'.[36] Meanwhile, *The Blackcoat's Daughter* is 'built around elliptical vagaries' but is unable 'to channel the story through emotion, spreading itself thin across themes of alienation, mourning and fears of abandonment'.[37] Furthermore, 'setting a bunch of people loose on the screen and telling them to mope until something supernatural emerges, then calling it a tone poem about loss, is no way to keep an audience entertained'.[38] And '[t]hose expecting a horror movie that's filled with a *lot* of those gross and scary moments will likely be disappointed' by *It Comes at Night*,

> while those who might appreciate the film's less horrific storytelling will probably be scared away by the marketing. One thing's for sure: No one who sees this is going to come out of it thinking it was any kind of fun; it's one of the bleakest movies to be released this year.[39]

In short, for nonplussed viewers both professional and casual, these films may be stylish, moody and technically accomplished – but they are not conventionally 'fun'. Their affective tone may feel more oppressive or alienating than sensational, and their narratives may read as 'yet another would-be art piece that mistakes ambiguity for complexity'.[40]

Horror fans who self-identify with higher amounts of genre literacy and subcultural capital, however, are the ones most likely to be regular posters on horror-centric discussion boards and are more likely to rank these among the best horror films of the year. On Reddit's 'Horror' board, for instance, *It Follows* and *The Witch* topped the fan rankings of 'Top 20 Films' for 2015 and 2016 respectively, with the other new prestige horror movies ranking highly as well.[41] If these films' detractors cannot adequately reconcile art cinema with horror cinema, their high-minded defenders (in the words of one reviewer) 'argue that you need to reconsider your expectations for "horror", but I can understand if the mainstream movie-goer would take the upcoming *Annabelle: Creation* [David F. Sandberg, 2017] over a more contemplative film'.[42] As Hills observes, it is common for horror fans to justify their love for a devalued genre by privileging connoisseurship – whether framed through auteurism, aesthetics, genre history, etc. – and hence their ability *not* to be scared like more 'naive' viewers or non-fans. This often means privileging certain horror films for their capacity to inspire affects beyond fear, particularly when those other affects allow fans to uphold horror as more of a 'mind genre' than a 'body genre'.[43] It is not difficult to see how the new prestige horror films, with their minimalist emphasis on tone and ambiguity over the crude mechanics of delivering scares, would seem ready-made for this fan-cultural rhetoric.

Yet, the outsized critical acclaim earned by these few examples of a genre that has been so often pilloried by critics has also inspired some backlash among long-time horror fans who either accuse these films of being overrated or being guilty of not representing 'straight-up horror' – a strategy of intra-subcultural distinction that largely hinges upon these films' apparent distance from some imagined generic 'core'. As one fan writer astutely observes, 'By calling something "prestige horror" or "smart horror", we [fans] are inadvertently (or maybe intentionally, for some) putting down other equally valid movies in the genre – and subsequently the fans who like them.'[44] In other words, by occupying the intersection of art cinema and genre cinema, these slow-paced and sometimes gore-averse films may have become 'safer' for middlebrow reclamation, albeit at the expense of films that may also be worthy of critical attention but lack such a rarefied aesthetic. On the one hand, then, some fans may prefer generically 'purer' horror films with more minoritising potential to *épater la bourgeoisie*; but, on the other hand, some fans resent how the critical praise lavished on these select films does not so much universalise the genre's overall cultural standing as preserve the genre's status as a 'bad object' transcended by the prestige few.

In sum, fans, critics and casual viewers all remain haunted by the dominant association of horror as a populist genre – albeit for different reasons. These films' divisive reception demonstrates that art-horror's disrepute may have less to do with horror's appeals to the body than its expected appeals to entertainment value. If even viewers who self-identify as possessing high degrees of (sub)cultural capital are far more likely to engage with one side of the art/genre binary when considering culturally 'lower' genres than higher genres, then horror's cultural disrepute will remain largely in place. But the fact that generic appeals can allow the new prestige horror films to find larger audiences beyond the art-house circuit does offer some hope that aesthetically different uses of the genre can achieve some (limited) mainstream visibility. Whether broader, more populist audiences will adjust their generic expectations accordingly, as the new independent prestige horror trend continues, remains an open question.

Notes

1. See Indie Film Maker, 'Horror Musical Instrument – The Apprehension Engine', *YouTube* (30 September 2016), *https://www.youtube.com/watch?v=lzk-l8Gm0MY* (accessed 29 August 2019); and Great Big Story, 'Sounds of the Nightmare Machine', *YouTube* (20 June 2017), *https://www.youtube.com/watch?v=1lTYPvArbGo* (accessed 29 August 2019).
2. L. Birnbaum, '*The Blackcoat's Daughter*: The film you aren't ready to see (but should)', *Film Inquiry* (1 July 2016), *https://www.filminquiry.com/blackcoats-daughter-2015-review/* (accessed 29 August 2019).
3. See Rhona J. Berenstein, *Attack of the Leading Ladies: Gender, Sexuality, and Spectatorship in Classic Horror Cinema* (New York, NY: Columbia University Press, 1996); Kevin Heffernan, *Ghouls, Gimmicks, and Gold: Horror Films and the American Movie Business, 1953–1968* (Durham, NC: Duke University Press, 2004); T. Snelson, '"From Grade B Thrillers to Deluxe Chillers": Prestige Horror, Female Audiences, and Allegories of Spectatorship in *The Spiral Staircase* (1946)', *New Review of Film and Television Studies*, 7/2 (2009), 173–88; S. Abbott, 'High Concept Thrills and Chills: The Horror Blockbuster', in I. Conrich (ed.), *Horror Zone: The Cultural Experience of Contemporary Horror Cinema* (London: I. B. Tauris, 2009), pp. 27–44; M. Jancovich, 'Relocating Lewton: Cultural Distinctions, Critical Reception, and the Val Lewton Horror Films', *Journal of Film and Video*, 64/3 (2012), 21–37; K. Edwards, '"House of horrors": Corporate strategy at Universal Pictures in the 1930s', in R. Nowell (ed.), *Merchants of Menace: The Business of Horror Cinema* (London: Bloomsbury, 2014), pp. 13–29; and M. Jancovich, 'Beyond Hammer: the first run market and the prestige horror film in the early 1960s', *Palgrave Communications*, 3 (2017), *https://doi.org/10.1057/palcomms.2017.28* (accessed 29 August 2019).
4. Joan Hawkins, *Cutting Edge: Art-horror and the Horrific Avant-garde* (Minneapolis, MN: University of Minnesota Press, 2000).
5. Hawkins, *Cutting Edge*, p. 66.
6. D. Bordwell, 'The art cinema as a mode of film practice', in T. Corrigan, P. White and M. Mazaj (eds), *Critical Visions in Film Theory: Classic and Contemporary Readings* (Boston, MA: Bedford/St. Martin's, 2011), pp. 560–4.
7. D. Pye, 'Movies and tone', in J. Gibbs and D. Pye (eds), *Close-Up 02* (London: Wallflower Press, 2007), pp. 7, 21, 23, 28, 76.
8. Julian Hanich, *Cinematic Emotion in Horror Films and Thrillers: The Aesthetic Paradox of Pleasurable Fear* (London: Routledge, 2010), pp. 179–80, 187.

9. A. Billson, 'Cheap thrills: The frightful rise of low-budget horror', *The Telegraph* (6 May 2015), http://www.telegraph.co.uk/film/it-follows/rise-of-low-budget-horror-movies-babadook/ (accessed 29 August 2019); J. Crucchiola, 'Why Do Prestige-Horror Trailers Keep Lying to Us?', *Vulture* (13 June 2017), http://www.vulture.com/2017/06/it-comes-at-night-why-are-horror-trailers-lying-to-us.html (accessed 29 August 2019).
10. J. Sconce, 'Irony, Nihilism, and the New American "Smart" Film', *Screen*, 43/4 (2002), 359, 368.
11. C. Alexander, 'TIFF 2016 Review: I Am the Pretty Thing That Lives in the House', *ComingSoon.net* (12 September 2016), http://www.comingsoon.net/horror/reviews/766113-tiff-2016-review-i-am-the-pretty-thing-that-lives-in-the-house (accessed 29 August 2019).
12. J. Crucchiola, 'Let's Talk About the Ending of *The Blackcoat's Daughter*', *Vulture* (31 March 2017), http://www.vulture.com/2017/03/blackcoats-daughter-ending.html (accessed 29 August 2019); emphasis in the original.
13. K. Rife, 'Horror is a Trojan horse for *The Blackcoat's Daughter* director Oz Perkins', *AV Club* (30 March 2017), http://www.avclub.com/article/horror-trojan-horse-blackcoats-daughter-director-o-252538 (accessed 29 August 2019).
14. S. Rose, 'How post-horror movies are taking over cinema', *The Guardian* (6 July 2017), https://www.theguardian.com/film/2017/jul/06/post-horror-films-scary-movies-ghost-story-it-comes-at-night (accessed 29 August 2019).
15. See D. Church, 'Queer Ethics, Urban Spaces, and the Horrors of Monogamy in *It Follows*', *Cinema Journal*, 57/3 (2018), 3–28; and B. Ashley, 'In horror film "The Witch", terror stems from patriarchal control of women', *Bitch* (3 March 2016), https://www.bitchmedia.org/article/horror-film-witch-terror-stems-puritanical-control-women (accessed 29 August 2019).
16. Noël Carroll, *The Philosophy of Horror or Paradoxes of the Heart* (London: Routledge, 1990), pp. 28–30.
17. See Matt Hills, *The Pleasures of Horror* (London: Continuum, 2005), pp. 34–6.
18. Hills, *The Pleasures of Horror*, pp. 25–7.
19. M. Hills, 'An event-based definition of art-horror', in S. J. Schneider and D. Shaw (eds), *Dark Thoughts: Philosophic Reflections on Cinematic Horror* (Lanham, MD: Scarecrow Press, 2003), pp. 142–4, 148–50.
20. A. A. Dowd, '*The Blackcoat's Daughter* finally rises from release-date purgatory to give everyone the creeps', *AV Club* (30 March 2017), http://www.avclub.com/review/blackcoats-daughter-rises-release-date-purgatory-g-252881 (accessed 29 August 2019).

21. R. Spadoni, 'Carl Dreyer's Corpse: Horror Film Atmosphere and Narrative', in H. M. Benshoff (ed.), *A Companion to the Horror Film* (Chichester: Wiley-Blackwell, 2014), pp. 157–9, 165; emphasis in the original.
22. R. Spadoni, 'Horror Film Atmosphere as Anti-narrative (and Vice Versa)', in R. Nowell (ed.), *Merchants of Menace: The Business of Horror Cinema* (London: Bloomsbury, 2014), pp. 109–12.
23. Hills, *The Pleasures of Horror*, p. 28.
24. On these shifts, see Y. Tzioumakis, '"Independent", "Indie", and "Indiewood": Towards a periodisation of contemporary (post-1980) American independent cinema', in G. King, C. Molloy and Y. Tzioumakis (eds), *American Independent Cinema: Indie, Indiewood, and Beyond* (London: Routledge, 2013), pp. 28–40.
25. J. Sexton, 'US "Indie-Horror": Critical Reception, Genre Construction, and Suspect Hybridity', *Cinema Journal*, 51/2 (2012), 69–71, 81–3.
26. F. Blichert, 'What's next for the indie horror movie wave', *Vice* (9 June 2017), https://www.vice.com/en_us/article/kzq7kz/heres-what-to-watch-next-if-youre-riding-the-prestige-horror-wave (accessed 29 August 2019).
27. Z. Baron, 'How A24 is disrupting Hollywood', *GQ* (9 May 2017), http://www.gq.com/story/a24-studio-oral-history (accessed 29 August 2019).
28. Figures from *The Numbers*, 'Box Office Performance for Horror Movies in 2015', http://www.the-numbers.com/market/2015/genre/Horror; and 'Box Office Performance for Horror Movies in 2016', http://www.the-numbers.com/market/2016/genre/Horror (accessed 29 August 2019).
29. J. Kendrick, 'A return to the graveyard: Notes on the spiritual horror film', in S. Hantke (ed.), *American Horror Film: The Genre at the Turn of the Millennium* (Jackson, MS: University Press of Mississippi, 2010), pp. 142–4, 155–6.
30. J. Hawkins, '"It fixates": indie quiets and the new Gothics', *Palgrave Communications*, 3 (2017), https://doi.org/10.1057/palcomms.2017.88 (accessed 29 August 2019).
31. See B. Davis and K. Natale, '"The pound of flesh which I demand": American horror cinema, gore, and the box office, 1998–2007', in S. Hantke (ed.), *American Horror Film: The Genre at the Turn of the Millennium* (Jackson, MS: University Press of Mississippi, 2010), pp. 46–9.
32. Although far from exhaustive, the list of 'High Jump Scare Movies' on the fan-made website *Where's the Jump?* is dominated by films made since 2003, and suggests a sharp upward trend in such scare tactics since 2009. See 'High Jump Scare Movies', *Where's the Jump?*, https://wheresthejump.com/high-jump-scare-movies/ (accessed 29 August 2019).
33. Billson, 'Cheap thrills'.

34. Alexander, 'TIFF 2016 Review'; K. McLoone, '*It Comes at Night* and the power of the unseen horror', *Cultured Vultures* (12 July 2017), https://cultured-vultures.com/it-comes-at-night-horror/ (accessed 29 August 2019).
35. Crucchiola, 'Why Do Prestige-Horror Trailers'.
36. E. Sacks, '"The Witch" casts a spell on critics even though it's not very good', *New York Daily News* (17 February 2016), http://www.nydailynews.com/entertainment/movies/witch-casts-spell-critics-not-good-article-1.2529738 (accessed 29 August 2019); W. Leitch, '*The Witch*: Suffer the Little Children', *The New Republic* (19 February 2016), https://newrepublic.com/article/130182/witch-suffer-little-children (accessed 29 August 2019).
37. J. Smith, 'The Blackcoat's Daughter', *RogerEbert.com* (29 March 2017), http://www.rogerebert.com/reviews/the-blackcoats-daughter-2017 (accessed 29 August 2019).
38. J. Hoffman, 'February review – Pseudo-intellectual horror of the dullest kind', *The Guardian* (14 September 2015), https://www.theguardian.com/film/2015/sep/14/february-film-review-kiernan-shipka-osgood-perkins-horror (accessed 29 August 2019). Originally titled *February* during its festival run, *The Blackcoat's Daughter* was subsequently re-titled by its distributor.
39. R. Jokinen, 'Bleak "It Comes at Night" is a thoroughly unpleasant experience', *SFist* (9 June 2017), http://sfist.com/2017/06/09/bleak_it_comes_at_night_a_thoroughl.php (accessed 29 August 2019); emphasis in the original.
40. R. Lawson, '*It Comes at Night* is a pretty but pointless downer', *Vanity Fair* (6 June 2017), http://www.vanityfair.com/hollywood/2017/06/it-comes-at-night-review (accessed 29 August 2019).
41. See 'Dreadit's Top 20 Films of 2015' (*https://www.reddit.com/r/horror/wiki/bestof2015*) and 'Dreadit's Top 20 Films of 2016' (*https://www.reddit.com/r/horror/comments/5re1dl/dreadits_top_films_of_2016/*) (accessed 29 August 2019).
42. McLoone, '*It Comes at Night*'.
43. Hills, *The Pleasures of Horror*, pp. 74–6, 82.
44. J. Hicks, 'Everybody be cool: How to rise above genre-fan backlash', *Blumhouse.com* (5 July 2017), http://www.blumhouse.com/2017/07/05/everybody-be-cool-how-to-rise-above-genre-fan-backlash/ (accessed 29 August 2019).

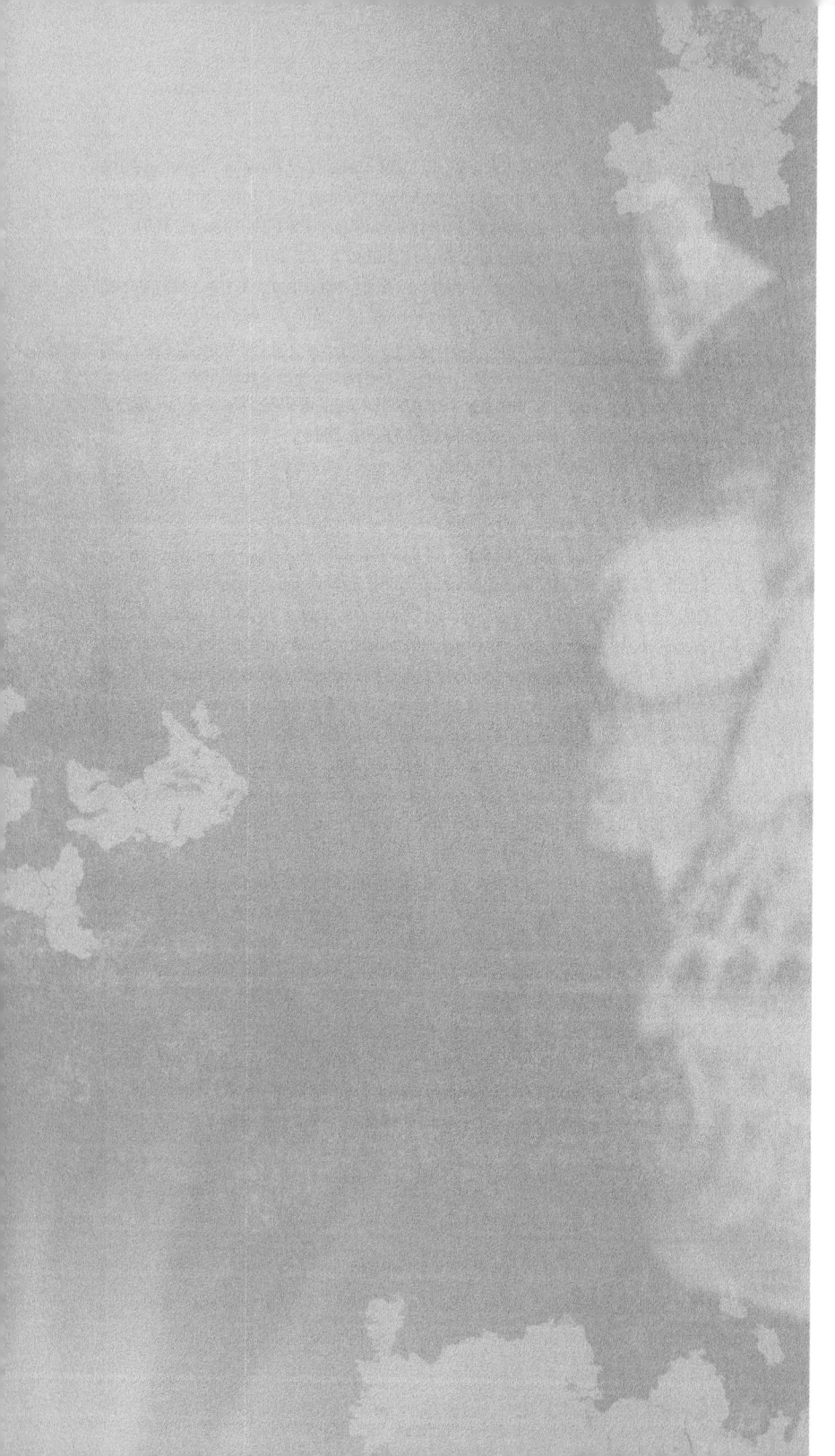

2

Hardcore Horror

Challenging the Discourses of 'Extremity'

Steve Jones

THERE HAS BEEN a notable increase in the production and discussion of extreme film (particularly extreme horror) in the cultural sphere over the last fifteen years. Extreme horror production and distribution has flourished thanks to the accessibility of digital film-making, crowdfunding and the global online marketplace. The box-office successes of films such as *Saw* (James Wan, 2004) and *Hostel* (Eli Roth, 2005) attracted the attention of press critics, who dubbed such films 'extreme'.[1] Controversial releases such as *A Serbian Film* (Srđan Spasojević, 2010) attracted the attention of censors in numerous countries, including the UK.[2] Within this context, some film-makers have carved a niche, producing gory, micro-budget horror that embraces content that censors find problematic. In previous work, I referred to these micro-budget productions as 'hardcore horror'.[3] Hardcore horror's 'extremity' is confirmed by its unavailability in major retail outlets such as chain stores and multiplex theatres.

This chapter explores the relationship between 'hardcore horror' films and the discursive context in which mainstream horror releases are being dubbed 'extreme'. This chapter compares 'mainstream' and 'hardcore horror' with the aim of investigating what 'extremity' means. I will begin by outlining what hardcore horror is and how it differs from mainstream horror (both in terms of content and distribution). I will then dissect what 'extremity' means in this context, delineating problems with established critical discourses about 'extreme horror'. Print press reviewers focus on theatrically released horror films, ignoring micro-budget direct-to-video horror. As such, their adjudications about 'extremity' in horror begin from a limited base that misrepresents the genre. Moreover, 'extremity' is not a universally shared value, yet it is predominantly presented as if referring to an objective, universally agreed-upon standard. Such judgements change over time. Moreover, in contrast to marketers' uses of 'extreme', press critics predominantly use the term as a pejorative. Although academics have sought to defend and contextualise particular maligned films and directors, scholars have focused on only a handful of infamous examples, and academic publishers implicitly support that narrow focus. As such, the cumulative body of scholarly work on 'extreme horror' inadvertently replicates print press critics' mischaracterisation of the genre. These discursive factors limit our collective understandings of 'horror', its ostensible 'extremity' and of 'extremity' qua concept. Given that the discourse of 'extremity' is so commonly employed when censuring representations that challenge established genre conventions, it is imperative that horror studies academics attend to peripheral hardcore horror texts, and seek to develop more robust conceptual understandings of extremity.

Contextualising hardcore horror

Associations between contemporary visceral horror and extremity have been confirmed in the marketing materials of recent horror titles and re-releases of contentious twentieth-century films.[4] Whether for DVD covers or digital platforms, promotional images routinely boast that a given horror title is being made available in an 'uncensored', 'uncut', 'unrated' or 'extreme' version. When films were censored for the theatrical release or previously banned, such claims signal which version of the film is being made available to prospective consumers. For example, *I Spit on Your Grave* (Meir Zarchi, 1978) has been released in multiple versions in the UK, including a 'Special Edition . . . Fuller Version' (Screen Entertainment, 2003) and an 'ultimate . . . most complete version ever released in the UK' (101 Films, 2010). Both versions are expurgated, in contrast to the 2004 Australian Force Entertainment DVD, which proclaims to be 'completely uncut'. However, in many cases the proclamation that a film is 'uncut' is a misnomer inasmuch as no cuts were required prior to release. For example, the 2007 Entertainment in Video UK DVD release of *Flight of the Living Dead* (Scott Thomas, 2007) boasts of being 'uncut', despite not being subject to censorship in the UK.[5] The US New Line Home Video release of the film is similarly emblazoned with an 'unrated' stamp even though it did not receive an R-rated theatrical release to warrant a distinction.[6]

Posturing towards 'extremity' in this manner is now a commonplace marketing strategy. To offer another example in the UK context, several films released by Technicolor Home Entertainment – including *Pig Hunt* (James Isaac, 2008) – were classified with a '15' certificate, but were rated '18' on DVD. Technically, this is due to the disc containing 'additional material' that was 'classified at a higher certificate than the main feature': in this case, the material was a trailer for *Pig Hunt* itself, which was classified at '18' even though the film was classified '15'.[7] Including the trailer appears to have been a tactic to secure the higher age rating. Given that the certification excludes a section of the population (thereby potentially reducing the sales-base), Technicolor Home Entertainment seem to have intentionally used the '18' certification marker to present *Pig Hunt* as if it contains more extreme content than it actually offers.

These marketing strategies illustrate the ways in which notional unacceptability is routinely embedded into the discourses that surround visceral horror films. Two implications follow. First, such constructed unacceptability signals that these films are products of a liberal moment, at least in terms of horror film censorship. Uncut versions of banned horror films (such as *I Spit on Your Grave*) are commonly sought after for their notoriety, and because they were at one time unavailable.[8] Rhetorically aligning newer, uncensored films with these illicit, sought-after products is a way of artificially generating cultural capital. The implicit claim made by labelling a horror film 'extreme' is that it contains material that could (perhaps 'should') trouble censors, even when it has not been censored. Secondly, the context in which these films are offered also belies their ostensibly controversial status. DVDs that are labelled as 'extreme' versions – such as the DVD release of *Saw III* (Darren Lynn Bousman, 2006) – are widely available in chain retail stores. Although the marketing implies unacceptability, the context reveals quite the opposite; that the content is permissible, and that is why it is abundantly accessible. Where films have traversed those boundaries – providing unacceptable content – they have been censored or outright banned. For instance, *The Human Centipede II (Full Sequence)* (Tom Six, 2011) was initially banned in various countries, including Australia, New Zealand and the UK. The censored 2011 UK DVD version by Bounty Films may lean on that controversy in its packaging (dubbing it 'the film they didn't want you to see'), but its wide release and legal permissibility undercuts, or at least dampens, any implied claim that the DVD release is 'extreme'.

Against (and perhaps in response to) this context, a subset of micro-budget film-makers have produced films that contain the kinds of imagery promised by the above marketing strategies (i.e. fictional content that would be rejected by censors). I have previously dubbed such films hardcore horror. This term implies comparisons to hardcore pornography, thereby highlighting three broad characteristics that distinguish hardcore horror. The first is industrial. Just as porn exists as a film-making 'industry' apart from 'legitimate' feature film-making, hardcore horror is the ghettoised, stigmatised and fragmented Other to studio-based horror film-making. The second characteristic is aesthetic. As with pornography, hardcore horror film-makers routinely deploy genitally explicit sex to mask the film's performative aspects. However, in hardcore horror, sex is usually combined or juxtaposed with violence. Thus, genitally explicit sex connotes that the dramatised violence is also real(istic), authentic and unplanned, rather than carefully crafted and staged.[9]

Before moving on to the third characteristic, it is worth noting that the combination of sex and violence is a step too far for major censorship bodies such as the Motion Picture Association of America (MPAA) and the British Board of Film Classification (BBFC).[10] For example, films such as *Murder-Set-Pieces* (Nick Palumbo, 2004), *Grotesque* (Kōji Shiraishi, 2009) and *The Bunny Game* (Adam Rehmeier, 2011) were banned by the BBFC because they contain prolonged depictions of sexual violence, or juxtapositions of sex and violence. To illustrate, *Hate Crime* (James Cullen Bressack, 2012) was refused classification because it 'focuses on physical and sexual abuse' in an 'unremitting manner'.[11] Since none of the films listed have yet been resubmitted for classification in censored forms, they cannot be sold legally in the UK. Many other films containing similar content have avoided official bans in the UK simply because they have not been submitted for classification (and thus still cannot be sold in the UK). Given the precedent set by banning films such as *Hate*

Crime, it would be fruitless to submit films such as *Prison of Hell: K3* (Andreas Bethmann, 2009) or *Faces of Snuff* (Shane Ryan et al., 2016) to the BBFC, since both contain significantly more frequent, sustained and explicit depictions of sex, violence and sexual violence than films that have been banned.[12] Little narrative context is provided for the depictions of violence in films such as *Women's Flesh: My Red Guts* (Tamakichi Anaru, 1999) and *Murder Collection V.1* (Fred Vogel, 2009), which follow a structure that is more commonly located in gonzo porn than in horror. Here, extremity is marked by eschewing the causal narrative resolution and character development that typifies normative Hollywood storytelling.[13] It is clear that censorship bodies such as the BBFC typically look to narrative context to provide a rationale for explicit violence.[14] Minimising that context increases the chances that a hardcore horror film would be banned if submitted for classification.

Hardcore horror's third distinguishing characteristic is commercial. In contrast to moderately budgeted independent horror that seeks to emulate larger studio productions' aesthetic standards and trappings, hardcore horror is differentiated from 'mainstream' horror by its graphic (genitally explicit) depictions of sex and lo-fi visuals. Hardcore horror is typically shot on micro budgets. For example, *Flowers* (Phil Stevens, 2015) was reputedly made 'for a mere $20,000', and was largely shot in the director's own home.[15] This location itself suggests a degree of intimate control over the project, which Stevens confirms in his DVD commentary where he refers to *Flowers* as 'the movie I've been always trying to make . . . that I . . . love personally and with all my heart'.[16] Stevens's comment – suggesting that movie-making is a compulsion rather than being motivated by profit – is typical of how hardcore horror film-makers routinely align budgetary limitations with integrity, distancing themselves and their films from the profit-driven commercialism connoted by studio film-making.

Flowers is distributed by specialists Unearthed Films, but many other hardcore horror films are distributed independently by the film-makers themselves. In this respect, contemporary hardcore horror film-makers take their lead from late twentieth-century film-makers such as Andreas Schnaas, Heiko Fipper and Shinji Imaoka who used VHS technology to release micro-budget sex-and-gore films to an international marketplace. Twenty-first-century hardcore horror film-makers follow a similar path, although digital technology has arguably amplified film-makers' ability to shoot and edit higher quality products on lower budgets, while digital platforms have facilitated new routes to international markets. For instance,

Italian independent horror company Necrostorm not only produce and distribute their own products, but also run crowdfunding campaigns through their own website, maximising the yield from those campaigns. Recognising that filmic content precludes them from the funding mechanisms and distribution chains even minor studios and DVD distribution labels have at their disposal, companies such as Necrostorm thrive because of their self-publication model.[17]

This model leaves film-makers in a vulnerable position. For example, Ryan Nicholson (Plotdigger Films) opened a successful Indiegogo campaign for *Gutterballs 2* in 2014, and in February 2016 Nicholson was hospitalised to remove a brain tumour. The film was not completed and pre-orders for various Plotdigger projects remain unfulfilled (much to the chagrin of backers who accuse Nicholson of stealing their money).[18] Given that the staff of Plotdigger primarily consisted of Nicholson and his spouse, his illness virtually halted the company's business. Furthermore, such companies depend on maintaining a dedicated fan base's interest and loyalty, not least because the content necessarily limits its commercial potential. Nicholson's illness and the resultant delays clearly damaged the fan/film-maker relationship and Plotdigger's viability prior to Nicholson's untimely death in 2019.

Moreover, with limited budgets and without the support of established distributors, these film-makers are reliant on social media to market their work. However, these avenues can be precarious. Film-maker Shane Ryan articulates this on his public Facebook page, protesting 'FACEBOOK moderator assholes . . . I joined ONLY to promote my films. But you goddamn fucking jackasses don't even allow me to . . . Don't I at least deserve to be able to let people know my films even exist . . .?'[19]

Promoting and distributing films via digital streaming platforms is just as frustrating for Ryan: 'It seems like almost nothing of mine is allowed on any major vod/streaming/etc site. Which is actually making me consider how I should make/edit my films. But . . . That's not art. These aren't studio films . . . we shouldn't have to censor ourselves.'[20] Ryan's comments indicate that working outside the studio system ought to translate into increased artistic freedom, but if the resultant movies contain extreme content, even these alternative routes to market are severely restricted.

A distinction needs to be drawn here between these limitations and other forms of banning. Prohibition can augment an extreme horror film's reputation insofar as censorship indicates that a given film contains material 'not found in the average Hollywood film'.[21] Censors aim to reflect majority values,[22] and so censorship serves as a promise to hardcore horror consumers that a film features the extreme content that they seek (which is not available in mainstream products). Such movies have limited commercial prospects, and banning can alert potential consumers to a project that might have otherwise gone unnoticed. By having to seek out a copy of a banned film, fans signal their investment in hardcore horror. However, in order to harness that potential, the film has to be available for purchase in some form.

Hardcore horror film-makers make a trade-off between profitability and artistic control, then. The word-of-mouth infamy film-makers can generate potentially yields greater (if necessarily more modest) fortunes than broader distribution can. By carving a niche apart from the mainstream commercial sector, hardcore horror film-makers avoid the market saturation that stifles many who seek fame in the world of studio-based horror. However, compared with an indie studio horror movie like *Hostel* – which had a budget of $4.8 million and has yielded over $82.2 million (worldwide, unadjusted)[23] thanks to its theatrical exhibition and subsequent home-media distribution – hardcore horror's budgets and returns seem insignificant. In this context, hardcore horror film-makers react against mainstream movies' profitability by suggesting that commercial success equates to curbing content to fit within the sector's commercial and censorial remits. Such curbing has an impact on hardcore horror's very essence: its horrific elements.

Extremity and its contingencies

By tracing its various characteristics, one can observe how hardcore horror is distinguished by its conscious negation of major studio film-making's industrial, commercial and aesthetic conventions, and therein lies its appeal as an alternative to mainstream horror. In this regard, hardcore horror film-makers might appear reactionary, railing against normative standards simply to shock or upset. Film criticism's dominant voices are preoccupied with theatrical releases and so routinely ignore peripheral horror. Nevertheless, hardcore horror is implicated in the broader discourses that surround gory studio horror.

To illustrate, critics have referred to certified, theatrically released visceral films such as *mother!* (Darren Aronofsky, 2017) as 'extreme horror'.[24] Here, 'extremity' indicates that the film in question contains too much gore or violence for the reviewer's tastes and seeks to shock simply for shock's sake.[25] Some critics suggest that visceral horror film-makers endeavour to outdo one another by creating ever-gorier or more explicit images.[26] Moreover, if a film-maker's aim is simply to outdo their peers, this game of 'one-upping' has no endpoint. Therefore, critics such as Lenore Skenazy suggest that '[i]f we start accepting this kind of movie as just "extreme" horror, the baseline will change'.[27] In this view, unless curbed, critics believe 'extreme' horror will have detrimental impacts on culture. Although they refer to theatrical releases as 'extreme', hardcore horror is implicated because the latter is distinguished by including content that is too affronting (or 'extreme') for the multiplex context.

Several problems follow from these premises. First, hardcore horror's very existence undercuts critics' complaints about mainstream horror's supposed extremity. A film such as *mother!* may be 'extreme' by the standards of certified films exhibited in cinemas but not by the standards of the genre as a whole. An individual who considers *mother!* extreme because it features infanticide[28] may change their assessment of its relative excessiveness after seeing *A Serbian Film*'s 'newborn porn' sequence (in which an infant is raped). However, that does not mean *A Serbian Film* is extreme and *mother!* is not. After all, the sequence in which a newborn is raped, beaten, dismembered, eaten and regurgitated in *Slow Torture Puke Chamber* (Lucifer Valentine, 2010) eclipses *A Serbian Film* in terms of prolonged violence and graphic detail, ensuring that it could not be released in the multiplex context in anything other than a heavily truncated form. Print press critics' broad proclamations about 'horror' misrepresent the genre by focusing almost exclusively on the mainstream studio system. Without explicit recognition of that limitation or a fuller synchronic understanding, Skenazy's illustrative complaint about the state of 'extreme' horror is only half-formed.

The second problem is that there is no universally shared value or absolute measure against which extremity is judged. For example, Todd Brown qualifies his description of *Martyrs* (Pascal Laugier, 2008) by adjudicating that it is '*incredibly* extreme';[29] Che Gilson deems that the violence in *Misogynist* (Michael Matteo Rossi, 2013) 'is often *highly* extreme';[30] Ronny Carlsson considers the finale of *Maskhead* (Fred Vogel, 2009) to be '*really* extreme';[31] reviewer 'Blacktooth' describes *Flowers* as 'a *very* extreme horror flick';[32] and Peter Bradshaw declares that *Irreversible* (Gaspar Noé, 2002) is an '*ultra-extreme* movie'.[33] If the adjective 'extreme' referred to an absolute standard, qualifiers such as 'ultra' would be unnecessary (since both 'ultra' and 'extreme' indicate excessiveness). Most overtly, David Edelstein's proclamation that film-maker 'Eli Roth is *extremely* extreme' demonstrates both the redundancy of such qualifying adjectives and how ineffective 'extreme' has become in contemporary discourse.[34] These phrasings reveal that 'extreme' is a relational judgement; it is a comparative measure that is contingent on the receiver's shared agreement about that to which it is being compared. Moreover, what a majority consider to be extreme (which is to some extent reflected in censorial standards) also changes over time. 'Extremity' indicates that which is unacceptable according to the cultural, political and social values of the moment, and those underlying values are not static. Thus, some previously banned films such as *Salò, or the 120 Days of Sodom* (Pier Paolo Pasolini, 1975) have subsequently been released uncut.[35]

What remains static, however, is the conceptual meaning of 'extremity'. The term is applied to that which is taboo or which breaches contemporaneous acceptability standards. The specific attributes, traits or themes that amount to extreme content change with time, but when critics point out differences between past and present, they routinely package such shifts with valuations, as if what is considered 'extreme' now is 'worse' than previous 'extreme' content. The latter is patently false insofar as if content was considered 'extreme' in the past, it violated acceptability standards in that moment. Present 'extreme' content is guilty of the same infringement, just as future 'extreme' content will be. Thus, discourse surrounding horror's 'extremity' reveals little about the elements that are being compared, since the term is commonly used to reassert (transient) normative value-judgements. The contingencies that would illuminate critics' judgements about extremity – such as the comparison between hardcore and multiplex horror – typically remain unexamined.

Without a more detailed understanding of the work 'extremity' does in relation to horror or a wider understanding of the genre, print press critics' proclamations about 'extreme horror' amount to little more than proposals about what horror films ought to be, packaged as if those assertions are objective descriptions.[36] This is entirely different from other uses of the term: in censorial contexts, 'extreme' usually indicates that content has infringed legal standards; in horror marketing, 'extreme' routinely promises that a film's content will suit some consumers' tastes (regardless of the veracity of such claims); hardcore horror film-makers and distributors additionally use the term to signal difference from studio horror.

Academic responses to extreme horror

Press critics almost universally use the term 'extreme horror' as a pejorative, tending to quickly dismiss films such as *The Human Centipede II (Full Sequence)* as disgusting, superficial 'shock films'.[37] A minority of academics have sought to counter these assertions by engaging with allegedly 'extreme' low-budget, theatrically released horror films. By subjecting such films to serious intellectual scrutiny, these scholars have challenged the notion that 'extreme' horror films are one-dimensional. Much of that work has assimilated discussion of these films into horror studies' established paradigms, such as allegorical, reflectionist approaches to textual analysis (paralleling films such as *Hostel* with a post-9/11 American mind-set, and so forth).[38] Where extreme horror has been approached by scholars, discussion routinely orients around several established thinkers – Antonin Artaud, Maurice Merleau-Ponty, Vivian Sobchack, Susan Sontag, Linda Williams – whose ideas are returned to again and again. It is somewhat perverse that these theoretical approaches are recycled given that extreme film is 'by definition, dependent on the idea of newness' because shock arises out of unexpectedness.[39]

Although academic work typically counters one shortcoming of print press criticism – the tendency to dismiss 'extreme' horror films – it frequently replicates another: the tendency to focus on a handful of theatrically released 'extreme' films.[40] Academics have been preoccupied with perceived trends such as 'Asia Extreme'[41] and 'New European Extremity'[42] and a small number of movies such as the *Human Centipede* series,[43] *Irreversible*[44] and *A Serbian Film*.[45] This scholarly work is valuable in its own right. However, little attention has been paid to hardcore horror within these discussions.[46] Cumulatively, scholars risk replicating the same mistake that undercuts print press criticism. Without a broad enough account of the horror genre, claims made about 'horror' or its 'extremity' are limited.

The academic publishing system supports the bias towards examining theatrically released, prominent 'extreme' films. Understandably, peer reviewers are encouraged to consider appeal to a journal's broader readership when commenting on articles, for example. As such, films and directors with recognisable names are an easier 'sell' to the prospective readership and editorial team than lesser-known micro-budget films and film-makers. Although press critics rebuke 'extreme' film-makers and censors actively suppress extreme materials, admonishment in the press and censorial controversy raise awareness about particular films. Those films become the very objects that academics then step in to examine or defend. The significance of such discursive analysis is apparent for peer reviewers, publishers and readers who have an awareness of the broader controversy arising out of press complaints and/or censorship.

Although some academics have sought to challenge the press's inadequacies then, the discursive system in which academics operate encourages canonisation of particular 'extreme' movies and the exclusion of others. In contrast to the small number of directors such as Michael Haneke,[47] Catherine Brellait[48] and Lars von Trier,[49] who have been scrutinised in multiple studies of 'extreme' film, hardcore horror auteurs such as Marcel Walz, Olaf Ittenbach, Kasper Juhl, Daisuke Yamanouchi, Andrey Iskanov and Andreas Schnaas remain virtually ignored within the scholarly literature. The existing work on 'extreme' horror (including Neil Jackson's chapter in this collection) is valuable and necessary. However, a handful of well-documented films such as *Irreversible*, *Antichrist* (Lars von Trier, 2009) or *A Serbian Film* have garnered most of the scholarly attention in this area, while equally interesting hardcore horror films such as *Atroz* (Lex Ortega, 2015), *...And Then I Helped* (Michael Todd Schneider, 2010) or *Collar* (Ryan Nicholson, 2014) remain neglected. As such, scholarly work to date somewhat misrepresents the volume and diversity of 'extreme' horror that is available.

Little attention has been paid to hardcore horror movies precisely because these films are marginal by definition. Indeed, hardcore horror film-makers flourish only because of the relative inattention paid to their work. If too much attention were drawn to the content produced by hardcore horror film-makers, they may fall foul of the law. The obscenity charges brought against FX artist Remy Couture for creating works depicting extreme forms of violence (chronicled in the documentary *Art/Crime* (Frédérick Maheux, 2011)) demonstrate the consequences that can result from spotlighting extreme horror fiction. Scholars publishing on these films risk admitting that they have engaged with potentially illegal or obscene materials.[50] These external pressures discourage scholars from engaging with materials that skirt the boundaries of acceptability.

Nevertheless, academic work cumulatively (presumably unintentionally) tends to marginalise most hardcore horror film-makers, who are already limited to the cultural peripheries because of the content that they produce. Those scholars who seek to defend hardcore horror's maligned texts should take care not to inadvertently reproduce pejorative attitudes towards these films. For example, affect-based analysis of 'extreme' horror might aim to suggest that visceral responses are valuable, but such interpretations imply that extreme film is principally characterised by providing transient bodily reactions. This commonplace approach essentially replicates the pejorative associations between extremity and superficial shock that critics employ to vilify these films.

Without greater focus on the concept of extremity or the variety of peripheral texts that constitute 'extreme horror', scholarly discourse risks homogenising all manner of representations that disrupt established genre conventions. Consequently, the term 'extreme' is often rendered banal, amounting to little more than an author's declaration that they personally found the representation distasteful. Virtually any depiction of sex or violence could be considered extreme compared with established genre conventions, the individual's prior viewing experiences and/or the industrial, commercial and sociopolitical context in which the film is situated, precisely because extremity is a contingent value rather than an absolute standard. In conclusion, extreme horror's depictions are particularly notable because these contentious images enliven our understanding of values that underpin our social and political beliefs.[51] That contentiousness is, after all, what makes these images seem 'extreme'.

Notes

1. See, for example, S. Tobias, 'Of thee I scream: How horror films reflect politics', *The Washington Post* (2 July 2016); K. Cochrane, 'For your entertainment', *The Guardian* (1 May 2007); C. Tookey, 'Antichrist: The man who made this horrible, misogynistic film needs to see a shrink', *Daily Mail* (24 July 2009).
2. See S. Jones, 'The Lexicon of Offence: The Meanings of Torture, Porn, and "Torture Porn"', in F. Attwood, V. Campbell, I. Q. Hunter and S. Lockyer (eds), *Controversial Images: Media Representations on the Edge* (Basingstoke: Palgrave Macmillan, 2012), pp. 186–200; J. Aston, '"A Malignant, Seething Hatework": An Introduction to US 21st Century Hardcore Horror', *Senses of Cinema*, 80/1 (2016).
3. Steve Jones, *Torture Porn: Popular Horror after Saw* (Basingstoke: Palgrave Macmillan, 2013). The term has since been adopted by others, including James Aston, *Hardcore Horror Cinema in the 21st Century: Production, Marketing and Consumption* (Jefferson, NC: McFarland, 2018).

4. For a detailed discussion of the following trends, see Mark Bernard, *Selling the Splat Pack: The DVD Revolution and the American Horror Film* (Edinburgh: Edinburgh University Press, 2014).
5. 'Flight of the Living Dead: Outbreak on a Plane', *BBFC* (2007), *www.bbfc.co.uk/releases/flight-living-dead-outbreak-plane-2007-1* (accessed 29 August 2019).
6. Moreover, the 'unrated' version of *Saw VI* (Kevin Greutert, 2009) is different to the theatrical version in multiple ways, but barely any of the changes re-establish controversial elements. Rather, the alternate footage consists of alternative takes, different dialogue and pacing changes (for a detailed breakdown, see *https://www.movie-censorship.com/report.php?ID=5170383* (accessed 29 August 2019)).
7. 'Pig Hunt', *BBFC* (2008), *https://www.bbfc.co.uk/releases/pighunt-2008* (accessed 29 August 2019).
8. See David Kerekes and David Slater, *See No Evil: Banned Films and Video Controversy* (Manchester: Critical Vision, 2001), p. 289: the list of titles banned by the Director of Public Prosecutions in the early 1980s 'remains something of a "shopping list" for collectors'.
9. This distinction is crucial: although these film-makers push taste boundaries, and such pushing has led to some films being outlawed (as obscene), hardcore horror does not contain footage of genuine crimes.
10. See M. Barker, '"Knowledge-U-Like": The British Board of Film Classification and its Research', *Journal of British Cinema and Television*, 13/1 (2016), 127; E. Pett, 'A New Media Landscape? The BBFC, Extreme Cinema as Cult, and Technological Change', *New Review of Film and Television Studies*, 13/1 (2015), 84.
11. 'Hate Crime', *BBFC* (2015), *http://www.bbfc.co.uk/releases/hate-crime-vod* (accessed 29 August 2019).
12. For a (non-exhaustive) list of films that are 'self-censored', which have 'not been formally rejected by the BBFC but are still effectively banned as it is pointless and expensive to submit films that won't pass', see 'Banned: Self-Censored', *Melon Farmers*, *http://melonfarmers.co.uk/banned.htm* (accessed 29 August 2019).
13. See David Bordwell and Kristin Thompson, *Minding Movies: Observations on the Art, Craft, and Business of Filmmaking* (Chicago, IL: University of Chicago Press, 2011), pp. 127–8.
14. See, for example, the BBFC's rationale for banning *Grotesque*: 'The work has minimal narrative or character development and presents the viewer with little more than an unrelenting and escalating scenario of humiliation, brutality and sadism', 'Grotesque', *BBFC* (2009), *http://www.bbfc.co.uk/releases/grotesque-video* (accessed 29 August 2019).

15. A. Ettinger, Liner notes for *Flowers*, DVD release (Unearthed Films, 2015).
16. 'Audio Commentary', *Flowers*, DVD release (Unearthed Films, 2015).
17. For the sake of full disclosure, I currently act as a script editor and translator for Necrostorm.
18. See R. Nicholson, 'Gutterballs 2: The Reel Deal', *Indiegogo* (2015), https://www.indiegogo.com/projects/gutterballs-2-the-reel-deal#/comments (accessed 29 August 2019).
19. S. Ryan, https://www.facebook.com/shane.ryan.77 (15 February 2018); emphasis in the original.
20. S. Ryan, https://www.facebook.com/shane.ryan.77 (17 February 2018).
21. Eric Schaefer, *"Bold! Daring! Shocking! True!" A History of Exploitation Films, 1919–1959* (Durham, NC: Duke University Press, 1999), p. 124.
22. See D. Harries, 'Watching the Internet', in D. Harries (ed.), *The New Media Book* (London: BFI Publishing, 2002), pp. 171–82; Michele White, *The Body and the Screen: Theories of Internet Spectatorship* (Cambridge, MA: MIT Press, 2009).
23. See 'Box office history for Hostel Movies', *The Numbers*, https://www.the-numbers.com/movies/franchise/Hostel#tab=summary (accessed 29 August 2019).
24. See, for example, P. Howell, 'Stranger Danger', *The Toronto Star* (15 September 2017).
25. This is a common trait among critics who deal with such material; see also S. Schiesel, 'No Mercy and Ample Ways to Die', *The New York Times* (12 October 2009); L. Terrell, 'The Brutal and the Banal Become Us', *The Star-Ledger* (8 March 2009).
26. For examples of this discourse in action, see S. Holden, '"Bliss": Cultures and Sexes Clash in the Aftermath of a Rape in Turkey', *The New York Times* (7 August 2009); M. Orange, 'Taking Back the Knife', *The New York Times* (6 September 2009); D. Thomson, 'If these Walls Could Talk, They'd Scream', *The Washington Post* (4 January 2008); W. Ide, 'The Life Before Her Eyes', *The Times* (26 March 2009).
27. L. Skenazy, 'It's Torture! It's Porn! What's Not to Like? Plenty, Actually', *AdAge* (28 May 2007), https://adage.com/article/lenore-skenazy/torture-porn-plenty/116897 (accessed 29 August 2019); see also Wendy Shalit, *Girls Gone Mild* (New York, NY: Random House, 2007), p. 101.
28. See P. Cooley, '"Mother!" is so controversial Paramount had to defend its decision to release the movie', *Cleveland* (18 September 2017), http://www.cleveland.com/entertainment/index.ssf/2017/09/why_is_mother_so_controversial.html (accessed 29 August 2019).

29. T. Brown, 'TIFF Review: Martyrs', *Screen Anarchy* (7 September 2008), *https://screenanarchy.com/2008/09/martyrs-review.html* (accessed 29 August 2019); emphasis added.
30. C. Gilson, 'Misogynist Review', *UK Horror Scene*, *http://www.ukhorrorscene.com/tag/horror-review/page/20/* (accessed 29 August 2019); emphasis added.
31. R. Carlsson, 'Maskhead review', *Film Bizarro*, *http://www.filmbizarro.com/view_review.php?review=maskhead.php* (accessed 24 March 2020); emphasis added.
32. Blacktooth, 'Flowers (review)', *Horror Society* (15 January 2015), *https://www.horrorsociety.com/2015/01/14/flowers-review/* (accessed 29 August 2019); emphasis added.
33. P. Bradshaw, 'Enter the Void', *The Guardian* (23 September 2010), *https://www.theguardian.com/film/2010/sep/23/enter-the-void-review* (accessed 29 August 2019); emphasis added.
34. D. Edelstein, 'In *Green Inferno*, Eli Roth Honors the Cannibal-Gore Tradition With Bravura', *Vulture* (25 September 2015), *https://www.vulture.com/2015/09/movie-review-green-inferno-goes-for-the-kills.html* (accessed 29 August 2019); emphasis added.
35. On *Salò*'s censorship history in the UK, see 'Salo', *BBFC* (2008), *http://www.bbfc.co.uk/case-studies/salo120-days-sodom* (accessed 29 August 2019). On marketing the uncut version, see S. Hobbs, '*Salò, Or the 120 Days of Sodom*: The Contemporary Distribution of Sexual Extremity', *Cine-Excess*, 2 (2016).
36. The same is true in scholarship. See, for instance, Elena Del Rio, *The Grace of Destruction: A Vital Ethology of Extreme Cinemas* (London: Bloomsbury, 2016). Del Rio uses phrases such as 'extreme pain' or 'extreme violence' in a discussion of 'extreme film' without defining what extremity is (or what normative standard is being compared to).
37. D. Itzkoff, 'Surgery Helps Lift British Ban on *Human Centipede 2* Film', *The New York Times* (7 October 2011); see also E. Shortall, '"Torture Porn" Horror Film Sequel Seeks Irish Release', *The Sunday Times* (16 October 2011).
38. See B. Kattelman, 'Carnographic Culture', in M. Canini (ed.), *The Domination of Fear* (New York, NY: Rodopi, 2010), pp. 3–16; D. Lockwood, 'All Stripped Down: The Spectacle of "Torture Porn"', *Popular Communication*, 7/1 (2008), 40–8; Kevin J. Wetmore, Jr., *Post-9/11 Horror in American Cinema* (London: Continuum, 2012).
39. T. Horeck and T. Kendall, 'Introduction', in T. Horeck and T. Kendall (eds), *The New Extremism in Cinema: From France to Europe* (Edinburgh: Edinburgh

University Press, 2011), p. 5; see Alison Taylor, *Troubled Everyday: The Aesthetics of Violence and the Everyday in European Art Cinema* (Edinburgh: Edinburgh University Press, 2017).

40. See Aaron Kerner and Jonathan L. Knapp, *Extreme Cinema: Affective Strategies in Transnational Media* (Edinburgh: Edinburgh University Press, 2016); Pramod K. Nayar, *The Extreme in Contemporary Culture* (Lanham, MD: Rowman and Littlefield, 2017).

41. See C. Y. Shin, 'The Art of Branding: Tartan "Asia Extreme" Films', in J. Choi and M. Wada-Marciano (eds), *Horror to the Extreme: Changing Boundaries in Asian Cinema* (Hong Kong: Hong Kong University Press, 2009), pp. 85–100; Daniel Martin, *Extreme Asia: The Rise of Cult Cinema from the Far East* (Edinburgh: Edinburgh University Press, 2015); O. Dew, '"Asia Extreme": Japanese Cinema and British Hype', *New Cinemas: Journal of Contemporary Film*, 5/1 (2007), 53–73.

42. G. Hainge, 'A full face bright red money shot: Incision, wounding and film spectatorship in Marina de Van's *Dans ma peau*', *Continuum: Journal of Media & Cultural Studies*, 26/4 (2012), 567; Alexandra West, *Films of the New French Extremity: Visceral Horror and National Identity* (Jefferson, NC: McFarland, 2016); W. Brown, 'Violence in Extreme Cinema and the Ethics of Spectatorship', *Projections*, 7/1 (2013), 27.

43. See E. Brinkema, 'Violence and the Diagram; Or, *The Human Centipede*', *Qui Parle*, 24/2 (2016); M. Smith, 'Revulsion and Derision: *Antichrist*, *The Human Centipede II* and the British Press', *Film International*, 13 (2015); K. Weir and S. Dunne, 'The Connoisseurship of the Condemned: *A Serbian Film*, *The Human Centipede 2* and the Appreciation of the Abhorrent', *Participations: Journal of Audience & Reception Studies*, 11 (2014).

44. C. Birks, 'Body Problems: New Extremism, Descartes and Jean-Luc Nancy', *New Review of Film and Television Studies*, 13/2 (2015), 131–46; A. Butler, 'Sacrificing the Real: Early 20th Century Theatrics and the New Extremism in Cinema', *Cinephile*, 8/9 (2012), 27–31; M. Brottman and D. Sterritt, 'Irreversible', *Film Quarterly*, 57 (2004), 37–42.

45. See M. Featherstone, 'Coito Ergo Sum: Serbian Sadism and Global Capitalism in *A Serbian Film*', *Horror Studies*, 4/1 (2013), 127–41; M. Featherstone and B. Johnson, '"Ovo Je Srbija": The Horror of the National Thing in *A Serbian Film*', *Journal for Cultural Research*, 16/1 (2012), 63–79; S. Kimber, 'Transgressive Edge Play and *Srpski Film/A Serbian Film*', *Horror Studies*, 5/1 (2014), 107–25. The limitation is also found in fan circles. See M. Betz, 'High and Low and in Between', *Screen*, 54/4 (2013), 495–513; as Betz finds, fan lists of 'extreme films' return to a small number of titles. This might seem

counter-intuitive given that familiarity with extreme texts carries subcultural capital among self-identified fans (see Pett, 'A New Media Landscape?'). It might appear reasonable that lesser-known titles would carry greater potential for attaining subcultural capital, and so unfamiliar titles ought to be a regular feature of such lists. However, some shared agreement is necessary among members of a subculture so that knowledge can be translated into capital; unfamiliar titles do not necessarily lend themselves to such valuation.

46. There are some exceptions, including David H. Fleming, *Unbecoming Cinema: Unsettling Encounters with Ethical Event Films* (Bristol: Intellect, 2017), which discusses Lucifer Valentine's films. Much of the work I have published in the area has been difficult to pitch to editors, for reasons outlined below.

47. Catherine Wheatley, *Michael Haneke's Cinema: The Ethic of the Image* (New York, NY: Berghan, 2009); B. Price, 'Pain and the Limits of Representation', *Framework: The Journal of Cinema and Media*, 47/2 (2006), 22–9; L. Coulthard, 'The Violence of Silence: Vocal Provocation in the Cinema of Michael Haneke', *Studies in European Cinema*, 9/2–3 (2012), 87–97.

48. See Taylor, *Troubled Everyday*; Troy Bordun, *Genre Trouble and Extreme Cinema: Film Theory at the Fringes of Contemporary Art Cinema* (Basingstoke: Palgrave Macmillan, 2017); D. Keesey, 'Split Identification: Representations of Rape in Gaspar Noé's *Irréversible* and Catherine Breillat's *A ma soeur!/Fat Girl*', *Studies in European Cinema*, 7/2 (2010), 95–107.

49. L. J. Marso, 'Must We Burn Lars von Trier? Simone de Beauvoir's Body Politics in *Antichrist*', *Theory & Event*, 18/2 (2015); J. Choi, 'Sentimentality and the Cinema of the Extreme', *Jump Cut*, 50/1 (2008).

50. For instance, I removed more than 20,000 words of my PhD thesis while the UK government was drafting Section 63 of the Criminal Justice and Immigration Act 2008 (the 'Dangerous Pictures Bill'), since it was not clear at that time whether the pornographic and horror-based content I was discussing would fall within the law's remit.

51. For a more detailed discussion, see S. Jones, 'Sex and Horror', in F. Attwood and C. Smith with B. McNair (eds), *The Routledge Companion to Media, Sex and Sexuality* (London: Routledge, 2018), pp. 290–9.

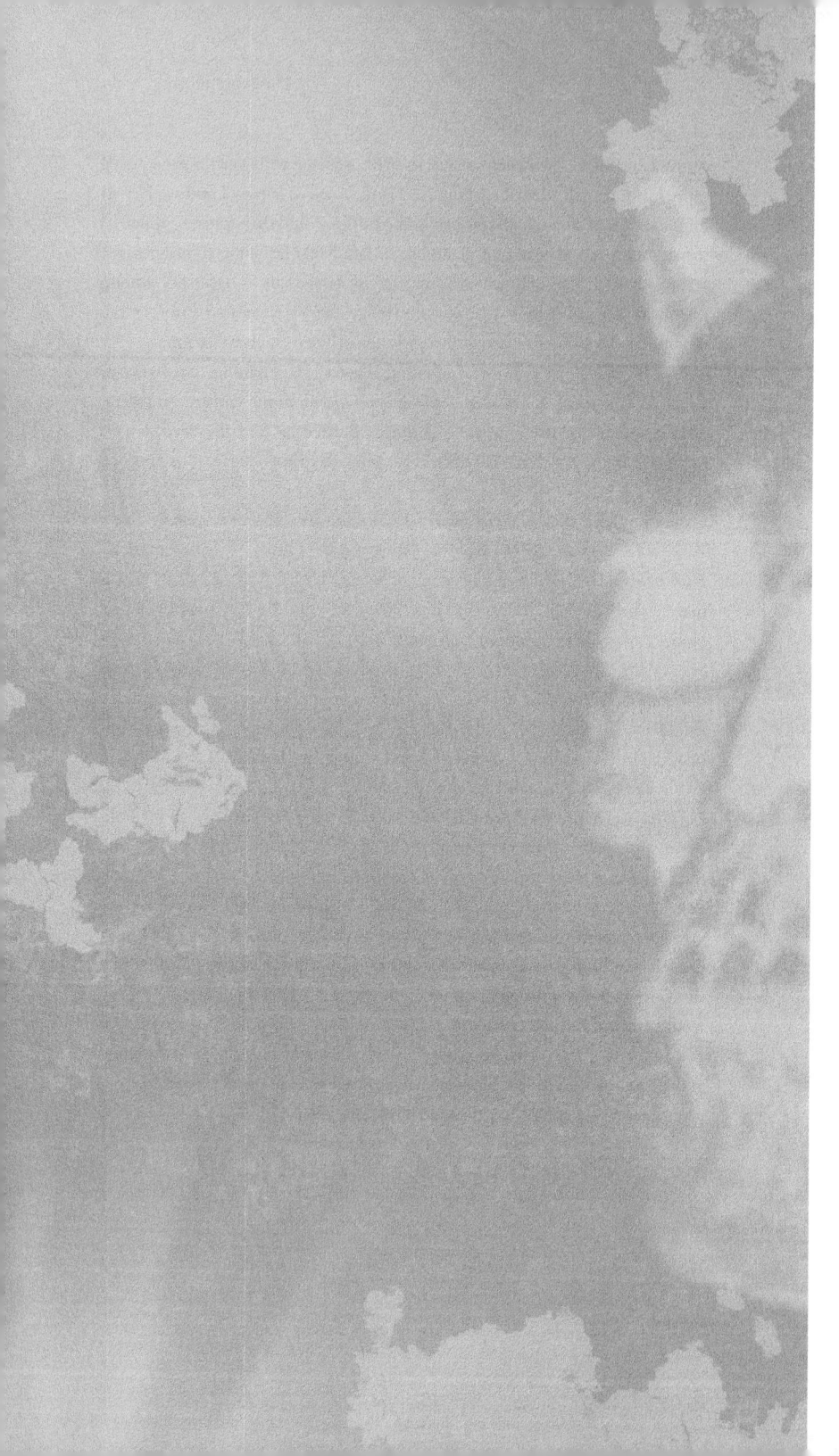

3

From Midnight Movies to Mainstream Excess

Cult Horror Festivals and the Academy

Xavier Mendik

> Cult films largely stand outside what James English (2005) has called 'the economy of prestige': the framework of valuation through award, ceremonies, and prizes . . . However, in recent decades there has been a proliferation of cult cinema that has seen it partly being co-opted by official culture. Therefore its position these days no longer lies uniquely outside the economy of prestige, but partly inside it.
> Ernest Mathijs and Jamie Sexton, *Cult Cinema: An Introduction*[1]

Introduction

AS WITH OTHER AREAS explored within *New Blood*, film festivals provide a further case study through which to consider the increased mainstreaming and 'respectability' of cult- and horror-themed material within the twenty-first century. Indeed, it can be argued that over the last twenty years the exhibition circuit for cult, horror and related 'extreme' film festivals has undergone a significant degree of evolution, with the proliferation of a number of events whose organisational structures, curatorial practices, esteem markers and transnational networks increasingly resemble more established modes of cinema exhibition beyond the genre circuit. If cult does now partly reside within more mainstream structures of prestige, as Mathijs and Sexton's opening quote suggests, then these trends have also been reciprocated by an increased interest in cult- and horror-oriented film festivals within the academy. While a number of academics (including Matt Hills, and more recently Rosana Vivar)[2] have translated a regular attendance at horror film events/conventions into important studies of subcultural film audiences, other scholars have also made inroads into this circuit by adopting roles as organisers and programmers of film festivals within this sphere.

My own interventions into this field have very much revolved around efforts to develop exhibition platforms that allow for the revaluation of cult and horror film traditions within their aesthetic, cultural and historical contexts. The key format through which this has occurred is *Cine-Excess*, a hybrid international film festival and academic conference that I have been running on an annual basis since 2007. As a result of this long-standing involvement, any commentary I provide in this chapter inevitably remains as much reflective as it does analytical, as I seek to situate my own event into this body of knowledge around cult cinema and its exhibition strategies.

Any requirement to locate *Cine-Excess* within a wider set of academic debates is far from coincidence, as the festival was initially launched to promote the UK's first taught MA in Cult Film and TV that I helped to develop at Brunel University in 2006. Given its close connection to postgraduate film education, *Cine-Excess* sought to combine elements of film festival activity (such as UK theatrical premieres, visiting international film-makers, awards ceremonies and film industry panels) with those of more 'traditional' academic conferences (through the provision of a three-day symposium showcasing current debates around cult and horror cinema within the academy). In its first year of operation, this hybrid film festival/conference format saw *Cine-Excess* anchored into the existing film festival Sci-Fi London, before it began operating as an annual stand-alone event from 2008 onwards. Between 2007 and 2012, the festival was held in a range of corporate cinema chains and regional film theatres across Central London, before effectively shifting regions to Brighton and the West Midlands to reflect my subsequent job postings. These geographical alterations also coincided with differing stages of the festival's evolution, and specifically the addition of subsidiary activities including a *Cine-Excess*-themed DVD label (2009–11), a documentary production arm (2010–present) and a peer-reviewed e-journal (2013–present), all of which were developed to compliment the ongoing event.

In all of its London/Brighton/Birmingham iterations, *Cine-Excess* has not only been influenced by alternative models of festival practice, but also by the emergence of a body of film and media research seeking to theorise previously derided examples of cult, horror or 'trash' cinema. Therefore, in order to discuss more fully how such events can be aligned to the mainstreaming of cult and horror film festivals (both inside and outside of the academy), I wish to outline some of the research that has been undertaken on subcultural festival strategies before reflecting on the potential impact that these debates have had on the development of *Cine-Excess*.

Taking trash seriously: cult, festivals and the academy

In order to provide an introductory context for the wider theoretical influences on *Cine-Excess*, it seems appropriate to highlight that the frequent tagline associated with the event was 'taking trash seriously'. This statement was used as an anchor to the annual festival and the subsequent DVD label, which released a range of film titles screened at the event (see Figure 3.1).

Here, 'taking trash seriously' not only underscored an intention to reclaim previously derided films via a more scholarly approach, but specifically referenced one of the earliest and most influential accounts of cult cinema: Jeffrey Sconce's article 'Trashing the Academy: Taste, Excess and an Emerging Politics of Cinematic Style'. First published in 1995, Sconce's article identified certain classes of marginal film that are frequently shunned on the grounds of their technical or representational 'excess', or simply because they are deemed as an affront to the boundaries of 'good taste'. Using the term 'paracinema' as a catch-all title for a wide range of unorthodox cinematic activity, Sconce defines cult film as 'a most elastic textual category',[3] which can cover disparate marginal film cycles that include:

> entries from such seemingly disparate subgenres as 'bad film', splatter-punk, 'mondo' films, sword and sandal epics, Elvis flicks, government hygiene films, Japanese monster movies, beach-party musicals,

Figure 3.1. The image from the Nouveaux-Pictures *Cine-Excess* DVD release of *Suspiria* reproduced in this volume is courtesy of its present distributor CultFilms.co.uk.

and just about every other historical manifestation of exploitation cinema from juvenile delinquency documentaries to soft-core pornography.[4]

For the author, what unites this uneven array of celluloid entries remains the fact that the paracinema text often problematises the boundaries of good taste, and here Sconce turns to Pierre Bourdieu's notions of cultural capital to explain how the cult film's potential appeal can intersect with a wider politics of taste, culture and distinction. For Sconce (citing Bourdieu directly), 'Tastes are perhaps first and foremost distastes, provoked by horror or the visceral intolerance of the tastes of others.'[5] Arguably, it is this ability to provoke unease that turns disreputable cinematic entries into objects of fascination for the attuned and highly educated subcultural audiences that Sconce identified as the idealised cult consumer. By endorsing the idea that paracinema represents a challenge to dominant ideologies and taste arbiters, Sconce famously argued that the cult film text represents 'an aesthetic of vocal confrontation',[6] whose narrative features and specific patterns of audience identification required further investigation.

It is the interrogation of these unwieldy texts, marginal film-makers and subcultural audiences that has preoccupied cult film theorists following the publication of Sconce's article. As a result of more than a decade of sustained theoretical enquiry, the academy has now been well and truly trashed, and this process of ransacking has also sought to examine how cult and horror material can circulate through a range of alternative modes of exhibition. Traditionally, the favoured format of cult film viewing remained the midnight movie screening, as referenced by early scholars such as Bruce A. Austin. In his 1981 study 'Portrait of a Cult Film Audience: *The Rocky Horror Picture Show*', Austin identified specific modes of exhibition and distinct codes of audience affiliation as the two key features that help solidify cult film status. In terms of the screening component, he argues that:

> the cult film may be defined as a motion picture which is exhibited on a continuing basis, usually at midnight, and gathers a sizeable repeat audience. This working definition of cult films emphasizes the importance of the repeated regular screenings for the build-up of a regular, returning audience which characterizes the cult film phenomenon.[7]

The author bases this analysis of alternative exhibition as the trigger for generating cult appeal on a study of late-night screenings for *The Rocky Horror Picture Show* (Jim Sharman, 1975). For Austin, it was these events that generated the film's notable fan following, effectively eclipsing the muted reception that accompanied its original release. Initially, the film was 'poorly distributed and unenthusiastically promoted, and very few reviews, outside of industry publications, appeared'.[8] It was only from mid-1976 onwards that *The Rocky Horror Picture Show* began to transform into a cult phenomenon, with a series of late-night screenings initialising a further pattern of Halloween-themed events alongside the formation of a designated fan club. Central to Austin's analysis of this subcultural appeal is the role of the film's fans as active participants in these viewings, which he considered through an audience-based study of 562 *Rocky Horror* viewers assembled for a screening at the Rochester film theatre in New York. As a result, the author identified three distinct categories of fan affiliation for the film, which he distinguishes as first time, veteran and regular attendance groupings. In addition to these active spectator subsets, he also identifies ancillary activities (such as the use of props as a precursor to attendance, and the pleasures of costuming as communal acts during the event), which further help in distinguishing the midnight movie viewing experience from more regularised mainstream modes of film participation. As he concludes, 'it is the event that attracts and continues to support the popularity of a cult film'.[9]

From midnight movies to mainstream excess: cult on the festival circuit

Austin's account of *The Rocky Horror Picture Show* phenomenon reveals the midnight movie phenomenon as event, where cult appeal is 'uniquely characterized by the repeated attendance of a group of certain individuals'.[10] His comments around the annexing of alternative sites of exhibition to active fan affiliation have been reaffirmed by Matt Hills, whose 2010 study of horror film festivals and conventions highlights an important aspect of live embodiment, based on a fan's physical proximity to visiting genre talent as well as their exclusive access to trailers, premieres and contentious releases not widely available through mainstream circulation. As a result, Hills argues that these horror-themed events provide an element of 'circulating capital', based on a process of 'periodic and "live" recognition'.[11] In her 2016 account of audiences for the San Sebastian Horror and Fantasy Film Festival, Rosana Vivar replaces Hills's notion of live embodiment with the concept of 'play' to explain a set of behaviours undertaken by what she terms as an 'expert audience of regular horror and fantasy film viewers' that attend the festival 'with previous experience and esoteric knowledge of the event'.[12] While both authors highlight the acquisition of subcultural capital based on regularised attendance at these events, their studies also indicate that the midnight movie phenomenon has been superseded by the emergence of distinct festival networks dedicated to the exhibition of cult- and horror-themed content on an annual basis.

Echoing Sconce's earlier comments about cult cinema's challenge to official taste and boundary markers, this new cult/horror festival scene can be seen as operating through what Mathijs and Sexton have defined as an 'alternative network of validation',[13] which simultaneously valorises and subverts wider notions of cultural currency and prestige found within more mainstream exhibition strategies. This often paradoxical celebration of marginal movie cultures is further complicated by what the authors see as an explosion in 'the celebration of badness'[14] that has taken place in recent decades, with an increased cult appreciation being directly traceable to two modes of activity: cult in festivals versus niche festivals for cult.

The first category of cult in festivals refers to a complex and often contradictory process of programming marginal film content within more established exhibition outlets. Given that the mainstream festival circuit remains dominated by what Mathijs and Sexton call 'colleges of influence', namely 'juries, programmers, boards, subscribers, sponsors, policy makers',[15] cult often circulates on its ability to be innovative, esoteric and ultimately offensive. In the authors' case study of David Cronenberg's controversial 1996 release *Crash*, the film was both derided and applauded when it entered into official competition at the Cannes Film Festival. That the film was eventually awarded a prize in the newly invented category of 'audacity' confirms that the classification of such cult material often has an abrasive relationship with wider concepts of taste and morality.

While the above example points to the potential of cult in festivals to revolve around an uneasy strategy of co-option, Mathijs and Sexton also point to a second category of 'self-sustaining cult events', where 'the interrogations of and confrontations with processes of valuation are built into the fabric of the festival'.[16] This niche cult festival circuit clearly indicates a differing set of criteria for the allocation of prestige, which can be linked back to the earlier midnight movie traditions outlined by scholars such as Sconce and Austin. Here, alternative prestige functions to celebrate established horror auteurs (such as Cronenberg); and, where prizes are awarded by niche cult festivals, they often operate through a system of mock awards, which attribute esteem and prestige in a distinctly ironic or parodic manner. These prizes often target those cult genres or creatives largely shunned by mainstream festivals, while promoting the markers of excess as factors that unite festival programmers and attuned audiences in this area. These are the shared features that Mathijs and Sexton define as more of the transgressive same: 'more blood, more gore, more full moons, more sorcery, more time travel and more vampires'.[17]

This preference for parodying the conventions of cultural value associated with mainstream events also extends to the award categories under which juries and audiences can allocate esteem. For instance, the Boston Underground Film Festival, which occurs annually every March, follows the format of many mainstream festivals by facilitating a directed number of competition entries. It then allocates prizes for both audiences and programming teams to review across four substrata, with best feature film and short entries providing prestige bandings comparable to mainstream film festivals. However, other classifications in circulation quickly reveal the degree of divergence from this more conventional sphere, particularly through the director's choice category of 'Most Effectively Offensive', which underscores the visceral and unsettling qualities long associated with cult material. Equally, the nature of the prizes allocated, which the festival widely promotes as the world's only demonic bunny award, reveals a degree of irreverence to the wider process of competition and prestige within the more established festival circuit.

Indeed, Boston's 'Most Effectively Offensive' award itself finds parity with the allocation of prize-giving for viscera that is prevalent in other international examples of niche cult film events. For instance, Florida's Freak Show Horror Film Festival (which occurs every Halloween weekend) dedicates at least one of its ten competition categories to 'Best Special FX Makeup', while the annual Atlanta Horror Film Festival simplifies these substrata of unease under their award category of 'Best Gore'. In addition, Atlanta's dizzying array of competition categories (which peaked at thirty-nine separate bandings in 2017) effectively functions to ridicule wider notions of festival prize-giving in general, with categories such as 'Best Short, Short' evidencing a type of self-knowing festival category fatigue included as a parodic joke to fans and consumers of the horror-oriented event.

Fine wine, federations and new cult capital on the festival circuit

While the Boston and Atlanta events clearly orient critic- and audience-defined awards to niche effect, other cult film programming strategies even challenge the boundaries of what should define a normal film festival. In the case of Slovakia's Grossman Fantastic Film Festival, a horror film competition is incongruously paired with a wine tasting event on an annual basis. While the festival's pairing of gross-out horror with an appreciation of fine wines might at first appear anachronistic, it actually highlights the fact that, despite a disdain for cinematic orthodoxy, the paracinema audience remains, in the words of Sconce, 'rich with "cultural capital" and thus possesses a level of textual/critical sophistication similar to . . . their nemeses'.[18]

While it would be easy to overstate the parodic nature of the programming and competition strategies that occur in such niche cult festivals, I would concur with Mathijs and Sexton's conclusions that 'when the mock celebration of badness takes on cult status, it ceases to be mere mockery', and instead 'clashes with the seriousness of genre specific awards'.[19] The seriousness of this awards system is itself evidenced by the promotion by the European Fantastic Film Festivals Federation (EFFFF) of the Méliès d'Or Award as one of the key prize categories at the Grossman event. The EFFFF's influence exceeds the remit of this one event, and instead points to the existence of a high-profile and highly organised transnational network of festival affiliations whose 'protocols and procedures exude a desire to be taken seriously'.[20] Although the EFFFF was formed in 1987 from a loose affiliation of five European events, it now numbers twenty-two festivals (from micro to large-scale events) that span Europe, and include the UK's Abertoir: The International Film Festival of Wales (held annually in November). The Federation also hosts a range of affiliated networks across the USA, Canada, South Korea and Mexico. Differing member festivals are bound together by a number of common practices that include the mutual sharing of a Méliès d'Or Award for most creative short and feature productions, which is hosted annually on a circulating basis by member sites within the network, who often share key personnel for programming and jury duties.

The degree of intra-organisation that subsequently exists within the network parallels many of the key features associated with mainstream, non-genre film festivals, to the extent that they often share many press and PR outlets with the more niche-oriented events, as well as drawing on comparable structures of guest liaison/talent booking. The existence of such professional mechanisms confirms the emergence of what programmer Hannah McGill has termed as 'cupcake and geek'[21] alternatives to the dominant festival orthodoxy, while also evidencing that subcultural audiences have, in the author's words, 'shuffled in from the sidelines to form a significant market'.[22]

Further evidence of this potential 'geek' intervention into mainstream event strategy can be evidenced by some of the programming practices that circulate within the EFFFF. For instance, Espoo Ciné is a medium-sized affiliated event that takes place in Finland every August, generating an average audience attendance of around 20,000 delegates each year. Although the festival confirmed its cult credentials by hosting 'major retrospectives of leading European masters of fantasy, horror and violence',[23] programmer Tuomas Riskala has also noted the existence of a much wider screening strategy that includes a children's film strand, art-cinema retrospectives and a focus on 'acclaimed US indies'.[24] If this broadened programming remit points to potential overlaps between mainstream and niche cult events, it is further underscored by the ancillary events and accreditation structures that accompany Espoo Ciné and related Federation members. In terms of these allied activities, Riskala identifies a set of annual seminars that are often 'restricted to film and cinema professionals',[25] and at which a range of film industry, aesthetics and educational debates are given prominence. The inclusion of these seminars not only replicates the industry-oriented/corporate networking sessions found in non-genre/corporate film events, but also references the increased importance that higher education strategies have played in adding credibility to the cult exhibition domain. Thus, the sentiments expressed by Riskala are echoed by other member organisations, such as Sweden's Fantastisk Film Festival, which is another medium-sized annual event that runs for ten days every September. Here, founding organisers such as Magnus Paulsson have identified 'film-business and filmmakers' as key demographics that complement the cult fan,[26] while also echoing the importance of integrating educational perspectives to its annual schedule:

> I strongly believe that entertainment value goes hand in hand with the educational when it comes to the fantastic film . . . At the Festival they get a proper critical and contextual introduction to each screening . . . Festival goers can also go and listen to related seminars and lectures given by film theorists.[27]

The importance of inculcating an educational component as festival esteem markers also demarcates the working practices of the larger Federation member organisations, such as the Brussels International Festival of Fantastic Film (BIFFF). Here, both education and scholarly audiences form an important component for an event that, in the words of former programmer Dirk Van Extergem, counts 'three quarters' of its demographic as students, and where 'the level of education is high (70 per cent higher and university studies)'.[28] As well as confirming the importance of the academy to cult- and horror-themed festivals, the development of the Brussels event also underscores the practice of co-opting the strategies of mainstream festival practices within the Federation. The festival originated as a midnight movie outlet, but BIFFF has now evolved to embrace a degree of infrastructural and organisational delivery comparable with the workings of mainstream film festivals. For instance, the cultist (and often retrospective) programming that defined early antecedents to the Brussels festival has been expanded to a larger team of dedicated programmers, whose duties are directed towards differing global categories of cult content as well as the responsibility for overseeing premiere submissions and high-profile releases that will be in competition. According to Van Extergem, '[t]he Festival, which has its roots in the post-punk (hard rock and heavy metal) era . . . comes dressed in the most sophisticated magic finery with an increasing international public'.[29] This so-called sophisticated transition is marked not only in terms of widespread audience numbers (tagged average of 65,000 visitors per annum), but also an enlarged screening rota that Van Extergem estimated in 2004 to stand at around 150 titles per year, around 80 of which tend to be first-run premieres. Arguably, the drive towards the provision of this premium viewing rota also results in a process of cultural zoning, with prestigious premieres being located at high-profile buildings, while more marginal or 'cult' retrospective showings take place in separate venues more comparable to the traditional midnight movie venue. As Van Extergem comments:

> At the Passage 44 – the bigger, more comfortable and technically advanced of the two – the Festival's prestigious guests, the films in competition and the ones intended to please a large audience make their stand. Meanwhile, at Cinema Nova – a theatre that looks both like a bunker and a sex shop – one could see more demanding pictures.[30]

This strategy of zoning of differing levels and intensities of cult material across mainstream and alternative cinema sites is a phenomenon found in other large festival sites within the Federation (such as the alternative Brigadoon section hosted by the Sitges International Festival of Catalonia), as well as the smaller outlets that exist within the framework. For instance, Espoo Ciné directs its premieres to two out of its three associated venues, with the focus falling on more prestigious screenings located within the Espoo and Helsinki cultural quarters, which in turn facilitates a high level of international prestige and press coverage for these activities. As programmer Tuomas Riskala has noted: 'The number of accredited journalists, local and international, attending the Festival every year is over 150. Espoo Ciné is also sure to attract at least as many industry professionals during the 6 day event.'[31]

'A salivate-all-over-your-chin event': the *Cine-Excess* International Film Festival

Having previously attended several festivals within the EFFFF (both in a professional and academic capacity), it is undeniable that this format had a distinct influence on the launch of *Cine-Excess* in 2007. The impact of this model was seen through the formation of the following three features that were devised for the festival:

1. The participation of visiting international film-makers, whose attendance is anchored by both retrospective screenings and a wider set of academic discussions/conference activity.
2. A dedicated screening season comprising up to eight UK theatrical premieres drawn from key global cult film regions or genres.
3. The inclusion of industry-oriented events that dissect key business and innovation trends in the field.

In terms of the first criterion, Mathijs and Sexton have identified niche cult festivals as portals that celebrate and revere the careers of cult film-makers whose work has not yet been fully recognised by the cinematic mainstream. For instance, they have identified a 'midnight movie heritage'[32] as the basis of the BIFFF, which began in 1983 as an event designed to introduce

Belgian audiences to visiting international horror film-makers such as David Cronenberg. Equally, the Sitges International Festival of Catalonia was one of the first European film festivals to confer acclaim on Cronenberg, awarding his debut feature *Shivers* (1974) at the same time as the film was being discussed by the Canadian parliament as an example of tax-funded obscenity.[33]

Comparable to the process of venerating visiting international filmmakers within the EFFFF, a similar process of career revaluation was initiated at the first *Cine-Excess* in 2007, which was attended by John Landis (director of *An American Werewolf in London* (1981)). The event also featured the first joint UK film festival appearance by the American filmmaker/producer team of Stuart Gordon and Brian Yuzna, who participated in an academic discussion on their 1985 horror film *Re-Animator* (Stuart Gordon). The contextualisation of such visiting film-makers within this forum of critical debate and discussion not only draws parity with the pronounced educational components identified within the EFFFF, but also explains the wider critical reception of *Cine-Excess* as a hybrid film event. As the *Guardian Guide* commented in 2011, '[t]reating cult film with the respect it doesn't always crave but often deserves, this is less a salivating fan event than a chin stroking academic one. Actually, there's a bit of both, so call it a salivate-all-over-your-chin event.'[34]

This celebration of visiting cult film-makers to illustrate wider academic discussions undertaken at the festival was further replicated through the development of a *Cine-Excess* Lifetime Achievement Award from 2008 onwards. This prize was used to recognise those cult creatives whose influence transcends the cult domain to retain wider aesthetic, cultural or historical importance. The first recipient of the *Cine-Excess* Lifetime Achievement Award was the American director and production head Roger Corman, who was given his award by actress Jane Asher, whom he had previously directed in *The Masque of the Red Death* (1964).

Later recipients of this annual *Cine-Excess* award included Italian horror director Dario Argento (together with his long-time film composer Claudio Simonetti), who attended the festival in 2009 to coincide with a high-definition UK re-release of their influential 1977 film *Suspiria* (Dario Argento). Further film-making recipients of the *Cine-Excess* Lifetime Achievement Award have been linked to an exclusivity of exhibiting rarely seen films at the event, as in the case of Joe Dante, who was invited by *Cine-Excess* in 2010 for a screening of his early collage film

Figure 3.2. Roger Corman receives his *Cine-Excess* Lifetime Achievement Award from actress Jane Asher at the festival in 2008.

The Movie Orgy (1968). Other award winners have also been aligned to the themed academic conference component of the festival as a promotional focus for their visit – when film-maker Catherine Breillat attended in 2013, for instance, her Lifetime Achievement Award was linked to the three-day academic conference component 'European Erotic Cinema: Identity, Desire and Disgust'.

Beyond the veneration of cult and horror film-makers whose work has yet to be fully realised within the mainstream, the award allocation strategies at *Cine-Excess* also echo Mathijs and Sexton's comments that niche festivals can provide a platform for minor stars and cult performers 'snubbed by the mainstream' to be 'championed' as 'ground breaking artists'.[35] As a result, a number of cult stars have been celebrated through the *Cine-Excess* Lifetime Achievement Award for their original contributions to cult performance, and the wider cultural and social dynamics raised by such physicality.

Recipients have included the European actor Franco Nero, who visited the festival in 2011 to receive both a *Cine-Excess* award and an honorary doctorate from Brunel University for himself and long-term collaborator Vanessa Redgrave. The ceremony included a special screening of Elio Petri's rarely seen thriller *A Quiet Place in the Country* (1968), in which the pair appear. (The fact that the Nero/Redgrave awards ceremony and screening took place at London's Italian Cultural Institute is also significant, as it further indicates the practice of cultural zoning of award components in prestige venues as highlighted in the EFFFF's model of niche festivals.) More recently, the 2018 edition of *Cine-Excess* further celebrated the centrality of cult performance by awarding its first posthumous Lifetime Achievement Award to actor Vincent Price. The award was timed to coincide with the fiftieth anniversary of his role as the villainous Matthew Hopkins in *Witchfinder General* (Michael Reeves, 1968), and was accepted by his daughter Victoria Price.

Beyond the allocation of awards as prestige markers, the second way in which the EFFFF format influenced the development of *Cine-Excess* is through the remit of programming. Here, two strategies are pertinent: programming against the grain of film/state bodies, and programming premieres as prestige markers. In terms of programming against the grain of film/state bodies, niche cult festivals have long held a reputation for exhibiting extreme or contentious materials as mechanisms through which to challenge the cultural orthodoxy. In this respect, it comes as little surprise that many of the festivals aligned to the Federation are themselves in

Figure 3.3. Cult performer Franco Nero receives his *Cine-Excess* Lifetime Achievement Award at the festival in 2011.

Figure 3.4. Author Victoria Price receives a posthumous *Cine-Excess* Lifetime Achievement Award for her father, actor Vincent Price, in 2018.

regions that have previously been subject to viewing restrictions imposed by official bodies and film censorship boards. For instance, programmer Tuomas Riskala has situated the development of Finland's Espoo Ciné event against a 'dark period of celluloid repression',[36] during which the festival gained prominence as a venue for otherwise censured materials thanks to special screening dispensations given to such outlets at this time. Many other Federation festivals situate their early development against similar historic battles with the censor, often merging these conflicts with wider political forces of the time. Rosana Vivar's discussion of the San Sebastian Film Festival, for example, situates the development of the event against a 1990s Basque territory 'immersed in a wave of nationalist violence and controlled by radical separatists'.[37] While such struggles constitute part of the legacy and fan memories attached to these festivals, it does not preclude the niche cult event from being the focus of contemporary controversies surrounding the 'extreme' image. For instance, when Ángel Sala, director of Sitges, programmed the controversial horror release *A Serbian Film* (Srđan Spasojević, 2010) for a special adult-only premiere screening at the event in 2010, the Spanish prosecutor initialised court action that threatened Sala with imprisonment on the grounds of exhibiting child pornography. The legal proceedings not only generated international publicity, but also garnered a strong campaign of rebuttal from international film reviewers and festival directors alike.[38] As a result, the prosecution was dropped when it became apparent that the images of child brutalisation contained in *A Serbian Film* were in fact fictionalised, with Sitges's own press response also pointing out that the film had previously been screened at prestigious film markets including Cannes and the American Film Market.[39]

While always mindful of the requirement to work within the legal and licensing regulations that govern the commercial exhibition of materials within the UK, *Cine-Excess* has still sought to provide a forum through which controversial cult cinema releases can be revaluated by filmgoers and academic audiences alike. In 2011, for instance, the festival hosted the world theatrical premiere of the new 'redemption cut' of Ruggero Deodato's film *Cannibal Holocaust* (1980), which had previously been either banned or severely cut by UK censors on the grounds of animal cruelty and presumed scenes of sexual violence. The screening generated considerable media publicity and was accompanied by a special panel discussion between director Deodato, academic researchers and BBFC representatives responsible for classifying his work.[40] This screening and panel discussion (which was itself also released as a DVD ancillary extra) confirms the importance of the horror fan's proximity to the otherwise banned or censored object at such festivals, as:

> seeing a special screening of a banned or heavily censored film at a festival years before the same film's eventual certification and re-release would place the fan closer to an 'originary moment' (the history of the film's censorship/banning).[41]

The festival has managed to secure additional screenings of rare or contentious titles, using its reputation as a critically inclined festival in key dialogues with local licensing authorities. Such negotiations generated a special screening of Richard Robinson's unsettling race conflict thriller *Poor Pretty Eddie* (1975) in 2014, as well as helping to secure the first uncut UK theatrical screening of the controversial rape and revenge drama *Death Weekend* (1976), which played at *Cine-Excess* in 2015 with a Skyped introduction from its director William Fruet.

Beyond screenings as representing a challenge to censorship restrictions, a further way in which the EFFFF influenced the curatorial practices of *Cine-Excess* is through the practice of programming premieres as prestige markers. As indicated above, programming strategies within such organisations have co-opted the market orientations of more mainstream festivals, while retaining the genre focus associated with the cult/horror domain. As a result, all Federation members share a common quest to secure a sizeable number of premiere titles (which then often circulate between the differing territorial sites that comprise the organisation). Commenting on this drive to secure premieres for Federation events, former Brussels International Festival of Fantastic Film programmer Dirk Van Extergem noted that while curatorial teams 'look at hundreds of new films every year before making their choices for the Festival's next edition', they also 'dwell on film markets (Cannes and Mifed) and festivals'.[42] The value of the premiere remains the fact that 'first-hand experience is the premium value of the festival experience'.[43] Here, the premiere is a pivotal point in the film's release and exhibition cycle, functioning within the niche circuit to further solidify an early cult reputation to the films in selection.

It is a similar drive towards programming a range of UK theatrical premieres that has become a distinctive annual feature of *Cine-Excess*, where up to eight exclusive screenings are drawn from distinct global regions or subcultural film cycles on an annual basis. During this selection process, curatorial decisions are made through what Mathijs and Sexton have defined as 'cultist programming',[44] with new releases being linked to national traditions, icons or genre patterns that have currency within the circuit. For instance, given the importance that a number of scholars have attached to Italian cult film traditions,[45] *Cine-Excess* has sought to both celebrate and interrogate these European formats through a range of tie-in UK film premieres. Gabriele Albanesi's *The Last House in the Woods* (aka *Il bosco fuori*, 2006), for instance, received its UK theatrical premiere at *Cine-Excess* in 2007, where it was promoted as a contemporary rendition of the Italian *giallo* thriller format popularised during the 1970s. In 2012, Giorgio Amato's *Closed Circuit Extreme* was programmed as another UK premiere, not only as a European example of the found footage horror cycle, but also as a release from the leading Italian distribution house Dania Film, co-owned by director Sergio Martino, who was also a *Cine-Excess* guest for that year. Later in 2013, Federico Zampaglione's erotic murder mystery *Tulpa* (originally released 2012) was re-edited by the director so that it could be programmed as a *Cine-Excess* UK premiere, facilitated by a local licensing proviso warning of unsettling content.

Beyond programming in the European domain, *Cine-Excess* has also celebrated emergent American traditions of cult horror, including a focus on the work of Texan film-makers Duane Graves and Justin Meeks. The festival hosted a number of UK premieres by the pair, including their 'bigfoot' feature debut *The Wildman of the Navidad* (2008), while the festival later screened their 2012 urban slasher film *Butcher Boys*, as well as the recent gothic horror western *Kill or Be Killed* (2015). Interest in the duo's work resides not only in their use of 1970s horror tropes and the frequent cameo casting of established cult film icons (such as Edwin Neil and Michael Berryman), but also because both are former film students of Kim Henkel (writer of the 1974 cult release *The Texas Chain Saw Massacre* (Tobe Hooper)), and continue to collaborate with him on a range of independent productions that recapture a spirit of 1970s Southern 'trash' cinema. Henkel's own support for *Cine-Excess* as a festival has been demonstrated by his assistance in securing potential UK premieres to screen, while his own work-in-progress documentary *Beset by Demons: The Lou Perryman Story* (which examines the life and brutal murder of the Southern cult actor) was itself a *Cine-Excess* premiere in 2017. Equally, this interest in emerging voices has extended beyond specific film-makers to encompass wider political/activist elements in film exhibition (such as the current women-in-horror-cinema movement); the festival has promoted new female horror auteurs such as Lou Simon, and hosted the UK theatrical premieres of her female-led backwoods thriller *All Girls Weekend* in 2016, and her recent revisionist vendetta film *3* in 2017.

In addition to the above programming strategies, *Cine-Excess* remains receptive also to new trends in non-Western cinema, responding to the established focus on Asian cult cinema traditions demonstrated by other niche cult festivals. In their analysis of Udine's Far East Film Festival, for instance, Nikki J. Y. Lee and Julian Stringer have identified a process of 'counter-programming'[46] in the event's quest to bring Asian cinema traditions to European fan audiences. Although residing beyond the EFFFF network, Udine similarly exists as a hybrid 'major international film festival' and a 'specialist fan convention targeted at devotees of genre cinema'.[47] The festival's remit seeks to elide the traditional divisions between auteurist and subcultural products as boundary markers for competition entries, thus seeking to ensure a broad programming remit from a range of Asian cultures including South Korea, Japan, China and Thailand. In addition, its embedded programming teams also attempt to problematise the classification of existing film genres to better reflect the tastes of their audience. *Cine-Excess* has sought to provide similar strategies of geographical 'counter-programming' from 2010 onwards, demonstrating a specific screening focus on Mexican and Argentinian film titles that not only reflects an upturn of genre production in these territories, but also replicates similar curatorial packages to those of other niche cult European events that have influenced its development.

Just before leaving the topic of programming, it is worth acknowledging that premieres and exclusive screenings not only act as festival esteem indicators, but also function to promote the annual *Cine-Excess* industry panel. This component represents a third element that finds parity with the practices undertaken by the EFFFF organisations, which frequently host industry-oriented events dissecting key business and innovation trends in the fields of horror and cult film. For *Cine-Excess*, the annual industry panel functions to situate cult cinema activity alongside emergent business or technology trends, with panel members drawn from film-making guests, industry representatives, innovators and applied researchers. The significance of this component for the festival's wider promotion can be judged by the fact that the first national publicity afforded to *Cine-Excess* came through the journal *Cinema Business*. The journal's review of the 2007 event focused on the 'Distributing Excess' industry panel, which they felt represented 'independent distributors, TV and multi-media producers', and also 'offered an insight into the challenges involved in pushing a specialist and often hard-to-sell product'.[48] Other examples of the *Cine-Excess* industry panel include the 2012 screenwriting industry panel, which was organised in conjunction with *Time Out* magazine. Further topics discussed on an annual basis have included the role of cult film within digital new technologies (2013), as well as considerations of how alternative film-making can be used as a trigger for educational inclusion (2017).

From new blood to new outlets: cult horror festivals as content producers

As can be indicated from the above discussion, the midnight movie phenomenon identified by the first wave of cult film studies has been replaced by a mature and transnational festival network, whose working practices increasingly mirror key features found in mainstream modes of film exhibition. In tandem with this transition, while niche programming strategies continue to promote classic cult, horror and marginal film content, they also increasingly integrate these crowd-pleasing formats alongside the quest for more esteemed and international premieres, while the inclusion of educational and business networking components ensure both credibility and wider market exposure than had been possible within the traditional grindhouse cinema format.

While I have demonstrated that a small niche event such as *Cine-Excess* bears the traces of these alternative festival practices, by way of conclusion, it is also worth commenting on how the increased proliferation and professionalisation of the niche cult film circuit shifts their primary role as exhibition outlets to increasingly becoming producers of cult content. Following Hills's 2010 account of the importance of the home entertainment market to the horror film convention scene, Mathijs and Sexton have similarly noted how the burgeoning cult film market on Blu-ray and DVD often relies on ancillary materials filmed at niche cult festivals, which affirms their exclusivity as venues for the exhibition and dissemination of alternative film materials. In addition, programmers from organisations such as the EFFFF have further expanded into this market by creating documentaries on cult film traditions, which subsequently circulate within this festival network as a precursor to wider release. Indeed, founding members from Sweden's Fantastisk Film Festival are just one example of an outlet that has used its organisational and programming experience to move from exhibition into documentary and then on to feature film production, releasing the acclaimed vampire fiction film *Frostbite* (Anders Banke, 2006) and the more recent supernatural drama *Sensoria* (Christian Hallman, 2015).

Following the evolution of this model, *Cine-Excess* has also been involved in a diversification from niche cult exhibition to content for exhibition. It did so initially through a collaboration with the art-cinema distributor Nouveaux Pictures between 2009 and 2011, which led to a number of film titles being released across the UK under a Nouveaux Pictures-*Cine-Excess* banner. These titles included the feminist retro sex comedy *Viva* (Anna Biller, 2007) and the Dutch thriller *Amsterdamned* (Dick Maas, 1988), with a 2010 high-definition re-release of Argento's *Suspiria* providing the most high-profile release for the label. Through such releases, the label promoted the pairing of cult feature film releases' ancillary DVD materials created by academics as research outlets and teaching tool extras. This format then prompted an additional strand of *Cine-Excess* diversification into documentary production, initially through working on commissioned projects for other home entertainment labels (such as a 2011 production analysing the controversial reception of *Cannibal Holocaust*). More recently, the festival's emergent reputation in this area of documentary production has facilitated educational funding to create long-form film projects exploring the historical and sociocultural tensions behind cult film traditions. To date, two productions have been completed through this funding stream. *Tax Shelter Terrors* (Xavier Mendik et al., 2016) was an hour-long production that linked a decade of controversial Canadian horror releases to the region's wider nationalistic tensions in the 1970s. The release was premiered at a horror event in Toronto, before enjoying a year-long international run across festivals and conferences, boosted by a Director's Choice award from Sydney's A Night of Horror International Film Festival. More recently, the *Cine-Excess* documentary production arm completed an 80-minute documentary, titled *That's La Morte: Italian Cult Cinema and the Years of Lead* (Xavier Mendik, 2018), which ties Italian cult film traditions of the 1970s to wider terrorist fears of the decade. This latest production has exhibited across a number of international cult film events, once again confirming how the midnight movie circuit has evolved into a complex network of niche cult and horror film festivals in the twenty-first century.

Notes

1. Ernest Mathijs and Jamie Sexton, *Cult Cinema: An Introduction* (Chichester: Wiley-Blackwell, 2011), p. 36.
2. See M. Hills, 'Attending Horror Film Festivals and Conventions: Liveness, Subcultural Capital and "Flesh-and-Blood Genre Communities"', in I. Conrich (ed.), *Horror Zone: The Cultural Experience of Contemporary Horror Cinema* (London: I. B. Tauris, 2009), pp. 87–103. For a more recent account of the cult and horror film festival phenomenon, see R. Vivar, 'A film bacchanal: Playfulness and audience sovereignty in San Sebastian Horror and Fantasy Film Festival', *Participations: Journal of Audience & Reception Studies*, 13/1 (2016), 234–51.
3. J. Sconce, 'Trashing the Academy: Taste, Excess and an Emerging Politics of Cinematic Style', in E. Mathijs and X. Mendik (eds), *The Cult Film Reader* (Berkshire: McGraw-Hill, 2008), p. 101.
4. Sconce, 'Trashing the Academy', p. 101.
5. Sconce, 'Trashing the Academy', p. 101.
6. Sconce, 'Trashing the Academy', p. 102.
7. B. A. Austin, 'Portrait of a Cult Film Audience: *The Rocky Horror Picture Show*', in E. Mathijs and X. Mendik (eds), *The Cult Film Reader* (Berkshire: McGraw-Hill, 2008), p. 394.
8. Austin, 'Portrait of a Cult Film Audience', p. 395.
9. Austin, 'Portrait of a Cult Film Audience', p. 402.
10. Austin, 'Portrait of a Cult Film Audience', p. 394.
11. Hills, 'Attending Horror Film Festivals', p. 93.
12. Vivar, 'A film bacchanal', p. 235.
13. Mathijs and Sexton, *Cult Cinema*, p. 36.
14. Mathijs and Sexton, *Cult Cinema*, p. 38.
15. Mathijs and Sexton, *Cult Cinema*, p. 39.
16. Mathijs and Sexton, *Cult Cinema*, p. 41.
17. Mathijs and Sexton, *Cult Cinema*, p. 41.
18. Sconce, 'Trashing the Academy', p. 103.
19. Mathijs and Sexton, *Cult Cinema*, p. 37.
20. Mathijs and Sexton, *Cult Cinema*, p. 37.
21. H. McGill, 'Film festivals: a view from the inside', *Screen*, 52/2 (2011), 285.
22. McGill, 'Film festivals', 285.
23. T. Riskala, 'The Espoo Ciné International Film Festival', in E. Mathijs and X. Mendik (eds), *Alternative Europe: Eurotrash and Exploitation Cinema Since 1945* (London: Wallflower Press, 2004), p. 229.

24. Riskala, 'The Espoo Ciné International Film Festival', p. 229.
25. Riskala, 'The Espoo Ciné International Film Festival', p. 230.
26. X. Mendik, 'The Fantastisk Film Festival: An Overview and Interview with Magnus Paulsson', in E. Mathijs and X. Mendik, *Alternative Europe: Eurotrash and Exploitation Cinema Since 1945* (London: Wallflower Press, 2004), p. 233.
27. Mendik, 'The Fantastisk Film Festival', p. 235.
28. D. Van Extergem, 'A Report on the Brussels International Festival of Fantastic Film', in E. Mathijs and X. Mendik, *Alternative Europe: Eurotrash and Exploitation Cinema Since 1945* (London: Wallflower Press, 2004), p. 223.
29. Van Extergem, 'A Report on the Brussels International Film Festival', p. 219.
30. Van Extergem, 'A Report on the Brussels International Film Festival', p. 219.
31. Riskala, 'The Espoo Ciné International Film Festival', p. 231.
32. Mathijs and Sexton, *Cult Cinema*, p. 42.
33. For an overview of the controversy raised by Cronenberg's film as a state-funded project, see B. Wright, 'Canada's Great Shame: Tax Shelters, Nationalism, and Popular Taste in Canadian Cinema', *Spectator*, 32/2 (2012), 20–5.
34. *The Guardian Guide* (21–7 May 2011), 23.
35. Mathijs and Sexton, *Cult Cinema*, p. 41.
36. Riskala, 'The Espoo Ciné International Film Festival', p. 231.
37. Vivar, 'A film bacchanal', p. 241.
38. S. Rowan-Legg, 'Charges against Sitges Festival & director Ángel Sala dropped', *Screen Anarchy* (22 February 2012), *https://screenanarchy.com/2012/02/charges-against-sitges-festival-director-angel-sala-dropped.html* (accessed 29 August 2019).
39. 'Press Note regarding charges against Ángel Sala, Festival Director, for the screening of *A Serbian Film* in 2010', *Sitges Film Festival* (9 March 2011), *https://sitgesfilmfestival.com/eng/noticies?id=1003040* (accessed 29 August 2019).
40. T. Masters, '"Video nasty" director Deodato debates censorship', *BBC News* (26 May 2011), *https://www.bbc.co.uk/news/entertainment-arts-13550879* (accessed 29 August 2019).
41. Hills, 'Attending Horror Film Festivals', p. 91.
42. Van Extergem, 'A Report on the Brussels International Film Festival', pp. 224–5.
43. Van Extergem, 'A Report on the Brussels International Film Festival', p. 225.
44. Mathijs and Sexton, *Cult Cinema*, p. 42.
45. See L. Hunt, 'A Sadistic Night at the Opera: Notes on the Italian Horror Film', in K. Gelder (ed.), *The Horror Film Reader* (London: Routledge, 2000),

pp. 324–36; Mikel J. Koven, *La Dolce Morte: Vernacular Cinema and the Italian Giallo Film* (Lanham, MD: Scarecrow Press, 2006); Xavier Mendik, *Bodies of Desire and Bodies in Distress: The Golden Age of Italian Cult Cinema 1970–1985* (Newcastle upon Tyne: Cambridge Scholars Publishing, 2015); and G. Needham, 'Playing with genre: An introduction to the Italian *giallo*', *Kinoeye: New Perspectives on European Film*, 2/11 (2002), 1–7.
46. N. J. Y. Lee and J. Stringer, 'Counter-programming and the Udine Far East Film Festival', *Screen*, 52/2 (2011), 303.
47. Lee and Stringer, 'Counter-programming', 303.
48. K. Noblett, 'Successful Excess', *Cinema Business*, 34 (2007), 27.

PART TWO

HORROR RECEPTION

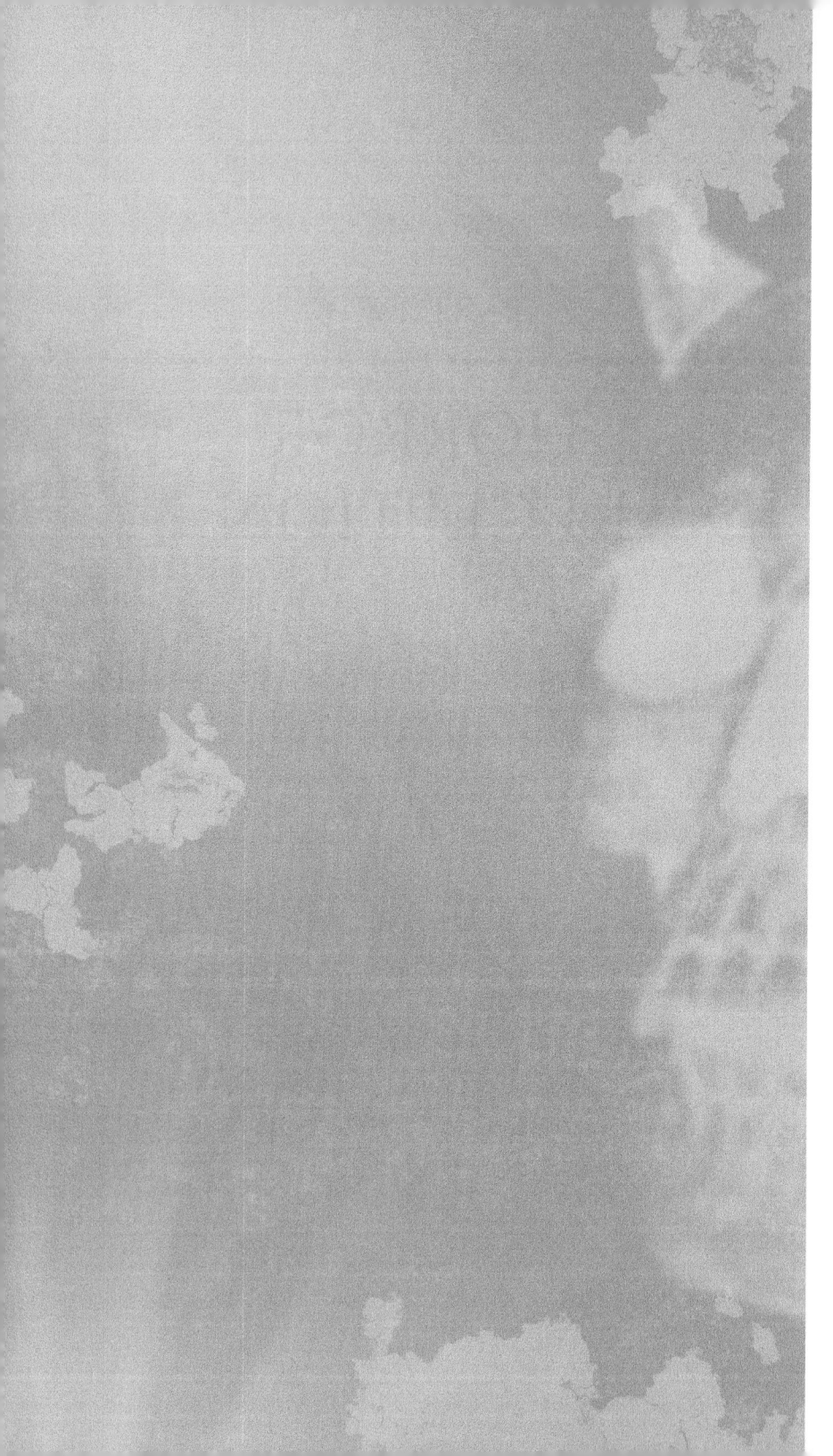

4

A Master of Horror?

The Making and Marketing of Takashi Miike's Horror Reputation

Joe Hickinbottom

THE LATTER HALF of the 2010s was a pivotal period for filmmaker Takashi Miike, arguably the most visible active Japanese director in Western film culture. In 2016, Miike received a Lifetime Achievement Award at the twentieth edition of Montreal's Fantasia International Film Festival, having been a staple at the festival since its inception (no other director's work has been screened at Fantasia more often than Miike's).[1] A year later, Miike was gifted an even more prestigious accolade in the form of an invitation to join the Academy of Motion Picture Arts and Sciences. Then, at the tail end of 2017 came the release of what was billed as the most significant film of his career: the live-action, samurai-oriented manga adaptation, *Blade of the Immortal*. Miike's most widely distributed film in the West in some years, *Blade of the Immortal* has been prominently positioned in promotional and critical discourse as a milestone in the director's expansive oeuvre, mostly for being his hundredth feature film. While this is actually an erroneous assertion (Miike does indeed currently hold over a hundred directing credits, but not all of these are for features), it has nevertheless been touted, and received, as a landmark in a career spanning over twenty-six years. It is fair to say, then, that Miike has never been more well known, and celebrated, among Western film critics and audiences.

What is so intriguing about Miike's current heightened visibility in the West – and what warrants him as a subject of investigation in this horror-themed collection – is that it is in large part owing to his reputation as a director of horror cinema. Ostensibly unremarkable (plenty of film-makers gain exposure for their work in the genre), Miike's case is in fact significant for its somewhat incongruous nature. Despite embracing a broad scope of genres across his body of work – including, but not limited to, those of *yakuza*, comedy, drama, action, samurai, musical, family, superhero, martial arts and horror – Miike possesses an enduring status as a horror auteur that has been built upon, and is maintained by, only a handful of titles, the most notable of which were released in the first half of the 2000s. Miike has focused very little on the horror genre over the last fifteen or so years, yet in the West the perception of him as a key producer of horror remains central to the discursive framing of the director and his releases. When a new Miike title is released in Western regions (regardless of its dominant generic elements), the film-maker's horror auteur status is leaned upon as a principal signifier in marketing practices, an approach often reflected in contemporaneous critical discourse. This positioning of Miike is symptomatic of the discursive genrification of his cinema outside his native Japan. As Miike's application of genre remains protean, Western distributors repeatedly return to the horror paradigm that characterised his early reception to present audiences with a suitable (and lucrative) means of understanding a diverse body of work: a method of reaching consumers that, in its process, bolsters his status as a horror auteur.

This chapter traces the trajectory of Miike's horror auteur reputation, charting the defining moments that forged the director's enduring position as a prominent figure in the wider discourse of horror cinema. I consider the (at times) contradictory and (at worst) cynical motivations at play in the construction, and exploitation, of Miike's repute as a horror auteur in marketing practices, before examining how it continues to be upheld in the face of the shifting contexts of Miike's film-making and reception. I posit that Miike's eminence in the West as a proponent of horror is primarily a discursive construct: a conceptual positioning curated by discourse that at once shapes, and is shaped by, patterns in the distribution and reception of his films.

Furthermore, I suggest that Miike's reputation as a horror auteur presents a valuable platform from which to consider the function of authorship on a broader scale in the distribution and reception of horror cinema today. The 'horror auteur' is a primary context in the dissemination and discussion of horror films in the twenty-first century, inflecting how horror cinema is sold, consumed and understood by distributors, audiences and critics. Miike's case is particularly notable, for the propagation of his horror authorship echoes (and, in some cases, intersects with) the enduring commercial and critical legacies of several other high-profile horror auteurs. The functions of Miike's horror authorship are performed in a similar manner to a select few who have preceded him: film-makers such as John Carpenter, Dario Argento, Tobe Hooper, George A. Romero and John Landis, whose reputations have, over many decades, served analogous discursive utilities. As we shall see later in this chapter though, beyond merely sharing parallels with their receptions, Miike has even been placed alongside these horror auteur titans through his inclusion in some significant horror productions – instances of canonisation that have, it seems, cemented the Japanese director as a true 'master of horror'.

'You are sick!' *Audition*, *Ichi the Killer* and the birth of a horror reputation

The foundation of Miike's horror auteur status – and the recognition of his work outside his native country more broadly – can largely be attributed to a pair of releases that arrived in the West in quick succession at the turn of the century, namely 1999's *Audition* and 2001's *Ichi the Killer*. The lively reception of these titles, especially at international film festivals, did much to carve out a place for Miike as a leading horror director in the minds of Western critics and consumers. Accompanied by considerable controversy, these two releases rapidly established Miike as a figurehead of modern Japanese horror (J-horror) cinema and of the contemporaneously burgeoning 'Asia Extreme' phenomenon. Much scholarship has been written on Asia Extreme elsewhere,[2] so there is little need to retread ground here; it is, however, important to recognise in this discussion Miike's centrality to the phenomenon and its lasting impact on his horror reputation.

Asia Extreme was a discursively constructed conceptualisation of a supposedly unified 'extreme cinema' from East Asia that proliferated in the West in the 2000s, a product of distributors' efforts to generate and supply audience demand for a seemingly violent, shocking and horrific cinema from the region. This aim was achieved through reductive marketing campaigns that packaged a wealth of disparate titles from many genres (most notably horror, action and thriller) into a homogenous brand. As Robert Hyland has justly noted, the classification of these titles was alarmingly amorphous in nature, often relying on the notion that 'if a film originates from Asia and looks extreme, then it must be exemplary of Asia Extreme'.[3] A principal tactic of these campaigns was to foreground certain titles and directors as representative of the Asia Extreme brand as a whole, and no other film-maker served as a more reliable point of reference than Miike. *Audition* and *Ichi the Killer* remain seminal films in the Asia Extreme canon, having become for many audiences demonstrative of Asia Extreme's established essential qualities: this was, it appeared, a violent, nasty and decidedly horrifying cinema trend.

One of the most salacious of all Asia Extreme films (and, ergo, one of the brand's most paradigmatic) was *Audition*, which swiftly gained Miike notoriety in the West, not least in horror circles. *Audition* was the first of Miike's features to be widely seen outside Japan, yet many spectators would likely have been unaware that the film was in fact the director's thirty-fifth in less than a decade. Of the hundred or so projects that currently constitute Miike's vast oeuvre, *Audition* can certainly be considered, as Steven Rawle proposes, his 'international calling card'.[4] The film's notorious appearances at festivals and theatres across Europe and the US garnered extraordinary media hype, firmly establishing Miike as an emerging director on the horror scene. Following its world premiere at the Vancouver International Film Festival in October 1999, *Audition* made its way to the Netherlands a few months later for its European opening, in January 2000. The film's reception at that year's International Film Festival Rotterdam – a festival with a reputation as a site of transgressive cinema – is infamous, and not without good reason. *Audition*'s shocking denouement (containing horrific scenes of torture and psychological torment) prompted an unprecedented number of Rotterdam audience members to walk out of screenings in disgust.[5] News of the upset spread quickly in the British media, with reports appearing in *The Guardian*, *Sight & Sound* and *The Mirror*, all claiming that one particularly disgruntled woman was so dismayed by Miike's film that, before leaving, she took the opportunity to verbally attack the director personally.[6] Miike recalls how the irritated punter, who was sitting directly behind him during the screening, 'made a point of it' to walk around the theatre and approach him to yell 'You are sick!' directly to his face.[7]

Further tales of audience aversion to *Audition* circulated as it continued to tour the festival circuit and later gained theatrical release throughout the West. Reports claimed that the film had been 'responsible for throngs of shaken filmgoers staggering out of theaters', and even had 'some viewers vomiting in the aisles'.[8] When it opened at the Irish Film Centre in Dublin in May 2001, managers resorted to placing warnings outside the cinema after two people fainted during a screening, and *The Mirror* claimed that up to twenty viewers a night were walking out of screenings.[9] Later that year, a notorious run at the Riffraff cinema in Zurich, Switzerland, garnered more sensational accounts of intense audience reactions to Miike's film. *The Guardian* reported that three spectators 'collapsed and the rest of the audience walked out in protest' during *Audition*'s premiere, proving so gruesome that 'a man had to be stretchered away' from the theatre. Frank Braun, the cinema's programme director, revealed that the film's debut screening was so calamitous that it led him to consider pulling it early on in its run, later changing his mind, tellingly, 'after being flooded with requests for tickets'.[10]

In spite of what such audience responses may indicate, *Audition* was well received by Western critics and tastemakers. It was awarded two critics' prizes at Rotterdam and gained a special mention in the judging of the International Fantasy Film Award at Portugal's Fantasporto Festival in 2001.[11] In the UK, support for *Audition* was displayed by *The Guardian*'s reviewers in particular: Peter Bradshaw praised the film as 'a modern-day Jacobean revenge nightmare', while Miike was celebrated as 'a master at manipulating audience expectations à la Buñuel and Polanski' and compared to Hitchcock and Lynch for 'reeling [viewers] in gently but expertly'.[12] Positive responses in the US came in the form of reviews in mainstream magazines and newspapers such as *Variety* and *The Los Angeles Times*, with Ken Eisner deeming *Audition* a 'lyrically paced' picture of 'haunting beauty' and Kevin Thomas applauding it as a 'gruesome but skillful' work from 'a compelling filmmaker'.[13]

These reviews foreshadowed the discursive framing of Miike as a provocative auteur that was to build momentum over the ensuing years, given impetus by another infamous Asia Extreme release: Miike's gory manga adaptation, *Ichi the Killer*. While not distributed by the leading proponent of the phenomenon, Tartan,[14] the controversy surrounding *Ichi the Killer* contributed greatly to the growth of Miike's horror reputation and the Asia Extreme discourse more broadly. Media coverage hyped the film's relentlessly graphic and sexualised violence, which plays out as the titular character, Ichi (Nao Ōmori), is pitted against Tadanobu Asano's sadomasochistic *yakuza* member, Kakihara, in an increasingly ferocious gang war. Hyperbolic reporting of the film's levels of violence was particularly rife in the UK, where it was subjected to substantial cuts by the British Board of Film Classification before it was permitted to be released. For instance, the BBC's Almar Haflidason wrote that, with the 'blood-soaked' *Ichi the Killer*, Miike attempts 'to push and tear at the levels of onscreen violence and take them to a terrifying new level', while *The Guardian*'s Bradshaw proclaimed it to be an 'ultra-violent' piece of work 'that really can only be viewed from between your fingers, or behind the sofa'.[15] The attention paid to *Ichi the Killer*'s depiction of violence further entrenched Miike's reputation as a provocateur, firmly positioning him as a figurehead of the Asia Extreme wave – a post that would see him, as we shall see later in this chapter, greatly influence one of the decade's most controversial horror subgenres.

Echoing *Audition*'s lively reception, festival screenings of *Ichi the Killer* whipped up quite the storm, which is perhaps unsurprising given the film's transgressive content. Importantly, the furore at these sites was not exclusively audience-generated; promoters and distributors were complicit in fostering controversy, having astutely recognised the lucrative potential of Miike's shock value after the persistent buzz left in *Audition*'s wake. At *Ichi the Killer*'s premiere at the Toronto International Film Festival's 'Midnight Madness' programme in 2001, festival organisers provided audience members with promotional 'vomit bags' – sporting a blood-spattered design, emblazoned with the film's '1' (Ichi) logo and exclaiming 'For Viewer Discomfort' – warning viewers of the film's likely nauseating effects. The same stunt was pulled during screenings at other events, including the Stockholm International Film Festival and the Hong Kong International Film Festival, illustrating the wide reach of Miike's reputation for the extreme. Significantly, as Oliver Dew rightly points out in his study of Asia Extreme marketing practices, such tactics relied heavily upon the traditional tropes of danger and dare central to the promotion of horror cinema. As an example of this, Dew draws attention to Medusa's home video release of *Ichi the Killer*, posters for which bore an image of a female viewer bound to a chair being forced to watch the film's scenes of terror, accompanied by the tagline 'at last, a volunteer'.[16]

During this early stage of exposure to Miike's cinema in the West, it made sense for the director's releases to be positioned for consumers within a horror framework. Although Miike's flexibility with genre is widely acknowledged today, in the early 2000s audiences were less familiar with the actual diversity of his work. With key releases such as *Audition* and *Ichi the Killer* making waves for their shocking content, it was logical for distributors to market his titles with the use of historically proven tropes of horror film promotion. Moreover, these two titles arrived before the trend of American remakes of J-horror classics – such as the hugely successful *The Ring* (Gore Verbinski, 2002) and *The Grudge* (Takashi Shimizu, 2004) – ignited Western interest in the Japanese originals and Asian horror more broadly. As such, the later-established familiarity with the assumed tropes of Asian horror cinema (what *The Guardian*'s Joe Queenan outlined in 2008 as 'water, hair, the trauma of secondary school, ghosts, and most especially creepy little girls')[17] could not yet be exploited, necessitating a more general discursive association with horror in order to increase the appeal of Miike's releases.

It is not the intent of this chapter to examine Miike's position in J-horror's domestic history. What is pertinent to this study, however, is the lasting impact of *Audition* and *Ichi the Killer* on Miike's horror auteur status and their abiding currency in the marketing of the director's cinema to certain audiences. More than any of his films, these two have acted as beacons in the framing of his releases within a horror context. This is of particular note, given that neither film fully adheres to the traditions of Asian horror that Western audiences had, rightfully or wrongfully, come to expect, coupled with the fact that Miike produced two other titles during this period that far more comfortably sit within the horror genre, yet lack anything approaching the same discursive power. *One Missed Call* (2003; one of six titles he directed that year[18]) was Miike's exercise in 'straight-up' J-horror film-making, following in the footsteps of the subgenre's seminal entries, such as *Ringu* (Hideo Nakata, 1998), *Pulse* (Kiyoshi Kurosawa, 2001) and *Ju-on: The Grudge* (Takashi Shimizu, 2002). As Rawle notes, *One Missed Call* shares many of the visual codes and narrative tropes typical of the Asian horror cycles popular among Western audiences around the turn of the century: an urban legend, a surprising denouement, vengeful apparitions, the abused child and menacing technologies.[19] Yet, arriving at the tail end of the J-horror boom, *One Missed Call* was shunned by Western critics as a hackneyed recycling of well-established conventions, and many derided the film for its departure from the kind of shocking and provocative cinema for which the director had become known. Following this, in 2004, Miike contributed to a horror anthology film, *Three... Extremes*, alongside other notable contemporary film-makers from East Asia, namely South Korea's Park Chan-wook and Fruit Chan of Hong Kong. Miike's segment, 'Box', is a slow-paced, complex and dream-like tale. Although the film received mostly positive reviews after a short run in theatres in 2005, it failed to reach audiences in the same way that *Audition*, *Ichi the Killer* or Park's *Oldboy* (2003) did, and was largely overlooked.

So, when one looks back at Miike's early reception in the West through a horror lens, two images of Miike come into focus: the 'actual' horror director, who engages directly with the genre and its tropes in films like *One Missed Call*, and the 'imagined' horror director, whose entire oeuvre is channelled through these recognisable tropes for the benefit of consumers, regardless of actual textual content. In the years following the release of *Audition* and *Ichi the Killer*, the line between these two versions of Miike would become increasingly blurred, with some productive results. With the discursive circulation of Miike as a purveyor of horror continuing to gain traction in the marketing and reception of his work, new creative opportunities within the genre would arise that, in their realisation, would further establish Miike in the horror sphere.

Miike makes a visit: influence and extreme capital in *Hostel*

In a scene in Eli Roth's 2005 horror film *Hostel*, a young American backpacker, Paxton, is searching for his missing friends. He arrives at a remote abandoned factory surrounded by tough-looking thugs in leather jackets and men in suits – they all appear to be waiting for something. In the background, out of focus, a businessman can be glimpsed leaving the building. Paxton stops the man, and the two engage in a short conversation:

Paxton:	Excuse me, I uh . . . Excuse me. How is it in there?
Businessman:	Be careful . . .
Paxton:	Why's that?
Businessman:	You can spend . . . *all* your money . . . in there.

The businessman is played by Takashi Miike, delivering his lines in slow, rehearsed English.[20] He gesticulates directly at Paxton (and, importantly, at the audience, momentarily breaking the fourth wall) as he gives his ominous warning of monetary indulgence, before pointing towards the derelict factory and walking off-screen with a knowing grin. The director is on-screen for a total of just 20 seconds, yet his appearance marks a pivotal turning point in the film's depiction of cruelty and violence. Upon entering the building, Paxton learns of its true purpose: it houses unwitting tourists kidnapped from the local area as prisoners, as subjects whom wealthy clients can pay for the privilege of torturing and killing. With this knowledge, we can ascertain that the Japanese businessman seen moments earlier has just been enjoying the heinous services offered inside the killing factory. Here, Miike's words shape audience expectation by signposting the kind of violent spectacle to follow, in a manner similar to the 'Quentin Tarantino Presents . . .' imprimatur donned by *Hostel*'s posters (Tarantino served as Executive Producer), albeit with less recognisability. Miike's admission that 'You can spend . . . *all* your money . . . in there' paints him as one who enjoys (as a character within Roth's film) and purveys (as a film-maker) the supposedly dubious pleasures of extreme violence. Knowing spectators – those familiar with Miike's cinema and its reputation for explicit content – can assume that what Roth has in store must be as gruesome as the horrors found in Miike's films.

As one of the key titles of the 'torture porn' horror subgenre, *Hostel* is often credited with bringing a new level of violence to Western mainstream cinema. What is commonly overlooked is the fact that the film is greatly indebted to Asia Extreme and to Miike's work in particular, which exhibits many of the tropes to be found in the torture porn canon. Operating essentially as a form of product placement, Miike's cameo in *Hostel* manifests the influence of his films (alongside those of his East Asian contemporaries) on an entire subgenre of modern mainstream horror. The short conversation between Paxton and Miike communicates a theme that runs throughout Roth's text – the moral implications of the consumption, and enjoyment, of extreme scenes of sex and violence – crystallised by Miike's very appearance.

This issue, and *Hostel* itself, would become central to the torture porn discourse. The phrase 'torture porn' was coined by *New York Magazine* critic David Edelstein in his discussion of a cycle of modern horror films, likening their graphic and extended scenes of violent torture to the act of sexual gratification incited by pornography.[21] Although its presence has since waned, torture porn was an important trend in popular horror cinema. Roth and his contemporaries were responsible for moving violence in mainstream horror cinema away from low-budget B-movie shock fare, towards higher-budget, profitable releases. Certainly, what was so striking about the torture porn canon was its popularisation of high levels of gore and protracted scenes of torture, the likes of which had never before been widely seen in multiplexes in the West. While many of the most commercially successful torture porn titles are American productions, the subgenre possesses a wider, international reach. As Steve Jones has argued, torture porn discourse has tended to focus on the violent images produced by US film-makers in their critiques of the country's political upheaval, overlooking the fact that 'images of torture and humiliation have also flourished in horror cinema from France, the UK, Australia, Korea, Japan and Thailand', as part of what Jones recognises as 'a globalized genre'.[22] Lindsay Hallam has also noted torture porn's international status, one that is 'closely linked to streams of new "extreme" cinema which has been coming out of Asia and France', singling out Miike's *Audition* and *Ichi the Killer* as chief examples.[23]

Miike's cameo in *Hostel* validates the Japanese director as an international horror auteur, pointing towards the interwoven, globalised nature of contemporary horror. Although fleeting, Miike's appearance in the film is a significant moment in an ongoing transnational exchange of creative and commercial stimulus between three global horror tastemakers – Miike, Roth and Tarantino – embodying the influence of Miike's cinema on Roth's own extreme horror film-making while illustrating Miike's active engagement in horror discourse.

Roth garnered attention in 2002 with the release of *Cabin Fever*, a film that, for Tarantino at least, established the new director as 'the future of horror'.[24] Roth has stated that Miike's cinema was of great inspiration to *Hostel*, in part due to the input of Tarantino. In an interview, Roth claimed that, when advising him on his ideas for *Hostel*, Tarantino encouraged him to 'make it as sick as you want to make it. Make it fucking balls-out. This could be your Takashi Miike film. This could be a classic American horror movie.'[25] Here, Miike is both heralded as the apogee of extreme film-making – someone to aspire to in the pursuit of creating 'sick' cinema – and positioned as a benchmark within the horror genre, with Tarantino conflating Miike's notoriety for extreme content with nationally specific horror film credibility. In the same interview, however, Roth attempts to elevate his work above mere imitation. He says, 'I didn't feel like there was any need to try to make *Ichi the Killer 2*. That's what Miike does, and let those guys do that. I kinda wanted to make something that felt influenced by that but was still an American movie.'[26] Alluding to Miike as an ambassador of Asia Extreme ('let those guys do that'), Roth at once expresses admiration for Miike's work (or, perhaps, what it represents) and displays a desire to distinguish it from his own cinema on the basis of its national specificity. Yet, Roth's casting of Miike in *Hostel* somewhat belies his claim of distinction; the placement of the Japanese director within his American horror movie connotes a desire to lend his work a level of credibility by exploiting Miike's extreme/horror capital.

The attachment of both Tarantino and Miike to *Hostel* illustrates the lucrative economic potential of the auteur in the spheres of horror production and reception, albeit in slightly different ways. There is, as many scholars have noted,[27] a Tarantino 'brand' – a kind of product to be expected when Tarantino is associated with a release – as drawn upon in promotional materials for Roth's film, billed as 'Quentin Tarantino Presents . . . *Hostel*'. In this case, Tarantino's name operates taxonomically, functioning, to follow Steve Neale's argument, 'as a "brand name", a means of labelling and selling a film and of orientating expectation and channelling meaning and pleasure'.[28] Tarantino's name invokes the director's established, discursively constructed auteur brand, bestowing upon the film his authorial approval and suggesting to viewers that, with *Hostel*, they can expect the same kind of violent, pop culture-conscious cinema (and its concomitant pleasures) produced by the auteur endorsing it.

The cameo appearance of Miike in *Hostel* goes even further, seeing the Japanese director's own auteur brand imprinted on the film itself through the rendering of his authorial presence visible on-screen. Timothy Corrigan suggests that auteurist marketing garners 'a relationship between audience and movie in which an intentional and authorial agency governs, as a kind of brand-name vision that precedes and succeeds the film, the way that movie is seen and received'.[29] Miike's cameo role in *Hostel* functions by these means. Distinct from that of the lead actors around which it emerges, Miike's appearance presents a transitory disruption to the narrative flow, temporarily pausing progression in its separation from the overarching structure. In essence, this cameo is an intentional intervention in the filmic structure that is disruptive (for those viewers who are familiar with director Miike) precisely *because of* the performer's recognisability.

Indeed, Miike has a recognisable star director image. His public presence at festivals, in interviews and in promotional material inflects the interpretation of the texts he authors or is associated with. Central to this is Miike's appearance, with his distinct visual facets – the sunglasses, the jacket, the leather trousers, the ubiquitous cigarette – becoming, through their repetition and consistency across a range of media, integral to his stardom. As Gary Bettinson writes of Wong Kar-wai, another prominent East Asian star director who shares Miike's penchant for spectacles, '[a]s a personality he is iconic, the omnipresent sunglasses an indelible trademark'.[30]

These 'trademarks' gesture towards, and grow to be synonymous with, the construct of the star and its associated meanings and expectations. In Miike's case, discussion of his appearance in film discourse often posits an interrelation between these recognisable traits and his status as an auteur.[31] His distinctive look at once *represents* and *is* his star director image; his appearance is thus a vital part of his authorial signature.

Miike's cameo in *Hostel* relies upon and contributes to his stardom in horror circles, bolstering his star director image. As Simon Dixon notes, cameo performances have 'a peculiar function in the spatial organization of stardom', proposing that '[t]he peculiar purpose of the star cameo is to *warp attentional space*, so that the minor becomes uncannily major'.[32] To follow this line, what is so significant about the minor role Miike plays in *Hostel* is its reflection of the star director image to be found in discourse, and particularly that surrounding horror cinema. Adorning a long brown trench coat, black t-shirt and dark sunglasses, he closely resembles the star figure to be found in interviews, television promos and magazines. In the brief seconds he is on-screen, Miike is foregrounded by Roth not as a character within the diegesis of the film but as himself, indicating the pair's awareness of the artifice of the former's star image via a referential, and reverential, display. Miike literally appears as 'Miike'.

Hard to watch: *Imprint* and the (re)making of a horror auteur

In the wake of *Hostel*, Miike's global reach continued to grow as his films began to cross boundaries in their production, distribution and reception. Miike's status as an international horror auteur was further cemented – in both a discursive and a pragmatic sense – when he was invited by Showtime, a premium US cable television network, to contribute an episode to their horror anthology series *Masters of Horror* (2005–7). The passion project of horror producer and director Mick Garris, *Masters of Horror* intended to showcase the film-making of thirteen contemporary horror directors in a series of newly commissioned hour-long episodes. Showtime offered contributors (including genre stalwarts and relative newcomers) free choice of material and 'freedom from corporate censorship', in return for adhering to tight budgets and schedules.[33] Cable networks such as Showtime (and its biggest competitor, HBO) occupy a particular sector within the landscape of American television, hospitable to recognised feature-film auteurs as a platform to exercise their film-making in the realm of television production.[34] *Masters of Horror* was accordingly billed as an opportunity for audiences to indulge in the nightmarish work of some of horror cinema's superlative directors: 'Experience terrifying visions from the greatest minds in the genre – these are the masters of horror!' proclaimed Anchor Bay's DVD release of the series.[35] Significantly for Miike, the show placed the Japanese director in the company of some of horror cinema's most well-established American and European auteurs – such as John Carpenter, Tobe Hooper, Joe Dante and Dario Argento – ratifying his position in the genre's auteur pantheon and ushering in an intensified level of acclaim in the West.

Miike's entry in the series, titled *Imprint*, stars US actor Billy Drago as Christopher, an American journalist who travels across nineteenth-century Japan in search of a past lover, Komono (played by Michie Itō).[36] During his investigation on a small, remote island populated by working girls and their masters, Christopher meets a woman who tells him that the other workers, driven by jealousy, tortured Komono by restraining her with rope, burning her arms with hot incense sticks and inserting needles under her fingernails and into her gums (in a moment reminiscent of *Audition*'s finale). As the story unfolds, a series of alarming scenes of further torture, rape, abuse, abortion and bodily deformity are revealed. Originally planned to air on 27 January 2006, *Imprint* was pulled from schedule at the eleventh hour. Reports suggested that Garris and the Showtime executives were so shocked by the film's content that they believed it to be unsuitable for broadcast. By his own account, Garris was equally impressed and disturbed by Miike's film: 'I think it's amazing', he told *The New York Times*, 'but it's even hard for me to watch'.[37] After the news broke that *Imprint* would not be shown, Showtime removed all reference to the film on its website, refused to comment further on the matter and replaced its broadcast slot with John McNaughton's *Haeckel's Tale* (2006), an adaptation of a short story by horror legend Clive Barker.

Showtime's refusal to air *Imprint* marked an important turning point in Miike's reception in horror circles, made all the more impactful by its contextual specificity. Cable networks such as Showtime have a reputation for broadcasting challenging material to its paying customers, yet *Imprint* was banned as it was deemed unsuitable even for such a tolerant market. Comments from both Garris and Miike indicate a disconnect between what the Japanese director believed to be acceptable for US audiences and what a cable television network was actually prepared to show. Garris has explained how his team 'made it clear [to Miike] that we were going on American pay cable television, and even though there wasn't as much control over content, there still were concerns', adding that 'when we got the first cut, it was very, very strong stuff'.[38] Approximately 8 minutes of footage was removed from the first submission, Garris states, almost all of which was from the scene in which Komono is tortured.[39] Despite the efforts made to tone down the flagged content, the final version of *Imprint* was ultimately rejected by Showtime. Speaking with Mark Schilling for *The Japan Times* a few months after the film was pulled from broadcast, Miike corroborated Garris's account, humbly admitting that he misjudged what was permissible on the network:

> I like being free, but I don't want my freedom to make trouble for others. I thought that I was right up to the limit of what American television would tolerate. As I was making the film I kept checking to make sure that I wasn't going over the line, but I evidently misestimated.[40]

Showtime decided that *Imprint* would be more likely to find an audience on home video, free from the restrictions of television network policies. Released on DVD later in 2006, *Imprint* garnered a considerable cult following, facilitated by the controversy surrounding it as the only banned episode of a horror television show proclaiming itself to be 'a ground-breaking, award-winning series that redefined terror'.[41] Exploiting Miike's reputation in the West as a purveyor of violent and disturbing content, the marketing campaign presented the film as too 'extreme' for American television, proudly stating that it was 'Banned From Cable Broadcast' and, tellingly, drawing attention to Miike as the director of *Audition* and *Ichi the Killer* while foregrounding the film's horrific imagery. Reflecting the tactics of the distributors of Asia Extreme, the promotion of *Imprint* emphasised its transgressive and shocking qualities, activating Miike's established extreme capital. The film is 'a tale of extreme cruelty and perverse vengeance', the DVD release claims, 'an unspeakable orgy of torment and depravity, where the lusts of the damned will inflict wounds that remain forever. This is IMPRINT'.[42]

Certainly, the video release offered cult horror fans – and, indeed, Miike fans – the alluring opportunity to view a film deemed inappropriate for television broadcast, enticing the cultist desire to indulge in content presumed to be offensive to the perceived mainstream. In an interview with Garris for the horror site *Icons of Fright*, Rob Galluzo recognises how *Imprint*'s troubled distribution garnered it a dedicated following. '[T]he thing I loved about it was it became the episode that you had to see', he says. 'Exactly', replies Garris.⁴³ It is important here not to overlook Showtime's own agency in cultivating this type of response. As a major television network invested in the project, there was much to gain from presenting *Imprint* in such a way as to maximise its potential audience reach. In spite of its supposed unsuitability for the broadcast platform on which the rest of the *Masters of Horror* series was hosted, the DVD release drew attention to the fact that it was available for the first time, uncut and unadulterated.⁴⁴ 'Too strong for cable TV! The sales angle is brilliant! Fans of Miike and his extreme side will rejoice; Imprint IS twisted', one reviewer cynically (yet astutely) posited of Showtime's intentions.⁴⁵

The designation of Miike as a 'master of horror' beside long-standing auteurs of the genre, such as Carpenter, Hooper and Argento, is indicative of the lasting impact of *Audition* and *Ichi the Killer* on his reputation in the West. Compared to a director like Carpenter, who has helmed some of the most influential horror films in American cinema – including seminal slasher flick *Halloween* (1978), unsettling ghost story *The Fog* (1980) and sci-fi horror tale *The Thing* (1982) – Miike has a relative lack of experience within the genre, and he does not truly share Argento's position as a pioneer of a 'foreign' subgenre of horror cinema, with his Italian *giallo* films, such as *The Bird with the Crystal Plumage* (1970), *Deep Red* (1975) and *Suspiria* (1977). Miike is known in the West as a horror film-maker on the back of just a handful of films, yet across his hundred or so releases to date the genre is hardly one that figures prominently. Even the director himself believes the association to be undeserved: 'Me, a "Master of Horror"? I'm the guy that made *Salaryman Kintaro!*' Miike has exclaimed.⁴⁶

Here, Miike amusingly casts aside the moniker by referencing one of his more accessible and child-friendly works – his 1999 family film, in which an ex-member of a biker gang makes his way through a series of white-collar jobs to provide for his young son and leave his life of delinquency behind. Yet, the director's dismissal of the title of 'master of horror' is more significant than its playfulness may suggest. His unwillingness to be confined by generic conventions – he claims to have 'a resistance towards being pigeonholed in one genre or category'⁴⁷ – is what ultimately makes *Imprint* a remarkable film both within the *Masters of Horror* series and in the trajectory of Miike's career internationally. While he had demonstrated with *One Missed Call* that he could produce a work of domestic mainstream horror cinema, *Imprint* is a much crueller, more challenging and problematic piece. Eschewing the contemporary Western stereotypes of

J-horror as a slow-burning site for ghoulish long-haired female ghosts and deadly cursed technology, Miike places his characters in the brothels of Meiji-period Japan and subjects them to horrendous torture and tragedy. With *Imprint*, Miike took an opportunity that further fuelled his reputation for pushing the boundaries of horror, signalling an increasing awareness of his notorious (and popular) global image in a manner that could be seen to contradict his reluctance to be labelled a master of the genre.

Conclusion

Charting the development of Miike's reputation as a horror auteur illustrates how the genre-positioning of certain texts in marketing campaigns can, at times, obscure the texts themselves – the perception of Miike as a predominantly horror director is, quite simply, inaccurate. Even if one considers *Audition* and *Ichi the Killer* to be, alongside *One Missed Call*, 'true' horror cinema (whatever that might mean), these titles constitute only a fraction of Miike's oeuvre. Moreover, if one were to focus on the percentage of output alone, it would be far more reasonable to label him as a producer of mainly *yakuza* fare (à la Kinji Fukasaku), or just as suitably as a prominent director of: family-friendly films, as evidenced by *Salaryman Kintaro*, the *Zebraman* superhero movies (2004, 2010), special effects blockbusters *The Great Yokai War* (2005) and *Yatterman* (2009), and the child-focused *Ninja Kids!!!* (2011); comedies, such as *Peanuts* (1996), *Shangri-la* (2002) and the *Mole Song* films (2013, 2016); manga adaptations, like the *Crows Zero* titles (2007, 2009), *As the Gods Will* (2014), *Terra Formars* (2016) and *Blade of the Immortal*; or even musicals, as with *Andromedia* (1998), *The Happiness of the Katakuris* (2001) and *For Love's Sake* (2012).

Despite his work's generic heterogeneity, the horror paradigm has figured centrally in shaping how Miike's cinema is understood in Western film discourse. With the diversity of his output posing difficulties for distributors hoping to promote his films to specific demographics, the categorisation of Miike's releases by means of horror tropes has proved an effective way of achieving more targeted marketability. Miike's cinema has been consistently curated by Western distributors to maximise its potential reach, eschewing certain titles in favour of his more sensationalistic films; texts which, more often than not, are amenable to horror promotion traditions. *Audition* was presented as a shocking 'discovery' at festivals, in theatres and on home video, and the focus on the explicit violence of *Ichi the*

Killer further strengthened his standing as a provocative horror maestro. The marketing of, and responses to, these films garnered Miike some vital creative opportunities – including a cameo role in a seminal American horror movie and an invitation to participate in an auteur-ratifying television series – that solidified his status as an international horror auteur.

Today, this reputation continues to be upheld (and exploited) in the taxonomy of the commercialisation of Miike's releases. Of particular note is the acquisition of both his back catalogue and more recent titles by Arrow Films, arguably the most influential current distributor of cult movies in the West. Horror cinema being their prime product, Arrow holds a prestigious gatekeeping position in the horror market and is thus well situated to sell (and re-sell) Miike's films directly to horror-inclined audiences. After continuing to find currency in Miike's earlier work by restoring and repackaging a slew of the director's titles – including his *Dead or Alive* (1999, 2000, 2002) and *Black Society* (1995, 1997, 1999) trilogies, *The Happiness of the Katakuris* and, of course, *Audition* – Arrow turned its attention to more recent films, such as the sci-fi action flick *Terra Formars* and his latest samurai epic *Blade of the Immortal*. While not horror titles themselves, appeals to horror tropes – and Miike's association with them – have helped Arrow reach their intended, knowing audiences, demonstrating the continuing power of Miike's horror capital.

The auteur is historically (and currently) significant in horror film discourse, and the case of the making and marketing of Miike's horror auteur reputation is a pertinent illustration of this fact. As Joe Tompkins has argued, there exists an important 'critical-industrial function of the horror auteur, which is to say the ways in which media industries use discourses of horror auteurism to marshal the critical and popular reception of films across various media'.[48] The capital of auteur-driven horror cinema – activated prosperously in the marketing of films by directors such as George A. Romero, Wes Craven and David Cronenberg – now circulates in the reception of more contemporary horror film-makers who are being positioned as emerging masters of the genre, as seen with, among others, Jordan Peele, Robert Eggers and Rob Zombie. Meanwhile, horror's current critical legitimation has prompted established auteurs renowned for other genres to produce original and reimagined contributions to the field: Darren Aronofsky's *mother!* (2017), David Gordon Green's *Halloween* (2018) and Luca Guadagnino's *Suspiria* (2018), to name but a few examples.

Although this chapter has focused on the specific case of the trajectory of Miike's horror auteur reputation, what it tells us about the functions of the horror auteur is applicable in a much wider context. Within the horror cinema landscape, the auteur continues to hold capital across the spheres of production, distribution and reception. Often, the commercial and critical power of the auteur can override filmic content; horror auteur reputations can, in the interest of marketability, be established and refined through discourse related not to textual qualities, but to promotional patterns. In many instances, a prevailing association with horror acts as a pillar upon which some directors' wider reception is built, as the structuring capacity of Miike's reputation for horror demonstrates. Indeed, Miike's name continues to find currency in the horror arena: alongside directors such as Romero and Landis, he is set to feature in *Untold Horror*, an upcoming documentary series helmed by Dave Alexander (editor-in-chief of international horror film magazine *Rue Morgue*) as part of a project 'dedicated to exploring the greatest horror tales almost told'.[49] As with Showtime's anthology series, Miike's inclusion here testifies to the lasting potency of his horror auteur status. Even two decades after *Audition*'s release, Miike is still considered to be – whether warranted on a generic basis or not – a valid, and valuable, master of horror.

Notes

1. At the time of receiving his award, screenings of Miike's work at Fantasia included twenty-nine features, two television series episodes, a portmanteau film and one short. For a comprehensive overview of Miike's influence at the festival, see R. Jordan (ed.), 'Twenty Years of Takashi Miike at the Fantasia International Film Festival' [special issue], *Off Screen*, 21/3 (2017), *https://offscreen.com/issues/view/volume-21-issue-3* (accessed 29 August 2019).
2. See G. Needham, 'Japanese Cinema and Orientalism', in D. Eleftheriotis and G. Needham (eds), *Asian Cinemas: A Reader and Guide* (Edinburgh: Edinburgh University Press, 2006), pp. 8–16; O. Dew, '"Asia Extreme": Japanese Cinema and British Hype', *New Cinemas: Journal of Contemporary Film*, 5/1 (2007), 53–73; C. Y. Shin, 'The Art of Branding: Tartan "Asia Extreme" Films', in J. Choi and M. Wada-Marciano (eds), *Horror to the Extreme: Changing Boundaries in Asian Cinema* (Hong Kong: Hong Kong University Press, 2009), pp. 85–100; S. Rawle, 'From *The Black Society* to *The Isle*: Miike Takashi and Kim Ki-Duk at the intersection of Asia Extreme', *Journal of Japanese and Korean Cinema*, 1/2 (2009), 167–84; Daniel Martin, *Extreme Asia: The Rise of Cult Cinema from the Far East* (Edinburgh: Edinburgh University

Press, 2015); and J. Hughes, 'The Festival Collective: Cult Audiences and Japanese Extreme Cinema', in C. D. Reinhard and C. J. Olson (eds), *Making Sense of Cinema: Empirical Studies into Film Spectators and Spectatorship* (London: Bloomsbury, 2016), pp. 37–56.
3. R. Hyland, 'A Politics of Excess: Violence and Violation in Miike Takashi's *Audition*', in J. Choi and M. Wada-Marciano (eds), *Horror to the Extreme: Changing Boundaries in Asian Cinema* (Hong Kong: Hong Kong University Press, 2009), p. 10.
4. Rawle, 'From *The Black Society* to *The Isle*', 170.
5. S. Hantke, 'Japanese Horror Under Western Eyes: Social Class and Global Culture in Miike Takashi's *Audition*', in J. McRoy (ed.), *Japanese Horror Cinema* (Edinburgh: Edinburgh University Press, 2005), p. 55.
6. J. Romney, 'Dutch treat', *The Guardian* (9 February 2000), http://www.guardian.co.uk/film/2000/feb/09/artsfeatures.rotterdamfilmfestival (accessed 29 August 2019); N. James, 'You have 15 minutes to crawl from the cinema', *Sight & Sound*, 10/3 (2000), 10; J. Friel, 'Warning as horror film shocks public', *The Mirror* (21 May 2001), 12.
7. In a 2012 interview conducted by Ard Vijn, Miike's anecdote is corroborated by Vijn's translator, who was present at that very screening: 'I was sitting next to him at the time', Luc van Houten says, 'and can testify this really happened'. See A. Vijn, 'IFFR 2012 Interview: Miike Takashi Talks Ace Attorney', *Screen Anarchy* (11 February 2012), http://screenanarchy.com/2012/02/iffr-2012-interview-miike-takashi-talks-ace-attorney.html (accessed 29 August 2019).
8. E. Mitchell, 'Film Review; Wife Hunting Sure Is a Sick and Frightful Business', *The New York Times* (8 August 2001), http://www.nytimes.com/movie/review?res=9B0CEEDB1F3CF93BA3575BC0A9679C8B63 (accessed 29 August 2019); S. Rose, 'Blood isn't that scary', *The Guardian* (2 June 2003), http://www.theguardian.com/film/2003/jun/02/artsfeatures.dvdreviews2 (accessed 29 August 2019).
9. Friel, 'Warning as horror film shocks public'.
10. 'Three collapse at Swiss horror premiere', *The Guardian* (10 January 2002), http://www.guardian.co.uk/film/2002/jan/10/news2 (accessed 29 August 2019).
11. *Audition* won both the FIPRESCI Award and the KNF Award at that year's Rotterdam festival.
12. P. Bradshaw, 'Audition', *The Guardian* (16 March 2001), http://www.guardian.co.uk/film/2001/mar/16/1 (accessed 29 August 2019); Romney, 'Dutch treat'; R. Mackie, 'Video releases: "Audition"', *The Guardian* (28 September 2001), http://www.guardian.co.uk/lifeandstyle/2001/sep/28/shopping.artsfeatures (accessed 29 August 2019).

13. K. Eisner, 'Review: "Audition"', *Variety* (31 October 1999), *http://variety. com/1999/film/reviews/audition-1200459973/* (accessed 29 August 2019); K. Thomas, '"Audition": Gruesome but Skillful', *The Los Angeles Times* (16 November 2001), *http://articles.latimes.com/2001/nov/16/entertainment/et-kevin16* (accessed 29 August 2019).
14. *Ichi the Killer* was acquired by Medusa for UK release on their Premier Asia label, and released in the US by Media Blasters on their Tokyo Shock label.
15. A. Haflidason, 'Review: Ichi the Killer', *BBC* (28 May 2003), *http://www.bbc. co.uk/films/2003/05/28/ichi_the_killer_2003_review.shtml* (accessed 29 August 2019); P. Bradshaw, 'Ichi the Killer', *The Guardian* (30 May 2003), *http://www. guardian.co.uk/culture/2003/may/30/artsfeatures1* (accessed 29 August 2019).
16. Dew, '"Asia Extreme"', 61–2.
17. J. Queenan, 'Bring on the creepy girls', *The Guardian* (22 February 2008), *http:// www.theguardian.com/film/2008/feb/22/worldcinema* (accessed 29 August 2019).
18. His other releases in 2003 were *Gozu*, the gangster flick *The Man in White* and its sequel *The Man in White 2: Requiem for the Lion*, his straight-to-video crime film *Yakuza Demon* and the hostage movie *The Negotiator*.
19. S. Rawle, 'Ringing *One Missed Call*: Franchising, Transnational Flows and Genre Production', *East Asian Journal of Popular Culture*, 1/1 (2015), 98–101.
20. The Japanese director is not proficient in English, so he learnt his lines phonetically; Miike's stilted conveyance draws particular attention to his dialogue, which he delivers in a careful (yet patently awkward) manner. See V. Musetto, 'Super "Hostel" – Asian Horror Master is Scared by New Film', *New York Post* (1 January 2006), *http://nypost.com/2006/01/01/super-hostel-asian-horror-master-is-scared-by-new-film/* (accessed 29 August 2019).
21. D. Edelstein, 'Now Playing at Your Local Multiplex: Torture Porn', *New York Magazine* (28 January 2006), *http://nymag.com/movies/features/15622/* (accessed 29 August 2019).
22. S. Jones, 'The Lexicon of Offence: The Meanings of Torture, Porn, and "Torture Porn"', in F. Attwood, V. Campbell, I. Q. Hunter and S. Lockyer (eds), *Controversial Images: Media Representations on the Edge* (Basingstoke: Palgrave Macmillan, 2012), pp. 195–6.
23. L. Hallam, 'Genre Cinema as Trauma Cinema: Post 9/11 Trauma and the Rise of "Torture Porn" in Recent Horror Films', in M. Broderick and A. Traverso (eds), *Trauma, Media, Art: New Perspectives* (Newcastle upon Tyne: Cambridge Scholars Publishing, 2010), p. 233.
24. Quentin Tarantino quoted in B. Enk, 'Hostel: Where Did Eli Roth Come From?', *Heavy* (15 October 2010), *http://heavy.com/movies/get-*

your-gore-on/2010/10/hostel-where-did-eli-roth-come-from/ (accessed 29 August 2019).
25. Eli Roth quoted in J. Condit, 'Roth, Eli (Hostel)', *Dread Central* (2 January 2005), *https://www.dreadcentral.com/news/3349/roth-eli-hostel/* (accessed 29 August 2019).
26. Roth quoted in Condit, 'Roth, Eli (Hostel)'.
27. For instance, see P. Hitchcock, 'Niche Cinema, or *Kill Bill* with *Shaolin Soccer*', in G. Marchetti and T. S. Kam (eds), *Hong Kong Film, Hollywood and the New Global Cinema: No Film is an Island* (London: Routledge, 2007), pp. 226–7; N. J. Y. Lee, 'Salute to Mr. Vengeance! The Making of a Transnational Auteur Park Chan-wook', in L. Hunt and L. Wing-Fai (eds), *East Asian Cinemas: Exploring Transnational Connections on Film* (London: I. B. Tauris, 2008), p. 212; and D. Martin, 'Body of Action, Face of Authenticity: Symbolic Stars in Transnational Marketing and Reception of East Asian Cinemas', in L. Wing-Fai and A. Willis (eds), *East Asian Film Stars* (Basingstoke: Palgrave Macmillan, 2014), pp. 28–32.
28. S. Neale, 'Art Cinema as Institution', *Screen*, 22/1 (1981), 36.
29. T. Corrigan, 'The Commerce of Auteurism', in V. W. Wexman (ed.), *Film and Authorship* (New Brunswick, NJ: Rutgers University Press, 2003), p. 96.
30. Gary Bettinson, *The Sensuous Cinema of Wong Kar-wai: Film Poetics and the Aesthetic of Disturbance* (Hong Kong: Hong Kong University Press, 2015), p. 1.
31. Meeting the director for an interview in 2003, Steve Rose writes how, '[i]n his trademark bug-eyed sunglasses, shaven-headed, chain-smoking, Miike cuts an impressively cool figure', and in her coverage of the 2011 Cannes Film Festival, Jane Dupont proposes that 'Mr. Miike, at 50, looks very much the cult auteur', and remarks that, '[s]itting in the shade on Majestic Beach with ruffled hair, an oilskin jacket, and leather pants and boots, he could almost be French'. See Rose, 'Blood isn't that scary'; J. Dupont, 'Takashi Miike's Heartrending Samurai Tale, Told in 3-D', *The New York Times* (20 May 2011), *http://www.nytimes.com/2011/05/21/arts/21iht-DUPONT21.html?_r=0*> (accessed 29 August 2019).
32. S. Dixon, 'The Figure in the Background: Stardom and Filmic Space', in K. R. Hart (ed.), *Film and Television Stardom* (Newcastle upon Tyne: Cambridge Scholars Publishing, 2008), p. 290.
33. D. Kehr, 'Horror Film Made for Showtime Will Not Be Shown', *The New York Times* (19 January 2006), *http://www.nytimes.com/2006/01/19/arts/television/19horr.html?_r=2&oref=slogin&* (accessed 29 August 2019).
34. As Tony Kelso notes, premium networks such as Showtime and HBO 'focus on risk and quality, "edgy" programming' and 'content that sparks lively

debate among journalists and academics alike'. For an in-depth explanation of the specificities of premium subscription television networks, see T. Kelso, 'And now no word from our sponsor: How HBO put the risk back into television', in M. Leverette, B. L. Ott and C. L. Buckley (eds), *It's Not TV: Watching HBO in the Post-Television Era* (London: Routledge, 2008), p. 54.

35. *'Masters of Horror: Season 1'*, DVD release (Anchor Bay, 2007).
36. Although the cast is almost entirely Japanese, all dialogue is spoken in English; in order to train the Japanese actors how to deliver their English lines, Miike worked closely with two Hollywood dialogue coaches.
37. Mick Garris quoted in Kehr, 'Horror Film Made for Showtime'.
38. Garris quoted in Kehr, 'Horror Film Made for Showtime'.
39. Garris quoted in R. Galluzo and M. Cucinotta, 'Fright Exclusive Interview: Mick Garris', *Icons of Fright* (8 September 2008), http://www.iconsoffright.com/IV_Mick.htm (accessed 29 August 2019).
40. Takashi Miike quoted in M. Schilling, 'Takashi Miike Makes His Mark', *The Japan Times* (23 June 2006), http://www.japantimes.co.jp/culture/2006/06/23/culture/takashi-miike-makes-his-mark/#.VxjhOHErLC0 (accessed 29 August 2019).
41. *'Masters of Horror: Season 1'*.
42. *'Masters of Horror: Imprint'*, DVD release (Anchor Bay, 2006).
43. Galluzo and Cucinotta, 'Fright Exclusive Interview: Mick Garris'.
44. *'Masters of Horror: Imprint'*.
45. N. Rucka, 'Review: Imprint', *Midnight Eye* (15 September 2006), http://www.midnighteye.com/reviews/imprint/ (accessed 29 August 2019).
46. Miike quoted in D. Brown, 'Report: Japan Premiere of Miike Takashi's *Big Bang Love, Juvenile A*', *Ryuganji* (22 May 2006), http://www.ryuganji.net/news/index.php?entry=entry060523-104118 (accessed 29 August 2019).
47. Miike quoted in T. Cook, 'Director Takashi Miike Discusses the Bizarre Absurdity of "Yakuza Apocalypse"', *Collider* (10 October 2015), http://collider.com/takashi-miike-yakuza-apocalypse-interview/ (accessed 29 August 2019).
48. J. Tompkins, 'Bids for Distinction: The Critical-Industrial Function of the Horror Auteur', in R. Nowell (ed.), *Merchants of Menace: The Business of Horror Cinema* (London: Bloomsbury, 2014), p. 203.
49. 'About – Untold Horror', *Untold Horror*, http://www.untoldhorror.ca/about/ (accessed 29 August 2019).

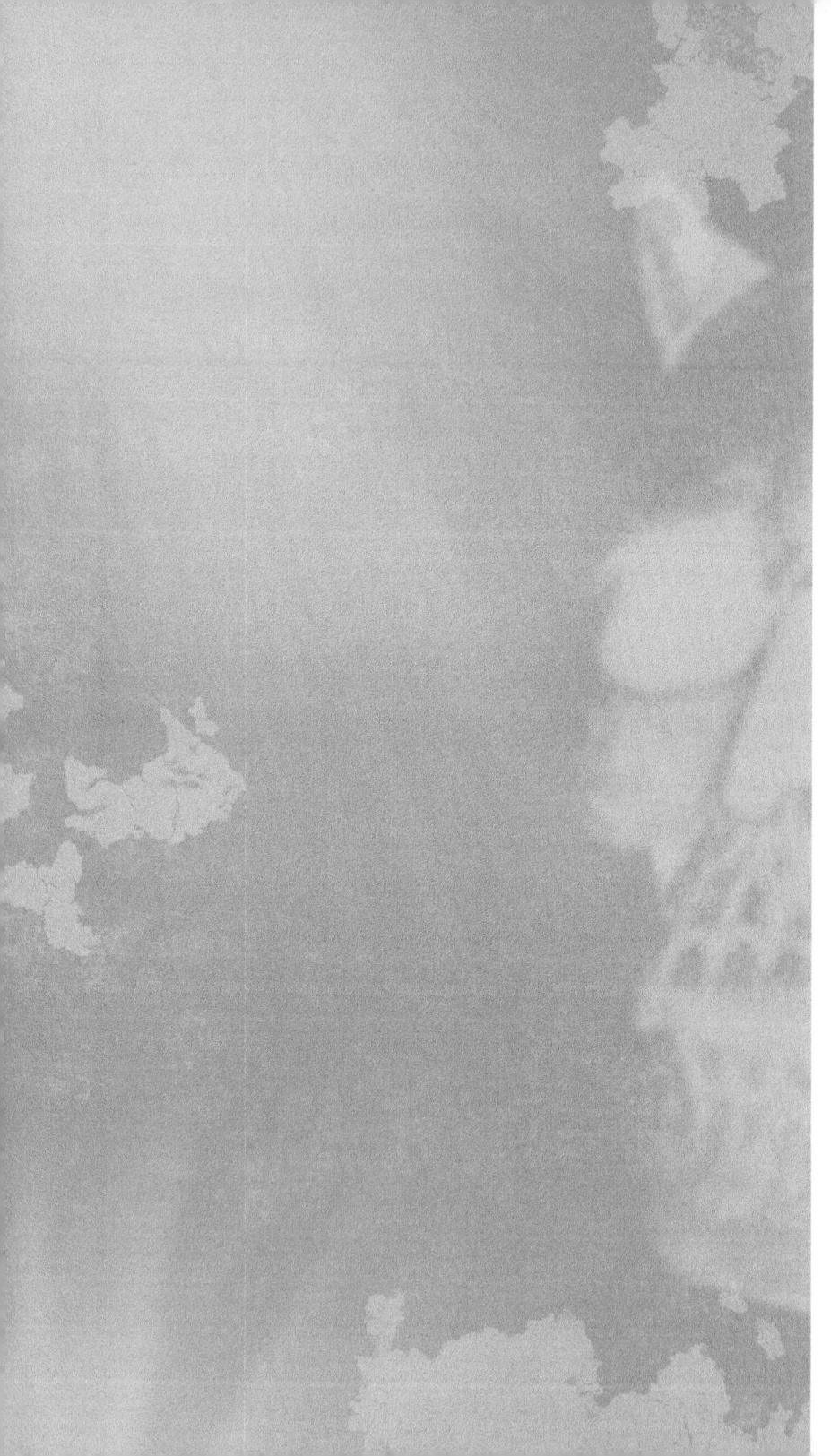

5

Bloody Muscles on VHS

When Asia Extreme Met the Video Nasties

Jonathan Wroot

UK HORROR FANS have enthusiastically received Japanese horror films over the last two decades – more so than any period before. A key catalyst for this trend was the release of *Ringu* (Hideo Nakata, 1998), in which a malevolent spirit fatally haunts unsuspecting viewers of a cursed video tape. Alongside the acclaim and success of *Audition* (Takashi Miike, 1999) and *Battle Royale* (Kinji Fukasaku, 2000), *Ringu* helped establish the UK sub-label, Asia Extreme, as a successful brand for Tartan Video. Though Tartan's success in this venture only lasted until 2008,[1] the term Asia Extreme has been adopted by other labels and still has a considerable influence on perceptions of Asian horror films within the UK.[2] This has provided ample opportunities for the promotion of later titles, as can be seen with *Bloody Muscle Body Builder in Hell* (Shinichi Fukazawa, 2014), which will henceforth be referred to as *BMBBIH*.[3] Completed over a fifteen-year period, starting in the late 1990s, *BMBBIH* was shot on 8mm tape to keep costs down, giving it a distinctive low-quality aesthetic. Not only do the film's visuals bring to mind the infamous cursed video tape of *Ringu* and, adjacently, Tartan's Asian horror reputation, but they also provided a cue for UK distributor Terracotta to make *BMBBIH* available through a limited-edition VHS release. This particular promotional strategy for *BMBBIH* positions the film within various cultural contexts and film reception discourses, both inside and outside J-horror. Subtitled *The Japanese Evil Dead* in many regions outside Japan, implications of exoticism and comparisons to Western horror films are clearly evident, though the distribution and marketing materials do not only demonstrate these discourses. The VHS format, memories of it within the UK, and related promotional practices, became central to the marketing strategy for *BMBBIH*.

J-horror has been of particular interest to academics in recent years. Kate Egan and Emma Pett have explored the discourses associated with these films following Tartan's bankruptcy. Other labels have emphasised older Japanese titles according to authorship and production contexts,[4] and regular consumers of Asian films either still use the category of Asia Extreme or reject it in favour of other classifications.[5] Egan's and Pett's research forms part of a special edition of the journal *Transnational Cinemas*, which attempts to readdress definitions of cult cinema within the global context. Cult is a fluid and shifting category of film and is often simplified to refer to the devoted behaviour of fans towards films that are outside the mainstream. The journal edition shows how even this definition has to change when considering various national and cultural contexts. For example, Jamie Sexton critiques existing studies of certain cult audiences, especially judgements made towards viewers of Asia Extreme.[6] The research of Oliver Dew, Daniel Martin and Chi-Yun Shin has tended to emphasise discourses of exoticism and otherness, often in comparison with the reception of Western horror films, in order to theorise the appeal of Asia Extreme films.[7] This evidence is largely drawn from the distribution and marketing materials of Tartan. While Sexton is right to critique this approach, the strategies of labels that have distributed Asian horror films in the UK after Tartan's bankruptcy are still under-researched. Egan's latest research focuses on Criterion, a label based in the USA. Terracotta's strategies for *BMBBIH* are particularly illuminating for the UK market.

Distribution and marketing materials provide rich resources for tracing the history of film releases – both in terms of the film itself, as well as how it was released to certain audiences. In 1997, Barbara Klinger specifically advocated the charting of films' availability and releases on platforms from cinema to television, as well as production, distribution and exhibition practices, in order to fully understand their history through discursive language and patterns.[8] Several articles have since provided detailed histories of distribution practice by analysing trailers, film posters and reviews, such as Jon Kraszewski's examination of blaxploitation films.[9] The study of these materials is necessary when researching home media releases of Asian films, which are most likely to be distributed in the UK via DVD and Blu-ray.[10] Sales figures for disc releases are notoriously difficult to source, with only annual amalgamations of UK sales figures being widely available.[11] Therefore, valuable insights can potentially be gathered from distribution and marketing materials, even for recent home media releases – especially when they are limited and exclusive to certain formats.

Within the contexts of home media and horror films, Egan has also provided insights from studying VHS packaging, film release histories and distributors' strategies. Terracotta was keen to imply that *BMBBIH* was a 'lost video nasty' in its marketing material. Egan's research, titled *Trash or Treasure?*, particularly illustrates what can be learnt from historical evidence linked to the video nasty period – a time in the 1980s when UK VHS releases of certain horror films were banned because they were deemed too offensive.[12] This evidence ranges from original video packaging, re-release packaging for later DVDs (after the ban was lifted), as well as the materials gathered by collectors and fans, either in their own personal archives or online. The term 'video nasty' has gained different connotations and meanings over time, through continued re-use following its initial emergence in the 1980s. Terracotta's use of the term in relation to *BMBBIH* highlights yet another reception context in which the marketing value of the phrase can be analysed. As detailed by Egan, promotional artwork, packaging and marketing material provide discursive evidence that can be examined through a reception studies approach.[13]

A further reason for applying Egan's approach, in addition to the wider reception studies methodology, is highlighted by the case-study film. *BMBBIH* was made widely available on DVD by Terracotta, but also as a limited-edition video tape, despite being released in 2017, well after the disappearance of VHS from UK shelves. When asked why they chose this platform, Clare Dean (product manager for Terracotta) emailed this response in July 2017 – three months after the UK release of *BMBBIH*:

> It was our decision to make the VHS tape with the intention of using it as a marketing tool. As the film has been made to look like it was shot on video, along with the obvious nod to the EVIL DEAD films, it seemed fitting! Little was known about the film when we first came across it, but we found out that it had a long and interesting production history, so we positioned it as a lost video nasty (with tongue

firmly in cheek). Incidentally, the cost of tapes and cases is high these days, making our cost per unit equally high, so releasing films on VHS tape is not easy (despite the retro format renaissance)![14]

By drawing comparisons to Western horror films, particularly Sam Raimi's *The Evil Dead* (1981), Terracotta is clearly eager to align *BMBBIH* with recognisable horror titles. Daniel Martin notices the alignment of Eastern horrors with Western equivalents in the critical reception of *Ringu* in the UK after its release by Tartan.[15] *Ringu* was immediately compared to *The Blair Witch Project* (Daniel Myrick and Eduardo Sánchez, 1999), which was in cinemas at a similar time. This was also used as a point of difference – *Ringu* offered similar shocks, as well as different ones, due to its cultural particularities. The marketing and promotion of *BMBBIH* can be argued to be operating along similar lines, though the VHS platform adds another perspective.

Shinichi Fukazawa began production on *BMBBIH* almost during the same year as the release of *Ringu*. Following its release on DVD in 2017, Fukazawa detailed in one interview how production initially began on the film seventeen years earlier. It took so long to complete and release as he had a very limited budget and resources.[16] The older format of VHS was also used as part of the film's UK release. Through this release tactic Terracotta clearly intends to make a connection to the UK video nasties trend from the 1980s. The intention, it seems, was not to present an anachronistic view of history, as the distributor is quick to emphasise the VHS collector's edition was treated as a tongue-in-cheek promotional strategy. But what it does evidence is the complex market for horror films in the UK. Fans of video-nasties-style horror and Asia Extreme are clearly targeted through the marketing of *BMBBIH*, as well as nostalgia for certain home media formats and promotion. This latter market may seem particularly minimal. Clare Dean detailed how only ten VHS editions of *BMBBIH* were made – with one given to the director, one used as a competition prize and eight being put on sale (which quickly sold out). Nonetheless, the DVD release contained the same artwork and extra material that appeared on the VHS tapes after the feature film. Clearly, Terracotta's strategy for *BMBBIH* aimed to promote the film through the familiarity and memory of older distribution practices. Given that, for many, VHS collecting has passed from practice to mere memory, the use of marketing ploys such as this provides fascinating evidence of the ways in which nostalgia and (sub)cultural literacy feed into horror fandoms operating today.

A limited-edition VHS: production-informed distribution in the marketing of *BMBBIH*

In April 2017, press releases for *BMBBIH*, for both the DVD and VHS releases, were widely circulated online. Many horror websites and critics not only reported on the film, but also provided Terracotta with several marketing slogans:[17]

> 'gory, insane and fun. Sayonara, baby' – *Infernal Cinema*
> 'Shinichi Fukazawa's splatter masterpiece' – *Attack from Planet B*
> 'a stand out cult classic in the making. 8/10' – *The Rotting Zombie*
> 'A cracking, gory, Japanese slice of horror heaven 7/10' – *Geek Legion of Doom*
> 'you will be clapping and beaming from ear to ear' – *Sex Gore Mutants*
> 'a terrific blood-splattered comedy' – *Cinehouse*
> 'as fun as it sounds' – *The Forbidden Room*

It was not only this reception that allowed Terracotta to plan its unique distribution strategy for *BMBBIH*; a key catalyst for its VHS release was the film's production history. Fukazawa's limited resources allowed Terracotta to conceive of the unique selling point of *BMBBIH* as a 'lost video nasty'. Furthermore, its gory aesthetics and promoted status as part of the 'splatter' subgenre situated the film within contemporary perceptions of Japanese horror films, as well as offering insight into the UK markets for horror films in general.

The production history of *BMBBIH* is of central significance in a promotional interview that Terracotta facilitated, in which the director elaborates on his influences and production resources.[18] A Super 8 camera was the only equipment that Fukazawa could get hold of. Shooting difficulties, along with a lack of finances for digitisation, meant that a lot of early footage had to be scrapped, leading to more time being taken up due to the need to re-shoot almost 80 per cent of the filmed scenes. In addition, Fukazawa mentions specific films that ended up encouraging him to make his own low-budget feature:

> *Evil Dead 3* and *Brain Dead* inspired me. While writing the screenplay, I tried to reach as much gore as seen in *Evil Dead* and the comedy in *Evil Dead 2*. Other horror movies that motivated me are *Night of the Living Dead*. That was my very first horror film that I watched

in the theatre. Also, Lucio Fulci's *Zombi 2*, Dario Argento's *Deep Red*, and John Carpenter's *The Fog*.[19]

These influences can clearly be seen in the aesthetics and the narrative of the film. In the tradition of *Night of the Living Dead* (George A. Romero, 1968) and *The Evil Dead*, almost all of the scenes take place in one house. Shinji (played by Fukazawa) owns the house, which his ex-girlfriend and a medium want to explore, as they believe it is haunted. Unfortunately, their suspicions are verified, and a violent ghost kills and possesses the medium, which the remaining characters then have to fight off. The retro effects in the film match the low-budget aesthetic of the above titles, as does the film's cinematography, due to the use of a Super 8 camera.

Terracotta have done much to emphasise the film's gruesome effects. As can be seen on the label's featured webpage for the film, bloody and ghoulish faces fill out the image and appear larger than the title character (seen heroically flexing his muscles in a black vest).[20] Both the hero and the ghoulish foes tower over the haunted house and the film's extended title – *Bloody Muscle Body Builder in Hell: AKA the Japanese Evil Dead* – which has been used by distributors outside Japan. Blood drips over these faces and words. Egan analyses several images in-depth throughout *Trash or Treasure?*, including the poster of *The Driller Killer* (Abel Ferrara, 1979). For *The Driller Killer*, the key narrative image of the film – a blood-drenched electric drill – emerges from the tagline and title (one that in fact contrasts with the actual content and status of the film as a 'psychological art-house film').[21] The original packaging for the video nasties capitalised on the films' gruesome posters, and was often the source of some of their controversy, sometimes even more than the films themselves, as is the case with *The Driller Killer*. Terracotta clearly recognised the potential advantages of reviving such strategies for new releases, but diverges from *The Driller Killer*'s precedent by offering a narrative image that aligns with the film's content.

I have conducted previous work on Terracotta's use of marketing terms such as Asia Extreme.[22] When they began to add other national cinemas to such categories, and moved beyond mainly focusing on horror films from Japan and South Korea, these terms have come to encompass a range of different types of film-making. It has particularly achieved this aim through a dedicated sub-label, Terror-cotta, which has released titles from Thailand, the Philippines and several other countries, including *BMBBIH* from Japan. The video nasties aesthetic utilised by Terracotta for the VHS packaging release of *BMBBIH*, in correspondence with the film's alignment with Asia Extreme, demonstrates another layer of discursive interplay within Terracotta's marketing strategy. The history of video nasties and labels such as Tartan's Asia Extreme demonstrate distribution tactics that Terracotta believes UK horror fans will recognise. Though these filmic categories existed in different historical moments, Terracotta suggests these fandoms have much in common, especially through their distinctive marketing aesthetics. This is evident not only through the limited-edition release of *BMBBIH*, but also through extra materials (on both the VHS and DVD releases of the film) which foreground the work of the artist who created the film's distinctive marketing images.

Graham Humphreys and the art of British horror and VHS promotion

'From Sketch to Scary: "Groovy" Artwork by Graham Humphreys' is a feature that runs for less than a minute on both the VHS edition (after the feature film) and DVD disc. An initial sketch transitions to the cover art for *BMBBIH* and then to the fully coloured version as it appears on Terracotta's final packaging (Figure 5.1). Details are given regarding the creator of this artwork, Graham Humphreys, a famous UK-based poster designer known for working on the UK promotional materials for horror films including *The Evil Dead* and *A Nightmare on Elm Street* (Wes Craven, 1984). This short special feature provides a promotional platform for both the artist and Terracotta, as it is listed in all the press releases for *BMBBIH*. Terracotta's marketing strategies for this title are intertwined. The label attempts to appeal to fans of VHS tapes, video nasties and Asia Extreme through not only the film content and the VHS platform but also through artwork that clearly aligns with VHS aesthetics.

Several years after advocating reception studies approaches within film research, Barbara Klinger examined the vast range of home media that could be explored, including DVD releases.[23] Though extra material within disc releases is often realised as an extension of other promotional media, Klinger argues that such material acknowledges its audience as seekers of trivia who are hoping to be treated to 'insider knowledge' by such content.[24] In the case of *BMBBIH*, this extra material overlaps with the cover art's aesthetic which clearly targets fans of the video nasties. Thomas Stubblefield claims that posters illustrate the appeal of film titles

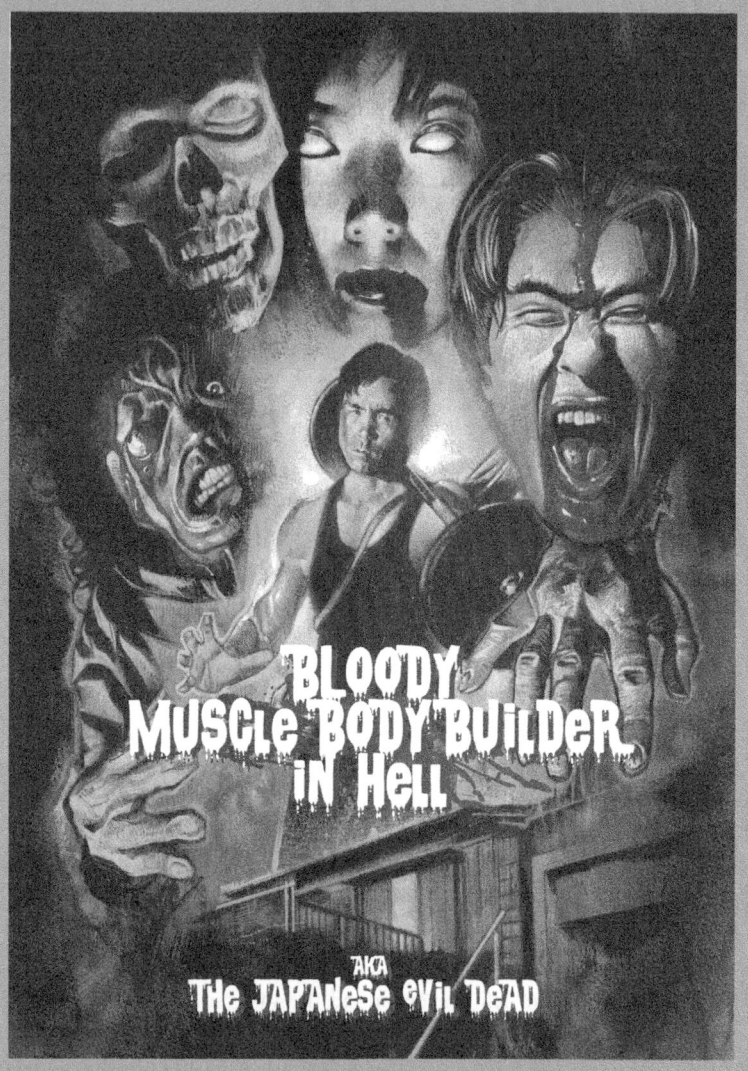

Figure 5.1. Graham Humphreys's artwork for *Bloody Muscle Body Builder in Hell* © Stand Entertainment.

beyond their primary textual content, something that has been evident in the migration of films from theatrical to digital platforms.²⁵ *BMBBIH*'s extra material emphasises the importance of Humphreys's artwork, in a manner similar to the promotion of a film via posters. Klinger has also argued that posters assist in the tracing of film history.²⁶ In the instance of *BMBBIH*, the 'retro' aesthetics illustrate how UK horror fans were being targeted by Terracotta, by way of the artist's recognisable name and through the film's alignment with a crucial context for UK horror distribution.

An information page on Humphreys's website details the artist's long association with the video nasties and horror films in general.²⁷ It illustrates how Humphreys worked initially with Palace Pictures to help design the UK marketing materials for many notorious 1980s horror films, such as *The Evil Dead*. In addition to marketing work extending to films outside the horror genre, Humphreys later provided storyboards for a few film productions, before going on to design promotional material for several releases for Tartan Films (including *Audition*) and, later, Arrow Video. Humphreys has also created new artwork for Anchor Bay for many of their releases, especially their 2003 re-release of the *Evil Dead* trilogy. These images can be found among the samples that Humphreys provides on his website. These materials not only demonstrate how Terracotta picked the right man for the job for the release of *BMBBIH*, but Humphreys's appointment conveys the capital extricable from recognisable horror aesthetics, as well as the cultist forms of media consumption that operate in horror fandom today.

That such aesthetics are being revived for recent horror releases such as *BMBBIH* is significant for a number of reasons. Ongoing fan commitment to the horror genre and to uncovering its often-guarded history (due to scarcity and censorship battles over the likes of the video nasties) is perhaps the most obvious reason that the use of such imagery resonates with collectors of horror media. Peter Hutchings specifically details horror's long and popular history, which distributors are happy to exploit in any number of re-releases on DVD and other home media formats – from Universal Studios' monster films to 'previously banned' features.²⁸ Collecting and ownership, argues Hutchings, is inherently tied up with memory.²⁹ But in addition to nostalgia for such films, the repackaging and re-release of such titles can also invoke the memories of fans' interaction with historic distribution and exhibition methods, whether this is through theatrical venues, TV broadcasts or other platforms.

Prestige horror releases and the subcultural potential of older distribution practices

Terracotta's release strategy for *BMBBIH* could be interpreted as making that which is old 'new' again – a principle that, as noted by Hutchings, is important to horror film collectors, especially those dedicated to the history of the video nasties. Egan again has found similar principles at work in later re-releases of the titles originally banned under the 1984 Video Recordings Act, which were particularly prominent in the late 1990s and 2000s:

> In this respect, the nasty marketing images (once considered to represent 'the extremes of violence and exploitation' in the British video market) could also appear, from the point of view of the VPRC or the BBFC, as past artefacts which, like the films themselves, have lost their power to shock or inspire letters of complaint and instead can be used for the benefit of perfectly acceptable retro 'humour'. Because of the liberalisation of censorship regimes in Britain and the diminishing nature of public complaints about the re-release of previously contentious titles, the theatrical play with nasty marketing images on re-release covers therefore suggests that such covers hold the potential to amuse rather than shock: a kind of discursive approach which Vipco, at the very least, seems particularly aware of.[30]

Rather than being used for shock value, Terracotta's distribution strategies appeal in terms of amusement, memory and nostalgia. However, the re-release of older titles through new promotional materials and packaging can also be significant for other reasons:

> if the fracturing of, and play with, old nasty marketing images is one way in which the 'tongue-in-cheek' quality of the retro can be productively tapped into, another is the adoption of marketing materials which weren't used in the original nasty marketing campaigns, but which seem to convey an essence of the nasty era perhaps more dramatically and effectively than the original marketing materials themselves.[31]

Egan states that newly designed promotional material can act as a historical record of previous distribution strategies, particularly in the case of the video nasties. While other researchers have noted similar trends, Terracotta has gone further in their bid to revive older marketing practices and aesthetics by making *BMBBIH* available on a 'dead' format.

This revival of older distribution practices and conventions is a significant contrast from previous horror and home media formats. The genre's continued popularity, and critical appraisal (both for new titles and older ones), has meant that certain horror films have been raised in their regard and attained certain canonical distinctions. Raiford Guins hypothesises that the re-release of films on DVD, as seen in the prestige re-releases of the works of Dario Argento, elevates the films' status, especially when transferred from low-quality VHS editions.[32] Similarly, Mark McKenna argues that the luxurious re-releases of low-budget films from years gone by, as demonstrated by Arrow Video, problematise the establishment of critically appreciated canons and suggest new categories of films that are deserving of acclaim and reappraisal.[33] In fact, some of Humphreys's work has been used in some of these re-releases.

Egan argues that new releases of older Japanese titles present them as both cult and art. This simultaneous critical re-evaluation and targeting of niche markets is achieved by detailing the film's production history within Criterion's Blu-ray re-releases, by way of extra features on the disc and in the packaging (e.g. through booklets).[34] *BMBBIH*'s release on VHS and as a lost video nasty goes further, suggesting a withstanding appreciation for older distribution and marketing tactics.[35] That Terracotta has revived aesthetics that tend to be associated with the distribution of VHS tapes suggests that there remains a group of collectors nostalgic for older types of horror film and older release formats.

While *BMBBIH* is not promoted as high art in the way that Criterion re-releases have reified cult films, as identified in Egan's work, the distribution and marketing materials are nevertheless presented as a treat for horror collectors. Humphreys is clearly a star in the release of *BMBBIH*, with his name featuring heavily in the promotional material, as well as in the disc and VHS extra content. A retro aesthetic is also clearly a unique selling point, though Terracotta is not establishing an original trend. In addition to the cursed video tape context and the history of the video nasties, the VHS format has been undergoing a small revival over the last ten years. Since what is widely recognised as the final studio title to be released on VHS – *A History of Violence* (David Cronenberg, 2005) in 2006 – several horror titles, including *BMBBIH*, have been released for VCR for a variety of reasons.

Shortly before *A History of Violence* came out in March 2006, several horror titles appeared on VHS,[36] including *Saw II* (Darren Lynn Bousman, 2005), *The Cave* (Bruce Hunt, 2005), *Red Eye* (Wes Craven, 2005), *The Fog* (Rupert Wainwright, 2005) and *Doom* (Andrzej Bartkowiak, 2005). The horror genre has helped to continue a niche consumer interest in the format, as well as initiatives to archive and store films that have only ever been available on VHS, for which various collectors have amassed their own considerable personal archives.[37] Niche distributors such as Bleeding Skull! (based in the USA) have specialised in releasing obscure VHS-only films either for VCRs or digital downloading/streaming.[38] Horror anthology films *V/H/S* (various, 2012) and *V/H/S 2* (various, 2013), which play upon the association between horror and the bygone format, have also received special-edition videotape releases. Furthermore, UK retailer HMV have released a string of 1980s classics, including horror *The Thing* (John Carpenter, 1982), in VHS-style packaging.

However, this resurging interest in VHS is not just about the films themselves. Helen O'Hara, in a 2015 article for *The Telegraph*, states that according to some estimates approximately 50 per cent of all films released on VHS have not been released on DVD. Accordingly, collectors have sought to retain, and in some cases recreate, the cover art for the video releases, as well as preserve and exhibit extra content. Such practices of remediation demonstrate revived interest in anachronistic forms of media and its consumption. Video collector Dale Lloyd, who runs the Midland-based Viva VHS, adds, 'It's not just the films. A lot of the trailers that play beforehand are extremely sought after and could be lost forever if not preserved . . . I am constantly baffled by so-called movie lovers who dislike videotape.' He continues, 'I mean, what self-respecting film fan would close the door on the mere notion of extra material? You should want to be able to see everything.'[39]

Viva VHS and Bleeding Skull! are two entrepreneurial business ventures that have risen in response to an ongoing demand to maintain video culture and preserve sought-after tapes. Further evidence of these practices exists in online discussions, such as *DVD Talk Forum*. Though dedicated predominantly to discussions of disc-based releases and extra content, some threads have taken to recognising that special features were also found on VHS tapes, especially when the format overlapped with the rise in popularity of DVD.[40] For *BMBBIH*, such tactics demonstrate the broader cultural (and subcultural) significance of what may appear to be a very niche marketing strategy. Not only has Terracotta revived VHS marketing aesthetics, targeting those who remain nostalgic for the era associated with them, but they have also preserved an outmoded yet still popular distribution practice to target new and existing audiences. While Egan has recognised similar patterns relating to video nasty re-releases,[41] *BMBBIH* provides evidence that such practices do not have to be limited to that category of films.

Named after VHS despite being disc-based, Arrow Video has made a name for itself by releasing prestige editions of cult horror films. Part of a larger distribution company, Arrow Films, the Arrow Video sub-label has grown in popularity due to its focus on a range of exploitation films from across the world. In recent years, it has released several titles in the UK that were formerly only available through the Tartan Asia Extreme label. In some circles, Arrow Video has developed a reputation as 'the Criterion of Shit Movies',[42] a designation that distinguishes the 'quality' of their output from those released by Criterion as 'cult-art'.[43] In his comparative analysis of Criterion and Arrow releases, McKenna concludes that the binaries between cult and art, or good and bad taste, clearly do not exist – at least not according to these labels.[44] Regardless of the 'quality' of the films, Arrow gives its titles equal treatment to Criterion by offering lavish, dual-format DVD and Blu-ray releases, a generous supply of extras and original artwork commissioned from the likes of Humphreys and others. As with the films that comprise Egan's research, McKenna details how many of Arrow's re-releases (such as the films of Lucio Fulci) were previously banned following the moral panic over the video nasties. If anything, what Arrow can refer to as canonical is the original distribution strategies for these films. Arrow has also provided UK re-releases of films previously distributed under the former Tartan Asia Extreme label, including *Dark Water* (Hideo Nakata, 2002), *Battle Royale* and *Audition*. In addition to redesigning the cover art and making the film available on Blu-ray, Arrow also created a promotional trailer for the new release of *Audition*. Arrow goes to great lengths to detail the work that has been carried out for a re-release, in order to highlight its work as a distributor alongside the reputations of specific titles.[45] McKenna concludes his overview of Arrow's recent practices by claiming that they do more than simply provide access to films, that they in fact facilitate 'an ever-evolving canon'. This is clearly evident in any of Arrow Video's prestige releases, and yet Arrow's reference to and utilisation of preceding distribution materials and strategies shows that they too pay special attention to the release history of their titles.

Conclusion

BMBBIH may not fully represent a continuation of the VHS revival, as only ten limited-edition copies were made available. However, the argument can be made that this release functions as much more than a commercial gimmick. By recalling both the video nasties and J-horror and Asia Extreme, the case of *BMBBIH* reveals the different demands and tastes of the UK horror market. Clearly, the memory of VHS plays a substantial role in the subcultural appreciation of horror, as films and marketing strategies exhibit nostalgia for VHS-specific contexts such as the arrival and censorship of the video nasties. In addition, the distribution and marketing materials themselves highlight a further allure for horror connoisseurs that extends beyond the specific context of a film's production. Terracotta's promotion for *BMBBIH* capitalises on perceptions of both Asia Extreme and video nasties, and in the process reveals the significance of distribution models and marketing materials beyond the reception of particular film texts.

The extra material provided for *BMBBIH* offers evidence of these trends. These appear on both the DVD and VHS versions of *BMBBIH*, suggesting that consumers would find value in these materials as well as in the process of their creation. However, *BMBBIH* also signifies wider trends taken up by distributors, particularly for Asian horror films on DVD and Blu-ray. Indeed, as this chapter observes, Terracotta is not the only UK label reviving older marketing strategies, or resituating films within new or existing discursive frameworks. Other distributors are demonstrating how reviving older promotional practices and materials can be successful, especially within the UK market.

Similar strategies have been noted in this chapter concerning VHS releases of horror films through specialist distributors. If nothing else, this chapter demonstrates further evidence of Hutchings's views on the significance of horror film re-releases and the links between collecting films, memory and nostalgia.[46] These are important factors for consumers that distributors can utilise. Furthermore, alongside older titles, Arrow is releasing new films, as Terracotta has done with *BMBBIH*. Distribution and marketing strategies can clearly be revived to match current trends within media consumption. These revivals may be most evident in relation to horror films, as avid fans are clearly nostalgic for older distribution and marketing practices and materials as well as the films themselves. Nevertheless, when looking beyond the horror label, *BMBBIH* shows that certain periods of film history and release platforms can play an important role in the minds of passionate film viewers and collectors.

Notes

1. O. Dew, '"Asia Extreme": Japanese Cinema and British Hype', *New Cinemas: Journal of Contemporary Film*, 5/1 (2007), 53–73; Daniel Martin, *Extreme Asia: The Rise of Cult Cinema from the Far East* (Edinburgh: Edinburgh University Press, 2015); C. Y. Shin, 'The Art of Branding: Tartan "Asia Extreme" Films', in J. Choi and M. Wada-Marciano (eds), *Horror to the Extreme: Changing Boundaries in Asian Cinema* (Hong Kong: Hong Kong University Press, 2009), pp. 85–100.
2. K. Egan, 'The Criterion Collection, cult-art films and Japanese horror: DVD labels as transnational mediators?', *Transnational Cinemas*, 8/1 (2017), 65–79; E. Pett, 'Transnational cult paratexts: exploring audience readings of Tartan's Asia Extreme brand', *Transnational Cinemas*, 8/1 (2017), 35–48.
3. The official theatrical release year of the film was 2014, at selected cinemas. It did not get released on DVD in Japan and the UK until 2017.
4. Egan, 'The Criterion Collection'.
5. Pett, 'Transnational cult paratexts'.
6. J. Sexton, 'The allure of otherness: transnational cult film fandom and the exoticist assumption', *Transnational Cinemas*, 8/1 (2017), 5–19.
7. Dew, '"Asia Extreme"'; Martin, *Extreme Asia*; Shin, 'The Art of Branding'.
8. B. Klinger, 'Film history terminable and interminable: recovering the past in reception studies', *Screen*, 38/2 (1997), 107–28.
9. J. Kraszewski, 'Recontextualizing the Historical Reception of Blaxploitation: Articulations of Class, Black Nationalism, and Anxiety in the Genre's Advertisements', *The Velvet Light Trap*, 50 (2002), 48–62.
10. J. Wroot, 'Distributing Asian Cinema, Past and Present: Definitions from DVD Labels', in A. H. J. Magnan-Park, G. Marchetti and T. S. Kam (eds), *The Palgrave Handbook of Asian Cinema* (Basingstoke: Palgrave Macmillan, 2018), pp. 201–19.
11. J. Wroot and A. Willis, 'Introduction', in J. Wroot and A. Willis (eds), *DVD, Blu-ray and Beyond: Navigating Formats and Platforms within Media Consumption* (Basingstoke: Palgrave Macmillan, 2017), pp. 1–8.
12. Kate Egan, *Trash or Treasure? Censorship and the Changing Meanings of the Video Nasties* (Manchester: Manchester University Press, 2007), p. 3.
13. Egan, *Trash or Treasure?*, pp. 6–7.
14. Email from Claire Dean (July 2017).
15. D. Martin, 'Japan's *Blair Witch*: Restraint, Maturity, and Generic Canons in the British Critical Reception of *Ring*', *Cinema Journal*, 48/3 (2009), 35–51.

16. K. Wynne, 'An Interview with Director Shinichi Fukazawa – Bloody Muscle Body Builder in Hell', *Attack From Planet B* (4 January 2017), https://www.attackfromplanetb.com/2017/04/an-interview-with-director-shinichi-fukazawa/ (accessed 29 August 2019).
17. 'Films – Bloody Muscle Body Builder in Hell', *Terracotta Distribution*, http://terracottadistribution.com/films/bloody-muscle-body-builder-in-hell (accessed 29 August 2019).
18. Wynne, 'An Interview with Director Shinichi Fukazawa'.
19. Wynne, 'An Interview with Director Shinichi Fukazawa'.
20. 'Films – Bloody Muscle Body Builder in Hell'.
21. Egan, *Trash or Treasure?*, p. 54.
22. Wroot, 'Distributing Asian Cinema, Past and Present'.
23. Barbara Klinger, *Beyond the Multiplex: Cinema, New Technologies and the Home* (Berkeley, CA: University of California Press, 2006), pp. 54–90; B. Klinger, 'The DVD Cinephile: Viewing Heritages and Home Film Cultures', in J. Benett and T. Brown (eds), *Film and Television after DVD* (London: Routledge, 2008), pp. 19–44.
24. Klinger, *Beyond the Multiplex*, pp. 68–74.
25. T. Stubblefield, 'Disassembling the Cinema: The Poster, the Film and In-Between', *Thresholds*, 34 (2007), 84–8.
26. B. Klinger, 'Digressions at the Cinema: Reception and Mass Culture', *Cinema Journal*, 28/4 (1989), 3–19.
27. See 'About', *Graham Humphreys Limited*, http://www.grahamhumphreys.com/ (accessed 29 August 2019).
28. P. Hutchings, 'Monster Legacies: Memory, Technology and Horror History', in L. Geraghty and M. Jancovich (eds), *The Shifting Definitions of Genre: Essays on Labelling Films, Television Shows and Media* (Jefferson, NC: McFarland, 2008), pp. 216–28.
29. Though Hutchings is specifically addressing horror films, similar trends are evident with revived interest in other outdated media formats such as vinyl and cassette tapes.
30. Egan, *Trash or Treasure?*, p. 211.
31. Egan, *Trash or Treasure?*, p. 211.
32. R. Guins, 'Blood and Black Gloves on Shiny Discs: New Media, Old Tastes, and the Remediation of Italian Horror Films in the United States', in S. J. Schneider and T. Williams (eds), *Horror International* (Detroit, MI: Wayne State University Press, 2005), pp. 15–32.
33. M. McKenna, 'Constructing the Economic Canon: Technological Capability

and Perceptions of Value in DVD and Blu-ray Distribution', in J. Wroot and A. Willis (eds), *Cult Media: Re-packaged, Re-released and Restored* (Basingstoke: Palgrave Macmillan, 2017), pp. 31–47.
34. Egan, 'The Criterion Collection'.
35. McKenna, 'Constructing the Economic Canon'.
36. J. Squires, 'What Was the Final Horror Film Officially Released On VHS?', *Bloody Disgusting* (4 May 2017), *http://bloody-disgusting.com/news/3435649/last-horror-film-officially-released-vhs/* (accessed 29 August 2019).
37. 'VHS Special Features That Have Yet to Be Released on DVD or Blu ray', *DVD Talk Forum* (2012), *http://forum.dvdtalk.com/hd-talk/603442-vhs-special-features-have-yet-released-dvd-Blu-ray.html* (accessed 29 August 2019); W. Cook-Wilson, 'It's been 10 years since the last major VHS release. Is there a future for the format?', *Inverse* (29 March 2016), *https://www.inverse.com/article/13482-it-s-been-10-years-since-the-last-major-vhs-release-is-there-a-future-for-the-format* (accessed 29 August 2019); J. Johnson, 'The End of an Era: Last VHS Tape Shipped', *Hot Hardware* (24 December 2008), *https://hothardware.com/news/the-end-of-an-era-last-vhs-tape-shipped* (accessed 29 August 2019); H. O'Hara, 'Is VHS making a comeback?', *The Telegraph* (23 April 2015), *http://www.telegraph.co.uk/culture/film/film-news/11555663/Is-VHS-making-a-comeback.html* (accessed 29 August 2019).
38. 'About – Bleeding Skull!', *Bleeding Skull!*, *http://bleedingskull.com/about/* (accessed 29 August 2019).
39. O'Hara, 'Is VHS making a comeback?'.
40. 'VHS Special Features That Have Yet to Be Released on DVD or Blu ray'.
41. Egan, *Trash or Treasure?*, p. 211.
42. C. Bickel, 'The Criterion of Shit Movies: Arrow Video's Lionization of Lowbrow', *Dangerous Minds* (22 April 2016), *http://dangerousminds.net/comments/the_criterion_of_shit_movies_arrow_videos_lionization_of_lowbrow* (accessed 29 August 2019).
43. Egan, 'The Criterion Collection'.
44. McKenna, 'Constructing the Economic Canon'.
45. For example, see J. Wroot, 'The Stories of Arrow Video, as told by Trailers for their DVDs', *Watching the Trailer* (29 April 2015), *http://www.watchingthetrailer.com/trailers-blog/the-stories-of-arrow-video-as-told-by-trailers-for-their-dvds* (accessed 29 August 2019).
46. Hutchings, 'Monster Legacies'.

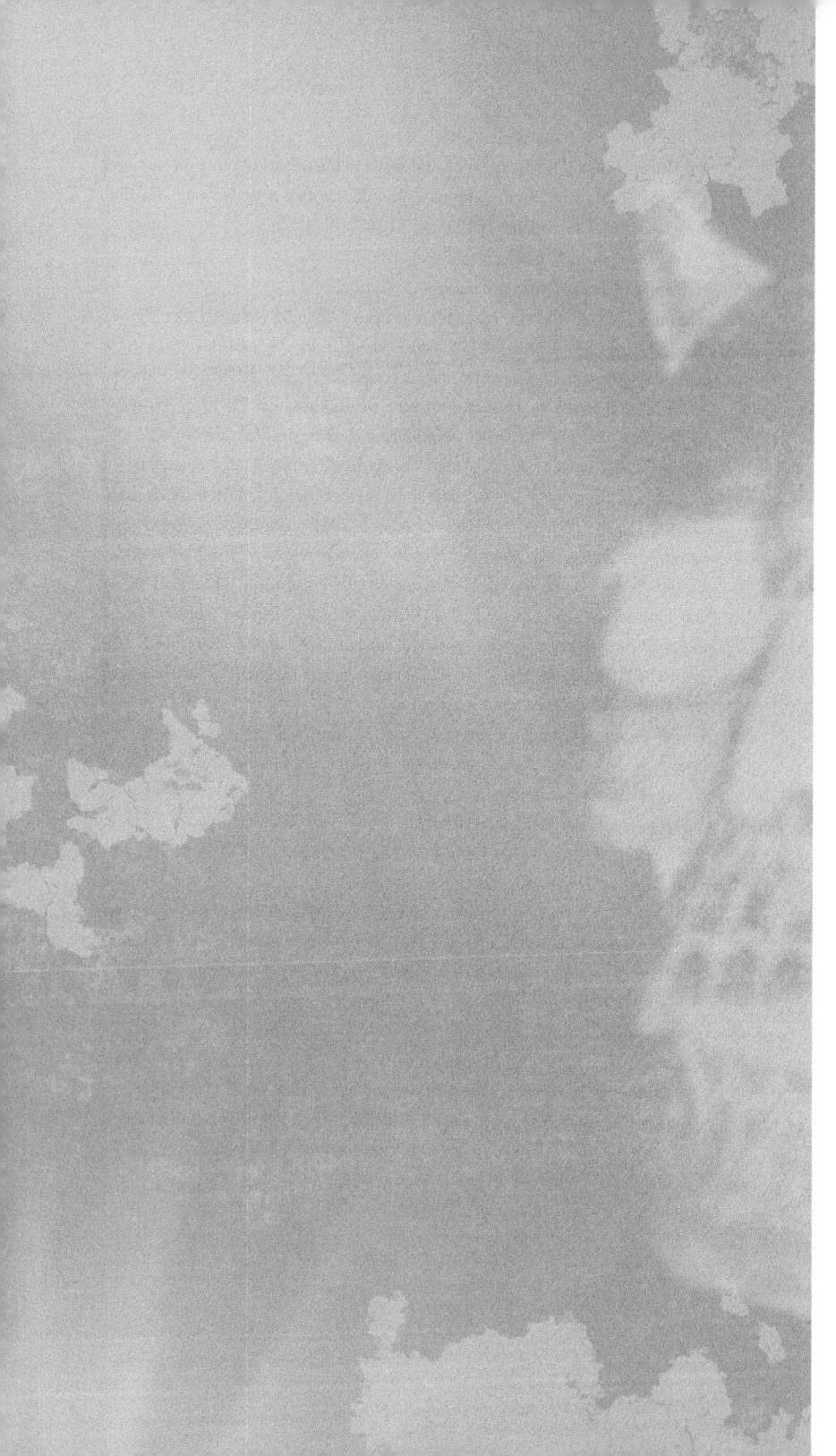

6

Streaming Netflix Original Horror

Black Mirror, Stranger Things and Datafied TV Horror

Matt Hills

IN THEIR 2013 MONOGRAPH *TV Horror*, Lorna Jowett and Stacey Abbott distinguish between 'single play dramas' or 'singular horror', such as *The Twilight Zone*, *The Outer Limits* and *Masters of Horror*, and horror in 'TV series and serialised soap opera', such as *Kolchak: The Night Strangler*, *The X-Files* and *True Blood*. In this chapter, I will follow their example by focusing on a flagship 'singular' Netflix original horror (the anthology show *Black Mirror*) and an instance of Netflix's high-profile 'serialised' horror (*Stranger Things*).[1] It has been argued that Netflix's genre TV productions may represent an entirely new phase in television horror, thus calling for analysis of the company's individualising construction of audiences and shift towards TV as a discursive object traversing digital media devices.[2] As a streaming service that has become emblematic of its type, Netflix has already attracted a raft of academic commentary, unlike niche horror-oriented streaming services, such as Shudder.[3] While it is true that smaller streaming services like Shudder do require further study, I want to maintain a focus on Netflix for a number of reasons.

First, I want to consider notions of the 'new' which have circulated around Netflix and how these have been coded through high theory that employs terms such as 'post-postmodern' or 'hyper-postmodern' to describe the type of horrors they offer. Secondly, I want to examine how Netflix's normalisation of binge-watching has impacted on constructions of television horror. I will argue that rethinking TV horror in relation to the binge or the post-postmodern has, in fact, failed to address issues of datafied horror. Hence, we need a more detailed analysis of potential shifts in the horror genre's (para)textual circulation and consumption via streaming – one that pays attention to how algorithmic gatekeeping functions can impact on horror's subcultural capital. The new blood of streaming Netflix horror therefore requires a concept of remediated subcultural capital, by which industrial processes aim to convert the genre's subcultural capital into more broadly recognised popular cultural capital[4] in a way that validates, rather than erodes, subcultural distinctions. As should hopefully be clear, by 'television' I am referring to what has been theorised as a phase of the transnational TV industry dubbed 'TVIV', or the 'post-broadcast', non-linear, on-demand era.[5] Bingeing has been figured as the characteristic mode of consumption for this type of TV, and 'traditional' broadcast or linear TV texts can, of course, be recontextualised as post-broadcast when they are hosted on platforms such as Netflix. Although I am focusing on Netflix for the reasons given, datafied horror could also be analysed via a far broader range of services, platforms and TV texts. The arguments set out in this chapter should thus be read as one set of starting points in what I hope will develop into a far wider analysis of datafied horror (and, indeed, other datafied genres[6]) in future scholarship.

I will analyse Charlie Brooker's *Black Mirror* (2011–) as an instance of 'singular' streaming horror, given that this anthology show, originally produced by Channel Four in the UK, has become a 'Netflix Original'. I will discuss *Stranger Things* (Netflix, 2016–), created by brothers Matt and Ross Duffer, as an example of 'serialised' horror TV. My case studies have been chosen to cover Jowett and Abbott's two basic categories of television horror, specifically in relation to texts not only classified as 'Netflix Originals', but acting as flagship examples of this corporate discourse. Although Netflix promotes TV shows as 'Originals' in territories where it has exclusive screening rights, such programmes are not necessarily produced by the company. Yet, *Black Mirror* and *Stranger Things* are 'Originals' in terms of being Netflix-produced, thus allowing the streaming service to utilise its proprietary, non-transparent audience data in relation to their promotion and production. It is for this reason that I refer to both shows as 'datafied horror' – they utilise the genre (alongside hybridised others) in relation to audience practices which have been translated into computerised data, or datafied.[7] While Netflix has produced a range of horror series, such as *Hemlock Grove* (2013–15), *The Haunting of Hill House* (2018–), *The Rain* (2018–), *Chambers* (2019) and *Black Summer* (2019–), demonstrating its participation in the horror boom that can be traced to the rise of 'quality' premium cable TV, *Black Mirror* and *Stranger Things* represent flagship shows for the service.

First, then, and before I address binge-watching and streaming horror's forms of capital: how has postmodernism returned in theories of Netflix horror?

Missing horrality: Netflix Originals and the 'post-postmodern'

Analysing the textual form of *Stranger Things*, Tracey Mollet – following the 2005 work of Valerie Wee – argues that it displays 'hyper-postmodernism', that is: 'a heightened degree of intertextual referencing and self-reflexivity that ceases to function at the traditional level of tongue in cheek subtext, and emerges instead as the actual text'.[8] This hyper-postmodern (inter)textual quality also blurs media boundaries, something which is apparent in *Stranger Things*'s conceptualisation for series one as an 'eight-hour movie',[9] and given its reliance on intertextualities linked to 1980s fantasy blockbusters and horror/slasher movies. Mollet is not alone in aligning Netflix's rise with an intensified version of postmodernism. Mareike Jenner has also drawn on postmodern theorising in her discussion of industrial shifts linked to Netflix,[10] while the editors of *Horror Television in the Age of Consumption* note that horror 'is quite at home in this new media culture'.[11] Jenner argues that Netflix builds 'on models of individualised viewing practices and self-scheduling of TV . . . in line with what Jeffrey T. Nealon . . . argues is post-postmodern capitalism'.[12] Rather than being text-focused, as in Mollet's analysis, Jenner/Nealon's approach is concerned more with the capitalist use of textual referencing in ways that align popular culture with individualised, commercialised authenticity.

However, the evocation of retooled postmodernism in Mollet's and Jenner's work can be called into question, or at least complicated. There is the issue of what Tim Jelfs has called 'linguistic convenience', where neoliberalism could just as well be substituted for '"(post)postmodernity", or "(post)postmodernism"', enabling analysts to consider continuities between 1980s neoliberalism and today's, rather than emphasising contemporary novelty.[13] Indeed, Nealon has gone on to re-describe 'post-postmodernism' as a matter of 'neoliberal biopolitics' instead, where values of personalised authenticity have become 'coincident with the logic of mainstream American economic life'.[14]

The textual distinctions of hyper-postmodernism can also be queried, given that intertextual referencing and self-reflexivity were argued in 1986 to characterise the then-contemporary horror film: 'contemporary Horror . . . knows that you've seen it before; it knows that you know what is about to happen; and it knows that you know that it knows you know'.[15] Demonstrating 'a violent awareness of itself as a saturated genre', Philip Brophy terms this 'horrality', or the 'deployment and manipulation of horror . . . as a textual mode'.[16] For hyper-postmodernism to stand out, critics seemingly have to reduce 1980s postmodernism to a flattened caricature. Continuities between 1980s horror film and current TV horror are hence downplayed in order to make the likes of *Stranger Things* textually readable as the horror genre's new blood. There is a risk here of scholarship reinforcing Netflix's brand value as a creator of innovative horror, when alternative critical readings might instead emphasise continuities of genre production across Netflix's practices and previous TV industry eras.

Jenner's scholarly engagement with Netflix has moved in this direction. Her 2018 monograph argues that *Stranger Things* would seem to fit

> neatly into conceptions of postmodern texts, presenting intertextuality and referencing a readily available (Hollywood) cinema history. Another reference point is the (. . . translocal) history of technology. Through this decentring of history, Netflix neglects constructions of a specifically American history. Thus, the idea of 'our' nation or history is neglected in favour of more transnational (cinema) history . . . *Stranger Things* use[s] genre . . . to formulate a 'transnational' version of history which often eschews more problematic aspects of . . . Reaganism.[17]

In this argument, Netflix references Hollywood horror texts that have enjoyed international success to lend *Stranger Things* a transnational legibility and currency, just as recognisable genres have functioned in this way across prior phases of TV history. *Black Mirror* works in a similar way, with its emphasis on 'translocal . . . technology' and its horror/SF extrapolations similarly working to address a 'global Netflix audience'.[18] Rather than TV horror being dispersed into a proliferation of micro-tags via Netflix's practices of micro-genre identification,[19] or reworked as post-/hyper-postmodern, Netflix uses TV horror to target and sustain cult followings across different national territories. Viewed in this light, Netflix's status as a 'disruptor' of established TV industry practices may have been somewhat overstated. Texts such as *Black Mirror* and *Stranger Things*, despite contrasting in terms of their singular/serial constructions, can both be addressed as strong examples of how 'genre functions as a central marker of the "grammar of transnationalism"'.[20] Both are 'heavily derivative', whether of Spielberg/slasher movies or anthology shows, such as *The Twilight Zone*.[21] To merely read *Black Mirror* as postmodern, or as if it could have been written by Jean Baudrillard,[22] is therefore a reductive projection of high theory onto the text, and one which fails to consider the transnational, TV-industrial value of making contemporary technologies central to the show's narratives.

As has been argued, *Black Mirror* has a strong fit with Netflix as a brand: 'each *Black Mirror* episode has its own finely crafted world, and most feature a shocking *Twilight Zone*-esque twist, making them perfect to pass around among friends, like urban legends'.[23] Moreover, despite David Sims suggesting, when it was first announced that Netflix had bought *Black Mirror*, that '[n]o doubt Brooker's already working on an episode about the . . . streaming giant that knows far too much about the habits of its customers', it is striking that episodes which have most centrally focused on vast data have involved bittersweet or happy endings rather than adopting dystopian tonalities.[24] Episodes such as 'San Junipero' (with its simulated lives) or 'Hang the DJ' (with its algorithmic processes for finding true love) starkly demonstrate this. Indeed, *Black Mirror* broadly mirrors Netflix's brand values, even including a Netflix logo in 'Bandersnatch' and thus trumpeting the service along with notions of groundbreaking interactive storytelling.

I am not arguing that streaming horror has no distinctiveness whatsoever in relation to previous TV eras. Rather, I hope to suggest that identifying streaming horror's differences purely through high-theoretical invocations of postmodernism might be at the cost of missing some key features. At the very least, the tendency of such perspectives is to disregard 1980s horrality only to make the same basic argument offered by Brophy back in 1986: that previous horror was less self-aware while current horror has become a saturated genre marked by increased knowingness. Offering up such a reading of the contemporary moment depends on overlooking the horrality that has been embedded in the horror genre's past.

Having said that, Netflix has been culturally positioned, and academically analysed, as distinctive in other ways, not merely via the post-postmodern. It is binge-watching and its impact on TV horror that I will now move on to consider: are fans of television horror series now bingeing on fear in new ways?

Bingeing horror: Netflix Originals and the 'genre bubble'

In the past, it has been assumed that television cannot hospitably host the affective intensities of the horror genre – either because of taste and decency guidelines linked to broadcast/network TV, the 'least objectionable programming' edicts of mass audience programming, or the upbeat, commercial interruptions of advertising.[25] Clearly, all of these presumed obstacles differ widely from the context of 'TVIV' and Netflix's favoured model of TV production, distribution and consumption. But Jowett and Abbott's *TV Horror* demonstrates that horror has always flourished, in a variety of ways, across the UK/US histories of TV drama, though it has arguably become more prevalent as 'quality' TV producers seek to mark out their 'edgy' difference compared to traditional US network television.[26] How, then, might Netflix's normalisation of bingeing alter aspects of contemporary TV horror, given that the genre has a newfound industrial value in the era of 'on-demand' viewing? Helen Wheatley has argued of gothic television that it draws much of its textual impact from the way that it places the domestic reception context (that is, the home) into discursive dialogue with textual codings of 'the home' in TV horror:

> Gothic television can be characterized by the meeting of two houses: the textual domestic spaces of Gothic television (haunted houses . . . permeable family homes under threat from within and without) and the extra-textual domestic spaces of the medium (the homes in which Gothic television is viewed) . . . [Through] the dialogue between these two houses . . . structures of identification are laid in place which potentially render the Gothic on television as one of the most affective of genres.[27]

Binge-watching has been argued to intensify audiences' emotional connection to texts, having the potential to render 'the most affective of genres' even more potent. Practices of fandom can also separately operate as amplifiers of affect – whether this involves communal speculation, collective sharing of textual moments as GIFs/memes or the identifying of 'Easter eggs' – but this does not alter the argument that bingeing can function as one mode of affective intensification for audiences. Indeed, this has been a key finding of in-depth empirical audience study, such as that offered by Lisa Glebatis Perks in her 2015 book *Media Marathoning*.[28]

Companies like Netflix and Sky are acutely aware of audiences' preferences to binge and of the investment that audiences make in shows watched in this way. Sam Ward concludes that, in order to compete with Netflix and older formats, such as DVD box-sets, Sky positioned itself as catering to the contemporary binge-watching audience. This was particular to the UK market and the company's use of Idris Elba to promote its on-demand service, however it did promote a lot of American and non-English titles through this campaign.[29] Other researchers theorise that the terms binge-viewing and marathoning are likely to be used for many years to come.[30] To give a further example, in relation to marathoning:

> [T]he fictive world holds greater power in marathoning than in other media engagement patterns . . . Although [Victor] Nell crafts an image of a delicate simulated experience . . . media marathoning creates a more stable and solid [fictional] world . . . The marathon[ing] version of Nell's delicate house would be an entire world made of narrative brick and reader mortar to create a stronghold in which readers blissfully play.[31]

From a 'delicate house' to a sturdier construction of bricks and mortar, the implication is that a more powerful sense of immersive belonging is created for TV audiences via bingeing. Anthropologist Grant McCracken makes a similar point, again drawing on discourses of the home: 'we binge . . . to craft . . . an immersive near-world . . . We may have made the world "go away" for psychological purposes . . . but . . . we have built another in its place. The . . . screen in some ways becomes our second home'.[32] Bingeing TV horror, then, facilitates a greater affective sense of the diegetic world as 'home', making narrative threats within this world more resonant for bingeing fans. Binge-watching, we might say, prompts a stronger sense of *Heimat*, as described by Cornel Sandvoss: 'these spaces differ from the territorial place conventionally understood as *Heimat*. Rather . . . they can be . . . textual, and hence can be accessed by fans in different mediated . . . ways, at different times, and from different localities'.[33] The result is a 'mobile *Heimat*' which resembles what Raymond Williams has termed 'mobile privatisation'.[34]

But to only celebrate the bingeing of TV horror as an invitation to a mobile *Heimat*, and thus to a sense of homeliness within which narrative threats can become more potent, is to neglect the critical anxieties that have circulated around Netflix's datafication of audiences. The mobile *Heimat* is what Netflix promises its users and, if instantiated, we can see how horror's generic affects can be intensified in relation to serialised texts such as *Stranger Things*. After series one, fans were moved to campaign online for 'justice for Barb', indicating a powerful connection with the show's characters.[35] The reaction to series two emphasised how 'The Lost Sister' interrupted many fans' experience of 'insulated flow' within bingeing, pulling them out of narrative immersion or the mobile *Heimat*.[36] Meanwhile, *Black Mirror* fans on Reddit have debated whether they prefer to binge the show or savour it an episode at a time, demonstrating that even supposedly 'singular' horror can be consumed as-if-serialised via bingeing.[37] *Black Mirror*'s brand, and Easter eggs spotted by fans which imply a coherent '*Black Mirror* universe', have provided an overarching sense of *Heimat* in this case.[38] This is something played up by series four's 'Black Museum' (which contained many references back to earlier episodes) and by the interactive episode 'Bandersnatch', which encapsulated, in one branching narrative, the variety of tones (bittersweet; dark; nihilistic; meta) previously linked to the show on Netflix.[39]

However, thinking about binged TV horror as a kind of mobile *Heimat* – within which the *unheimlich* can be generated effectively – does not address how Netflix uses proprietary data gathered from audiences to recommend subsequent titles to them and populate their home screens. This algorithmically driven process, where audiences are datafied and treated as 'measurable types' via an array of data points, has been argued to lead to 'filter bubbles' of consumption.[40] Through this process, audiences see more of the kinds of TV shows that they have already binged and enjoyed, and fewer other forms of Netflix content. TV studies scholar James Bennett has anecdotally described his own Netflix profile as offering 'up a database of black and muted colour palettes, often punctuated with visceral red titles that reveal my penchant for dark dramas and horror', while discussing how algorithms dictate this 'echo chamber'.[41]

Rather than only viewing Netflix Originals and their designed-for-bingeing as an intensification of horror's affects, it is important to also consider how Netflix's datafication of horror can lead to individualised, personalised genre bubbles. Of course, the niche target marketing of services like Shudder, where a community of genre fans is interpellated, might seem to resemble this generic enclosure. And yet, a niche service such as Shudder is consciously chosen for its focus on a particular genre; Netflix's genre bubbles, by contrast, emerge out of the datafication of individual consumption choices, and as such are never explicitly chosen by the viewer. Furthermore, Netflix personalises the paratextual artwork and graphic design through which users encounter its recommendations, meaning that generic hybrids such as *Stranger Things* can be paratextually toggled towards (or away from) horror genre identifications on the basis of viewers' previous choices.[42] This may be, for instance, via the selection of conventional horror imagery, or alternatively via emphases on teen romance, childhood friendship, the mystery of a missing child or more science-fictional graphic design. (For some examples of these personalisations, see online commentaries such as Mark Wilson's 2017 discussion for *Fast Company*.[43]) Genre bubbles can thus occur not only at the level of recommendations, but also through *how* recommendations are paratextually framed on a person's profile.

It is possible that Netflix's use of algorithmic gatekeeping (meaning what users see on their profile is data-driven) could generate new genre or micro-genre patterns. As Catherine Johnson has argued: 'Algorithmic analysis of large datasets generated from actual user behaviour enables novel patterns of viewing, taste cultures and genre categories to be identified that were not previously visible.'[44] In turn, this can also 'enable content and viewers to be valued in new ways'; such is the case with the moving away of the horror genre, and its fandoms, from a position of cultural disreputability, surrendering the status of a supposedly marginal niche in favour of being valued by the likes of Netflix.[45] Such fans will reliably binge, especially when a series is initially dropped, and hence they can act as good, predictable consumers contributing to the brand value of Netflix by championing newly released content, as well as recognising the affective power of horror bingeing. As Jenner has pointed out, it is therefore unsurprising that 'Netflix heavily relies on genre to structure its interface. Its generic categories are based on an already existing consensus about genre, which . . . [it] does not challenge.'[46] For instance, *Black Mirror* was bought as a genuine Netflix Original because the Channel Four episodes had already found a transnational audience on the streaming service, and thus Netflix sought to build on its pre-established SF/horror genre identity. To give some examples of this genre positioning: Netflix-produced episodes such as 'Shut Up and Dance' focused on dark, realist horror; 'Playtest' cast Kurt Russell's son, Wyatt Russell, and referenced John Carpenter's *The Thing* (1982); 'Hated in the Nation', also from the first Netflix-produced season, emulated the horror of Alfred Hitchcock's *The Birds* (1963). Likewise, *Stranger Things* is designed to be quickly identifiable as fantasy-horror. Indeed, its season one opening

> immediately makes inroads into the horror and science fiction genres. We are introduced to the sinister atmosphere of the Hawkins Laboratory . . . [and] see a scientist running for his life, away from an (as yet) unseen foe. The scientist reaches apparent safety in the elevator; however, a point-of-view shot and a monster's 'chittering' alert us to the fact that the scientist is being preyed upon . . . *Stranger Things* . . . plays into the generic conventions of Noël Carroll's suggested horror plot structure, establishing the monster's presence by an attack and by immediately linking the children to its discovery.[47]

TV horror is thus valuable to Netflix because its community of knowledgeable fans will generate seemingly individualised 'genre bubbles' which are nonetheless culturally, communally and algorithmically predictable as sources of brand difference and value. But how does the popularity of *Black Mirror* and *Stranger Things*, along with their status as datafied horror, threaten to alter the 'subcultural capital', or insider fan knowledge, of TV horror?[48] I will conclude by considering this question.

Knowing horror: Netflix Originals and subcultural/popular cultural capital

Subcultural capital is knowledge that has group validity, hence conferring status 'in the eyes of the relevant beholder'.[49] As the name suggests, subcultural capital belongs to subcultures of fans and cannot typically be acquired through formal education. Despite the assumption that subcultural capital might be opposed to the 'mainstream' of pop culture, Sarah Thornton argues that it is partly circulated by mass media, and although this can sometimes result in fans determining that subcultural distinction has been 'sold out', such an outcome is not inevitable.[50] Having said that, David Beer has argued that the algorithmic extension of subcultural capital – such as Netflix's circulation of *Stranger Things* or *Black Mirror* to audiences who would not identify as genre fans – adds a new dimension to the mediation of subcultural capital, since this now occurs without human decision-making[51] and via a corporate, privatised process:

> If . . . cultural knowledge now finds-us, then cultural know-how might be decoupled from the types of socialisation processes that are more dependent on . . . the consumption of the right type of broadcast media outputs. We might wonder where this might leave something like . . . 'subcultural capital', if these forms of knowledge can now circulate outside of subcultural groups and as they find a new audience through algorithmic processes.[52]

I have previously argued that horror texts can be analysed in terms of their differential levels of intertextual subcultural capital,[53] in which a horror film or TV show's references to other genre products will presuppose forms of audience knowledge. But this assumes that texts circulate socially within genre-based subcultures, rather than via datafied gatekeeping, where audiences may find *Stranger Things* or *Black Mirror* on their Netflix profile by virtue of the shows' star actors, say, rather than as a matter of genre.

It is therefore important to consider how datafied horror complicates the genre's relationship to subcultural capital by seeking to reach audiences who are relatively low in such (fandom-centred) capital. With this in mind, and following Beer's argument above, Craig Haslop has analysed the role of star casting in cult television such as *Stranger Things*, and the same process is evidently at work in *Black Mirror*, not only via the casting of Wyatt Russell but also through season five's casting of Miley Cyrus. Haslop argues that Winona Ryder's casting was crucial to enabling *Stranger Things* to circulate outside genre fandoms. It should be noted that Netflix executives can be involved in shows' casting decisions, utilising the service's proprietary data,[54] although no such admission has been made on the record in relation to Ryder's casting as Joyce Byers. Haslop observes how 'Ryder's star image was particularly relevant given its mix of signifiers . . . connect[ing] her to cult and the mainstream', drawing on her presence in 1980s cult films such as *Heathers* (Michael Lehmann, 1989) to authenticate *Stranger Things*'s '80s pastiche, as well as her wider Hollywood cachet via non-genre roles in *The Age of Innocence* (Martin Scorsese, 1993) and *Reality Bites* (Ben Stiller, 1994) in the 1990s.[55] The result is that 'Netflix positioned her star image as one that was not out of place in association with the programme's cultish objectives but could still appeal to wider audiences, otherwise deterred by the series' . . . cultish associations'.[56]

Such casting enables Netflix to use its datafication of audiences along non-genre dimensions, potentially transforming the subcultural capital of a series like *Stranger Things* into a more widely recognised 'popular cultural capital'.[57] And though this does partly hinge on intertextual forms of capital – just as *Black Mirror* arguably featured Jodie Foster as a director of one episode to broaden its reach, as well as the director of British social-realist horror movie *Eden Lake* (2008), James Watkins, as a bid to shore up its hard-hitting genre credentials[58] – such moves remain subject to algorithmic support via the Netflix interface.

Netflix's use of datafied horror has also complicated or remediated genre-oriented subcultural capital in other ways. For instance, Joe Tompkins has analysed horror's subcultural capital in relation to twenty-first-century remakes of 1970s/1980s horror movies. Tompkins argues that, in order to avoid being seen as mainstreamed 'sell-outs' among fans, such remakes typically emphasise their directors' horror fandom: 'the horror franchise reboot effectively enables industry personnel to cultivate notions of aesthetic distinction and subcultural capital, and thus reward audience competencies in accordance with the logic of media brands'.[59] At the same time, it has increasingly become apparent that 'fans and critics are often quite critical of contemporary reboots on the grounds that they . . . exploit valued subcultural materials . . . assimilating fan attachments with commercial imperatives'.[60] Such remakes might thus be seen as risky for Netflix's attempts at algorithmically disseminating subcultural capital, especially as Netflix seeks to remediate this into more widely recognised popular cultural capital without alienating subcultural genre fandoms. As Paul Driscoll has proposed, *Stranger Things* is a kind of anti-remake: 'In marked contrast to the movie remake which retells an existing story using contemporary forms . . . *Stranger Things* sets out to tell a new story by conservatively adhering to bygone forms.'[61] By emulating anthology shows from a similarly 'bygone' era, *Black Mirror* also combines originality with a derivative genre position, but in a way that renders it 'authentic'. The trick to these anti-remakes is that they are consequently able to combine recognised subcultural capital with algorithmically circulated popular cultural capital. Unlike the botched horror movie remake, which repackages edgy horror as 'saleable, multiplex-friendly fodder' and so surrenders subcultural status in fans' eyes, Netflix's canny retooling of the televisual uncanny has not generally suffered such a fate.[62]

However, if subcultural capital has taken on a less exclusive colouration through its algorithmic (re)circulation and recontextualisation as popular cultural capital – of the type linked to TV shows such as *I Love the 80s*[63] – then how have genre fans recuperated their sense of distinction? Crucial here has been the listing of 'Easter eggs', or hyper-detailed, fleeting content that fans isolate from a show's narrative context. As Tanya Horeck et al. have noted, 'binge-watching is a . . . part of wider listicle culture', and nowhere is this more apparent than in cases of reclaimed subcultural capital.[64] Fans of *Stranger Things* make videos listing horror/fantasy intertextualities and discuss such connections online, while *Black Mirror* fans list the Easter eggs connecting episodes together, as well as spotting moments where the production team has baited them by self-reflexively adding fan-oriented details. Driscoll has recognised that there is almost a 'listmania' at work here, a point affirmed by Paul Booth: 'Fans' list-making . . . becomes a way of approaching the canon text; an access [route] rather than an artifact in and of itself.'[65] Such list-making can objectify subcultural capital and fans' distinctive ways of reading these TV horror shows, acting as an alternative mode of listing to that carried out by Netflix:

> We can draw an important distinction between . . . institutional lists . . . that materially measure, trace, and map the field (storing and processing its data), and what I will call 'memory' lists – subjective and participatory lists that are about taste and lived experience . . . On both ends, institutional and participatory, lists process the distinctions and inscribe the categories through which . . . culture . . . is generated.[66]

It follows, then, that the big data owned by Netflix works institutionally to remediate subcultural capital as popular cultural capital, whereas fans' participatory lists of *Stranger Things* and *Black Mirror* Easter eggs act as a differential form of what might be termed small data list-making. Such data is freely available, always amendable by other fans and necessarily exists at a human scale of accessibility, whether compiled into an official guide or shared in a subreddit.

I have argued here that analysing the emergence of horror-oriented Netflix Originals requires thinking about TV horror in specific ways. Rather than falling back on accounts of post-postmodernism/hyper-postmodernism, datafied horror – where the commissioning, circulation and promotion of horror TV draws on audience practices coded through big data – calls for discussion of the personalised 'genre bubbles' linked to Netflix's brand value, as well as ways of understanding horror's subcultural/

popular cultural capital. This latter shift is not merely a mainstreaming of 'authentic' horror. Fans' subcultural capital, in the guise of *Black Mirror* and *Stranger Things* Easter-egg-hunting and list-making, co-exists with these shows' popular cultural capital as flagship Netflix programming, accessible through notions of techno-cultural anxiety and/or 'retro' 1980s pastiche.

Datafied genre TV is likely to become more culturally significant as other major streaming services go live, but we should take care not to substitute the promotional discourses surrounding algorithmic culture for its actualities. As Jonathan Cohn has argued:

> If . . . [Netflix] algorithms recommended it make or purchase its less hyped series, such as *Hemlock Grove* . . . [then] should we necessarily assume its technologies are intelligent, or just occasionally lucky? . . . [T]he rhetoric around algorithms and recommendation systems is often much more influential than the algorithms themselves.[67]

Yet, both textually and paratextually, horror's new blood in the twenty-first century remains recognisable precisely as horror – a genre that enables Netflix to position itself as affectively immersive, subculturally 'authentic', transnationally cultish and supposedly user-driven. Not bad going for diegetic monsters and uncanny technologies.

Notes

1. Lorna Jowett and Stacey Abbott, *TV Horror: Investigating the Dark Side of the Small Screen* (London: I. B. Tauris, 2013), pp. 40, 44.
2. L. Belau and K. Jackson, 'Introduction: Binging on Horror', in L. Belau and K. Jackson (eds), *Horror Television in the Age of Consumption: Binging on Fear* (London: Routledge, 2018), p. 3; S. Gerrard, 'Introduction', in S. Gerrard, S. Holland and R. Shail (eds), *Gender and Contemporary Horror in Television* (Bingley: Emerald Publishing, 2019), p. 2.
3. See, for example, Mareike Jenner, *Netflix and the Re-invention of Television* (Basingstoke: Palgrave Macmillan, 2018) and Ramon Lobato, *Netflix Nations: The Geography of Digital Distribution* (New York, NY: New York University Press, 2019).
4. J. Fiske, 'The cultural economy of fandom', in L. Lewis (ed.), *The Adoring Audience* (London: Routledge, 1992), pp. 30–49.

5. M. Jenner, 'Is this TVIV? On Netflix, TVIII and binge-watching', *New Media & Society*, 18/2 (2016), 257–73.
6. For a related study, see Tanya Horeck, *Justice on Demand: True Crime in the Digital Streaming Era* (Detroit, MI: Wayne State University Press, 2019).
7. Arne Hintz, Lina Dencik and Karin Wahl-Jorgensen, *Digital Citizenship in a Datafied Society* (Cambridge: Polity, 2019), p. 146.
8. Valerie Wee cited in T. Mollet, 'Looking through the upside down: Hyper-postmodernism and transmediality in the Duffer Brothers' *Stranger Things*', *Journal of Popular Television*, 7/1 (2019), 59.
9. Trisha Dunleavy, *Complex Serial Drama and Multiplatform Television* (London: Routledge, 2018), p. 148.
10. Jenner, 'Is this TVIV?', 257–73.
11. Belau and Jackson, 'Introduction', p. 3.
12. Jenner, 'Is this TVIV?', 267.
13. Tim Jelfs, *The Argument about Things in the 1980s: Goods and Garbage in an Age of Neoliberalism* (Morgantown, WV: West Virginia University Press, 2018), pp. 19, 142–3.
14. Jeffrey T. Nealon, *I'm Not Like Everybody Else: Biopolitics, Neoliberalism and American Popular Music* (Lincoln, NE: University of Nebraska Press, 2018), p. 32.
15. P. Brophy, 'Horrality – the Textuality of Contemporary Horror Films', *Screen*, 27/1 (1986), 5.
16. Brophy, 'Horrality', 5.
17. Jenner, *Netflix and the Re-invention of Television*, pp. 228–9.
18. Charlie Brooker and Annabel Jones with Jason Arnopp, *Inside Black Mirror* (London: Ebury Press, 2018), pp. 217, 311.
19. Jenner, *Netflix and the Re-invention of Television*, pp. 132–3.
20. Jenner, *Netflix and the Re-invention of Television*, p. 228.
21. Dennis Broe, *Birth of the Binge: Serial TV and the End of Leisure* (Detroit, MI: Wayne State University Press, 2019), p. 110; R. Butler, 'The Eaten-for-Breakfast Club: Teenage Nightmares in *Stranger Things*', in K. J. Wetmore, Jr. (ed.), *Uncovering Stranger Things: Essays on Eighties Nostalgia, Cynicism and Innocence in the Series* (Jefferson, NC: McFarland, 2018), pp. 72–83. And see also I. Berriman, 'Charlie Brooker Talks the Twilight Zone and Technology', *GamesRadar* (1 February 2013), *http://www.gamesradar.com/charlie-brooker-talks-the-twilight-zone-and-technology/* (accessed 29 August 2019).
22. M. Jiménez-Morales and M. Lopera-Mármol, 'Why *Black Mirror* Was Really Written by Jean Baudrillard: A Philosophical Interpretation of Charlie Brooker's Series', in A. M. Cirucci and B. Vacker (eds), *Black Mirror and Critical Media Theory* (Lanham, MD: Lexington Books, 2018), p. 103.

23. D. Sims, '*Black Mirror* Is the Perfect Show for Netflix', *The Atlantic* (8 September 2015), *https://www.theatlantic.com/entertainment/archive/2015/09/netflix-and-black-mirror-a-match-made-in-digital-heaven/404275/* (accessed 29 August 2019).
24. Sims, '*Black Mirror* Is the Perfect Show for Netflix'.
25. Matt Hills, *The Pleasures of Horror* (London: Continuum, 2005), pp. 115–16.
26. Jowett and Abbott, *TV Horror*, p. 10.
27. Helen Wheatley, *Gothic Television* (Manchester: Manchester University Press, 2006), p. 200.
28. Lisa Glebatis Perks, *Media Marathoning: Immersions in Morality* (Lanham, MD: Lexington Books, 2015).
29. S. Ward, 'Box Sets on the Set-Top Box: The Promotion of on Demand Television in Britain', in J. Wroot and A. Willis (eds), *DVD, Blu-ray and Beyond: Navigating Formats and Platforms within Media Consumption* (Basingstoke: Palgrave Macmillan, 2017), pp. 177–96.
30. M. Pittman and K. Sheehan, 'Sprinting a media marathon: Uses and gratifications of binge-watching television through Netflix', *First Monday*, 20/5 (5 October 2015), *https://firstmonday.org/ojs/index.php/fm/article/view/6138* (accessed 29 August 2019).
31. Perks, *Media Marathoning*, p. 8.
32. Grant McCracken cited in Belau and Jackson, 'Introduction', p. 2.
33. Cornel Sandvoss, *Fans: The Mirror of Consumption* (Cambridge: Polity, 2005), p. 64.
34. Sandvoss, *Fans*, p. 64.
35. Gina McIntyre, *Stranger Things: Worlds Turned Upside Down* (London: Century, 2018), p. 101.
36. Perks, *Media Marathoning*, p. xxii; McIntyre, *Stranger Things: Worlds Turned Upside Down*, p. 182.
37. M. Hills, '*Black Mirror* as a Netflix Original: Program Brand "Overflow" and the Multidiscursive Forms of Transatlantic TV Fandom', in M. Hills, M. Hilmes and R. Pearson (eds), *Transatlantic Television Drama: Industries, Programs, & Fans* (Oxford: Oxford University Press, 2019), pp. 213–38.
38. E. Whitney, '24 Easter Eggs From All Three Seasons of "Black Mirror," Plus a Timeline Connecting Every Episode', *Screen Crush* (26 October 2016), *http://screencrush.com/black-mirror-easter-eggs-theory/* (accessed 29 August 2019).
39. M. Hills, '*Black Mirror*: "Bandersnatch" and "The Affair" of Re-Narration in (Gendered TV) Taste Cultures', *CST Online* (18 January 2019), *https://cstonline.net/black-mirror-bandersnatch-and-the-affair-of-re-narration-in-gendered-tv-taste-cultures-by-matt-hills/* (accessed 29 August 2019).

40. John Cheney-Lippold, *We Are Data: Algorithms and the Making of Our Digital Selves* (New York, NY: New York University Press, 2017), p. 99; Eli Pariser, *The Filter Bubble* (London: Penguin, 2012).
41. J. Bennett, 'Public Service Algorithms', in D. Freedman and V. Goblot (eds), *A Future for Public Service Television* (London: Goldsmiths Press, 2018), pp. 111–12.
42. A. Chandrashekar, F. Amat, J. Basilico and T. Jebara, 'Artwork Personalization at Netflix', *The Netflix Tech Blog* (7 December 2017), *https://medium.com/netflix-techblog/artwork-personalization-c589f074ad76* (accessed 29 August 2019).
43. M. Wilson, 'Netflix is Even Personalizing its Graphic Design to You Now', *Fast Company* (18 December 2017), *https://www.fastcompany.com/90154608/netflix-is-even-personalizing-its-graphic-design-to-you-now* (accessed 9 February 2020).
44. Catherine Johnson, *Online TV* (London: Routledge, 2019), p. 150.
45. Johnson, *Online TV*, p. 150.
46. Jenner, *Netflix and the Re-invention of Television*, p. 132.
47. Mollet, 'Looking through', 61. And see Butler, 'Eaten-for-Breakfast Club', pp. 79–80 on the show's use of additional horror tropes.
48. Sarah Thornton, *Club Cultures: Music, Media and Subcultural Capital* (Cambridge: Polity, 1995), p. 11.
49. Thornton, *Club Cultures*, p. 11.
50. Thornton, *Club Cultures*, pp. 116–17.
51. T. Striphas, 'Algorithmic culture', *European Journal of Cultural Studies*, 18/4–5 (2015), 406.
52. David Beer, *Popular Culture and New Media: The Politics of Circulation* (Basingstoke: Palgrave Macmillan, 2013), pp. 95–6.
53. Hills, *Pleasures of Horror*, p. 179.
54. Hills, '*Black Mirror* as a Netflix Original', p. 220.
55. C. Haslop, '"Do you wanna come with me?" The role of the star image as brand for the commodification of cult in mainstream telefantasy', *Celebrity Studies* (2019), 10–11.
56. Haslop, '"Do you wanna come with me?"', 10.
57. Fiske, 'The cultural economy', p. 33.
58. J. Walker, 'A Wilderness of Horrors? British Horror Cinema in the New Millennium', *Journal of British Cinema and Television*, 9/3 (2012), 447–8.
59. J. Tompkins, '"Re-imagining" the canon: examining the discourse of contemporary horror film reboots', *New Review of Film and Television Studies*, 12/4 (2014), 383.
60. Tompkins, '"Re-imagining" the canon', 396.

61. Paul Driscoll, *Stranger Things – Season 1* (Edinburgh: Obverse Books, 2019), p. 27.
62. Mark Kermode cited in Tompkins, '"Re-imagining" the canon', 396.
63. C. Soukup, '*I Love the 80*s: The Pleasures of a Postmodern History', *Southern Communication Journal*, 75/1 (2010), 83.
64. T. Horeck, M. Jenner and T. Kendall, 'On binge-watching: Nine critical propositions', *Critical Studies in Television: The International Journal of Television Studies*, 13/4 (2018), 502.
65. Driscoll, *Stranger Things – Season 1*, pp. 22–3; P. Booth, 'Fans' list-making: memory, influence, and argument in the "event" of fandom', *MATRIZes*, 9/2 (2015), 96.
66. Liam Cole Young, *List Cultures: Knowledge and Poetics from Mesopotamia to BuzzFeed* (Amsterdam: Amsterdam University Press, 2017), p. 49.
67. Jonathan Cohn, *The Burden of Choice: Recommendations, Subversion, and Algorithmic Culture* (New Brunswick, NJ: Rutgers University Press, 2019), p. 86.

PART THREE

EMERGING SUBGENRES

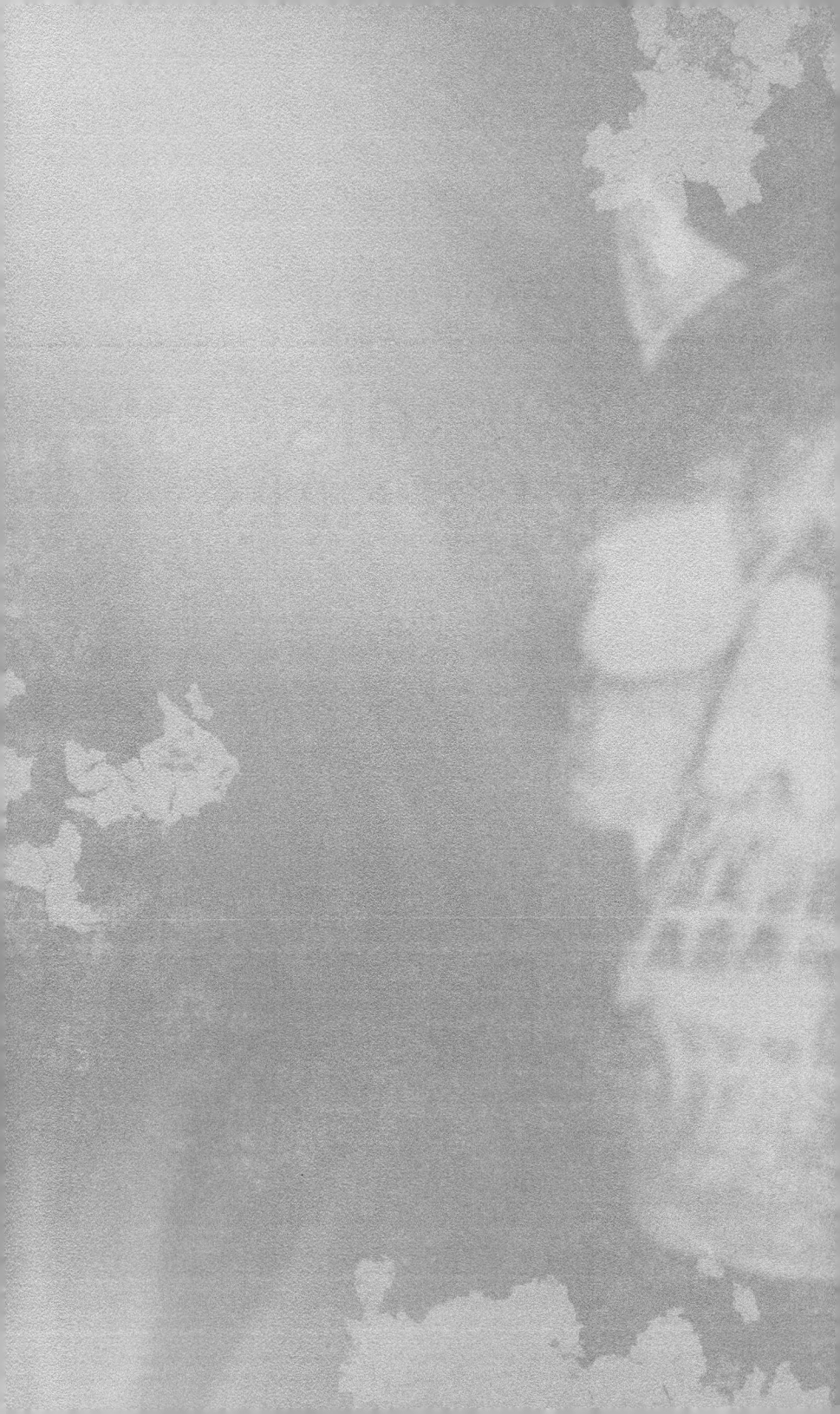

7

The digital gothic and the Mainstream Horror Genre

Uncanny Vernacular Creativity and Adaptation

Jessica Balanzategui

THROUGHOUT THE twenty-first century, the mainstream televisual and cinematic horror genre has increasingly engaged with vernacular modes of horror and Gothic cultural production on the internet. This type of internet storytelling tends to be known broadly as 'Creepypasta' and extends upon both early Web 2.0 viral narrative practices such as chain emails and 'cursed' social media posts, as well as the pre-digital folkloric storytelling traditions upon which these digital folk narratives draw, particularly the ghost story and urban legend. As I have argued elsewhere, Creepypasta stories can be categorised as the 'digital gothic': these multimodal online narratives deliver a distinctively digital rendition of horror and Gothic fiction, drawing upon vernacular aesthetics and narrative forms to craft uncanny dread and eerie frisson.[1] The lower-case 'g' gestures to the vernacularity of this fiction, and also to the way mainstream horror and Gothic forms are appropriated and rearranged by this collaborative approach to storytelling.

In previous work, I have explored the dialectical 'uncanny nostalgia' for obsolete analogue media technologies at the core of the digital gothic.[2]

In this chapter, I turn to an examination of the ways that these digital gothic stories have started to exceed their previously niche online communities to influence mainstream media and entertainment cultures. As a result, the vernacular formal properties and collaborative circuits of authorship that underpin the digital gothic interact with the 'official' horror genre produced and circulated by mainstream screen industries, as studio-produced films with global cinema releases and television programmes on cable and network stations bear the influence of this informal mode of cultural production.

The visibility and profile of vernacular internet horror stories was propelled by a disturbing crime in Wisconsin in 2014, in which two tween girls attempted to kill one of their friends to appease popular digital gothic figure the 'Slender Man', believing themselves to be acting as his 'proxies'. Subsequent to this troubling event, which sparked a moral panic about internet horror stories with global resonance,[3] three Slender Man feature films have been released: the documentary *Beware the Slenderman* (Irene Taylor Bordsky, 2016) and horror features *Always Watching: A Marble Hornets Story* (James Moran, 2015) and *Slender Man* (Sylvain White, 2018). In addition, a Creepypasta-themed anthology television series was released in 2016, SyFy's *Channel Zero*, which adapts a well-known digital gothic story each season.

Beginning with an analysis of the aesthetic devices of the digital gothic and the authorship conditions that shape them, this chapter proceeds to consider how mainstream adaptations of digital gothic stories remediate in troubled ways the style, narrative structures and thematic preoccupations of their online source material. Through an analysis of the first season of *Channel Zero*, I position the current trend of film and television adaptations of digital gothic tales as a key flashpoint in the shifting relationships between online, vernacular cultural expression and the industrial mechanics of mainstream entertainment. This chapter outlines how these processes of exchange illuminate complex cultural tensions between the internet's function as, to use Trevor Blank's terms, the primary contemporary 'system of and . . . storehouse for folklore',[4] and the formalised production, distribution and consumption channels of mainstream entertainment industries.

The digital gothic and vernacular, collaborative authorship

Key to both the creation and form of digital gothic narratives is a self-consciously vernacular style, undergirded by the kinds of '"ordinary" and "popular" cultural formations' and modes of discourse that Jean Burgess posits as central to digital vernacular creativity.[5] As Burgess outlines, vernacular creativity entails 'creative practices that emerge from highly particular and non-elite social contexts and communicative conventions', including 'vernacular speech, thought or expression', and 'everyday language' as distinguished from 'institutional or official modes of expression'.[6] As will be seen, the digital gothic foregrounds a conversational, vernacular style on a number of levels, and the stories tend to be produced and distributed by a nebulous community of anonymous or pseudonymous creators, making it difficult for consumers to identify a tale's origins, contexts and authors. This ambiguously collaborative dynamic infuses the tales with a sense of both mystery and authenticity.

Indeed, Creepypasta stories – a term that derives from the portmanteau 'copypasta', which stands for 'copy' and 'paste' – are designed to be virally shared and developed across multiple platforms. Thus, the informal and rhizomatic digital distribution process that fuels Creepypasta stories is key to their form and function, as it obfuscates the conditions of their authorship and thus lends the tales a folkloric quality. The vaguely defined collaborative processes that underpin these tales in turn roots them in the everyday, creating different epistemic expectations around these stories – namely a suspension of disbelief stemming from uncertainty about the tale's precise relationships to reality – when compared to mainstream horror and Gothic fiction.

For instance, the now infamous internet bogeyman the Slender Man emerged on a forum called Something Awful in 2009, which invited users to create 'Paranormal Images' using Photoshop and other photo-editing software. One of the most widely known bogeymen of the twenty-first century, Slender Man is a tall, faceless creature in a suit with spindly, elongated arms who abducts and possesses his victims, who are primarily children. The Slender Man was influenced by characters drawn from mainstream art and entertainment, including the 'Tall Man' from the film *Phantasm* (Don Coscarelli, 1979) and the 'Gentlemen' creatures from the infamous episode 'Hush' of *Buffy the Vampire Slayer* (Joss Whedon, 1999). As Andrew Peck suggests,

> Slender Man drew upon an existing matrix of belief that included mass media representations of paranormal creatures, the user's personal experiences and fears, and the influence of previous posts on the discussion thread. In other words, the Slender Man was not an

entirely new creation and was influenced by a vast network of vernacular and institutional performances that had directly and indirectly preceded it.[7]

As forum users shared and discussed their photographs, constructed a backstory for the character and pinpointed his defining characteristics, Slender Man gradually developed a complex lore and relatively consistent narrative logic. The bogeyman's crystallisation was not only characterised by a blurring of boundaries between the producers and consumers of this artistic and narrative content – a blurring that Limor Shifman has described as a key element of vernacular digital genres[8] – but also by a playful shrouding of the lines between mundane online communication and fantasy, aided by the anonymity and pseudonymity of forums like Something Awful. As Shira Chess points out, 'many of those on the Something Awful thread . . . confessed fear of the very things they had created', citing user Phy who remarked as the character was being formed, 'Jeez. Slender Man's been entirely made up by this thread, but he's already having an effect. He steals your sleep'.[9] This is a strangely Gothic incarnation of what George Ritzer and Nathan Jurgenson (drawing on Alvin Toffler) have called 'prosumption': a dissolution of the distinction between producers and consumers that in parallel combines the processes of consumption and production, a condition that Ritzer and Jurgenson contend is central to the participatory Web 2.0 age.[10]

The eerie qualities of this Gothicised prosumption-based model of authorship are also related to the fact that while working as a digital community to collaboratively develop internet horror stories, the real-world identities of users are generally not known to each other. The anxieties that this multilayered, somewhat contradictory process of authorship creates in turn tend to be refracted in the stories themselves. For instance, as the Slender Man character developed, a key tenet of his mythology eventually became that he could possess people, rendering them his proxies to perpetuate his image and manipulate media technologies.[11] This narrative conceit renders uncanny the formal and technical qualities of vernacular digital storytelling, as the collective creative practices behind the Slender Man's expanding mythos become implicated in the creature's supernatural powers: according to Slender Man lore, it can be unclear which anonymous or pseudonymous contributors to the creature's narrative world are regular internet users building upon a story that they enjoy; which contributors are 'victims' of the beast recounting traumatic encounters with him; which are 'proxies' of the bogeyman mechanically acting out the monster's whims to extend his influence; or which may be the monster himself. The combination of creative community and haunting uncertainty that underpins the collaborative circuits of digital gothic cultural production thus contributes to the phenomenon that Chess describes, whereby 'audiences often became terrified by their own tales'.[12]

The uncanny qualities of this Gothic prosumption-based authorship are also associated with the viral proliferation of Creepypasta tales, as stories quickly expand beyond and evade the original authors' control. While the origins and development of a Creepypasta narrative can often be traced quite precisely, these origins tend to be quickly obscured by the viral sharing that digital gothic style fosters. In the case of the Slender Man, the creature quickly spread beyond the Something Awful forum to become a pervasive online presence and Creepypasta icon, his mythos perpetuated by amateur web series like 'Marble Hornets' (Joseph DeLage and Troy Wagner, 2009–14) and indie video games like freeware game *Slender: The Eight Pages* (Mark Hadley, 2012), which led to a commercial video game release, *Slender* (Blue Isle Studios, 2013). Thus, the Slender Man is characterised by a reciprocal relationship between vernacular, collaborative modes of cultural production and institutional media forms.

The narrative dynamics of the digital gothic thus accord with Russell Frank's suggestion that the 'folk' sector of cyberspace is 'a communication underground that runs parallel to and often comments on the "above-ground" communication of the mass media'.[13] Chess has aptly theorised the complex authorship processes at the heart of Creepypasta tales like the Slender Man as an 'open-sourcing' of the horror genre, as Slender Man is 'established, debugged, and negotiated through a complex set of generic yet evolving expectations'.[14] As Chess outlines, the Slender Man's formation accords with the cultural logic and poetics of open-source software, as users co-develop and share the generic and narrative 'code' that underpins the bogeyman, drawing from the established generic templates of 'above-ground' horror and Gothic fiction to build and modify his semantic and syntactic formula. Significantly, this creative process displaces concerns with intellectual property rights, visible and appropriate credit for creative work and, ultimately, the anchoring of narratives and fictional creations to specific authors and their associated material, cultural and spatio-temporal contexts. In fact, Creepypasta narratives depend for their functioning upon a dismissal of such traditional definitions of authorship in order to cast an eerie shadow over the lines between producer and consumer, authors and their creations.

Contributing to this subversive textual and epistemic play is the key role performed by digital platforms in shaping Creepypasta stories. As Heather Duncan explains, internet horror stories often 'reveal a heightened awareness of the extent to which nonhuman agents are a part of our individual and collective identities', and by extension, are central to our stories and popular culture.[15] As Duncan suggests, 'amateur digital narratives composed in interactive spaces like Reddit are especially fertile ground for sprawling stories that quite literally take on a life of their own', an independent agency in part enacted by the technical affordances of the online spaces themselves.[16] For instance, on message board site 4Chan – one of the original homes of Creepypasta – many users opt for the default username 'Anonymous' due to the distinctively ephemeral qualities of the website, which has no archive and from which posts with little activity are promptly deleted. As Asaf Nissenbaum and Limor Shifman explain in their examination of meme creation on the site,

> [w]hat makes the site different from most other forum websites is the absence of marked identity and history. *There is no way to create a stable identity on 4chan* . . . 4chan's discourse exists only in the present – there is no record of people or the past, just the current conversation.[17]

Similarly, Reddit – another of the primary platforms for digital gothic prosumption – is structured by ranking algorithms that display certain content on the site's 'front page' and prioritise particular comments and threads. These ranking algorithms in turn shape the informal mechanics of distribution that underpin digital gothic content, because certain stories spark discussion, while others may receive few comments, if any.

The development of these stories is thus tied to the platforms that structure processes of creativity and collaboration, not just the activity of their human authors. These digital tools – forums, discussion boards, wikis – can operate as 'black boxes', their internal workings to some extent veiled from users, even as their infrastructure operates in tandem with users' creative processes. The numerous forums discussing Reddit's ever-changing 'front-page' algorithm illuminate the anxieties this dialectic can provoke.[18] As Duncan suggests, 'black boxes are uncomfortable reminders of the instability inherent in the networks of objects and systems that we operate inside of without necessarily being conscious of them, until something goes wrong'.[19] Built into stories like those that surround the Slender Man is this very threat that the tools used to craft these tales have the potential to defy or evade the prosumer's mastery, as the bogeyman is the product of an alliance between (generally anonymous) human authors and artificially intelligent digital platforms.

'Candle Cove'

As some of the most successful and famous digital gothic stories are remade in mainstream entertainment, the tensions between digital vernacular cultural production and official modes of entertainment creation and distribution are illuminated. The story 'Candle Cove' provides an intriguing example of such frictions, for it was one of the first Creepypasta tales to be remade for television, as season one of Creepypasta-themed SyFy anthology series *Channel Zero*. 'Candle Cove' is one of the most popular types of Creepypasta stories, those about lost episodes of television programmes, usually popular children's television programmes, in a haunting corruption of childhood nostalgia. 'Candle Cove' is a rare instance in which the author of the original version of the story, Kris Straub, is now relatively widely known: the story was originally published in 2009 on his own website *IchorFalls* under a Creative Commons license. Such intellectual property considerations are rare in digital gothic storytelling. Indeed, as will be outlined later in this section, Straub's lack of anonymity was a key reason that 'Candle Cove' was selected to be the source material for the first season of *Channel Zero*.

The famous story is about an eponymous forgotten television show from the 1970s that may or may not have really existed: as is key to the construction of the hazy boundaries between reality/fiction and authenticity/artifice that underpin the digital gothic's form and function, the story rests on an ambiguity as to whether or not the television show it describes actually exists or is entirely a fiction invented for the purposes of the story. This ambiguity fuelled the viral and open-source nature of the story, as it successfully invited further vernacular creativity across a wide range of digital spaces as netizens contemplated whether or not the show 'Candle Cove' really existed;[20] shared their apparent 'memories' of the programme;[21] and created – or, according to some examples, simply 'found' and uploaded – videos on YouTube of the television programme.[22] Like the Slender Man, the mysterious television show from the story took on a life of its own that exceeded Straub's story, propelled by rhizomatic digital networks in a way that harnessed the deepest fears expressed by the original story. In essence, the premise is that online material can facilitate a disorienting collapse of the boundaries between the individual, the collective and the technologies that draw them together. Rather than being positioned as an official adaptation of a vernacular digital gothic tale, the televisual reconstruction of 'Candle Cove' purports to take part in this uncanny participatory dynamic, as series creator and executive producer Nick Antosca has pointed out in interviews: rather than adapting the stories to create 'canonical versions of the Creepypastas', the creators think of each season of *Channel Zero* as 'like a nightmare that you have after reading the story it's based on. It's our fan fiction of the original Creepypasta.'[23] This rhetoric suggests that the show's creators aim to engage in the uncanny prosumption that underpins the digital gothic.

Straub's original publication of 'Candle Cove' was presented on a discussion board called the 'NetNostalgia.Forum'. This mode of delivery parallels the television show 'Candle Cove' at the centre of Straub's tale, fostering uncertainty as to whether such a forum actually once existed or is a fictional creation of the author (many similarly named web forums, such as 'netnostalgia.board-directory.net', do exist). The story unfolds as a conversation between various forum users, beginning with a post by user Skyshale033, who invites other forum users to help them firm up their recollection of the hazily remembered television show from their childhood:

> Does anyone remember this kid's show? It was called Candle Cove and I must have been 6 or 7. I never found reference to it anywhere so I think it was on a local station around 1971 or 1972. I lived in Ironton at the time. I don't remember which station, but I do remember it was on at a weird time, like 4:00 PM.

Other forum users join in the conversation, gradually filling in details and adding to Skyshale033's vague memories of the show. While initially the tone of the conversation is warm and nostalgic, the discussion becomes increasingly uncanny as the sinister nature of the programme surfaces. The users describe a cheaply made pirate show, constituting of crude puppets and sets, which featured a menacing, skeletal character called 'Jaw Bone' and another ominous figure called 'The Skin Taker', who threatened to take the skin of other characters. The show also featured inexplicable, elongated moments of despair, as is initially described by original poster Skyshale033 as a 'bad dream' about the show that the other posters point out must actually be a memory based in real experience, since they too share it:

The opening jingle ended, the show faded in from black, and all the characters were there, but the camera was just cutting to each of their faces, and they were just screaming, and the puppets and marionettes were flailing spastically, and just all screaming, screaming. The girl was just moaning and crying like she had been through hours of this.

When considered in relation to the themes of 'Candle Cove', Antosca's comments about the television adaptation's aim to function like 'a nightmare that you have after reading the story' gesture to *Channel Zero*'s intended continuation of the digital story's murkily defined interplay between fictional cultural production and genuine memories and experiences. Antosca's rationale also highlights how the show seeks to extend the story's eerie obfuscation of the distinctions between individuals and an amorphously defined collective of forum posters. In Straub's tale, the eerily indeterminate boundaries between childhood nightmares and shared, lived experience position the dynamics of vernacular digital communication and collaborative, open-source storytelling as a source of uncanny dread. This fictional forum conversation facilitates porous boundaries between the singular identities of the various users, and renders uncertain their status as human agents with a firm grasp on their realities and memories.

Emphasising this anxiety, the story ends with a post by 'mike_painter' that reveals that the show may have only existed in the minds of the forum posters. He recounts a recent conversation with his mother in which she mentioned that when watching 'Candle Cove', he 'would tune the tv to static and just watch dead air for 30 minutes'. Thus, just as the status of the story itself would be unclear to the many readers who first encounter it on Reddit, YouTube or Yahoo Answers, the status of the television show within the story is unclear both to the 'characters' (or forum posters) themselves, and to the reader. Beneath this broader question about the story's position along the continuum from fiction to genuine web forum exchange, within its diegetic world the story impels the reader to question whether or not 'Candle Cove' was simply a product of false or corroded memories created by anonymous corroboration on a digital forum; a shared delusion rooted somehow in the forum users' pasts; or the product of vague but malevolent technological agency, either via the 'NetNostalgia' platform or haunted 1970s television sets (or some strange combination of both). 'Candle Cove' is thus a quintessential example of the digital gothic, as it is designed to function somewhat as a 'black box': the motives underlying its authorial and contextual mechanics hidden, propelling its uncanny power.

While 'Candle Cove' thus exhibits the key characteristics of the digital gothic, by contrast to the anonymous authorial dynamics of most digital gothic stories, the author of the original version of the story, Kris Straub, is relatively widely known, and, as highlighted above, Straub published the story under a Creative Commons license.[24] Indeed, the fact that this particular tale has a clearly identifiable author and original source played a role in the creators' decision to adapt it for season one, as it avoids the legal issues likely to emerge if a story was adapted without the author's permission. As the show's creator Nick Antosca explains, 'in the case of *Candle Cove* and *No-End House* [the story on which season two is based], those authors are actually pretty well known'.[25]

Yet the legal negotiations central to the creative processes of screen entertainment industries conflict with the folkloric dynamic of the digital gothic, which has resulted in ongoing challenges for the show's creative team. Antosca explains that the authors of the tales chosen for adaptation in seasons three and four – Kerry Hammond's 'Search and Rescue Woods' and Charlotte Bywater's 'Hidden Door' – were much 'harder to track down' because their stories were published anonymously (and expanded upon collaboratively – a point that Antosca does not raise), necessitating a lengthy process of internet research.[26] At this stage, the creative team, in Antosca's words, 'haven't tried too hard to adapt stories where we can't identify the author' as a result of uncertainties about how to handle the legal processes. Antosca's comments imply that a single, definitive author and source can be identified for all Creepypasta tales, repudiating the viral circulations of vernacular creativity that underpin the digital gothic. Yet all of the stories adapted for the series, even those like 'Candle Cove' that were not originally published anonymously or pseudonymously, became popular tales of digital gothic culture via processes of informal dissemination and expansion that parallel the birth of the Slender Man. In the case of 'Candle Cove', soon after appearing on Straub's website, the tale was quickly copied, pasted and modified across numerous websites including 4chan, Reddit, IGN and Horror. com, often without reference to the original source and author. 'Candle Cove' was thus developed and established according to the same opensource, folkloric dynamics as the Slender Man.

The digital gothic and the official horror genre

All of these unique properties of the digital gothic mode result in particularly subversive and complex relationships with the 'above-ground' horror genre, to return to Frank's term for the industrial channels of mainstream, profit-driven cultural production.[27] In particular, the aesthetics and formal conventions of mainstream adaptations of sprawling digital gothic tales expose the contortions that emerge with exchanges between vernacular digital and institutional modes of cultural production. For instance, SyFy's television retelling of the story 'Candle Cove' adheres to some of the standard strictures of horror and Gothic screen texts, yet it is also meandering, fractured and loose, suggesting the creative team's struggle to weld the polyphonic amorphousness of the digital gothic into a teleological narrative that unfolds coherently over six episodes.

Emphasising collisions between vernacular creative dynamics and institutional modes of production and distribution, the first season of *Channel Zero* is preoccupied with determining a human origin to the mysterious TV show 'Candle Cove', and positions this quest as central to the show's narrative. The show follows protagonist Mike (a version of the original story's forum user 'mike_painter') as he travels back to his childhood home and (re-)encounters the television programme from his youth that was previously an eerie, decaying fragment of his childhood memories. Tied vaguely to a series of murders that occurred in the 1980s – including the death of Mike's own twin brother Eddy – the television programme continues to have a sinister influence over both Mike and his hometown. Through a focus on the origins and material roots of 'Candle Cove', *Channel Zero* is fixated with drawing firm epistemic boundaries around the Creepypasta story's mysterious television show, and ambiguously dwells upon whether 'Candle Cove' is borne of human, technological or spiritual agency.

After many red herrings in which props from the TV show – masks, puppets, costumes – are found in different characters' homes and environments around the town (suggesting that certain characters or groups were behind the sinister programme's production), the source of 'Candle Cove' is ultimately revealed in the final episode to be an ill-defined combination of human, technological and supernatural forces, in the form of Mike's long-dead twin, Eddy. Mike killed Eddy when they were children, after the twin murdered another child while seemingly under the supernatural influence of 'Candle Cove'. Ever since, Eddy – whose precise supernatural form remains unclear throughout the series – has been dwelling in an indistinct space accompanied by an analogue television, and projecting 'Candle Cove' onto the town's television screens and into the minds of the children. Thus, while *Channel Zero*'s narrative revolves around identifying the television show's origins and contexts, it also constantly defers this possibility. Just as Eddy himself remains a nebulously defined figure throughout the series, the nature and origins of 'Candle Cove' are never comprehensively clarified, in a symbolic expression of the impossibility of coherently tracing contexts, distribution channels and authors in the rhizomatic web of digital gothic production upon which *Channel Zero* is based.

This dialectic tension is augmented by the status of 'Candle Cove' as an analogue television programme, broadcast before the era of digital signals. As both Dominik Schrey and Thomas Elsaesser have pointed out, analogue media is culturally defined as oppositional to digital media because of the material, indexical origins of the images it projects, and also because of the tangible mechanical workings of analogue technologies. As Elsaesser suggests in relation to the digital image's challenge to traditional definitions of cinema, 'the digital image is not part of cinema or film history, and the reason seems to be an absence: the lack of "roots" and "texture", which is to say, materiality and indexicality'.[28] Accentuating the contrast between digitality and the indexical and mechanically rooted filming and recording processes of analogue television, digital gothic storytelling is underpinned by almost infinitely replicable and modifiable narrative, aesthetic and binary codes. In addition, as described above the digital gothic is subject to the 'black box' dynamics of the participatory platforms on which it appears, which can displace or conceal the material and human origins of these stories. Throughout *Channel Zero*, the television show 'Candle Cove' seems to rest in an unsettled slip-zone between these two visual media traditions, suggesting cultural tensions related to the different relationships between authorship, technology and creative production that they each represent.

Even though its source and origins are immaterial, the analogue, tangible nature of 'Candle Cove' is emphasised throughout *Channel Zero* by its excessively tactile style. 'Candle Cove' features rough-hewn, crudely made puppets filmed interacting in front of clunky, homemade sets and props, seemingly accentuating the indexical nature and human-derived origins of the images. The tension between analogue and vernacular digital modes of authorship is also symbolically gestured to by repeated references to the book *Treasure Island* (Robert Louis Stevenson, 1883) throughout the series – for instance, Mike is seen reading the book to his daughter, Lily. The preoccupation with both analogue television and the classic book suggests an anxiety about the impending obsolescence of these analogue narrative modes in the face of ephemeral digital creativity: as Schrey suggests, in the digital age, 'even media formats with a strong tradition like the book (as a material object) or cinema (as a specific "dispositif") are now perceived to be threatened by obsolescence and seem to be outpaced by their increasingly ephemeral digital successors'.[29]

Throughout *Channel Zero*, the dialectic tension between the seemingly material origins of 'Candle Cove' and its supernatural ephemerality are symbolically aligned with anxieties about human agency and control, fears primarily expressed through a recurring puppet motif. This motif is particularly emphasised during a set piece in the show's penultimate episode, in which protagonist Mike wakes up in an abandoned water park, his arms strung up and tied to an unseen apparatus like a puppet. The antagonist behind Mike's mistreatment remains ambiguous, just as it remains impossible to pinpoint a single 'puppet-master' orchestrating the sprawling fictional world of digital gothic narratives like 'Candle Cove' and the eponymous TV show at the centre of the story. While *Treasure Island* is a story with a well-known author and exists as a material object that Mike can touch, hold and read to his daughter in a linear fashion, the story within which Mike himself exists – constructed to play out like a 'nightmare' sparked by a polyphonic digital gothic story – operates more according to what Lev Manovich has described as a 'database logic', expanding, layering and spreading out in a multidirectional manner.[30] On a metatextual level, *Channel Zero* constantly struggles to incorporate this database logic into its teleological, linear structure, which sustains the show's vague Gothic tensions.

Showcasing the mechanics of database narrative logic, throughout *Channel Zero* numerous different characters and devices become 'channels' for the perpetuation of 'Candle Cove': the eerie characters of 'Candle Cove' appear on television sets and computer screens all over town, and are also manifested by children wearing masks and costumes, adornments that position these characters not as human individuals but as mere agents of the influence and propagation of 'Candle Cove'. The show's central reoccurring monster embodies the horrors of the show's uncontrollable, uncontainable spread. This grotesque being is covered head-to-toe with teeth that shoot off haphazardly in many different directions, concealing the child's face, physical form, and thus identity. As the show progresses, Mike himself starts to grow extra teeth, which sprout out at odd angles from his gums and which he is forced to pull out in front of a mirror. The endless proliferation of teeth – along with the vaguely defined flock of masked and costumed characters who work with the television and computer screens to propagate the 'Candle Cove' mythos – function as visual metonyms for the collective, rhizomatic narrative mechanics of the digital gothic.

Indeed, most of the central monsters in *Channel Zero* are depicted as frightening for their symbolic association with database logic, being seemingly interchangeable and constantly modifiable. In the climactic episode, Mike encounters a being who condenses all of the different monsters who have haunted the series. At first the creature looks to be The Skin Taker – a patchwork constellation of hessian and human skin-like material – which stands at the end of a hallway and jitters as if afflicted by a glitch. As Duncan points out, 'glitches' often appear uncanny because they render visible the previously invisible, black-box functioning of digital code, impelling our sudden awareness of code's agency over and involvement in our interaction with media devices and platforms.[31] After glitching in an uncanny manner, The Skin Taker transforms into an even more shapeless figure which nevertheless seems to have a human, material core: embodying the show's overarching symbolic dialectic of materiality/authorship and digitality/black-box ephemerality, the figure seems to be made up only of a sack-like outer layer with no physical core, yet materiality is eerily suggested when the figure hits its head repeatedly (and inexplicably) against the wall, resulting in a crushing sound that evokes visceral physical contact. The creature then runs towards Mike, before melting into the ether before his eyes, only to reappear at the end of the hallway in a different form, a hybrid of a scarecrow and a pirate with its head on fire. Having changed forms once again, the figure walks slowly down the hall, its head burning into embers, smoke and bits of flesh, finally dissipating into a formless smoke cloud before Mike's eyes. Like the Slender Man, the form and identity of this monstrous being is impossible to grasp, a subversively violent ephemerality and erratic modifiability that is key to the creature's horrors.

As well as invoking the digital uncanniness of glitch, this creature suggests the unnerving visual effect of 'morphing', in which an image mutates into the image of something else through digital editing, animation or error. As Laura Marks explains, the aesthetic of morphing visualises the unnerving potentials of database logics and aesthetics:

> The morph effaces mortality and replaces it with the endless recuperability of the database [. . .] The uncanniness of morphing speaks to a fear of unnatural, transformable bodies [. . .] Untroubled about its naturalness (is it indexical or simulacral?), digital video refuses the doomed search for origins . . . What digital video loses in indexicality, it gains in flexibility.[32]

Later, Mike encounters this monster once again in Eddy's mysterious 'room'. Eddy tells Mike the creature's name is Jaw Bone, before immediately changing his mind and saying that the beast's name is actually The Skin Taker: the monster is seemingly representative of a number of the hazily defined tormentors of 'Candle Cove'. At this moment, the creature morphs yet again, pulling his face open to briefly reveal the aforementioned Tooth Monster dwelling inside. Following the dynamics of open-source creative production, this character has no stable identity, and, like the internet story from which he emerged, is endlessly modifiable and replicable, exhibiting the uncanny poetics of database logic.

Conclusion

The vernacular, collaborative and open-source creative circuits of the digital gothic – which collapse the distinctions between producers and consumers, technological and human agents, and reality and fiction – sit in dialectic tension with the entertainment industry's institutional creative practices. The digital gothic's subversively mysterious approach to authorship, which is symbolically positioned as a key source of uncanny dread throughout the first season of *Channel Zero*, troubles institutional channels of cultural production and distribution, as is evidenced by the creative team's struggle to select and settle agreements around digital gothic content. In some ways, the informal, prosumption-driven flows of the digital gothic operate as a Gothic antithesis to the corporate, profit-driven processes of mainstream entertainment, which is a particularly significant and perhaps cathartic distinction in an era in which the 'above-ground' entertainment industries tend to prioritise expansive franchises that are meticulously orchestrated by large teams, and undergirded by a complex array of intellectual property agreements. Digital gothic tales, often gleefully, work through cultural anxieties about how digital modes of communication and creative production challenge dominant constructs of authorship in a cultural moment in which the corporate management of creativity is highly visible. As the digital gothic increasingly influences the themes, aesthetics and narrative structures of mainstream horror and Gothic media, perhaps open-source approaches to genre storytelling will further unsettle the producer/consumer, professional/amateur dichotomy.

Notes

1. See my article on the aesthetics of the 'digital gothic', in particular the dialectic between nostalgia and uncanny dread for obsolete analogue media: J. Balanzategui, 'Creepypasta, "Candle Cove", and the Digital Aesthetics of Uncanny Analogue Nostalgia', *The Journal of Visual Culture*, 18/2 (2019), 187–208.
2. Balanzategui, 'Creepypasta'.
3. For more on this moral panic and the Slender Man case, see J. Balanzategui and N. Later, '"Dark and Wicked Things": The Slenderman, Tween Girlhood and Deadly Liminalities', in M. Bohlmann (ed.), *Misfit Children: An Inquiry into Childhood Belongings* (Lanham, MD: Lexington Books, 2016), pp. 71–88.
4. Trevor Blank, *Folklore and the Internet: Vernacular Expression in a Digital World* (Logan, UT: Utah State University Press, 2009), pp. 2–4.
5. J. Burgess, 'Hearing Ordinary Voices: Cultural Studies, Vernacular Creativity and Digital Storytelling', *Continuum: Journal of Media & Cultural Studies*, 20/2 (2006), 205.
6. Burgess, 'Hearing Ordinary Voices', 206.
7. A. Peck, 'Tall, Dark and Loathsome: The Emergence of a Legend Cycle in the Digital Age', *The Journal of American Folklore*, 128/509 (2015), 339.
8. L. Shifman, 'The Cultural Logic of Photo-Based Meme Genres', *The Journal of Visual Culture*, 13/3 (2014), 342.
9. S. Chess, 'Open-Sourcing Horror: The Slender Man, *Marble Hornets*, and Genre Negotiations', *Information, Communication & Society*, 15/3 (2012), 389.
10. G. Ritzer and N. Jurgenson, 'Production, Consumption, Prosumption: The nature of capitalism in the age of the digital "prosumer"', *Journal of Consumer Culture*, 10/1 (2010), 13–36.
11. This element of his mythos was solidified in particular by the influential YouTube series 'Marble Hornets' (Joseph DeLage and Troy Wagner, 2009–14).

12. Chess, 'Open-Sourcing Horror', 389.
13. R. Frank, 'Caveat Lector: Fake News as Folklore', *The Journal of American Folklore*, 128/509 (2015), 316.
14. Chess, 'Open-Sourcing Horror', 375.
15. H. Duncan, 'Human "ish": Voices from Beyond the Grave in Contemporary Narratives', *English Language Overseas Perspectives and Enquiries*, 15/1 (2018), 85.
16. Duncan, 'Human "ish": Voices from Beyond the Grave', 91.
17. A. Nissenbaum and L. Shifman, 'Internet memes as contested cultural capital: The case of 4chan's /b/ board', *New Media & Society*, 19/4 (2017), 487; emphasis in the original.
18. See, for instance, 'r/TheoryOfReddit', *Reddit* (2010), https://www.reddit.com/r/TheoryOfReddit/comments/88disb/did_reddit_change_the_front_page_algorithm_again/ (accessed 29 August 2019).
19. Duncan, 'Human "ish": Voices from Beyond the Grave', 90.
20. See, for instance, the thread 'Candle Cove – does it exist?', *TV Forum* (2009), https://tvforum.uk/tvhome/candle-cove-does-exist-30175/ (accessed 29 August 2019).
21. See, for example, TheGothicLibrarian's reading of such a recounting on YouTube, https://www.youtube.com/watch?v=ga33xJ09Nm0 (accessed 29 August 2019).
22. See the video 'Creepypasta Archives: Candle Cove Screaming Episode', https://www.youtube.com/watch?v=qtAxK50boUw (accessed 29 August 2019).
23. Nick Antosca quoted in M. Rougeau, 'Horror Anthology *Channel Zero* and the Challenge of Hunting Down Creepypastas', *GameSpot* (20 September 2017), https://www.gamespot.com/articles/horror-anthology-channel-zero-and-the-challenge-of/1100-6453480/ (accessed 29 August 2019).
24. See K. Straub, 'Candle Cove', *IchorFalls* (2009), http://ichorfalls.chainsawsuit.com/ (accessed 29 August 2019).
25. Antosca quoted in Rougeau, 'Horror Anthology *Channel Zero*'.
26. Antosca quoted in Rougeau, 'Horror Anthology *Channel Zero*'.
27. Frank, 'Caveat Lector', 316.
28. T. Elsaesser, 'Truth or Dare: Reality Checks on Indexicality, or the Future of Illusionism', in A. Koivunnen and A. Soderbergh Widding (eds), *Cinema Studies into Visual Theory?* (Turku, Finland: D-Vision, 1998), p. 31.
29. D. Schrey, 'Analogue Nostalgia and the Aesthetics of Digital Remediation', in K. Niemeyer (ed.), *Media and Nostalgia: Yearning for the Past, Present and Future* (Basingstoke: Palgrave Macmillan, 2014), p. 27.

30. L. Manovich, 'Database as Symbolic Form', *Convergence: The International Journal of Research into New Media Technologies*, 5/2 (1999), 80–99.
31. Duncan, 'Human "ish": Voices from Beyond the Grave', 90.
32. Laura Marks, *The Skin of the Film: Intercultural Cinema, Embodiment and the Senses* (Durham, NC: Duke University Press, 2000), pp. 151–2.

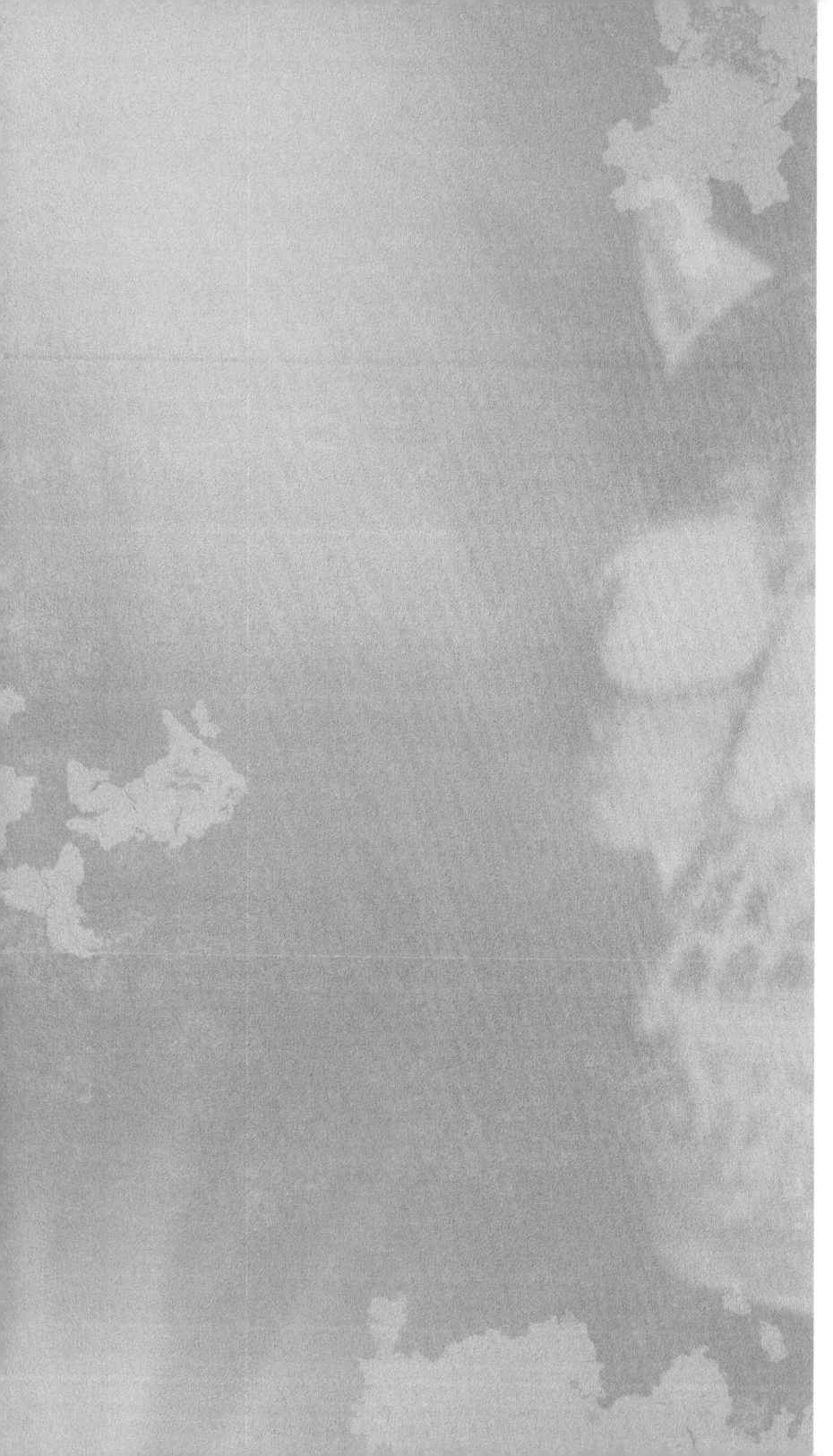

8

Nazi Horror, Reanimated

Rethinking Subgenres and Cycles

Abigail Whittall

NAZI HORROR HAS A LONG cinematic history. While an early example of the subgenre emerged during the Second World War in *Revenge of the Zombies* (Steve Sekely, 1943) – a film featuring a Nazi scientist raising the dead for the Third Reich – no further Nazi horror films were released for some decades.[1] Nazi horror re-emerged in films such as *The Frozen Dead* (Herbert J. Leder, 1966), *Shock Waves* (Ken Wiederhorn, 1977), *Death Ship* (Alvin Raeckoff, 1980), *Zombie Lake* (Jean Rollin, 1981) and *The Keep* (Michael Mann, 1983). In the same period, numerous Nazisploitation films were released depicting torture in concentration camps, culminating in the 1970s with examples such as *Ilsa, She Wolf of the SS* (Don Edmonds, 1975). David A. Frank and Caroline Joan Picart have also identified variants of the Nazi monster in what they refer to as 'The Hollywood Nazi-as-Monster Flick', citing texts such as *Apt Pupil* (Bryan Singer, 1998).[2]

As this chapter will outline, Nazi horror has seen its largest resurgence in the twenty-first century, with a slew of films reigniting the subgenre, including *Hellboy* (Guillermo del Toro, 2004), *Frostbite* (Anders Banke, 2006), *Unholy* (Daryl Goldberg, 2007), *Outpost* (Steve Barker, 2008),

Dead Snow (Tommy Wirkola, 2009), *The Devil's Rock* (Paul Campion, 2011), *Ratline* (Eric Stanze, 2011), *Iron Wolf* (David Bruckner, 2013), *Frankenstein's Army* (Richard Raaphorst, 2013) and, more recently, *Overlord* (Julius Avery, 2018). While this chapter will not have the space to consider the popularity of the mode across other media (for example, the increase of Nazi zombies in video games following the reception of *Call of Duty: World at War*'s side-game mode), it is evident that Nazi horror is prolific and diverse and as such poses interesting questions about established generic labels. This chapter will help to illustrate when Nazi horror films have been reanimated and in what monstrous guises. It will also explore reasons why such antagonists have been resurrected again and again, in order to reflect our deepest, darkest fears throughout history, and in contemporary society.

Situating Nazi horror

Nazi horror illustrates the problem of determining generic boundaries, as it blurs horror with other genres including science fiction, fantasy, war, thriller and even comedy. Peripheral genre films featuring 'horrific' Nazis, such as *Raiders of the Lost Ark* (Steven Spielberg, 1981), *Hellboy* or, more recently, *Captain America: The First Avenger* (Joe Johnston, 2011), further complicate generic distinctions. Moreover, Nazi horror draws attention to the relationship between horror and the war genre; as Jeanine Basinger argues, the two share many themes as 'each contains a world gone mad with violence'.[3] Defining such a varied corpus of films has consequences, as the labels we apply have the potential to include certain films and omit others, impacting our understanding of those films and their relationship to other texts. I should acknowledge here that labels can be defined by, and for, different groups of people: film-makers and audiences use and understand generic labels in different ways, as do scholars. Though a more radical approach might be to do away with such labels altogether, these terms are pervasive and determine patterns of consumption and reception, and can therefore be usefully interrogated and employed. In this chapter, I will make the case for Nazi horror as a subgenre, one that has often been underestimated and critically neglected due to the use of generic labels, an exploration of which can reveal Nazi horror's cultural significance and the reasons behind its longevity.

It is important, then, to situate Nazi horror in relation to the wider genre. For Brigid Cherry, subgenres divide the horror genre 'along lines of plots, subject matter or types of monster', a focus that is valuable for identifying horror's recurring themes and iconography.[4] Cherry's definition is significant for it indicates that monsters are key identifiers not just of the horror genre, but of its subgenres. Similarly, both Noël Carroll and Bruce Kawin base their entire understanding of horror around taxonomies of the monster.[5] As Kawin suggests, monsters lend themselves to immediate categorisations, and he identifies three horror subgenres – monsters, supernatural monsters and humans – within which more specific creatures constitute sub-subgenres. While this structure is useful for recognising that horror films can be grouped along different lines of specificity, Kawin's precise use of the term 'subgenre' is contestable because his categorisations are at once too large and too restrictive. Nazi monsters are not considered in Kawin's work, nor would they neatly fit into the broad categories that he describes, with some titles at risk of occupying all three camps.[6] Problems can thus arise when scholarship organises horror according to such strict and broad categories, making Cherry's definition the more fitting for a study such as this.

This chapter identifies Nazi horror as a subgenre as opposed to a cycle. It is important to make this distinction, as these terms have been used interchangeably despite being inaccurate synonyms. For instance, Carroll identifies cycles as historical periods, referring to 'the Hollywood movie cycle of the thirties' and 'the horror cycle within which we find ourselves', suggesting that cycles are distinguished by their period and do not necessarily belong to the same subgenre.[7] Cherry, following Steve Neale's definition, identifies cycles as 'groups of films made within a specific and limited time-span, and founded, for the most part, on the characteristics of individual commercial successes'.[8] These definitions are similar in one respect, for in both instances the term 'cycle' refers to films from a specific period. In contrast to Carroll, though, Neale's definition suggests that cycles can be distinguished from subgenres according to specific characteristics; to this end, it is the more commonly used definition. Peter Hutchings places a similar emphasis on periodisation, writing that cycles 'exist in relation to particular times and particular places', grouping films according to both historical and geographical specificity.[9] Hutchings's use of the term has repercussions for how we understand films, as it focuses analysis on a key trope utilised in a particular period and national context, an issue for a mode that includes British (*Outpost*), Norwegian (*Dead Snow*), American

(*Blood Creek* (Joel Schumacher, 2009)), Swedish (*Frostbite*) and New Zealand (*The Devil's Rock*) productions.

Moreover, most definitions of cycles group films around specific economic contexts, often identifying the intent of a series of films to 'cash in' on a commercial success.[10] In relation to horror in particular, groups of films may be linked by their desire to convert low production budgets into high profits on release. As Mark Jancovich argues, even by the 1940s horror films were making greater profits than other contemporaneous genres due to their often low budgets, with a prime example being the unanticipated success of horror B-movies such as *Cat People* (Jacques Tourneur, 1942).[11] Such claims have been made for Nazi horror, as Marcus Stiglegger argues of the 1960s–1980s 'sadiconazista' films, to be followed by Julian Petley who writes that '*Shock Waves* spawned a brief Nazi zombie cycle'.[12] Here, focus on cycles places emphasis on a profitable urtext. Twenty-first-century Nazi horror films, however, range considerably in terms of their production context, from Hollywood blockbusters such as *Hellboy* and the recent *Overlord*, to independent productions and direct-to-DVD offerings like *Fantacide* (Shane Mather, 2007). Among these disparate films, there is no obvious urtext that initiated either low- or high-budget copies.

That Nazisploitation has been considered a cycle is significant. This choice of word is noteworthy due to, as Ernest Mathijs and Jamie Sexton argue, exploitation's dual meaning: first, 'a purely commercial manner of exploiting a property for as much money as possible'; secondly, exploiting 'taboo topics as a key appeal of the films'.[13] Nazisploitation, then, demonstrates how horror and exploitation cinema overlap in the form of commercially driven horror cycles. Yet, exploitation is a loaded concept that also demonstrates why the term 'cycle' poses potential dangers, for it may be used as a judgement on what is perceived to be a commercially (rather than artistically or sociopolitically) driven film. Indeed, Mathijs and Sexton warn of the 'constant shifting and sloppiness of "exploitation cinema" as a concept', noting that all commercial cinema is profit-aware and that even Hollywood will employ taboo themes 'if they prove popular'.[14] Exploitation is therefore a contestable and highly loaded categorisation that illustrates both content and commercial strategies. For Hutchings, cycles offer an 'intermediate' point of reference between individual films and the subgenres from which they hail.[15] While it is important not to lose sight of particular economic patterns, one should avoid situating films only along economic lines – for example, failing to account for twenty-first-century Nazi horror films' relation to their twentieth-century progenitors.

Therefore, to understand Nazi horror films fully, one should consider the generic (and subgeneric) boundaries within which they operate.

Nazi zombies

Considering Nazi horror as a subgenre encourages recognition of its established history and its relationship to other subgenres and cycles. To think about these issues in more detail, we may consider the Nazi zombie, a monster with a particularly rich history. The rise and fall of the zombie film has been discussed by Kyle William Bishop, who credits films such as *White Zombie* (Victor Halperin, 1932), *Night of the Living Dead* (George A. Romero, 1968) and *28 Days Later* (Danny Boyle, 2002) for inspiring new cycles for the subgenre.[16] Cynthia J. Miller notes that the Nazi zombie has risen adjacently to the primary subgenre, with *King of the Zombies* (Jean Yarbrough, 1941) drawing on Haitian voodoo, *Shock Waves* employing slow-moving, Romero-esque zombies and *Horrors of War* (Peter John Ross and John Whitney, 2006) corresponding with 'a new era' of fast-moving zombies.[17] While Nazi zombies are the most prolific variation of the Nazi horror subgenre, *Horrors of War* was the twenty-first century's initial Nazi zombie film, yet it was not especially successful and could be situated as a product of the *28 Days Later* cycle rather than its own Nazi-oriented urtext.

The connection between twenty-first-century Nazi zombies and the *28 Days Later* zombie cycle is significant. Bishop has connected the latter to cultural anxieties, arguing that the zombie films that follow 9/11 have tended 'to emphasise certain end-of-the-world metaphors, including infectious disease, biological warfare, euthanasia, terrorism and even rampant immigration'.[18] This approach acknowledges the ways in which film interacts with pertinent sociopolitical contexts. Indeed, Nazi threats on screen can be considered in light of societal fears of the rise of far-right populism which has coincided with a tumultuous political landscape in several Western countries in recent years. As such, the Nazi zombie can be considered an expression of the resulting anxieties that have been building in the twenty-first century, offering an allegorical monster that signifies an undying fascist threat.

The extent to which Nazi horror can be considered a politically meaningful subgenre has been subject to debate: Petley argues that 'it would be unwise to look to such films for political or ideological analysis'.[19] This is especially the case for the Nazi zombie, as Miller suggests that the Nazi zombie is 'the embodiment of parody itself. . . . which, by its very existence, mocks its own origins', while Ben Kooyman views the symbolic use of Nazi zombies in *Dead Snow* as 'self-defeating' due to it 'wrongly perpetuating that Nazism, like zombiedom, is an easily containable, inconsequential, and routinely defeatable threat'.[20] These arguments suggest that Nazi zombies largely do not provide insights into the cultures from which they emerge, yet Sven Jüngerkes and Christiane Wienand have understood the zombies of *Dead Snow* to be 'memory fragments, vehicles or images of repression', while the protagonists represent a nation who 'only recently . . . developed an increasing discourse about their collective Nazi past'.[21] This is a persuasive account of the underlying, and culturally specific, meaning that Nazi zombies can convey in the twenty-first century.[22]

Not only would I contest the argument that the Nazi zombie's hybridisation is purely parodic, but I would argue that its hybridity actually constitutes an exception to the traditional zombie subgenre in meaningful ways. In *Dead Snow*, Nazi colonel Herzog returns from the dead to lead his soldiers in a mission to reclaim their gold. Bishop notes that 'the foes are more like *draugar*, animated corpses that protect burial sites and treasure'.[23] Elsewhere, the Nazi monsters of *Frankenstein's Army* are better described as 'zombots' than zombies. Synthesising soldier and machine, these creatures obey their creator, an errant Nazi descendant of Frankenstein. These twenty-first-century Nazi *draugar* and zombots, therefore, appear to be informed by the wider zombie subgenre while also diverging from it with instincts that surpass a simple hunger for human flesh.[24]

Moreover, these particular Nazi zombies do not desire flesh at all, and though the *draugar* of *Dead Snow* use their teeth, they continue to use their army-issued weapons. So, too, do the zombies of the *Outpost* series, which Bishop notes are 'powerful revenants with supernatural abilities (e.g., ghost-like teleportation) that torture and murder their human victims, usually with bayonets'.[25] The effect of this hybridity is that the monsters of *Outpost* are zombie-like in appearance, yet not mindless in the way that zombies often are. Led by Brigadeführer Götz, the equivalent of Herzog in *Dead Snow*, these Nazi zombies defy Jamie Russell's observation that 'there are no aristocrats, blue bloods or celebrities among zombies', as they both retain their ranks in the afterlife.[26] Moreover, these films imply that their wartime behaviour is the reason for their undead monstrousness, that in their reanimation they become doubly horrific. This is reinforced in *Outpost: Rise of the Spetsnaz* (Kieran Parker, 2013) when villain Colonel Strasser sends in 'the child killer', signifying a correlative indicating the more heinous the Nazi, the more effective the zombie. Although Russell notes the typical zombie 'returns to "life" without regaining any of its former personality', the Nazi zombies by contrast retain their characteristics, providing a fear of the former person as well as the fear of the supernatural process of revival.[27]

Such traits suggest that the Nazi zombie offers the 'ultimate' horror threat and that this is one reason for its cinematic longevity. Indeed, the mercenaries of the first *Outpost* film are brought together from various countries and conflicts, against which the Nazi zombie poses the most significant global danger. Yet, the portrayal of the mercenaries is a critical one, suggesting that legacies of violence belong to all nations. The men reflect on their past actions, with French Foreign Legionnaire Jordan concerned that those he killed will haunt him in the afterlife, while the Belgian peacekeeper Cotter has no time for religion, stating that 'we gave up that right when we started killing men who believe in things for money'.

The Russian protagonists of the third *Outpost* film are similarly violent characters: in the opening sequence, for instance, one soldier rips teeth from Nazi corpses to keep as trophies. This pattern of representation of violent Russians also features in *War of the Dead* (Marko Mäkilaakso, 2011). Helmed by a Finnish director, the film focuses on the period of the Second World War that found Russia advancing on Finland in order to gain land and defend Leningrad. From a Finnish perspective, Russia was an enemy, yet one that is distinct from the Nazi threat coming out of central Europe. While Russian soldier Kolya proves to be a hero in *War of the Dead*, Finnish Captain Niemi becomes the greater threat once he has been infected and turns against his own men, thus conveying the Nazi zombie as a uniting threat to all.[28] Both the *Outpost* series and *War of the Dead* utilise the Nazi zombie to at once bring nations together and tear them apart, a theme that (unconsciously, perhaps) comments on the shifting nature of war.

There are various reasons given for the revival of the Nazi zombie in the twenty-first century, but these do not always prove satisfying. That the Nazi has become a meaningless monster is an argument supported by Miller's interviews with directors of Nazi horror, suggesting that for film-makers 'Nazis are kitsch – Saturday matinee villains – archetypes'.[29] A similar yet subtly different explanation is that the Nazi zombie has been employed as 'shorthand' and (for Petley) rather than representing nothing represents 'everything that is vile and depraved', against which all other monsters pale in comparison.[30] Yet these explanations are undermined by the films' clear anti-war messages, characterised by persistent concerns about the blurring between human and monster, hero and villain. In this respect, the Nazi zombie is more complex than either the 'pantomime' or 'ultimate' villain explanation allows for. They borrow from zombie lore while exhibiting distinct characteristics, marking them out as a different monster to the zombie, and therefore part of a different subgenre, one that has been employed to literalise persistent fears regarding human cruelty and oppressive, fascist ideology.

Beyond zombies: Nazi werewolves, vampires and scientists

This chapter has clarified the importance of distinguishing between subgenres and cycles when considering Nazi horror films. However, further distinctions can be made to distinguish current Nazi zombies from other forms of Nazi monsters. Miller has implied this in her identification of a Nazi zombie subgenre, and yet that term risks overlooking the fact that Nazi zombie films operate as a sub-subgenre within a larger corpus of Nazi horror films. Observing them thusly – as variations on a common theme – will bring to light their relationship to other Nazi monsters. Miller alludes to werewolves in her analysis, arguing that like zombies they have 'brutal, arbitrary origins' that make them well suited to Nazi hybridisation. Given that there are both Nazi-created zombies and werewolves in *Horrors of War*, this might suggest that the two are deemed interchangeable in nature.[31] *Outpost: Rise of the Spetsnaz* notably also features a snarling zombie dragged around on a lead, while inside the Nazis' underground facility the protagonist comes across failed experiments locked behind doors, one of which is labelled 'wolf soldat' and from which ominous growls emanate. These examples demonstrate that the two bodies of films are not easy to unstitch from one another, with many slippages occurring between the various incarnations of the Nazi monster.

Such slippages between werewolves and zombies are evidence of the peculiar hybridity of the Nazi monster, while also implying a connection between the wolf and Nazi iconography. David J. Skal argues that this link stems from Hitler's fascination with the creature, illustrated in his insistence to name residences and the people around him after wolves, perhaps due to the wolf's currency as 'an ancient symbol, deeply linked to militarism and the battlefield, with special meanings in Norse and Teutonic mythology'.[32] Moreover, the popularity of *The Wolf Man* (George

Waggner, 1941) and its cultural legacy ensured that 'the wolf man's saga was the most constant and sustained monster myth of the war, beginning with the first year of America's direct involvement, and finishing up just in time for Hiroshima'.[33] The Nazi werewolf therefore deserves its own consideration, as it is at once thematically linked to the Nazi zombie and informed by its own distinct mythology and cinematic history. Yet, similar to Nazi zombies that respond to orders, the Nazi werewolf of *Iron Wolf* has been trained not to attack fellow Nazis and, as such, is utilised to further their fascist regime. Unlike the characteristically animalistic werewolf of horror lore, the Nazi werewolf is a unique creation that both conforms to, and subverts, the symbolism of the (were)wolf.

The vampire also adds another dimension to the Nazi villain. According to Miller's interviews with directors Steve Barker (the *Outpost* series) and Marko Mäkilaakso (*War of the Dead*), contemporary vampires are often portrayed as 'sexual beings, with personalities [that] suggest a more "elitist" quality', an element that would not necessarily offer up vampires as ideal Nazi monsters.[34] There is indeed some conflict in the relationship between Nazis and vampires as evident in *BloodRayne: The Third Reich* (Uwe Boll, 2011), though not in the way Miller suggests. In the film, a Nazi doctor comments that the vampire he has captured and vivisected could possibly have been ethnically Romani, yet despite this suggested impurity he is excited by the prospect of vampirism offering the Third Reich potential immortality. Conversely, *Frostbite* depicts a Nazi vampire who adopts the elitism of vampirism to amplify his Nazi ideology. He exclaims, 'When I'm done, our kind will rule over all of you, like the cattle you are!' This fascist plot to rule over the 'cattle' suggests that the vampire's genetic elitism is precisely what aligns it with Nazism, something Hutchings notes in his observation that 'the Nazi scientist vampire fits a certain generic template in his obsession with bloodlines and genetics'.[35] The vampire of *Frostbite* is also notable in that he changes form to a grey-skinned, deformed being that scuttles along walls and ceilings, an exception to the 'sexy' vampires of the contemporary subgenre. Therefore, it is clear that Nazi monsters transgress previously established archetypes of horror monsters, a matter which further exemplifies why we must move away from definitions based upon fixed characteristics and instead look for connections between subgenres and sub-subgenres.

As Hutchings's analysis of the Nazi vampire suggests, an understanding of Nazi horror as a hybridised subgenre is supported by its intersection with mad science, another horror subgenre with a long and complex history. Miller has noted the presence of a mad Nazi scientist in *Revenge of the Zombies*, and James J. Ward has observed how earlier Nazisploitation films of the 1960s and 1970s reveal a fear of technologically advanced Nazis.[36] That twenty-first-century Nazi zombies draw on cultural anxieties about improperly used science, old and new, is evident in the undead Nazis of *Outpost* that have been created using unified field theory, a pseudoscientific concept that distorts time and space so that the Nazi soldiers can live indefinitely. During an explanation of unified field theory, the characters reference the USS Eldridge and the Philadelphia experiment, a popular myth that an American-led experiment rendered the USS Eldridge invisible. This is significant for insinuating that both sides were pursuing potentially dangerous knowledge, thus invoking discussions over the ethics of scientific conquest through the ambiguous distinction between the Allies' 'good' and the Nazis' 'bad' uses of science. As Ward argues, 'the Nazis in these films remain a threat because the experiments they undertook seem to require continual vigilance to ensure that others don't attempt them'.[37] This fear is reinforced by the open endings employed by such Nazi horror films, including *Outpost: Black Sun* (Steve Barker, 2012), which concludes with an American scientist pursuing unified field theory technology, while *Frankenstein's Army* concludes with the Russians in possession of Frankenstein's head (and, presumably, knowledge).

Frankenstein's Army, a film which references Mary Shelley's urtext in its title, epitomises the 'mad Nazi science' sub-subgenre, utilising tropes of the Nazi horror subgenre while expressing myriad anxieties about abuses of technology. The invocation of Shelley's 1818 text, *Frankenstein*, suggests that fears of genetic engineering and the post-human have a significantly longer history. The hybrid nature of the zombots – created from corpses that have been combined with turbines representing developments in airborne weaponry, while naval mines and old-fashioned diving suits evoke the war at sea – is symbolic of the mounting arms race throughout the Second World War. Yet, there is also relevance to the twenty-first century. Daniel Dinello notes that technologies combining cameras and mechanical limbs with the human body are currently underway, and rather than being utopic, 'posthuman technologies – according to the requirements of war and profit – will have profoundly disturbing, perhaps revolutionary effects on our world'.[38] Moreover, *Frankenstein's Army* mostly takes place in a vast underground space resembling a factory. There, body parts are wheeled around in containers and dumped down chutes like discarded scraps of metal, with the zombots doubling as both killers and workers as they labour on the assembly line. This imagery recalls *Outpost: Black Sun*, which includes a Nazi facility working on an industrial scale. Arguably, such imagery offers the darkest subtext of these films, in that these spaces at the intersection of the Nazi, zombie and mad science horror subgenres give rise to memories of the Holocaust.

Nazisploitation: then and now

One of the most complicated relationships to be traced between twenty-first-century Nazi horror and previous cycles of Nazisploitation is their engagement with the Holocaust. Where the 'sadiconazista' Nazisploitation films, including *Ilsa, She Wolf of the SS*, centred around explicit depictions of the concentration camps, such transparent references to the Holocaust or anti-Semitism are rare in contemporary Nazi horror films. That is not to say that implicit references to the Holocaust are absent in the Nazi horror subgenre, as crimes are echoed in the images of piles of burnt bodies in *Frankenstein's Army* or the heaps of white naked bodies in *Outpost*. In the latter film, the Eastern European setting also evokes memories of the Bosnian war that collide with the more prominent Second World War association, perhaps creating the suggestion that acts of genocide radiate beyond a singular time or place. In this respect, it is significant that the examples of Nazi zombies given here are not perpetrator narratives (though these can be found in films like *Iron Wolf* and *Frostbite*), nor from countries that experienced the force of concentration camps first-hand. Perhaps the absence of explicit references comes down to a question of taste, as Aaron Kerner argues that 'the knee-jerk assumption that the Holocaust should be represented "as it really was" maintains a strong hold on the popular imagination'.[39] For twenty-first-century Nazi horror to evoke the same explicit themes as previous Nazisploitation is to risk backlash that, rather than capitalising on its taboo topic, might potentially lead to financial and critical neglect.

That is not to say that such films are entirely missing from contemporary Nazi horror. For instance, Nazi occult horror film *Fantacide* uses references to the Holocaust as part of its seeming rally against a perceived rise in political correctness.[40] Moreover, *Dead Snow* features a scene in which protagonist Martin is bitten and fears being infected, to which his friend Roy responds that as he is of Jewish descent the Nazis would not want to recruit him anyway. Such macabre humour suggests intent to shock similar to *Fantacide* but may also offer a way of confronting such memories. Indeed, it is striking that this explicit reference is framed through horror-comedy, as Christina M. Knopf has observed gallows humour in early Nazi horror film *Revenge of the Zombies*. For Knopf, the comedy of this film was 'a marker of strong morale and a spirit of resistance', and so the tongue-in-cheek aside in *Dead Snow* can be understood as a successor to that gallows humour, as much as it may be understood in relation to the more morally vilified Nazisploitation films.[41] Thus, while they are not immersed in the horrors of the Second World War in the way that previous Nazisploitation films were, twenty-first-century Nazi horror films still utilise implicit images of the Holocaust, demonstrating an ongoing unease of knowing how to handle Holocaust representation.

An examination of Nazi horror therefore illustrates the complicated process of tracing cycles and subgenres, but also its rewards. Nazi horror is not solely a financial, exploitative or meaningless cycle, but a large, complex subgenre of diverse films. These films have been impacted by their history, hybridity and various cultural contexts that convey the ever-shifting meanings of the Nazi as a recurring monster. It is possible to trace these films and observe their complex subgeneric heritage, a tactic that reveals how cycles and subgenres are connected in increasingly multifaceted ways. While Nazi horror has, indeed, been 'reanimated' in the twenty-first century, the Nazi monster never really died, and analysis of its most recent incarnations suggests that it is because Nazism invokes some of our deepest, most long-standing fears.

Notes

1. *Revenge of the Zombies* is a sequel of sorts to *King of the Zombies* (Jean Yarbrough, 1941), which depicted an Austrian, but not explicitly Nazi, scientist raising zombies.
2. David A. Frank and Caroline Joan Picart, *Frames of Evil: The Holocaust as Horror in American Film* (Carbondale, IL: Southern Illinois University Press, 2006).
3. Jeanine Basinger, *The World War II Combat Film: Anatomy of a Genre* (Middletown, CT: Wesleyan University Press, 2003), p. 124.
4. Brigid Cherry, *Horror* (London: Routledge, 2009), p. 3.
5. Noël Carroll, *The Philosophy of Horror or Paradoxes of the Heart* (London: Routledge, 2004); Bruce Kawin, *Horror and the Horror Film* (London: Anthem Press, 2012).

6. Kawin, *Horror and the Horror Film*.
7. Carroll, *The Philosophy of Horror*, p. 159.
8. Steve Neale, *Genre and Hollywood* (London: Routledge, 2000), p. 7.
9. Peter Hutchings also argues that 'horror can be seen as proceeding via successive waves of sequels and cycles as initial commercial hits are exploited', in Hutchings, *The Horror Film* (London: Routledge, 2014), p. 16.
10. 'Cash in' is the phrase used by Hutchings, *The Horror Film*, p. 16. Rick Altman also suggests that these terms can be distinguished according to financial and industrial context, as he argues that subgenres can be shared among multiple studios but cycles belong to one studio, in Altman, *Film/Genre* (London: BFI Publishing, 1999); however, as Barry Keith Grant notes, 'this claim is questionable, particularly after the decline of the studio system', in Grant, *Film Genre: From Iconography to Ideology* (London: Wallflower Press, 2007), pp. 36–7.
11. M. Jancovich, 'Horror in the 1940s', in H. M. Benshoff (ed.), *A Companion to the Horror Film* (Chichester: Wiley-Blackwell, 2017), p. 242.
12. M. Stiglegger, 'Cinema beyond Good and Evil? Nazi Exploitation in the Cinema of the 1970s and its Heritage', in D. H. Magilow, E. Bridges and K. T. Vander Lugt (eds), *Nazisploitation! The Nazi Image in Low-Brow Cinema and Culture* (London: Continuum, 2012), p. 27; J. Petley, 'Nazi Horrors: History, Myth, Sexploitation', in I. Conrich (ed.), *Horror Zone: The Cultural Experience of Contemporary Horror Cinema* (London: I. B. Tauris, 2009), p. 208.
13. Ernest Mathijs and Jamie Sexton, *Cult Cinema: An Introduction* (Chichester: Wiley-Blackwell, 2011), p. 154.
14. Mathijs and Sexton, *Cult Cinema*, p. 154.
15. Hutchings, *The Horror Film*, p. 16.
16. Kyle William Bishop, *American Zombie Gothic: The Rise and Fall (and Rise) of the Walking Dead in Popular Culture* (Jefferson, NC: McFarland, 2011).
17. C. J. Miller, 'The Rise and Fall – and Rise – of the Nazi Zombie in Film', in C. M. Moreman and C. J. Rushton (eds), *Race, Oppression and the Zombie: Essays on Cross-Cultural Appropriations of the Caribbean Tradition* (Jefferson, NC: McFarland, 2011), pp. 139–48.
18. Bishop, *American Zombie Gothic*, p. 26.
19. Petley, 'Nazi Horrors', p. 208.
20. B. Kooyman, 'Snow Nazis Must Die', in S. Hantke and A. S. Monnet (eds), *War Gothic in Literature and Culture* (London: Routledge, 2015), p. 125; Miller, 'The Rise and Fall', p. 148.

21. S. Jüngerkes and C. Wienand, 'A Past that Refuses to Die: Nazi Zombie Film and the Legacy of Occupation', in D. H. Magilow, E. Bridges and K. T. Vander Lugt (eds), *Nazisploitation! The Nazi Image in Low-Brow Cinema and Culture* (London: Continuum, 2012), p. 247.
22. The sequel, *Dead Snow: Red vs Dead* (Tommy Wirkola, 2014), complicates this representation of national identity as it includes Russian zombies and American protagonists. This is not necessarily detrimental, however, as the Americans act as a globalised version of Martin and his friends, suggesting that the Nazi zombie resonates with particular times and places, but also beyond.
23. K. W. Bishop, 'Nazi Zombies', in J. Pulliam and A. J. Fonseca (eds), *Encyclopedia of the Zombie: The Walking Dead in Popular Culture and Myth* (Santa Barbara, CA: Greenwood, 2014), p. 182.
24. *Shock Waves* features similarly purposeful zombies, giving this 'exception' precedent in the Nazi horror subgenre. See Miller, 'The Rise and Fall', p. 142; Petley, 'Nazi Horrors', p. 207.
25. Bishop, 'Nazi Zombies', p. 181.
26. Jamie Russell, *Book of the Dead: The Complete History of Zombie Cinema* (Guildford: FAB Press, 2005), p. 7.
27. Russell, *Book of the Dead*, p. 8.
28. The threat of contagion in *War of the Dead* is unusual in this respect, as though the zombie embodies a certain freedom to become part of a mass and act unrestrained by morality, zombies created by the Nazis remain part of an oppressive regime. It is perhaps for this reason so few Nazi horror films feature contagious zombies.
29. Miller, 'The Rise and Fall', p. 144.
30. Petley, 'Nazi Horrors', p. 205.
31. Miller, 'The Rise and Fall', p. 145.
32. David J. Skal, *The Monster Show: A Cultural History of Horror* (London: Plexus, 1993), pp. 211–12.
33. Skal, *The Monster Show*, p. 218.
34. Miller, 'The Rise and Fall', p. 145.
35. P. Hutchings, 'Northern Darkness: The Curious Case of the Swedish Vampire', in L. Hunt and S. Lockyer (eds), *Screening the Undead: Vampires and Zombies in Film and Television* (London: I. B. Tauris, 2013), p. 63.
36. Miller, 'The Rise and Fall', p. 141; J. J. Ward, 'Utterly Without Redeeming Social Value? "Nazi Science" Beyond Exploitation Cinema in Nazisploitation', in D. H. Magilow, E. Bridges and K. T. Vander Lugt (eds), *Nazisploitation! The Nazi Image in Low-Brow Cinema and Culture* (London: Continuum, 2012), p. 95.

37. Ward, 'Utterly Without Redeeming Social Value?', p. 95.
38. Daniel Dinello, *Technophobia! Science Fiction Visions of Posthuman Technology* (Austin, TX: University of Texas Press, 2005), p. 5.
39. Aaron Kerner, *Film and the Holocaust: New Perspectives on Dramas, Documentaries, and Experimental Films* (London: Continuum, 2011), p. 1.
40. Other exceptions include *BloodRayne: The Third Reich* and *Puppet Master: Axis Rising* (Charles Band, 2012), which demonstrate the particular pervasiveness of sexualised Nazisploitation and the Ilsa figure.
41. C. M. Knopf, 'Zany Zombies, Grinning Ghosts, Silly Scientists and Nasty Nazis', in C. J. Miller and A. B. van Riper (eds), *The Laughing Dead: The Horror-Comedy Film from Bride of Frankenstein to Zombieland* (Lanham, MD: Rowman and Littlefield, 2016), p. 27.

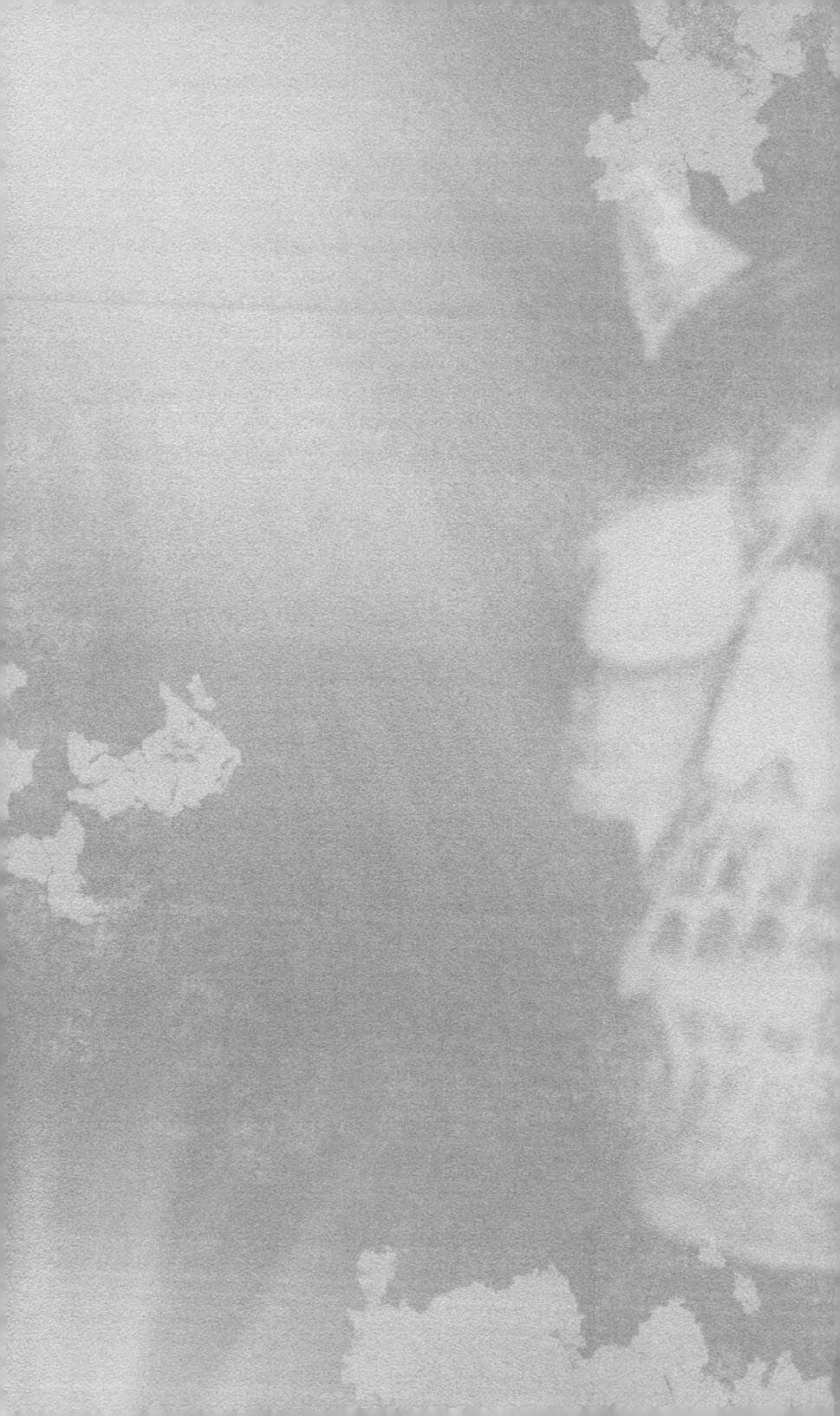

9

Digital Witness

Found Footage and Desktop Horror as Post-cinematic Experience

Lindsay Hallam

AS THE TORTURE PORN trend seemed to fade away as the first decade of the twenty-first century came to a close, another new subgenre of horror started to emerge: the found footage film. While torture porn played on the fears of international terrorism and torture brought about by the post-9/11 war on terror, found footage films – and their more recent form, the desktop film – evoke fear by focusing on another form of invasion, one that originates in the technology that has come to dominate our lives. We are all now producers of media as well as consumers of it, documenting, filming and sharing every moment, significant or otherwise. Some welcome the constant surveillance in quests for more likes, retweets and fleeting moments of fame. In turn, the films that explore the darker sides of this new cultural practice have begun to incorporate these new forms of media into their form, illustrating how cinema itself has undergone a transformation from an analogue product to a digitally integrated medium.

Found footage and desktop films are examples of what Steven Shaviro has called 'the post-cinematic', in that they are film texts that reflect how the cinematic form has 'transformed, over the past two decades, from an analogue process to a heavily digitised one'.[1] As Shaviro describes, '[d]igital technologies, together with neoliberal economic relations, have given birth to radically new ways of manufacturing and articulating lived experience'.[2] Cinema is no longer the 'cultural dominant', having been incorporated into new digital technologies, resulting in new cinematic expressions that communicate the sensations and intensities created in this media-saturated environment and its subsequent affects.[3] Found footage and desktop films in particular articulate this new 'media ecology', in which, as Shaviro explains:

> all activity is under surveillance from video cameras and microphones, and in return video screens and speakers, moving images and synthesised sounds, are dispersed pretty much everywhere. In this environment, where all phenomena pass through a stage of being processed in the form of digital code, we cannot meaningfully distinguish between 'reality' and its multiple simulations; they are all woven together in one and the same fabric.[4]

In such films, we see events after they have been 'processed' as 'digital code', before being transmitted to us (within the narrative) through the intermediary of a camera, mobile device or computer screen. These films are transmedia objects, often existing alongside other elements found across different platforms, as demonstrated by the internet advertising campaign and website that accompanied the pioneer of the found footage film format, *The Blair Witch Project* (Daniel Myrick and Eduardo Sánchez, 1999). In the desktop film, there are layers of visuals, windows upon windows of information, images and interfaces. By presenting the narrative in this way, these films provide 'an account of *what it feels like* to live in the early twenty-first century' by capturing the rush of affect and intensity that ensues when immersed in the interplay between reality and its recording.[5]

The affect evoked by these films is symptomatic of how our relationship with technology produces bodily responses. As Johanna Isaacson states: 'our hearts race when we are messaged or liked, an extra minute of waiting for a text stretches into timeless misery . . . The resonant, bright, droney, and dull sounds that accompany these gestures have now become part of our nervous system.'[6] Moreover, our devices have become extensions of ourselves, often causing anxiety when they are lost or forgotten. They prompt our need to document each moment according to the mantra 'pics or it didn't happen', a statement that demonstrates how authenticity is dependent upon photographic evidence, which is then viewed, rated and shared by others online. Our identity and sense of self, and certainly our fears, are now bound to the digital realm.

In this chapter, I will argue that the emerging subgenres of found footage and desktop horror are forms of post-cinema and that their effectiveness (and affectiveness) comes precisely from the integration of new digital media with traditional horror cinema conventions, expressing contemporary fears and anxieties via the very modes in which they are experienced. Through the examination of found footage and desktop films, it is possible to chart how our lived online experiences have informed new horror modalities and techniques, especially in the ways that they evoke new sensations of fear and visceral immediate responses. As a result, the forms of transmedia inspired by these films have come to shape the aesthetic of the films themselves, as the desktop screen becomes the film screen.

In order to demonstrate the development of post-cinematic horror from found footage to desktop films, I will first survey the different forms that have emerged since 1999 (see Table 9.1). I will then examine found footage films that have employed internet viral campaigns, where online digital space is used to extend the story of the film as a form of marketing and advertising. These films are part of a wider transmedia network of digital experience that has become increasingly indistinguishable from our lived reality. Indeed, as the final part of this chapter explores, the digital space is where much of our lives now take place; in turn, the digital space has become the location of the film itself, as seen in the desktop film. The internet, once a place to access material peripheral to the central film, is now a primary narrative space.

Table 9.1. Feature-length post-cinematic horror.

Form	Description	Key examples
Found footage	The events on-screen appear to have been captured on a camera, which is wielded by a character in the film. Other characters often speak directly into the camera and address the camera as though it were another person in that space with them. Footage from other devices, such as phones and laptop webcams, can also be included.	*The Blair Witch Project* (1999), *The Collingswood Story* (2002), *Diary of the Dead* (2007), *[Rec]* (2007), *Paranormal Activity* series (2007–15), *Cloverfield* (2008), *The Last Exorcism* (2010), *V/H/S* series (2012–14), *The Bay* (2012), *Creep* (2014), *Ratter* (2015), *Creep 2* (2017)

Form	Description	Key examples
Transmedia	Feature-length films that utilise internet viral campaigns through official websites and social media sites, with extra features released online or as DVD extras. These elements often broaden and extend the story of the original film, and also work as a form of marketing that drums up publicity and creates a fan base for a film before its release.	*The Blair Witch Project* (1999), *Paranormal Activity* (2007), *Cloverfield* (2008)
Social films	A term created by Intel and Toshiba to describe an interactive film released initially through social media sites. Segments are filmed and posted online, with viewers able to interact with the story and characters further through posts, comments and participation in gameplay.	*Inside* aka *The Inside Experience* (2011)
Desktop films	The film's location is the protagonist's desktop computer screen.	'The Sick Thing That Happened to Emily When She Was Younger' from *V/H/S* (2012), *The Den* (2013), *Open Windows* (2014), *Unfriended* (2014), *Searching* (2018), *Profile* (2018), *Unfriended: Dark Web* (2018)
Screenmovies/ Screen life	The terms 'screenmovie' and 'screen life' were coined by producer/director Timur Bekmambetov to describe specifically the desktop films released by his company, Bazalevs Productions.	
Snapchat films	Segments initially filmed and released through the Snapchat app, then later edited together as a feature-length film (with some additional material added). Presented in the portrait aspect ratio of a mobile phone.	*Sickhouse* (2016)

Internet advertising and the transmedia object

Richard Grusin argues that, in this new era of digital cinema, the time has come to 'recognise that a film does not end after its closing credits, but rather continues beyond the theatre to the DVD, the video game, the soundtrack, the websites, and so forth'.[7] In post-cinema, the lines between film and other media become especially blurred. Just as Grusin maintains that a film continues after the final credits, the transmedia marketing and advertising campaigns that begin before a film is even released have also become an integral part of the post-cinematic film form. The first major example of this approach was *The Blair Witch Project*, for which transmedia was used to create a story and a mystery in which consumers could become invested over time. People were essentially sucked into a puzzle in which the film was just the final piece. Brigid Cherry explains that, '[i]n the 11-month run-up to the film's release at least 20 fan sites, a web ring, an email discussion list and a newsgroup were established.'[8] As this illustrates, the film had a life on the internet before it was shown to the public, and people already designated themselves *Blair Witch* fans prior to actually seeing the film.

The overwhelming success of *The Blair Witch Project* was attributed in large part to its marketing campaign, which was primarily based on portraying the events of the film as real and the protagonists as actual missing people. Significantly, the film was marketed as a documentary, not as a traditional horror film. The official website, *blairwitch.com*, provided background mythology about the fabled Blair Witch, descriptions of the film-makers' disappearance and a catalogue of evidence that was recovered in the subsequent search for the missing trio. In his analysis of the use of the internet in making this film such a success, J. P. Telotte suggests that all of this online material led to the film being seen as 'just one more artefact' in a larger 'project'.[9] Co-director Eduardo Sánchez even stated that the website functions as 'a completely autonomous experience from the film. You don't have to see the film to actually have fun on the web site, and investigate it and get creeped out.'[10] Surprisingly, once the film was revealed to be complete fiction, there was little fan backlash: one can posit that people were unwilling to let go of something in which they had become so invested, even though they had been fooled.

In contrast to *The Blair Witch Project*'s aim to convince the audience that it is real, a post-2000 example of a found footage film, *Paranormal Activity* (Oren Peli, 2007) – the film that usurped *The Blair Witch Project*'s place as the most profitable independent film ever – used transmedia in a different way. The rise of YouTube has led to the significance of the trailer, rather than an official website, as a tool to create buzz. Rather than attempting to convince the audience that the film is real, this trailer focuses on the experience of watching the film in a communal cinema setting. In an era where viewers are seen as savvy and sceptical, footage of young adults looking genuinely scared demonstrates the film's power to override the initial disbelief and cynicism of its target audience. Their fear is 'real', even if the film itself is not. While the trailer does not try to convince the viewer that *Paranormal Activity* is a documentary, it makes use of similar techniques (for example, footage of real people watching the film) to market the film as an intense, frightening experience.[11]

Angela Ndalianis writes extensively of the affective response of viral marketing and transmedia storytelling, arguing that:

> As our favourite fictions enter our everyday world, as we become embroiled in adventures they throw our way with combined intellectual and sensory intensity, we forget that they're a marketing strategy devised to sell a product. What we do remember is the memory of the experience and how it seduces our sensorium.[12]

When viewing this trailer, the spectator sees the overwhelming fear and intensity that others feel when engaging with *Paranormal Activity*, and is encouraged to experience this themselves. The trailer also gives the viewer a perceived sense of control – they can personally 'demand' that the film be shown in their area – when, in fact, the viewer is performing the advertising and marketing for the product themselves. Through the use of social media, consumers had closer access to the film, and social networks created the buzz itself, with *Paranormal Activity* becoming a popular trending topic on Twitter immediately after the trailer's release. The film's distributor, Paramount, relied primarily on social media to market the film, saving vast amounts of money normally expended on TV spots and advertisements in traditional media. Therefore, as Ndalianis states, although people are in fact providing unpaid labour, the person partaking in such an act is so involved in the overriding and addictive interactive experience that they do not consciously realise that they are ultimately servicing a capitalist enterprise.

The *Cloverfield* (Matt Reeves, 2008) viral campaign was even more involved than *Paranormal Activity*'s, and, like *The Blair Witch Project*'s, its transmedia content provides a larger context and backstory that could almost stand on its own, independent of the film itself. In addition to giving each of the film's characters a Myspace page (providing character background not present in the film), a series of websites offer clues as to what the monster might be. A website for a fictional soft drink, 'Slusho', which is made with a secret 'deep-sea ingredient', leads to another website for Slusho's parent company, Tagruato, which is involved in deep-sea drilling. There is also a website for TIDO Wave, an environmental group believed to be involved in an attack on a Tagruato oil rig. Added to this is a series of video blogs of a girl, Jamie, who is addressing her boyfriend, Teddy, who works for Slusho in Japan.[13] He sends her a Slusho hat and a substance that may well be Slusho's secret ingredient, but is labelled with 'Jamie – don't eat this'. She thinks he is trying to break up with her, so she proceeds to eat the substance and then chronicles the strange after-effects. Interestingly, these videos, which originated online and were later included as DVD extras, foreshadow the desktop film, which relies heavily on webcam footage of characters talking directly to the camera. By following these narrative threads, it could be inferred that the monster in the film was perhaps created through human intervention with the deep-sea environment, just like Godzilla was made from radiation from the nuclear attack in Hiroshima (although this has been disproven in subsequent *Cloverfield* sequels, which depict the monsters as aliens). So, while the *Cloverfield* film shows us a completely subjective point of view of the monster attack, the viral campaign provides some possible answers to how the monster came to be that are not found in the film.

A further example of post-cinema transmedia storytelling came in 2011, when corporations Intel and Toshiba created what they termed a 'social film', *Inside* (D. J. Caruso, 2011). Released online through YouTube, Twitter and Facebook as a series of episodes over the course of eleven days (25 July–4 August 2011), *Inside* is ostensibly the story of a young woman, Christina Perraso, who finds herself trapped in a room with only a (Toshiba) laptop as a form of communication. Through the webcam and social media platforms, Christina pleads with viewers to help her figure out where she is and how she can escape. The filmed segments follow traditional cinematic conventions and techniques, showing Christina as she looks around the room and tries to figure out how to break out. Alongside these shots are images from the laptop webcam and of social media posts. Outside of these pre-filmed segments was the interactive gameplay and social media communication, creating a full multiplatform transmedia experience for viewers. As Sarah Atkinson notes:

> In many cases the audience members would seamlessly step from one 'level' of communication to another in conversational streams, making 'metaleptic' leaps between the ontological boundaries of fact, fiction, inside and outside of the diegesis, traversing the multi-layered diegetic and paratextual levels whilst maintaining a propensity towards a persistent and willing suspension of disbelief.[14]

Echoing Ndalianis's earlier statements, viewers would become swept up in the story and their own intense emotional experiences while engaging with the text – a text that is essentially an advertising campaign. Shaviro argues that the digital form of post-cinema is inseparable from its participation in neoliberal economic relations, for just as post-cinematic texts 'are *machines for generating affect*' they are also 'capitalising upon, or extracting value from, this affect'.[15] *Inside* can therefore be viewed as a logical progression for the post-cinema form: it was directed by an established film-maker, stars a well-known actress (Emmy Rossum) and uses traditional genre conventions, but these are mixed with new digital media formats, all for the primary purpose of selling a corporation's media technology.

Desktop films

Following on from *Inside*'s use of laptop webcam footage, in desktop films the entire film plays out on a desktop computer screen. There have already been several terms used in reviews to describe these films, such as 'laptop horror' and 'webcam horror', while the producer and director Timur Bekmambetov refers to them as 'screenmovies'.[16] The term 'desktop film' more fittingly encompasses the subtle variations already found in this form (not all of them take place on a laptop, or are shot from a webcam). While desktop films now incorporate different genres, such as the mystery-drama *Searching* (Aneesh Chaganty, 2018), early precedents are found within the horror genre. A specific earlier use is found in Chuck Tyron's *Reinventing Cinema: Movies in the Age of Media Convergence*. In a chapter titled 'Desktop Productions', the term 'desktop feature film' is used in relation to the found footage horror film *The Last Broadcast* (Stefan Avalos and Lance Weiler, 1998), which was 'the first feature-length motion picture filmed, edited, and screened entirely with digital technologies'.[17] As the place where film-makers, and now film spectators, interface with digital cinema technology, the desktop is central not only to how these films are made, but also more recently to how they are consumed. With the rise of streaming services like Netflix and Amazon Prime Video, such films are increasingly viewed on computer screens; moreover, both of these services also produce their own original content, most of which bypasses a traditional cinema release altogether (as Matt Hills's chapter in this collection explores).

Rising concurrently with these desktop horror films is what critic and film-maker Kevin B. Lee has termed 'desktop documentary', a form of non-fiction film 'which uses screen capture technology to treat the computer screen as both a camera lens and a canvas' and 'seeks both to depict and question the ways we explore the world through the computer screen'.[18] Lee's films, such as *Transformers: The Premake* (2014), interrogate the ramifications of the increased time spent with computers and online spaces and examine how consumers have also become film-makers and producers of their own visual content available online. This is expressed more directly than in fictional desktop horror films, which explore these themes as a subtext to the narrative and the eliciting of thrills and scares. Yet, these texts all utilise the desktop screen as the film's location rather than a physical space, reflecting how this online space is increasingly the location of where we, in essence, live our lives and play out our emotional experiences. For Shaviro, this dislocation from purely physical subjectivity 'leads precisely to a magnification of affect, whose flows swamp us, and continually carry us away from ourselves, beyond ourselves'.[19]

The first example of the desktop horror film format appears as a segment in the found footage anthology film *V/H/S* (establishing a link between found footage and desktop films), titled 'The Sick Thing That Happened to Emily When She Was Younger'.[20] The segment unfolds as a series of Skype conversations between a couple, Emily and James, who are separated while James is at medical school. Emily begins to confide in James that she believes her house is haunted, and through the conversations, a real threat is revealed. In a similar manner to *Paranormal Activity*, digital technology is used to document supernatural activity, eventually hinting at a larger conspiracy that may include alien lifeforms. Throughout the segment, poor lighting, off-centre framing and the incorporation of technical problems (such as glitching and pixilation) enhance realism. The film was made without the use of any traditional cameras, with the scenes captured directly onto the computer: director Joe Swanberg comments that 'it became like a weird I.T. problem . . . It was less like a movie problem to solve and more like we were managing Wi-Fi signals and computer frame rates.'[21]

Desktop horrors and thrillers have subsequently been expanded to feature-length format, in the films *The Den* (Zachary Donohue, 2013), *Open Windows* (Nacho Vigalondo, 2014), *Unfriended* (Levan Gabriadze, 2014) and its sequel *Unfriended: Dark Web* (Stephen Susco, 2018), *Searching* and *Profile* (Timur Bekmambetov, 2018), with *Variety* critic Peter Debruge branding these films 'Found Footage 2.0'.[22] *The Den*, *Unfriended* and *Profile* all take place on a character's desktop screen that stays static, while in *Open Windows* and *Searching* there is movement in the zooming into/out from the desktop screen and the tracking across various open windows, in addition to footage from various cameras and locations that are then transmitted onto the desktop. 'The Sick Thing That Happened to Emily When She Was Younger', *The Den* and *Searching* take place over a series of days and weeks, while the narratives of *Open Windows* and *Unfriended* play out in real time. *Sickhouse* (Hannah Macpherson, 2016) moves away from the computer desktop to another portable device, the mobile phone, filmed completely through the Snapchat app and presented in the aspect ratio of an upright mobile handset. The Netflix release *Cam* (Daniel Goldhaber, 2018) does not completely take place on a desktop, but key scenes are presented as the live-streaming performances of the protagonist, cam girl Alice.[23] The concept of 'identity theft' is then taken to an extreme, as Alice becomes locked out of her account while what appears to be a digitally created double of her continues to perform in her place. The protagonists in all of these films are dragged into a sequence of events that they engage with through their computer or mobile device, as opposed to their immediate physical surroundings. Urgency and isolation are emphasised, as the protagonists become bound to their screens as a means to survive.

The title of Nacho Vigalondo's *Open Windows* contains several puns on the new uses of the term 'windows' in the modern age: the prevalence of the Microsoft Windows programme, and the term used to denote the many different screens, or 'windows', that can be accessed on a computer desktop, allowing the user to alternate between different websites, clips and programmes. The desktop screen itself is also 'a window to the world', similar to how cinema was once described as a medium through which the viewer could see places that were geographically distant. It could be argued that the desktop screen/window is even more open than that of the cinema screen, given the increased interactivity and ability to communicate with, and influence, the objects of our engagement. Yet, there is a danger to this openness, as *Open Windows* demonstrates: with so much of our lives now lived online, we are often left vulnerable to attack in many ways, including identity theft, cyberbullying and hacking.

The film's first act has Nick Chambers situated in a hotel room, having won a contest to meet his favourite film star, Jill Goddard. An ardent fan, Nick has created a website dedicated to Jill that includes, in his words, 'pictures of Jill, scans, videos, articles'. Nick boasts in the introduction video that he records for the contest that 'some of my stuff is the first posted of her', even though he is not a reporter or working for an agency. Writing of the allure of pop culture stars, Shaviro posits how 'he or she is someone to who I respond in the mode of intimacy, even though I am not, and cannot ever be, actually intimate with him or her'.[24] Nick is portrayed as an obsessed fanboy, his website tellingly called jillgoddard-*caught*.com (emphasis added). Shaviro explains that stars are 'figures upon which, or within which, many powerful feelings converge; they *conduct* multiplicities of affective flows'.[25] In the film's opening scene, we see the trailer for Jill's latest movie with certain moments freeze-framed as Nick captures screen grabs: he hopes to 'catch' Jill in a particular affectively charged and potent moment, attempting to get closer to a figure that will always remain unattainable.

In *Open Windows*, there are no straight cuts from one shot to the next but instead movement across the desktop to another window (or shot), creating the illusion that the film is continuous with no edits (much like Hitchcock's 1948 film *Rope*). It is not so much that we are following the gaze as following the cursor, as it negotiates the different windows on the desktop, itself a form of editing in its organisation of visuals. The affective power of this movement between shots is similar to that created by the handheld camerawork of found footage films, in that there is a feeling of immediacy in the images and a sense that the characters are using technology to keep up as events spiral out of control. However, in a break from the conventions of other found footage films that only use diegetic sound, *Open Windows* incorporates a non-diegetic score to heighten emotional tension. Despite this intrusion from outside the diegetic world of the film, events play out in real time, with each choice that Nick makes leading to immediate consequences as he gets closer and closer to Jill yet is also manipulated by Simon Chord, who at first guides, and then later controls, Nick's actions.

The connection between window and screen goes back to Alfred Hitchcock's 1954 film *Rear Window*, made six decades before *Open Windows*. The narrative of *Rear Window* is commonly interpreted as mirroring the film-watching process, as, like the protagonist L. B. Jeffries, we too must collect clues and make inferences from what we see, as Jeffries does by watching his neighbours through adjacent windows. In Hitchcock's film, the window takes on many metaphorical dimensions relating to the cinematic apparatus, alluding to the lens of camera and projector, the window in the projection booth and the eye as window.[26] Vigalondo expands on many of these points, demonstrating that the metaphors in Hitchcock's film have not only become more relevant, but literal. Within the physical space of the home or workplace, people are often surrounded by as many screens as windows, each offering a view to different spaces, whether they be physical spaces or cyberspaces. Thus, the phrase 'opening a window' has now come to mean something new, a movement that leads to more information, more clues in an ongoing trail or narrative, similar to how one moves from scene to scene within a narrative film. Just as Jeffries collates more information by looking through windows located geographically across the street, in *Open Windows* Nick looks between a series of windows on his desktop in order to obtain information that will allow him – within a narrative trajectory echoing that of many Hollywood movies – to defeat the villain and save the girl.

As the film goes on, it takes on a quality similar to a video game, with Chord initially appearing only as a disembodied voice who presents Nick with choices and information, just as a voice directs play in video games such as *Portal*, *Transistor*, *The Talos Principle* and *Bioshock*. The 1992 Sega game, *Night Trap*, is also evoked. As Brian Walton explains, in *Night Trap*:

> you play as an outside observer watching a slumber party through hidden cameras, operating a system of traps to capture creatures intent on kidnapping the girls you are watching. Anyone who played the game will get a feeling of déjà vu as Chord and Nick go back and forth with Jill's life hanging in the balance.[27]

The internet has also become an arena for communal gaming, allowing players working as teams to communicate verbally across the globe and direct each other's actions, much in the same way that Chord guides Nick outside the hotel without being seen in *Open Windows*. The lack of straight cuts between shots is further akin to the experience of playing a game in that it unfolds in a continuous motion (which, in many games, often occurs from a first-person perspective), and the inclusion of a non-diegetic score in the film reflects another common video game technique.[28] This allusion to the experience of playing a video game is yet another example of how the desktop film integrates stylistic techniques from new forms of media, incorporating them into its own cinematic form.

A further echoing of video game mechanics in *Open Windows* is to be found in the series of moral choices that Nick must make, especially as he gets closer to Jill and is presented with an opportunity to get her to do whatever he desires. As Nick drives from the hotel room to near Jill's house, there is a move from references to Hitchcock's *Rear Window* to slasher film conventions. The desktop shows several windows containing images of Nick from his laptop webcam and of Jill at her computer at home, alongside a feed from a camera strapped to Chord's head that provides a subjective point of view, similar to that seen in many slasher films as the killer stalks their victims. Chord is wearing black gloves (a reference also to the killers found in Italian *giallo* films) and picks up a large knife. We still have not seen his face, and when the window opens, Nick asks Chord, 'Is that you?' There is a glimpse of Chord's eyes reflected in the knife as he replies, 'You're the one who wanted to see so badly'.

Imitating the actions of slasher movie killers, Chord compels Nick to obey his commands and forces him to take his place as Jill's tormentor. Chord makes it known to Nick that he is in Jill's house, as his camera shows that he is watching Jill as she strips to her underwear to take a shower. This shot recalls many similar images from slasher films, most famously the opening shot of *Halloween* (John Carpenter, 1978), in which a woman is in a state of undress unaware that she is being watched. It is always implied in these shots that the killer on-screen and spectator off-screen are complicit, that by sharing the killer's gaze the viewer is implicated in the violence that inevitably follows (as outlined by Carol J. Clover in her seminal study of the slasher film, *Men, Women, and Chain Saws*).[29] Here, the connection of the killer and the audience, and the character of Nick, is no longer implied but now explicit, due to the technological context of the narrative.

The notion of stalking, and the place of recording and photographing the victim as a form of violation, reflects the prevalence of paparazzi photographers and hackers who regularly target celebrities. This is another twenty-first-century horror of its own, for celebrities, in addition to the other personal and technological horrors that the desktop film exploits. While magazines and television shows are unable to display the full nude photographs of celebrities that are captured, these images are freely available to view online. At the beginning of *Open Windows*, Jill is already subject to rumours that she has appeared in a sex tape; an image of her with her breasts exposed (taken from the previously described scene) is used to take over several websites with the promise of an incoming video of the actress, accompanied by a looped recording of Jill saying 'I'll do anything you say'. The hacking of celebrity phones and internet cloud accounts has, in recent years, proliferated with wide-ranging and sinister results. Hollywood actress Jennifer Lawrence, herself a victim of such a hacking, has stated of the violation: 'It is not a scandal. It is a sex crime', asserting that '[a]nybody who looked at those pictures, you're perpetuating a sexual offense'.[30] In *Open Windows*, those who view the events online are, like Lawrence's example, perpetuating Chord's offences. By staying online, the viewers become complicit in Jill's attempted murder. Not content with just seeing Jill's body, the viewers want to see everything, including her death – indeed, they feel entitled to it.

The scene of Jill's forced striptease thus evokes conflicting responses, confronting us with our desire to be intimate with the alluring object, while also clearly illustrating that our fascination and obsession can never be reciprocated, only taken by force. Yet, there is still a titillating aspect to this enforcement. The expectation of seeing Jill's breasts is, according to Chord, 'the final frontier', with his commentary throughout the scene (consisting of 'Hey, hey! Look, look! Now we're talking!') most likely voicing what many in the audience are thinking. The casting of Sasha Grey as Jill Goddard adds a further dimension, as Grey became famous initially for her work as a porn star. Grey's casting also nods to the tradition in horror films of casting Playboy bunnies and porn stars such as Marilyn Chambers, the protagonist of David Cronenberg's *Rabid* (1977). Now, in the age of the desktop film, with pornography as one of the biggest internet-based industries, horror and desire become one and the same within *Open Windows*. The viewer's potentially personal and intimate desires are reflected back upon them and exploited – via Nick – within the film's fictional narrative.

In the film's final act, the carefully constructed story seems to break down into a series of events and plot twists that lack much sense. Along with this narrative fragmentation is a visual fragmentation, as somewhat preposterous devices such as 'ping pong cameras' relay visual information in an attempt to justify what we see. The physical space only becomes visible as the computer processes the space into digital code, phenomena existing only on the screen rather than in reality. Hence, this produces a different look – this is how we are now seeing and experiencing the world. The film only ends when Jill decides, in an act of defiance, to close the laptop.

As *Open Windows* and other found footage and desktop films demonstrate, the medium of cinema is reacting to the new media landscape, which now primarily consists of, and exists on, an online digital space. That so much of our lives – our experiences and interactions – take place digitally means that our emotions, and our fears, have also reacted to this change. We are now immersed in an intricate network of affective flows that traverse both physical and virtual realms. Films, video games and digital forms of communication have now all overlapped in terms of the influence they have on our perception of our everyday lives. Though *Open Windows* is perhaps an outlandish horror vehicle, its premise is still rooted within this contemporary context.

Media is now social, our relationships (sometimes with people whom we have never met physically) forged and broken through digital interactions. The desktop horror film thus expresses, in a post-cinematic form, a transformation of horror film conventions in a way that not only reflects, but connects into, the network of affect and emotion that we are currently experiencing. Our fears and anxieties are now becoming aspects of ourselves that exist beyond our own bodies, an integral part of our shared digital world.

Notes

1. S. Shaviro, 'Post-Cinematic Affect: On Grace Jones, *Boarding Gate* and *Southland Tales*', *Film-Philosophy*, 14/1 (2010), 2.
2. Shaviro, 'Post-Cinematic Affect', 2.
3. T. Grisham, J. Leyda, N. Rombes and S. Shaviro, 'Roundtable Discussion on the Post-Cinematic in *Paranormal Activity* and *Paranormal Activity 2*', *La Furia Umana*, 11 (2011).
4. Shaviro, 'Post-Cinematic Affect', 8.
5. Shaviro, 'Post-Cinematic Affect', 2; emphasis in the original.
6. J. Isaacson, '"Unfriended" Unpacks Cyber-Sociality', *Blind Field: A Journal of Cultural Inquiry* (16 February 2016), *https://blindfieldjournal.com/2016/02/16/unfriended-unpacks-cyber-sociality/* (accessed 29 August 2019).
7. R. Grusin, 'DVDs, Video Games, and the Cinema of Interactions', in S. Denson and J. Leyda (eds), *Post-Cinema: Theorizing 21st-Century Film* (Falmer: REFRAME, 2016), pp. 71–2.
8. B. Cherry, 'Stalking the Web: Celebration, Chat and Horror Film Marketing on the Internet', in I. Conrich (ed.), *Horror Zone: The Cultural Experience of Contemporary Horror Cinema* (London: I. B. Tauris, 2009), p. 80.

9. J. P. Telotte, 'The Blair Witch Project Project', Film Quarterly, 54/3 (2001), 35.
10. Telotte, 'The Blair Witch Project Project', 35.
11. The Paranormal Activity trailer can be viewed here: https://www.youtube.com/watch?v=F_UxLEqd074 (accessed 29 August 2019).
12. Angela Ndalianis, The Horror Sensorium: Media and the Senses (Jefferson, NC: McFarland, 2012), p. 166.
13. While the other Cloverfield-associated websites have since been taken down, you can still access these webcam messages at http://www.jamieandteddy.com/password.php using the password 'jllovesth'.
14. Sarah Atkinson, Beyond the Screen: Emerging Cinema and Engaging Audiences (London: Bloomsbury, 2014), p. 110.
15. Shaviro, 'Post-Cinematic Affect', 3; emphasis in the original.
16. T. Bekmambetov, 'Rules of the Screenmovie: The Unfriended Manifesto for the Digital Age', MovieMaker (22 April 2015), https://www.moviemaker.com/archives/moviemaking/directing/unfriended-rules-of-the-screenmovie-a-manifesto-for-the-digital-age/ (accessed 29 August 2019).
17. Chuck Tryon, Reinventing Cinema: Movies in the Age of Media Convergence (New Brunswick, NJ: Rutgers University Press, 2009), p. 93.
18. C. Grant, 'On Desktop Documentary (Or, Kevin B. Lee Goes Meta!)', Film Studies for Free (6 April 2015), http://filmstudiesforfree.blogspot.co.uk/2015/04/on-desktop-documentary-or-kevin-b-lee.html (accessed 29 August 2019).
19. Shaviro, 'Post-Cinematic Affect', 5.
20. The 2002 film The Collingswood Story (Michael Costanza, 2002) is an early example where webcam footage is used extensively, while Redacted (Brian De Palma, 2007), Megan is Missing (Michael Goi, 2011) and The Bay (Barry Levinson, 2012) also use different computer footage throughout. The short film Noah (Walter Woodman and Patrick Cederberg, 2013) is considered one of the first films to be completely presented in the desktop format.
21. M. Murphy, 'In "Unfriended," Horror Unfolds on a Desktop Screen', The New York Times (12 April 2015), http://www.nytimes.com/2015/04/12/movies/in-unfriended-horror-unfolds-on-a-desktop-screen.html (accessed 29 August 2019).
22. P. Debruge, 'Film Review: "Unfriended"', Variety (3 August 2014), http://variety.com/2014/film/festivals/film-review-cybernatural-1201274261/ (accessed 29 August 2019).
23. In this instance it should be further noted that, as a Netflix film, these scenes in Cam of live-streaming are most likely also being live-streamed at that very moment by the spectator.
24. Shaviro, 'Post-Cinematic Affect', 11.
25. Shaviro, 'Post-Cinematic Affect', 11; emphasis in the original.

26. R. Stam and R. Pearson, 'Hitchcock's *Rear Window*: Reflexivity and the Critique of Voyeurism', in M. Deutelbaum and L. A. Pogue (eds), *A Hitchcock Reader* (Chichester: Wiley-Blackwell, 2009), pp. 193–206.
27. B. Walton, 'Fantastic Fest Review: *Open Windows* with Elijah Wood and Sasha Grey', *Nerdist* (6 October 2014), *http://nerdist.com/fantastic-fest-review-open-windows-with-elijah-wood-sasha-grey/* (accessed 29 August 2019).
28. This influence of video games has led to some films playing out completely from a first-person perspective, in examples such as *Hardcore Henry* (Ilya Naishuller, 2015), *Pandemic* (John Suits, 2016) and *Let's Be Evil* (Martin Owen, 2016).
29. Carol J. Clover, *Men, Women, and Chain Saws: Gender in the Modern Horror Film* (Princeton, NJ: Princeton University Press, 1992).
30. 'Cover Exclusive: Jennifer Lawrence Calls Photo Hacking a "Sex Crime"', *Vanity Fair* (7 October 2014), *https://www.vanityfair.com/hollywood/2014/10/jennifer-lawrence-cover* (accessed 29 August 2019).

PART FOUR

HORROR IN THE WORLD

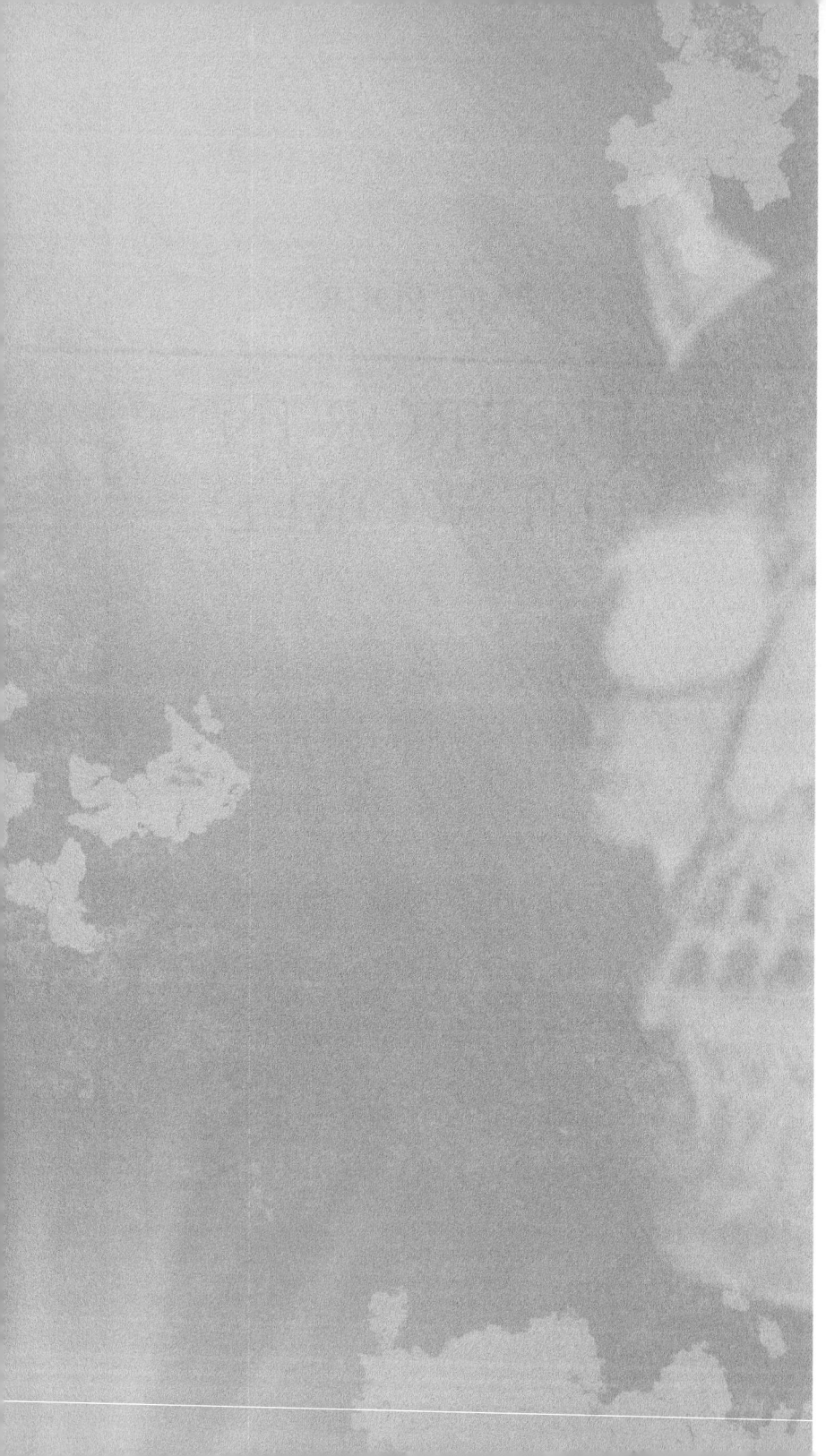

10

Revisiting the Female Monster

Sex and Monstrosity in Contemporary Body Horror

Eddie Falvey

HISTORICALLY, THE BODY has been utilised by horror filmmakers in diverse ways. It has functioned as an apparatus for trauma, torture, mutilation and death; a subject of possession; a source of sexual threat, violence and exploitation; a target for disease and disintegration; a platform for difference and monstrosity. That the genre has regularly used the body as the site of its horrors speaks to the body's value as a subject in the study of identity politics in the horror genre. Through the depiction of all manners of corporeal violation, many horror texts – which can be considered to collectively constitute the subgenre of body horror – employ bodies as vehicles to expose and comment on cultural formulations of otherness. This chapter offers a survey of contemporary body horror that focuses on the re-emergence of one particular mode of otherness as a significant element of (post)modern horror aesthetics, namely the exploitation, violation and destruction of the monstrous female body. It will consider how the female body functions in modern horror cinema in new and evolving ways as a primary locus for the expression of cultural anxieties about sex and violence, in ways that both exploit and challenge notions of the female as monster, as Other.

Twenty-five years after the publication of *The Monstrous-Feminine*, Barbara Creed's manifesto on feminine monstrosity, Creed's pivotal critique of scholarship foregrounding analysis of women as victims over women as monsters still resonates.[1] For Creed, such readings neglected proper discussion of how the female body operates as a site of monstrosity determined by biological difference. Creed claims that it is short-sighted to only consider horror's generic entrapment of women at the hands of monstrous men, proposing that such readings deny space to fully explore how monstrosity is recurrently evident in female horror bodies and often emerges from their sexed characteristics. Horror's tendency towards the monstrous has been conceptualised in many ways both before and since Creed. Noël Carroll's *The Philosophy of Horror* explored how a fascination with monstrosity, in its various forms, has sustained horror's standing at the discursive intersection of wider discussions on identity.[2] Lianne McLarty, in her discussion of David Cronenberg's cinema (central to the development of the body horror subgenre and also a component of Creed's work), writes that Cronenbergian horror forces introspection by 'render[ing] the Other impossible to disavow by collapsing the boundaries between them and us'.[3] Cronenberg's cinema brought corporeality, thematically entwined with sexual identity politics, to the forefront of horror aesthetics in the 1970s and 1980s, and critical interest in his work has been sustained, with Xavier Aldana Reyes observing that his 'cinema literalises the horrors of embodiment and the visceral quality of the mode is played with at a surface level and dissected at a structural one'.[4]

Cronenberg's tendency to foreground the body as a site of disintegration marks his cinema as one that exhibits the theme of pronounced corporeality that I will explore here. Through a selection of twenty-first-century case studies – including *Teeth* (Mitchell Lichtenstein, 2007), *Contracted* (Eric England, 2013), *It Follows* (David Robert Mitchell, 2014) and *Raw* (Julia Ducournau, 2016) – this chapter will examine how monstrous femininity has invited new modes of spectatorship, in addition to demonstrating horror's developing capacity to confront a range of sexual issues, including sexual difference, exploration, exploitation and trauma. As clearly politicised and culturally coded signifiers, bodies determined by difference provide more than just the site of horror: they go further, to offer evidence of the ever-shifting ways in which the body, and those represented by such bodies, figure discursively. Before examining this in relation to the selected case studies, however, it is important to first consider exactly how the body has come to function in this manner across the horror genre, particularly in recent years.

Gender, difference and sexual violence in contemporary horror

A prevailing theme in recent exercises in the body horror subgenre is the perpetration, and ramifications, of sexual trauma, especially that experienced by women. Writing on the pornographic sensations of extreme body horror, Jay McRoy notes that 'close-ups of bodily trauma, medium shots of mutilated or reconfigured corpses, and the application of disorienting editing effects add to a cinema of fragmentation in which the body of the viewer (re)enacts that horror on the screen'.[5] McRoy's discussion of the affective powers of horror conveys the genre's power to elicit responses to the body *through* the body. Certainly, feelings about the genre often come down to more than a matter of sheer preference; rather, horror is found to administer its power through reactions to it,[6] by eliciting fear, disgust and even trauma by way of the graphic content that is often central to its aesthetic, thematic and affective properties. Linda Williams's definition of cinematic excess observes it as a decentring of the body, one that leaves it '"beside itself" in the grips of . . . fear and terror'.[7] By leaving audiences disturbed, shocked and sickened by its various affective elements, horror throws the viewer out of balance and, in doing so, doubles the corporeal instability identifiable on-screen.

As seen in the recent revival of popular screen monsters, such as werewolves and vampires, images of monstrosity can be found to be fundamentally sexed, demonstrating the body's potential for imparting ideas about social and sexual difference. Rosalind Sibielski illustrates this in her chapter on contemporary werewolf films, expressing how monstrosity continues to provide currency for the presentation of sexual difference:

> Tales of monstrosity have frequently been deployed to give expression to cultural fears concerning the blurring of the boundaries between the masculine and the feminine by representing the breakdown of gender categories as 'monstrous.' In twenty-first-century werewolf texts, however, tales of monstrosity are instead deployed to shore up cultural meta-narratives of biological essentialism by insisting that sexual difference is so deeply ingrained that even monstrosity is governed by it.[8]

Sibielski's claims are supported by close analysis of a variety of contemporary werewolf narratives, yet her reading of monstrosity has wider application. Peter Odell Campbell has similarly argued as much in his discussion of HBO's *True Blood* (2008–14), identifying gender-coding as well as an inherent queerness in many contemporary screen monsters.[9] It is largely agreed upon that the horror genre's invocation of otherness is linked to the ways in which it frames the body.[10]

Staple monsters like werewolves and vampires have long acquired attention for symbolic rendering of biological and sexual difference. Through the abject lens of corporeal symbolism, monsters such as these figure as bodies out of balance, operating under the duress of unsanctioned and unchecked desire. Writing on Bram Stoker's *Dracula* (1897), Andrea Dworkin states that:

> Dracula . . . goes beyond metaphor in its intuitive rendering of an oncoming century filled with sexual horror: the throat as a female genital; sex and death as synonymous; killing as a sex act; slow dying as sensuality; men watching the slow dying, and the watching is sexual; mutilation of the female body as male heroism and adventure; callous, ruthless, predatory lust as the one-note meaning of sexual desire.[11]

Dworkin's claim for *Dracula*'s portentous symbolism demonstrates the way in which horror narratives have historically volunteered women's bodies as the literal and figurative bait for male sexual fantasies, played out with violence. The sticky legacy of Dworkin's reading is echoed in contemporary literature in E. L. James's loose reimagining of Stephanie Meyers's vampire saga, *Twilight* (2005–8), as a BDSM fantasy in the *Fifty Shades* trilogy (2011–12). Wrapped within the schema of vampirism, James's identification of what she perceives to be characteristics of a BDSM relationship articulates the ways in which horror narratives (even those directed towards younger audiences, as is the case with *Twilight*) have continued to embody sexual connotations that convey power dynamics.

Examples of horror films that carry pronounced sexual threats, both explicit and implicit, are too numerous to list here;[12] nevertheless, it is striking that violence, a core aesthetic property of horror cinema, has, in the century since *Dracula*, continued to carry a sexual gene. As evinced by Steve Jones, this is especially true of the particularly fraught subgenre that is torture porn. For Jones, the conflation of violence with sex that occurs in the very naming of the subgenre is fundamentally problematic, both for its vagueness and for its suggestion that violence may be functionally pornographic for some viewers.[13] *Dracula*'s precedent illustrates that horror has long maintained a central sexual component and that the sexing of monstrous bodies (such as the vampire) and monstrous acts (like extreme violence) underpins earlier horror traditions. If the sexing of monsters precludes their monstrosity, then Dracula's aggressive thirst for female throats serves also as a threat of rape, at least for Dworkin, for whom the throat acts as a symbolic vagina. If screen monsters continue to possess a sexual identity (and appetite) that is fostered in amplified gender characteristics, then it is clear that contemporary horror owes much to the precedent set by Stoker's *Dracula*, which presents sexual threat as a natural component of androcentric hegemony.

Harry M. Benshoff, in his survey of the queer modes of spectatorship that arise out of horror's subtextual elements, illustrates an ongoing attempt by scholarship to unpick 'the monster movie's underlying ideological project'.[14] This project is evidently multifaceted,[15] yet in its utilisation of the body to illustrate discontinuities in corporeal experiences – be they biological, sexual, social or psychological – body horror specifically can be found to embody the horror genre's capacity to convey various symbolic elements. Judith Butler's extensive work on gender approaches the body as a constructed site of meaning that is wholly subject to the cultural power relations determined by hegemony. Butler writes that 'the power regimes of heterosexism and phallogocentrism seek to augment themselves through a constant repetition of their logic'.[16] Within this vein, sexual violence, both explicit and implicit, manifests in the *logic* of the horror genre, with the corporeal destruction central to its imagery revealing the violent consequences of phallogocentric power. In keeping with Butler's desire to address 'power regimes' and challenge hegemonic privilege and oppression, body horror's symbolic concretisation of oppressive power dynamics offers a recurring indication that some people get to live easier than others, a matter that presents the subgenre as an unexpected enabler of her agenda to dismantle the prevailing heterosexist and phallogocentric logic. In essence, the body emerges from horror cinema as a discursive instrument for the contemplation of difference, otherness and structural systems of othering, as well as a testament to the genre's relatively unique ability to convey shifting ideas about the world through extreme imagery.

Horror's focal interest in bodies and the horrors of sexual threats and violence is far from a new phenomenon. As the previous discussion illustrates, a traceable continuity exists between body horror's earlier and later manifestations: from *Dracula* to Cronenberg and beyond, presentations of the sexed horror-body appear to have an overriding doctrinal authority within the genre's aesthetic and thematic superstructure. Following Carroll's and McRoy's suggestions that horror affectively repeats itself in viewer responses, if we are to accept that the affective properties of horror have a phenomenological effect on the viewer then it follows that watching particular types of horror produces particular types of effects. Compounding Gilles Deleuze and Félix Guattari's notion that affect does more than denote a personal response,[17] Eric Shouse writes that 'an affect is a non-conscious experience of intensity; it is a moment of unformed and unstructured potential'.[18] In keeping with this, the affective potential of horror does more than merely invite particular modes of spectatorship due to a series of symbolic elements; rather, horror films invoke the experience of being the Other, of existing outside, or in the shadow of, heterosexist and phallogocentric hegemonic frameworks.

Trauma in such films, then, does not merely function as thematic subtext but rather emerges as an affective response within viewers to specific textual elements. Just as queer politics may be located within the denotative properties of a classical horror film (as Benshoff argues), there is clear evidence that horror elicits a variety of different forms of spectatorship.[19] If trauma – a key consequence of horror spectatorship – destabilises the body, then it could be deemed that, in doing so, depictions of trauma in horror affectively elicit trauma within certain viewers. But, how does one source evidence of these modes of affect? In the next sections, I will attempt to offer an answer to this question by considering what viewers have made of films such as *Teeth*, *Contracted* and *It Follows*, provocative films with something to say about the female body and its oppression.

The female monster bites back in *Teeth*

Today, even after the many years that have passed since Creed's initial intervention, the concept of feminine monstrosity remains a staple theoretical model in horror studies as recent films continue to illustrate the acuity of her work. Over the last three decades, horror cinema has found currency in grotesque corporeality as a vehicle to explore social anxieties relating to the body. This theme emerges prominently in Mitchell Lichtenstein's *Teeth*, a horror-comedy in which a teenager, Dawn (Jess Weixler), finds herself in possession of a *vagina dentata* that savagely defends her from sexually aggressive men. Steven Shaviro has written that *Teeth* 'conveys a powerful feminist sense of how gender coding is not a personal or moral stance, but rather a socially produced, and socially diffused, framework within which we act and understand without even being aware that we are doing so'.[20] Shaviro's assessment rings true, in that *Teeth* does more than concretise a fantasy of violently castrating a sexually aggressive and socially privileged patriarchy at the hands, or teeth, of the *vagina dentata*. The film situates the body as a primary site through which power manifests – power that is conditioned by the privileges yielded by one's gender.

Naturally, given its approach, *Teeth* is somewhat contentious. Beyond the matter that the bloody castration at least partially victimises her attackers (running the risk of leading viewers to overlook their abhorrent behaviour in favour of empathy for their pain), the fact that Dawn's vagina becomes the involuntary site of a violent act of revenge can be seen to deny her direct ownership of it. As Emma Rees notes, Dawn's 'response [is] beyond her control, so through her revenge she is liberated and threatened in equal measure'.[21] Thus, if *Teeth*'s feminist status is largely engendered through its construction of Dawn's body as a site of resistance, then one should also consider the actual implications of that in regards to her agency as avenger. Ronald Allan Lopez Cruz writes that body horror 'relishes the destruction of the organic form to the point of unnatural evolutionary insignificance'.[22] Dawn's evolved vagina, however, is significant, with the *vagina dentata* operating as a symbolic reminder that women's bodies are are at risk of being taken by force. Yet, herein lies a problem of incompatibility – viewers are required to at once celebrate her body's ability to fight back against the threats posed to it and, conversely, accept the denial of her agency of it. Ultimately, then, Dawn's monstrosity manifests as an evolutionary response to the ongoing threat of sexual violence in a manner that may seem to pose more questions than it answers.

Notwithstanding this, *Teeth* has proved to be a significant film in popular horror discourse, not least for the claims of its value as a feminist text to be found in both scholarly and populist discourses. In an example of the latter, Cody Noble has written that '*Teeth* stands unrelenting as a feminist film, promoting female sexuality, sexual awareness and the notion of consent . . . viewers should come away from *Teeth* with the following truth: pussy does grab back.'[23] Noble channels the spirit of the #MeToo movement and draws clear linkages between *Teeth*'s critique of sexual violence and current US president Donald Trump's appalling advocacy of grabbing women by the genitals. Meanwhile, users discussing *Teeth* in subreddit forums echo Noble's reading of the film's defiance against male sexual aggression. As one user states, '*Teeth* is hilarious IMO. She turns into a dick biting superhero in the end'. Another insinuates a shared female pleasure in watching the film, stating that 'My girlfriends and I adored that movie in college', while a further user proclaims it is 'still [their] favourite movie to recommend to teenage boys'.[24] On Twitter, one woman expresses similar feelings, stating, 'I really like the movie *Teeth* because it's weirdly cathartic for me and I watched it during a time I sort of needed it', and another writes that they 'love teeth [*sic*] and whenever I watch it I come out with a sense of hope'.[25] Elsewhere, IMDb users have similarly found a common interest in the film's depiction of violence against abusive men. One reviewer writes, '[A]fter this movie . . . [you] kinda wish you could do that. a guys [*sic*] rapes you . . . no problem. just "bite" that puppy off.'[26]

The conclusion of this brief discourse analysis is that horror films, and especially those which overturn regular gender dynamics, can have a remedial effect on portions of their audiences, offering cathartic, even pleasurable, viewing experiences. While Mark Jancovich is right to observe the different pathways offered to viewers of a single horror film – writing that 'rather than a horror having a single meaning, different social groups construct it in different, competing ways'[27] – there is a common thread to be found in the above responses to *Teeth*. Yes, these positive reactions vary in intensity, but they do in fact all focus on, and mostly champion, the film's inversion of horror's tendency to present women as victims. As Dawn's *vagina dentata* defiantly repudiates a series of sexual oppressors, her body makes literal the desire to bite back against sexual violence and oppression, to become 'a dick biting superhero', no less. Her evolved body acts in response to this subjugation, imparting a modified sexual agency that has clearly resonated with those spectators fed up with women's on- and off-screen oppression at the hands of a sexually threatening patriarchy, and within a largely demeaning genre. It is to a great extent these feelings that were also the driving force behind many favourable reviews in the popular press (from the *Chicago Tribune*, *Entertainment Weekly*, *The Guardian*, *The New York Times* and *The Wall Street Journal* (all 2008), most notably), praising the film's message and Jess Weixler's central performance. This is an unusual popular reception, given the film's extreme graphic content: a characteristic that often denies a horror film critical legitimation.

Teeth, then, ultimately presents the female body as a site of strength that is distinguished by its characteristics, lending it a corporeal power so strong that men should fear it. Through its underscoring of sexual difference by means of a drastic reinvention of the genitals as monstrosity, the film shifts the body from its normative mode. By utilising embodied monstrosity as a vehicle to impart ideas about male sexual privilege and consent, *Teeth* emerges as a text that expresses a feminist agenda through its monstrous reconfiguration of the female body. Yet, of course, as anyone can confirm, vaginas are not in fact equipped with protective internal teeth, so the film's social utility only extends as far as its plea to dismantle, or at the very least acknowledge, sexual power dynamics that privilege men and oppress women. That the film's hardly radical message is deployed through imagery and representations that are patently corporeal (and latently subversive) speaks to body horror's capacity for social commentary, a quality that has continued to be exercised in many of the body horrors that have followed in *Teeth*'s wake.

Transmission and threat in *Contracted* and *It Follows*

In Eric England's 2013 film *Contracted*, we find an alternative approach to the female monster that bears its own comments on sexual trauma. The film charts the rapid decomposition of protagonist Sam's (Najarra Townsend) body after the contraction of a virus, presenting the female body as monstrosity by considerably different means to Dawn's *vagina dentata*.[28] While *Teeth* locates the female body as a site of resistance, *Contracted* conversely configures it as a site of disease and disintegration. In the film, the virus that brings upon the breaking down of Sam's body is sexually transmitted and, crucially, the specific mode of its transmission has implications for Sam that deny her the same opportunity of retribution afforded to Dawn in *Teeth*: Sam contracts the virus after being raped at a party, inflecting the nature of her body's destruction in troubling ways.

To expand: if the sexual violence inflicted upon Dawn in *Teeth* is immediately and, for some, reasonably punished, then Sam's sexual trauma in *Contracted* is denied any form of comparable cathartic response (for neither Sam nor the audience). This becomes starkly evident when examining *Contracted*'s reception, which is highly problematic for the fact that Sam's rape is not duly acknowledged as rape by a large proportion of the film's viewers. Despite Sam being drunk, drugged and repeatedly telling her attacker to stop, a disturbing number of online commenters discuss the sequence as merely a one-night stand. One writes that 'unprotected, promiscuous sex leads to unspeakable horror', while another states that 'Samantha gets together with a strange guy in a moment of drunken stupor and has unprotected sex.'[29] Yet, a further online reviewer does manage to identify the issue here, writing, 'I am pretty sure the writer might actually not understand that they wrote a rape scene.'[30] This sentiment certainly corresponds with the theatrical poster, which includes the tagline 'Not Your Average One Night Stand', suggesting either a lack of comprehension that the scene clearly depicts rape or, even more unsettling, the trivialisation of rape in search of the perfect promotional gambit.

While the above examples display a troubling level of toxic ignorance (from, it seems, both promoters and a segment of the film's audience), it is not difficult to see why *Contracted* was met with considerably less enthusiasm than *Teeth* was. *Contracted* distastefully punishes Sam for something out of her control, holding her physically accountable for the rape that she endures. It would be generous to argue that the film is subtly calling to attention the sad fact that, in many cases, women end up doubly abused in the aftermath of sexual assault, as blame is scrutinised and shame administered. If only that were the film's message. Given that Sam's attacker promptly disappears from the story after sexually and biologically assaulting her (he does, however, return for the sequel), it is clear that the film is more concerned with its spectacles of bodily disintegration than with sincerely handling its thematic subtexts. In *Contracted*, body horror's capacity to critique modern sexual dynamics in challenging and vital ways is passed up, eschewing the opportunity to comment on the devastating impact of male oppression on the female experience in favour of grotesque imagery.

Yet, it would be wrong to assert that there is an objectively proper manner in which *Contracted* should have conducted its handling of Sam's trajectory, given that rape-revenge plots in film and associated media is a fraught topic that has stirred much debate regarding the responsibility of texts depicting sexual violence. It is not in the interest of this chapter, and certainly not its place, to moralise or try to explain the dos-and-don'ts of screen representations of sexual violence. *Teeth* and *Contracted* take markedly different approaches to the presentation of rape's aftermath, which have engendered equally different patterns of reception. It is difficult not to argue that the former film is to be commended for offering portions of its audiences spectatorial pleasures stemming from its seemingly satisfying treatment of Dawn's attackers, whereas *Contracted* could be criticised for negating this possibility, for both Sam's character and the film's viewers, through its disabling of Sam's capacity for revenge. Megan Garber, writing on the cathartic pleasures of watching Sansa Stark's vengeance against her rapist in the final episode of season six of *Game of Thrones* (HBO, 2010–19), articulates the specific sense of fulfilment that scenes depicting victims' retribution can offer:

> The show . . . presented a vision of justice that was not just civic or karmic, but also warm and close and personal. In the end, it was Sansa and her abuser, alone again in a darkened chamber; in the end, it was Sansa making the decisions about who would be the victim.[31]

As Alexandra Heller-Nicholas notably contends, 'writing about rape – even fictional representations of it – is a formidable task, considering the ideological minefield and deeply subjective and emotional responses that the topic evokes'.[32] Certainly, scholarship must strictly avoid delegitimising the individual responses of those who have personally experienced such unimaginable trauma, as any pleasure experienced by viewers is principally phenomenological. Just as audiences may or may not find karmic satisfaction in Sansa's vengeance, viewers may respond to the rape-revenge dynamic of Dawn's and Sam's narrative arcs in any way they see fit. Rather than make claims for an untenable, distinct moral reality, it is more productive to defer to moral relativism and allow that a text's meaning will shift with each viewer. By failing to patently identify rape as rape though, *Contracted* does not appear to intend to inspire viewers to sympathise with Sam's trauma. Despite clearly rooting its horrors in the body, *Contracted* simply does not offer the same corporeal resistance displayed in *Teeth*; instead, the film only configures Sam as a victim, a matter that, as its reception demonstrates, impacted viewers' responses to it accordingly.

The theme of sexually transmitted afflictions and their threatening effects on the body is further explored in David Robert Mitchell's *It Follows*, albeit in a less patent manner than either *Teeth* or *Contracted*. One of the most critically and commercially successful horror films of recent years, *It Follows* finds protagonist Jay (Maika Monroe) stalked by a fatal curse that has been transferred to her during sex.[33] While ostensibly similar in plot to *Contracted*, the film in fact stands apart from all those previously discussed as one could reasonably argue that, strictly speaking, it is not a body horror film as, in the course of *It Follows*, the protagonists' bodies remain unchanged. However, closer analysis of the film reveals that it very much does include a devastating corporeal threat, but it is one that the protagonists manage to avoid for its duration (albeit with an uncertain conclusion). Instead of being acted out upon the bodies of the central characters in grotesque detail, as is common for body horror, the threat in *It Follows* is rather represented by a demonic entity, whose destructive power we see manifested in the disfigured bodies of those on the fringes.

In this sense, one could even stipulate that *It Follows* works as antibody horror, or even post-body horror, for the fact that the curse does not directly present itself in the protagonists' bodies, but rather, for the large part, remains outwardly invisible.[34] Such a reading offers an alternative, postmodern take on utilisations of the horror body as a means of conveying sexual politics. Indeed, *It Follows* exhibits pointedly artful characteristics typical of what has contentiously been labelled 'post-horror', a term that has rightly been met with suspicion for its suggestion of elitist taste cultures (see David Church's chapter in this collection for further discussion).[35] The film constructs an atmosphere of sustained dread through the uncertainty of its threat, and, while a strong case can be made for its status as a supernatural horror, the utilisation of sex as the source of its corporeal threat offers continuity with other body horror.

It Follows has been found to offer a less straightforward platform for closed critical readings and has been read as a simple supernatural slasher film, as well as a daring commentary on STDs, the dangers of unsafe sex, sexual conservatism and even sexual assault.[36] Irrespective of how one chooses to read *It Follows*, what remains is another horror text principally invested in sex and monstrosity, exploring how these two spheres might converge to dramatically, and devastatingly, alter the body as a result. By locating its horrors in the body (albeit mostly invisibly), *It Follows*, like the other films under discussion, illustrates the various ways in which contemporary horror uses threats against the body to mark difference, and to exchange ideas about diverging social and sexual experiences.

Raw and the monstrosity of adolescence

Thus far, the focus has been on examples of body horror primarily concerned with the causes and effects of female sexual trauma and threat, but other notable contemporary horror texts have employed the body's signifying capacity to examine sexual awakening and exploration. Met with considerable acclaim upon release, *Raw*, Julia Ducournau's cannibal body horror film, is a remarkable example of this.[37] *Raw* belongs to a long tradition of horror cinema – from *Carrie* (Brian De Palma, 1976) to *Ginger Snaps* (John Fawcett, 2000) to *Teeth* – that renders female coming-of-age as corporeal monstrosity. Indeed, Shelley Stamp Lindsey's reading of *Carrie*'s engagement with 'the language of fantasy to represent the terrain of female adolescence' can be aptly applied to the much later releases of *Ginger Snaps*, *Teeth* and *Raw*.[38] Reading the monstrosity of *Carrie*'s titular character as a literalisation of sexual and social difference, Lindsey observes how:

> Conflating questions of femininity and the supernatural, the film renders Carrie's puberty not simply in the hyperbolic language of melodrama, but in the violent terms of horror, where unarticulated excess is not so much placed onto the mise-en-scène as it is written on her body.[39]

Both *Carrie* and *Raw* similarly structure their horrors around educational settings: the former employing the social dynamics of high school, the latter engaging with the undergraduate experience, and in particular the trials of leaving the home. Ducournau's film follows Justine (Garance Marillier) through her first semester at a prestigious veterinary school in rural France. Justine is a supremely bright, if shy, 16-year-old who, having been a lifelong vegetarian, experiences considerable change after eating a raw rabbit kidney during a hazing ritual led by a cohort of older students. She soon finds herself craving meat; following an incident in which her sister, Alexia (Ella Rumpf), loses a finger, that hunger quickly transforms into a desire for human flesh. The hunger Justine feels worsens to the point that it starts to control her at an instinctual level. A particularly striking sequence finds Justine sinking her teeth into her own arm during sex with her queer roommate, Adrien (Rabah Naït Oufella), after he repeatedly restrains her from biting him. In the final act, the film reveals that Justine's condition is genetic as she becomes aware of her sister's similar hunger and murderous means of procuring flesh. Alexia is finally imprisoned for the murder and cannibalisation of Adrien. During the film's final scene, Justine's father tells her that it is neither her nor her sister's fault. Thumbing a scar on his lip, her father goes on to explain that it took a kiss to understand her mother's reluctance to be with him physically. He opens his shirt to reveal scars across his chest. He reassures Justine that she will find her own solution.

Raw, like *Carrie* before it, uses the quiet seclusion of the educational context to metaphorically render puberty through the monstrous devolution of Justine's body into cannibalism; in the course of her transformations,

Justine's new behaviours highlight the ways in which self-governing subcultures (social hierarchies, fraternities, sororities and so on) condition conduct in dangerously debilitating ways. A hermeneutic reading of *Raw*'s socio-spatial development of the eccentric subcultural cohort Justine becomes a part of reveals the pointed ways in which the film offers cultural criticism, at both micro and macro levels. As with many other body horrors (evidenced by *Teeth*, *Contracted* and *It Follows*), in *Raw* there occur transformations of oppressed bodies into grotesque cannibalistic spectacles of corporeal powerlessness as the bodies of the female protagonists begin to evade their control. In an interview with *The Independent*, the director states 'cannibalism is really interesting because it goes with my body obsessions . . . when you talk about the body, you talk about much more than the body – you talk about the human condition'.[40] In light of this statement, Ducournau's depiction of the corporeal reality of a single, outcast, 16-year-old girl can be seen to place the director's presentation of womanhood in dialogue with key works of gender theory. The legacy of Butler's desire to destabilise rigidly patriarchal, heterosexist identity frameworks emerges in Justine in her descent towards a life of cannibalism. If Justine's development is expressive of an array of formative teen experiences, then her journey is certainly illustrative of alternative understandings of corporeal normativity.

To return to *Carrie* once more: in her discussion of the institutional spaces of De Palma's film, Frances Pheasant-Kelly writes that 'the high school prom is a focal point of American socio-cultural tradition, important as a rite of passage and in establishing a coherent body image'.[41] Comparatively, the spaces of *Raw* are significantly less stable than in *Carrie*, emerging as a complex network of diverging social, and thus corporeal, possibilities for Justine. The manifold spaces within which the college experience unfolds in *Raw* are less rigidly determined than the comparatively fixed spaces of the high school prom, therefore formulating a heterotopic labyrinth of unfamiliar subcultural structures that offer new, formative and in some ways traumatic experiences for Justine. Writing on the characteristics of heterotopias, Michel Foucault states that:

> Heterotopias always presuppose a system of opening and closing that both isolates them and makes them penetrable. In general, the heterotopic site is not freely accessible like a public place. Either the entry is compulsory, as in the case of entering a barracks or prison, or else the individual has to submit to rites and purifications. To get in one must have a certain permission and make certain gestures.[42]

It is not difficult to see how Foucault's notion of the heterotopia might be mapped onto the spaces of *Raw* and its treatment of female adolescence. From subterranean parties shot with disorienting handhelds flooded with neon lighting, to rooftop rituals in which blood-drenched pledges consume raw meat, the film presents abject spaces of semi-regulated transgression made accessible by specific 'rites and purifications'. It is within these spaces – liminal spaces of erasure, otherness and monstrosity – that Justine's transformation occurs. On the surface, the eating of meat functions as a ritual introduction into the closed world of the cohort that Justine must join, but it also acts as a bloody rite of passage signifying a sexual awakening. Significantly, the film does not overlook the at times traumatic nature of puberty and the many changes, challenges and fears it can give rise to. When discussing the ritual of eating raw meat (the gateway to human cannibalism), Justine's sister insists it is safe because 'everyone does it'; but, after consuming the meat, Justine finds herself afflicted with a severe rash across her entire body that suggests otherwise. If the forced meat-eating is taken to represent coercion, sexual or otherwise, then the film's development of Justine's monstrosity makes literal the traumatic consequences of these events.

Rather than read *Raw*'s depiction of cannibalism as a critique of meat consumption (which is possible, if fairly redundant, given the broader themes) or see Justine's sexual proclivities as illustrative of S&M preferences, a more rewarding reading might consider the social dynamics of the somewhat cultist cohort that accelerates her monstrous transformation. If the vegetarianism imposed upon Justine by her protective parents is an allegory for abstinence to coincide with veritable lack of sexual knowledge, then one can see how *Raw* makes a case for the value of education and parental support in the development of sexual identity. Justine arrives at college an introverted virgin who soon finds herself plunged into an unfamiliar realm of shifting attitudes and social dynamics. The dynamics presented by the cohort offer Justine a wealth of social and sexual possibilities that correlate with the radical changes occurring within her (indeed, there is something positively Sadean about the excessive carnal possibilities provided by the new social order that Justine comes to inhabit).

Furthermore, it is easy to see how, especially if the forced meat consumption is read as sexual coercion, *Raw* can be understood as a critique of the ways in which subcultures, such as university fraternities and sororities, impact those not entirely ready or willing to participate in their dangerous games. One striking sequence finds Justine drunkenly trying to eat a corpse; some of the group members, unaware of her cannibalistic condition, observe and record this act to circulate among the cohort. The glee with which the other students witness Justine's humiliation, and the ostracism she suffers as a result, brings to mind how sexting images and videos of young people are parasitically and illegally shared to the social ruin of those involved. If Justine's monstrosity is the result of her corruption due to a lack of prior sexual knowledge, then perhaps the monstrosity that manifests in her predicates the universal message that the film shepherds: that such experiences have real impact on young people's lives. Moreover, if her journey is a metaphor for her sexual awakening, then it is sadly one marked by anxiety, coercion and trauma.

Conclusion

Collectively, *Teeth*, *Contracted*, *It Follows* and *Raw* demonstrate how monstrous corporeality provides a coherent vehicle for working through ideas relating to sex, power and identity. In particular, they illustrate how body horror's symbolic currency continues to be utilised by film-makers to articulate issues of female sexual experiences, specifically foregrounding sexual difference in ways that preclude their characters' respective monstrosity. As violent sexual encounters, unbidden transmissions and the pains of sexual awakening give way to corporeal trauma, these films depict extreme destabilisations of the body resulting in monstrosity that threatens the characters in more enduring ways. In such cases, the body symbolically renders difference by way of grotesque differentiation. Monstrous corporeality, as it functions in these case studies, offers a vehicle for communicating the message that, sadly, women's bodies continue to be dictated by harmful sociopolitical structures and subjected to (mostly male) oppression, the effects of which are felt, and rendered, both physically and discursively.

Furthermore, analysis of these films calls for the consideration of their affective potential for the people who view them. As preceding studies on horror, monstrosity and spectatorship (such as Benshoff's work) illustrate, horror born out of the body offers more than mere artifice, providing a mode of expressing divergent ways of navigating the world. Benshoff argues that the 'cinematic monster's subjective position is more readily acceded to by a queer viewer – someone who already situates him/herself outside a patriarchal, heterosexist order and the popular culture texts it produces'.[43] By identifying with monsters, as some viewers of *Teeth* clearly continue to do, viewers are left to explore their familiarity with the subtexts of what they see on screen. By assigning themselves the role of the monster, such viewers may experience how watching body horror offers a complex negotiation of themes revolving around sex, trauma and agency. Indeed, Benshoff's claim that queer viewers may express sympathy with outwardly monstrous characters is telling of how culturally marginalised and/or abused viewers might identify themselves in relation to hegemonic identity paradigms and prevailing forms of power. It is by these means that, as this survey demonstrates, contemporary horror continues to offer a lucrative platform to explore how gender politics come to light through embodied images of abjection, difference and trauma.

In the context of the real-world horror of sexual oppression and abuse – starkly amplified by the ongoing #MeToo movement – contemporary body horror films, such as *Teeth*, *Contracted*, *It Follows* and *Raw*, utilise monstrosity to articulate universal fears about the female experience and women's current place in the world. In *The Monstrous-Feminine*, Creed made the persuasive case for a new term to capture 'the importance of gender in the construction of [feminine] monstrosity'.[44] Even as the horror genre continues to develop in many ways, in the twenty-five years since *The Monstrous-Feminine*'s publication horror films have, in simple terms, enduringly expanded on Creed's original thesis. Locked within contemporary cinematic reinstitutions of the female monster are recurring attempts to reflect upon the horrors and consequences of sexual violence and trauma that both embolden and move forward Creed's model, making use of the body to provide dramatic and grotesque visualisations of new forms of sexual and social difference.

Notes

1. Barbara Creed, *The Monstrous-Feminine: Film, Feminism, Psychoanalysis* (London: Routledge, 1993). Also see Carol J. Clover, *Men, Women, and Chain Saws: Gender in the Modern Horror Film* (Princeton, NJ: Princeton University Press, 1992); B. K. Grant (ed.), *The Dread of Difference: Gender and the Horror Film* (Austin, TX: University of Texas Press, 2015).
2. Noël Carroll, *The Philosophy of Horror or Paradoxes of the Heart* (London: Routledge, 1990).

3. L. McLarty, '"Beyond the Veil of the Flesh": Cronenberg and the Disembodiment of Horror', in B. K. Grant (ed.), *The Dread of Difference: Gender and the Horror Film* (Austin, TX: University of Texas Press, 2015), p. 262.
4. Xavier Aldana Reyes, *Body Gothic: Corporeal Transgression in Contemporary Literature and Horror Film* (Cardiff: University of Wales Press, 2014), p. 58.
5. J. McRoy, '"Parts is Parts": Pornography, Splatter Films and the Politics of Corporeal Disintergration', in I. Conrich (ed.), *Horror Zone: The Cultural Experience of Contemporary Horror Cinema* (London: I. B. Tauris, 2009), p. 197–8.
6. See L. Williams, 'When the Woman Looks', in B. K. Grant (ed.), *The Dread of Difference* (Austin, TX: University of Texas Press, 2015), pp. 15–34; see also Vivian Sobchack's work on the kinaesthetic subject, in Sobchack, *Carnal Thoughts: Embodiment and Moving Image Culture* (Berkeley, CA: University of California Press, 2004).
7. L. Williams, 'Film Bodies: Gender, Genre, and Excess', in B. K. Grant (ed.), *Film Genre Reader III* (Austin, TX: University of Texas Press, 2003), p. 144.
8. R. Sibielski, 'Gendering the Monster Within: Biological Essentialism, Sexual Difference, and Changing Symbolic Functions of the Monster in Popular Werewolf Texts', in M. Levina and D. T. Bui (eds), *Monster Culture in the 21st Century: A Reader* (London: Bloomsbury, 2013), p. 117.
9. P. O. Campbell, 'Intersectionality Bites: Metaphors of Race and Sexuality in HBO's *True Blood*', in M. Levina and D. T. Bui (eds), *Monster Culture in the 21st Century: A Reader* (London: Bloomsbury, 2013), p. 99–101.
10. See Harry M. Benshoff, *Monsters in the Closet: Homosexuality and the Horror Film* (Manchester: Manchester University Press, 2004); Aldana Reyes, *Body Gothic*; M. de Valk (ed.), *Screening the Tortured Body: Cinema as Scaffold* (Basingstoke: Palgrave Macmillan, 2016).
11. Andrea Dworkin, *Intercourse* (New York, NY: Free Press, 1987), p. 119.
12. See Clover, *Men, Women, and Chain Saws*.
13. Steve Jones, *Torture Porn: Popular Horror after Saw* (Basingstoke: Palgrave Macmillan, 2013), p. 15.
14. Benshoff, *Monsters in the Closet*, p. 286.
15. For more examples of a reflectionist critical orthodoxy, see R. Wood, 'The American Nightmare: Horror in the 70s', in M. Jancovich (ed.), *Horror, the Film Reader* (London: Routledge, 2001), pp. 25–33; Clover, *Men, Women, and Chain Saws*; Richard Dyer, *The Culture of Queers* (London: Routledge, 2002).
16. J. Butler, '"Subjects of Sex/Gender/Desire" (1990)', in I. Szeman and T. Kaposy (eds), *Cultural Theory: An Anthology* (Chichester: Wiley-Blackwell, 2011), p. 487–8.

17. B. Massumi, 'Notes on the Translation and Acknowledgements', in G. Deleuze and F. Guattari, *A Thousand Plateaus* (Minneapolis, MN: University of Minnesota Press, 1987), p. xvi.
18. E. Shouse, 'Feeling, Emotion, Affect', *M/C Journal*, 8/6 (2005), *http://journal.media-culture.org.au/0512/03-shouse.php* (accessed 29 August 2019).
19. Benshoff, *Monsters in the Closet*, pp. 1–30.
20. S. Shaviro, '*Teeth*', *The Pinocchio Theory* (3 May 2008), *http://www.shaviro.com/Blog/?p=632* (accessed 10 January 2020).
21. Emma Rees, *The Vagina: A Literary and Cultural History* (London: Bloomsbury, 2013), p. 238.
22. R. A. L. Cruz, 'Mutations and Metamorphoses: Body Horror is Biological Horror', *Journal of Popular Film and Television*, 40/4 (2012), 167–8.
23. C. Noble, 'Vagina Dentata: Re-examining Teeth (2007)', *Diabolique Magazine* (29 January 2017), *https://diaboliquemagazine.com/vagina-dentata-re-examining-teeth-2007/* (accessed 29 August 2019).
24. To see the full comments from users 'meinnitbruva', 'Princess_kushlestia' and 'CigfranDu' (respectively), see 'Teeth, a 2008 indie film about a Christian girl that has razor sharp teeth in her vagina', *Reddit* (2017), *https://www.reddit.com/r/dontputyourdickinthat/comments/7wydx6/teeth_a_2008_indie_film_about_a_christian_girl/?utm_source=share&utm_medium=web2x* (accessed 10 January 2020).
25. Addison Peacock (@Addison_Peacock), *Twitter* (2018), *https://twitter.com/Addison_Peacock* (accessed 19 September 2019); Chrys (@Chrysanthmm), *Twitter* (2018), *https://twitter.com/chrysnathemm* (accessed 19 September 2019).
26. Kelly (@anomalousdarling), 'NOT what I expected', *IMDb*, *https://www.imdb.com/user/ur4034964/?ref_=tt_urv* (accessed 10 January 2020).
27. M. Jancovich, 'Genre and the Audience: Genre Classifications and Cultural Distinctions in the Mediation of *The Silence of the Lambs*', in R. Maltby and M. Stokes (eds), *Hollywood Spectatorship: Changing Perceptions of Cinema Audiences* (London: BFI Publishing, 2001), p. 43.
    Contracted is often compared to Éric Falardeau's *Thanatomorphose*, which was released a year before it in 2012. The plotting is indeed strikingly similar, yet with one key difference – in *Thanatomophose*, the protagonist discovers her affliction after awakening from a night of rough sex to find her body rotting, whereas in *Contracted*, Sam contracts the virus after being raped.
28. @dee.reid, '"Contracted" (2013) follows one week after "It Follows" (2014)', *IMDb*, *https://www.imdb.com/review/rw3338365/?ref_=rw_urv* (accessed 10 January 2020); Paul Magne Haakonsen (@paul_haakonsen), 'You will

catch somethings while watching this movie . . . And it will stick with you . . .', *IMDb*, *https://www.imdb.com/review/rw2978969/?ref_=tt_urv* (accessed 10 January 2020).

29. @Bexcellent, 'Good potential but disappointing', *IMDb*, *https://www.imdb.com/review/rw3261479/?ref_=tt_urv* (accessed 10 January 2020).

30. M. Garber, 'Justice for Sansa Stark', *The Atlantic* (20 June 2016), *https://www.theatlantic.com/entertainment/archive/2016/06/justice-for-sansa-stark/487814/* (accessed 29 August 2019).

31. Alexandra Heller-Nicholas, *Rape-Revenge Films: A Critical Study* (Jefferson, NC: McFarland, 2011), p. 7.

32. *It Follows* boasts a Rotten Tomatoes rating of 96 per cent positive reviews (*https://www.rottentomatoes.com/m/it_follows* (accessed 10 January 2020)) and a box-office sum of $23 million (*https://www.the-numbers.com/movie/It-Follows#tab=summary* (accessed 10 January 2020)).

33. This theme is explored in J. Hayward, 'No Safe Space: Economic Anxiety and Post-recession Spaces in Horror Films', *Frames Cinema Journal*, 11 (2017), *http://framescinemajournal.com/article/no-safe-space-economic-anxiety-and-post-recession-spaces-in-horror-films/* (accessed 29 August 2019).

34. See S. Rose, 'How post-horror movies are taking over cinema', *The Guardian* (6 July 2017), *https://www.theguardian.com/film/2017/jul/06/post-horror-films-scary-movies-ghost-story-it-comes-at-night* (accessed 29 August 2019).

35. See B. Morrow, '"It Follows" is Not About STDs. It's About Life As a Sexual Assault Survivor.', *Bloody Disgusting* (27 April 2016), *https://bloody-disgusting.com/editorials/3387893/follows-not-stds-life-sexual-assault-survivor/* (accessed 29 August 2019).

36. *Raw*'s aggregate score from popular critics places it at 91 per cent on Rotten Tomatoes, *https://www.rottentomatoes.com/m/raw_2017* (accessed 10 January 2020).

37. S. S. Lindsey, 'Horror, Femininity, and Carrie's Monstrous Puberty', in B. K. Grant (ed.), *The Dread of Difference: Gender and the Horror Film* (Austin, TX: University of Texas Press, 2015), p. 280.

38. Lindsey, 'Horror, Femininity', p. 280.

39. Julia Ducournau quoted in K. Aftab, 'Director Julia Ducournau on her cannibal film Raw: "I asked my actor, what do you think in principle about shoving your hand up a cow's arse?"', *The Independent* (15 April 2017), *https://www.independent.co.uk/arts-entertainment/films/features/julia-ducournau-raw-a7666871.html* (accessed 29 August 2019).

40. Frances Pheasant-Kelly, *Abject Spaces in American Cinema: Institutional Settings, Identity and Psychoanalysis in Film* (London: I. B. Tauris, 2013), p. 44.

41. M. Foucault, 'Of Other Spaces: Utopias and Heterotopias', *Architecture/Mouvement/Continuité* (1984), 7.
42. H. M. Benshoff, 'The Monster and the Homosexual', in H. M. Benshoff and S. Griffin (eds), *Queer Cinema: The Film Reader* (London: Routledge, 2004), p. 66.
43. Creed, *The Monstrous-Feminine*, p. 7.

11

The Kids are Alt-right

Hardcore Punk, Subcultural Violence and Contemporary American Politics in Jeremy Saulnier's *Green Room*[1]

Thomas Joseph Watson

THIS CHAPTER PRESENTS a critical case study of one horror film that was produced and released alongside the development of a contentious sociopolitical epoch in contemporary American culture. As such, I would like to begin with a quotation that addresses these wider contexts:

> [T]he night Barack Obama was elected President in 2008, the White supremacist web forum Stormfront lit up with posts about racial extremists' fantastical visions of violence to combat 'White racial genocide'. On election night 2016, Stormfront lit up again as White supremacists expressed triumph with Donald Trump's victory. They celebrated: 'we finally have one of us in the Whitehouse again!'[2]

Approximately two months prior to 20 January 2017, the day that Donald Trump was inaugurated as the forty-fifth president of the United States, alt-right originator Richard Spencer declared America 'a White country, designed for ourselves and our prosperity', before raising his arm, toasting the crowd gathered at the National Policy Institute national conference, and proclaiming 'Hail Trump! Hail our people! Hail victory!' This gesture was then met with a chorus of cheers and Nazi Sieg Heil salutes, blurring the semantic distinctions between white nationalism, white supremacy and neo-Nazism.

Approximately six months after Trump's inauguration, on 11–12 August 2017, protesters from 'activist groups' claiming affiliation with white supremacist, white nationalist, neo-Nazi and neo-confederate organisations descended on Charlottesville, West Virginia, justified for doing so in their unified opposition to the proposed removal of the statue of confederate commander Robert E. Lee. This apparent opposition evidenced what Kirsten Dyck has referred to as a toxic form of 'nostalgia for the slavery era'.[3] This so-called 'Unite the Right' rally was initiated by a torch procession, replete with chants of 'Jews will not replace us', 'Blood and Soil' and the rallying cries of 'White lives matter'.[4] The proposed removal of the confederate monument from Virginia's Emancipation Park was itself a response to the murders of nine African-American parishioners in Charleston, South Carolina, by white supremacist Dylan Roof in June 2015. It is in this respect that the alt-right movement in the US, gaining momentum since its inception in 2010, garnered a sense of public visibility that had been gestating systemically in different guises for over a decade. It is within this politically extreme climate that Jeremy Saulnier's *Green Room* (2016) was released, a horror siege narrative that has been framed in the contexts of the alt-right movement and the resultant casualties of their infractions. The actual 'horrors' of *Green Room* are positioned within narrative contexts of angry, racist ideology and the escalating violence that is created when such rhetoric masquerades as a substantial ideology. This horror is therefore granted a further degree of veracity and poignancy when it is placed alongside a very real, violent reality.

In the wake of the Charlottesville 'Unite the Right' rally, the Alamo Drafthouse Theatre located in the city organised a programme of films, titled 'Intolerable: Reflections of Bigotry and Hatred in Cinema', aiming to ruminate on the following questions: 'What are the socioeconomic conditions that have fostered this anger and hatred? What life experiences result in someone wielding a torch at a White supremacist rally? And most of all, how can we make our communities better for all?'[5] *Green Room* was included as part of this screening programme as a contemporaneous film perceived to address these issues. It depicts the aftermath of a hardcore punk band witnessing a murder at a venue owned by neo-Nazis, and their attempts to escape from further violent retribution.

Many reviews of the film have focused on the apparent connections between *Green Room* and an ultra-conservative allegorical moment, leading with reflective titles such as 'Watching Green Room after Charlottesville'[6] and '"Green Room" Is a Horror Movie for Trump's America',[7] thus framing the film as anticipating the prominence of the alt-right and their position concomitant with Trump's presidency. To add theoretical weight to such readings, Adam Lowenstein has defined the allegorical moment as the 'shocking collision of film, spectator, and history where registers of bodily space and historical time are disrupted, confronted, and intertwined'.[8] The allegorical moment is attributed to the way significant historical trauma, national historiographies and discourses relating to cultural identity are negotiated and reconciled.[9] In order to do this, Lowenstein questions how certain films 'access discourses of horror to confront the representation of historical trauma tied to the film's national and cultural context'.[10] *Green Room* can therefore be read as a representation of historical tensions and conflicts within a particular subcultural 'scene' and also as a film that exploits discourses of horror to confront the representation of pro-white racism, neo-Nazism and white supremacy in contemporary American culture.

The current chapter examines *Green Room* as an allegorical reflection, illustrative of racial tensions and fascist extremism in contemporary American culture. The chapter follows a two-pronged analysis that will examine how the film's aesthetics of violence punctuate the escalating ordeal narrative, responding to the film's 'discourses of horror' and how they may be interpreted through Foucauldian ideas of power, containment and control. Additionally, I aim to locate this violence historically, at a subcultural level, examining the position of the neo-Nazi in contrast to established punk/hardcore ideologies (albeit confined to the geographical limitations of the US for the purposes of this chapter).[11] As such, the current work aims to position *Green Room* alongside other representations of extreme, radical politics and the way such ideologies have been utilised as a source of horror.

Subcultures and representation: fascism and Nazism meet punk and hardcore

Petra Rau, in historicising the semantic conflation of Nazism and fascism, presents the following analysis:

In the popular discourse, historical specificities often fall by the wayside, and then the term fascism – and often 'fascism' – refers to any local versions of right-wing, authoritarian, totalitarian, ultra-nationalist and corporate rule . . . 'Fascism' assumes a common denominator but prefers Nazism as its most effective iconography. Nazism has simply become the synecdoche for fascism.[12]

Alongside popular discourse, as it is referred to by Rau, representations of skinhead subcultures across national boundaries have been relatively constant since the early 1980s, mirroring the emergence of the subculture in the UK and its exportation to wider Europe and the US. Filmic representations have located the subculture, and its presumed fascistic leanings, across a range of sociopolitical contexts (relating to both immediate and nostalgic iterations of Thatcher's Britain, the galvanisation of the far-right in Europe and the turbulent race relations and conservative politics that continue to affect contemporary American and Australian culture). As such, a tentative canon of 'skinhead cinema' may be formed encompassing the following films: *Made in Britain* (Alan Clarke, 1982), *Skinheads: The Second Coming of Hate* (Greydon Clark, 1989), *Romper Stomper* (Geoffrey Wright, 1992), *Pariah* (Randolph Kret, 1998), *American History X* (Tony Kaye, 1998), *The Believer* (Henry Bean, 2001), *This is England* (Shane Meadows, 2008), *Russia 88* (Pavel Bardin, 2009) and *Imperium* (Daniel Ragussis, 2016). With specific reference to *Romper Stomper*, *American History X* and *The Believer*, John Marmysz points to the characterisation of the violent skinhead as 'sophisticated and sympathetic' and suggests that there is a 'remarkable ambivalence towards skinheads' in popular cinema.[13] This ambivalence presents a contrast with the transgressive position of skinheads in subcultural discourse, especially in relation to instances of violence motivated by fascism. A similar conflation has also been attributed to skinheads and neo-Nazis in subcultural terms.

Two sides of the US hardcore scene are relevant to *Green Room* as a case study: first, bands have appropriated white-power imagery (and continue to do so) so that they may attack the wider ideologies of neoconservative culture; secondly, several bands and notable figureheads have also appropriated such imagery but do so to communicate a politics of hate (spreading rhetoric concerning violence and discrimination). As Kevin Borgeson and Robin Maria Valeri suggest, 'since the 1980s, skinheads and neo-Nazis have been treated as two sub-types of the same thing', and it is apparent that 'violence is an attribute common to all skinheads that join the movement, not just neo-Nazis'.[14] As such, *Green Room* also acknowledges the contentious presence of neo-Nazi skinheads in the American punk (and later hardcore) scene(s). For Borgeson and Valeri:

> Hardcore was also an outlet for white youth who felt discriminated against in post-civil rights America. Many white youths, growing up in an era where policies were designed to ensure equal rights under the law for all in America, began to feel that they were objects of discrimination. As the American economy took a downward turn, the middle-class families were experiencing the effects of layoffs and downsizing. The American dream seemed less and less achievable. Court decisions enforced policies aimed at promoting racial equality and few youths truly understood why such policies were necessary. Many simply thought of those policies as preferential to minorities.[15]

Green Room is a product of director Saulnier's own autobiographical experiences as part of the Washington D.C. punk and hardcore scenes of the late 1980s/early 1990s, and it is worth reflecting on the dominant political discourse that characterised the Reagan administration and a growing sense of disenfranchisement and politicisation within these scenes. The rise of hardcore punk in the early 1980s, amid the contemporaneous Reagan administration, developed in tandem with 'the emergence of the discursive paradigm of a so-called colour-blind society' where the illusion of racial equality was promoted.[16] In accordance with such a perspective, racism became 'a thing of the past' and 'the American myth of the seemingly limitless potential of the individual' became 'the sole basis for political discourse'.[17] This political discourse 'played to resurgent conservatism, to nationalism, and to fundamentalism – the emerging foundations of the New Right'.[18]

In response, various hardcore punk bands went on to adopt imagery associated with white supremacism to highlight the perceived hypocrisy of this paradigm (and it was this transgressive imagery that alluded to an apparent undercurrent of repression within the 'official' discourse). This 'subversive appropriation of white power imagery' adorned album covers, tour flyers and other ephemera, with the Texan band M.D.C. (Millions of Dead Cops) and the New York group Reagan Youth being some of the most visible, and vocal, in terms of both iconography and satire.[19] The back cover of M.D.C.'s eponymous first album, for example, depicts the amalgamation of a Klansman and a police officer pointing a gun directly at the audience, an image they adapted accordingly for their latest release, *Mein Trumpf* (2017), by replacing the figure of the police officer with the current president. These bands, alongside the Dead Kennedys, 'attacked President Ronald Reagan, the Christian neoconservative right, and white hate groups alike', and this attack on neoconservative values can be seen in contemporary political and subcultural contexts when considering the current Trump administration as an echo of the 1980s.[20]

White rage and inchoate whiteness: subcultural contexts of punk and hardcore

In the context of contemporary USA, and centred primarily around skinhead music and culture, white supremacists recast punk rock as a medium of intolerance. White power becomes a rallying cry for disenfranchised, often working-class, white youth who create an imagined community of racial purity through their music and their scene. For those on the political right, punk offers illusory pure-white-people's-music.[21] Daniel S. Traber suggests that 'part of popular music's allure is that it offers fans tools for identity construction'.[22] Recent studies of punk subcultures, and of the nature of DIY punk specifically, have addressed the ways individuals are provided with 'the resources with which to construct oppositional identities'.[23] Indeed, 'punk provides individuals with the opportunity of self-empowerment and disalienation' which can lead to potent forms of political resistance.[24] However, the politically progressive nature of punk, as alluded to here, casts this subculture in a romanticised light, and the possible negative aspects of this 'empowerment' need to be accounted for. Indeed, as Kevin Dunn concedes, 'there is nothing inherently progressive about the politics and political openings that punk engenders', and it is the case whereby 'many punks have constructed oppositional identities along racist, fascist, and neo-Nazi lines'.[25] *Green Room* explicates these tensions by placing two different iterations of punk within mutually shared subcultural spaces (the remote neo-Nazi club and the green room it contains). As such, 'punk provides the resources and the political openings for individuals to be politicized', but 'the actual character of that politicization is shaped by personal agency and other socio-economic and historical forces'.[26]

Cultural anxieties concerning the promotion and distribution of white-power rhetoric have often focused on the production and proliferation of white-power hate music in other subcultural scenes (specifically punk). As Matthew Worley and Nigel Copsey argue, movements within the far-right attempt 'to claim youth cultural styles and forms of popular music as conduits for fascist politics' and seek to utilise 'cultural spaces associated with punk to propagate racism and fascism'.[27] As a result, 'the far-right's appropriation of punk and skinhead styles forged a distinct subculture aligned instead to the politics of Nazism and ultra-nationalism', whereby such appropriation came to function as a recruitment tool.[28] This is alluded to in the film as *Green Room*'s white supremacist leader, Darcy Banker (Patrick Stewart), implores his followers to 'remember, it's not a party, it's a movement', when the crowd is gathered at his backwoods venue. For John M. Cotter, such 'propaganda seeks to incite violent activity by accentuating perceived threats from a conspiracy of enemies and by constructing a "warrior" subculture that glorifies aggression and sacrifice'.[29] This is again illustrated in scenes which depict willing 'true believers' as they stab themselves before they are taken into custody, thereby sacrificing themselves to cover up the initial murder in the film (a point I will explicate below). The supposed 'cause' promoted by this white supremacist faction is thereby ultimately protected from legitimate law and order.

Certain tensions emerge here. Previous positions of racial extremism have been rendered increasingly insidious in structural terms, but have also maintained a higher sense of visibility and mainstream crossover from their previous positions as prevalent online subcultures (as noted by cultural scholar Angela Nagle in reference to the alt-right).[30] As Dyck states, 'for many individuals who have joined pro-white hate groups in the postwar era, the radical, illicit, and stigmatized nature of white-power and neo-Nazi ideologies and practices is often part of their appeal'.[31] This then leads to the question as to whether those who have joined these groups have indeed done so on the basis that they harbour the same extreme rhetoric of hate and discrimination espoused by such groups (or at least sympathise with it), or whether it is the transgressive, outlaw nature of this subculture that serves as reason enough to join. In this sense, boundary-pushing and the testing of an individual's thresholds may account for membership as opposed to any racist ideology (and it is this sense of boundary-testing that is broached in several films detailing subcultures and neo-Nazi sensibilities).

Subcultural capital, authenticity and violence

In her book *Club Cultures: Music, Media and Subcultural Capital*, Sarah Thornton offers a critical reading of the different relationships existing between taste cultures and social structure: 'Subcultural ideologies are a means by which youth imagine their own and other social groups, assert their distinctive character and affirm that they are not anonymous members of an undifferentiated mass.'[32] Thornton draws on the foundational writings of Pierre Bourdieu, particularly his 1984 work *Distinction* and his formulations of cultural capital. Thornton's conceptions of subcultural capital are evidenced at several key points in *Green Room*, working to establish subcultural boundaries and the position of the characters within them. The first clear instance of Thornton's *objectified* subcultural capital relates to the way members of the film's focal band, The Ain't Rights, treat Tad (David W. Thompson), a local Oregon punk and gig promoter with whom they are staying on their tour, by scrutinising his music tastes. As Thornton notes, 'subcultural capital confers status on its owner in the eyes of the relevant beholder' and 'is objectified in the form of fashionable haircuts and well-assembled record collections'.[33]

The opening stages of the film progress in a way that expand these subcultural notions of authenticity and truth. As Tad begins to interview the band about their output and creative drives, he alludes to the band being 'hard to find' due to no 'social media presence', admiring this fact as he explains how he approves of their 'analogue style'. Bass player Pat (Anton Yelchin) offers the following contemplative response: 'no one wants to starve, but when you take it all virtually you lose the texture . . . you gotta be there, music is for effect, its time and aggression . . . and it's shared live. And then it's over, the energy can't last.' Pat's assertions reflect Thornton's discussion of authenticity and popular music, whereby 'music is perceived as authentic when it *rings true* or *feels real*, when it has *credibility* and comes across as *genuine*'.[34] The live show is what constitutes authenticity for Pat, and 'the essence or truth of music' is still located in the live performance as an embodied experience. This is in opposition to the commodity fetishism characteristic of contemporary music subcultures where subcultural capital is displaced onto coveted 7" vinyl, for example (hence the initial admiration of Tad and his record collection). It is, however, the live performance that leads to the demise of the band and the ensuing horror depicted in the film.

Due to a show cancellation about which Tad has failed to notify the band prior to their arrival, he offers them a replacement gig nearby in rural Portland set up by his skinhead cousin. Warning the band that they're 'mostly boots and braces down there', guitarist Sam confirms that 'They're not like burning crosses or anything, right?' Tad's assertions that the skinheads are 'Right Wing, technically ultra-left but not affiliated' does not seem to deter the band as Pat alludes to an awareness of DMs and SHARP skinheads that have populated their shows in the past.[35] When the band members arrive at the rural backwoods venue, they are taken to the green room of the film's title. After receiving precise instructions as to where to unload their gear ('the owner doesn't fuck around with the fire codes'), the band is led directly to the backstage area. The set-dressing immediately points to the white-power sensibilities welcomed in this location as the walls are adorned with insignia associated with racism (stickers and banners promote slogans like 'Anti-racist = Anti-white', 'Kaiser Crusade', 'Don't Forget who the Real Victims Are' and 'White Pride Worldwide').[36] Further reference is made by the band, rather flippantly, to the dubious leanings of their hosts ('They run a tight ship . . . except it's a U-boat').

The iconography of 1980s US hardcore is knowingly evoked throughout *Green Room*, not least in the clothing worn by the lead characters comprising the hardcore group The Ain't Rights (Minor Threat and Dead Kennedys shirts, for example), but also the imagery used to promote the film and the horror and violence to come (the severed arm on Oliver Barrett's limited-edition quad-poster variant stands as a warped appropriation of Raymond Pettibon's iconic 'four bars' logo for the seminal US hardcore band Black Flag). Perhaps one of the central homages to the 1980s hardcore scene in the film is the initial act of defiance offered by The Ain't Rights to the crowd gathered in the venue, the band taking to the stage for what happens to be their last show. The band tears into a knowing rendition of the Dead Kennedys' 'Nazi Punks Fuck Off', this track being one of the central anti-fascist songs of the subculture (the lyrics addressing the systemic, conservative politics governing society's institutions):

> Punk ain't no religious cult
> Punk means thinking for yourself
> You ain't hardcore 'cause you spike your hair
> When a jock still lives inside your head
> . . .
> You still think swastikas look cool
> The real Nazis run your schools
> They're coaches, businessmen and cops
> In a real fourth Reich you'll be the first to go

Nazi punks
Nazi punks
Nazi punks, fuck off!
Nazi punks
Nazi punks
Nazi punks, fuck off!

You'll be the first to go
You'll be the first to go
You'll be the first to go
Unless you think

The scene is therefore set for a slow increase in tension in the atmosphere inside the venue, as one punk subculture comes into ideological conflict with another. But what sets *Green Room* aside and marks it as a horror film is the unrelenting, cold sense of calculation and precision that characterises the film's main aggressors (attributes that present these figures as something more than obvious villains and monsters). Although the film does not depict any violence that is directly motivated by racial hatred, the violence enacted is justified by the neo-Nazis to maintain a sense of self-preservation and survival, regardless of the human cost (on both sides), to protect their ideology.

The initial off-screen murder of the film is discovered by Pat as he returns to the green room to retrieve a misplaced phone. The narrative reveals that the victim, a young girl named Emily, was a member of the white power movement and was plotting her escape with her boyfriend, with the assistance of her friend Amber. This escape attempt, upon discovery, results in a violent death, which is the catalyst for the violent maelstrom that permeates the film (referred to as a 'cluster fuck' in the film's narrative).[37] Theorist Michel Foucault made the following distinctions between power and violence:

> What defines a relationship of power is that it is a mode of action which does not act directly and immediately on others. Instead, it acts upon their actions: an action upon an action, on existing actions or on those which may arise in the present or the future. A relationship of violence acts upon a body or upon things; it forces, it bends, it breaks.[38]

Power is exerted by the figure of Darcy as he controls his underlings and perceives the incarcerated Ain't Rights as a threat to his organisation. Power is used to maintain control over the band as they remain incarcerated in the earlier stages of the film, utterances such as 'we're not keeping you here, you're just staying' and 'do you see a way out of it? For them . . . no' making this power implicit. It is crucial that the band not see Darcy until the end of the film, making his faceless proclamations of threatened violence all the more unnerving: 'Okay, now, you're trapped. That's not a threat, it's a fact'.

As Sabine Hake notes, this exertion of power and control has an ideological function whereby 'the Nazis' primary role is to personify the monopoly of violence and the power over life and death associated with the totalitarian state, to perform the suspension of the rule of law and its replacement by total surveillance'.[39] This is further instilled as Darcy's attack dogs are controlled by the German attack command 'Fass!' and his underlings are given the hierarchical identity of makeshift foot soldiers based on their 'Red Laces'.[40] As Hake continues in relation to the characterisation of the Nazi, 'confirming their status as absolute enemies, they remain identified with a complete lack of emotion – to be precise, the power to affect (i.e. someone or something) but not to be affected. All their attention is focused on the expansion and preservation of power.'[41] When Darcy realises that the escalating violence will indeed affect his interests, further violence is offered as the only recourse. Foucault also noted that 'where there is power, there is resistance', and it is this resistance that characterises the main points of violent rupture within the film, the band members being brutally murdered as they attempt to escape their captors (Reece, Tiger and Sam are stabbed, mauled and shot to death respectively). As explained in an interview with Saulnier, 'the assumption is that violence is a choice that ends choices: once characters commit to solving a problem with murder, they set off a chain of events that seems inevitable, and that draws more and more people into the maelstrom'.[42] As Reece says before he exits the green room, 'we won't all live, but, I dunno, maybe we won't all die'.

These relationships of violence become processes of action and reaction to structures of power, control and containment. This is both in a literal sense, given the limited confines of the film, and in symbolic terms, when ideology and self-preservation are threatened. These demonstrations of power, control and containment have also been evoked in the critical discourse around the film, with David Jenkins noting that '*Green Room* is about how modern politics is the process of averting a crisis', evoking a response to the current presidency as an administration of chaos by design.[43] Moreover, Trevor Johnston, while interviewing Saulnier directly, suggested that 'on the surface, *Green Room* . . . would seem to be warning about the far-right extremists festering in the country's rural heartlands'. In response, Saulnier offered the following commentary concerning the political subtext of his film:

> For me, it's actually using the Neo-Nazi extremists to highlight the problems of the American Right. What Patrick Stewart's authoritarian character is actually protecting, and what he's telling his minions they're actually fighting for, are clearly two different things. And that's the issue with the very corporate, elitist movement on the American Right, which uses all sorts of false ideology to start culture wars among the underlings, because it's about keeping them fighting each other rather than looking out for their own interests. Overall, it's not so much about the Neo-Nazis per se, though, as it is a critique of mainstream America . . . *Green Room* is still about delivering this very intense movie experience . . . Underneath, though, there's a story about stripping away ideology and affiliation so people can get back to being just human beings . . . The hatred is learned. It's channelled. And who's doing the channelling?[44]

Darcy therefore represents much more than a simple antagonist for the film's story. Though his actions may look selfish in the film's later scenes, his positioning earlier on means that he reveals much about the truth of the far-right ideology represented in the film. Their ideology is self-serving, self-interested and emphasises personal gains and superiority above all else.

One of the most sobering realisations in the film is indeed the false presentation of the unifying and brotherly ideology espoused by Darcy. As the film progresses and people are killed on both sides, it becomes apparent that Darcy is only really interested in protecting his own livelihood as a dealer of heroin, very much opposed to those who sell and consume 'that nigger dope'. For Saulnier, 'the theme is really about stripping people of their affiliation, their ideology, and their labels . . . Through this need to survive, they throw away all of their identities.'[45] This is also true of the surviving punks and remaining female skinhead as Pat and Amber become hyper-realised versions of the antagonistic skinheads in order to fight back and survive. For Darcy, any real sense of white supremacist ideology falls apart when he can no longer maintain a sense of order or control. As such, 'the larger, again critical suggestion is that for many in the skinhead subculture, neo-Nazism is no more than a pose, with the subculture being for those just a means of asserting power and/or expressing anger'.[46] The remaining punks can no longer remain true to their sense of self and authenticity; as they remark, 'if we can't play real war . . . let's pretend'. The finale of the film is the first time where Pat is able to see Darcy (as he is about to dispose of Pat's fellow bandmate's remains). In the cold light of day, stripped of his ideological leanings, Pat exclaims, 'Funny . . . you were so scary at night'. To refer back to Foucault, it is now the case whereby Darcy can no longer maintain his previous 'domination of the means of constraint'.[47] The discursive control he once exerted via the cold façade of white supremacist ideology has essentially given way to frantic desperation. To the terrorised band, Darcy was dangerously powerful precisely because he remained an invisible orchestrator of violence. Darcy was effectively a symbol of a wider systemic discourse of oppression and control, a figurehead espousing an extreme ideological position. As the emptiness and arbitrariness of his ideology is revealed, both to the survivors of his violent onslaught and the audience by proxy, this essentially marks the point in the narrative where Darcy is humanised prior to being executed.

Conclusion

Following the wider release of *Green Room* in 2016 and a variety of other sociopolitically charged genre films released throughout the year and into 2017, a number of film scholars and writers began to anticipate a tentative ground zero designated 'Trump-era horror cinema'.[48] Writing in *Sight & Sound* in his end-of-year summation, 'The Year in . . . Horror', Kim Newman began to interrogate whether contemporaneous genre cinema reflected wider social concerns. Newman posed the following question: 'In a year in which minorities have come under increasing attack, have horror films tried merely to reflect cultural concerns or do they share some culpability for encouraging the demonisation of "the other"?' In an expansion of these points, Newman asserts how:

> The all-too-evident horrors of 2016 will probably not be fully realised by horror cinema until later in 2017 and beyond – with the real world consistently one-upping its imagined, distorted reflection by being worse than anyone imagined . . . All of the op-ed pieces about the revenge of the disaffected, overlooked and ignored voter and the rising tide of plague-on-both-your-houses abstraction from the demographic process will inevitably feed into horror movies sooner or later . . . though there's always the question of how culpable the genre is for the way things are as a result of its demonisation of the 'other', even if in ambivalent tones.[49]

Green Room is positioned alongside *The Purge: Election Year* (James DeMonaco, 2016), *The Childhood of a Leader* (Brady Corbet, 2015), *10 Cloverfield Lane* (Dan Trachtenberg, 2016) and *Don't Breathe* (Fede Álvarez, 2016). These disparate examples represent the same core themes and tropes of 'being trapped in hard-to-escape homes that present nightmarish versions of family normality, with a dangerous, petulant, aggressively male tyrant enforcing a political agenda which provides a thin rationale for psychotic violence and exploitation'. With assertions of tyranny and political agendas relating to violence, Newman postulates that 'perhaps we can discern the beginnings of President Trump-era horror'.[50]

Critical discourse surrounding *Green Room* has described the film as a 'scary exploitation thriller',[51] an 'action horror' narrative, 'an anarchist punk exploitation film' and an 'ultra-violent backwoods horror'.[52] On the surface, the film adheres to common horror tropes and conventions, namely a situation in which a group of young protagonists leave an urban centre of normality and order, venturing into the rural unknown to face a monstrous Other. The fact that the film's antagonists are skinheads residing in contemporary America makes it easy to align this monstrous 'Other' with recent anxieties concerning race, fascism and ultra-conservatism. However, the film presents a more nuanced engagement with these contentious issues. The representations of both the protagonists and antagonists are complicated given the film's interpretation and representation of fractured subcultures, subcultural capital, ideology and resulting conflicts. Saulnier presents his characters as 'tortured innocents – flawed beings who freefall into unbreakable cycles of violence', and this is true of characters on both sides of the conflict.[53] In this respect, the film acts as a tentative arbiter of ongoing debates that have characterised punk and hardcore scenes for approximately four decades, in addition to recent instances of political violence and white terrorism. As Steven Duncombe and Maxwell Tremblay argue in relation to punk and its appropriation by white-power organisations:

> It's easy to condemn this music and culture, along with its violence and bigotry, and simply turn away, dismissing it as some sort of aberrant strain of an otherwise healthy organism; it's (self-) satisfying to chant 'Nazi Punks, Fuck Off!' along with the Dead Kennedys. But White Power punk's sense of victimization, its valorization of oppositional solidarity, its creation and mobilization of DIY cultural networks, its understanding of the desire of the forbidden and the shocking, and the simple raw emotionality and the anger of its expression are characteristics that *all* punk shares. Acknowledging this means accepting that there is no one, clear racial politics to punk and no simple 'we'.[54]

Green Room is therefore a reflection of recurrent underlying societal anxieties, which are, unfortunately, defining features of the present epoch. Central to its narrative is the violent clash between two punk music subcultures, similarly represented by Duncombe and Tremblay's statements.

Following *Green Room*, other examples of politically engaged contemporary cinema have responded to these concerns. Kaleem Aftab argues that Spike Lee's *BlacKkKlansman* (2018), following the director's other politically engaged films, passes 'judgement on the rise of neo-Nazis in the current era' amid the 'continuing strength of White hegemony'.[55] Aside from the film engaging with the real-life story of two police officers (one black and one Jewish) infiltrating David Duke's Ku Klux Klan in the 1970s, the ending of the film transitions from period fiction to documentary footage detailing the unrest in Charlottesville in 2017. We are presented with a montage featuring the speeches made by David Duke at the event, the comments made by Trump following the escalating violence at the 'Unite the Right' rally and the car attack resulting in the death of Heather Heyer.[56] Lee's commentary indicates that the cultural contexts of racism, fascism and violence are still very much present in contemporary culture and that those espousing such views (and actions) have again moved into the centre as opposed to occupying peripheral cultural spaces. As a coda to this chapter, recent comments made by Saulnier while promoting his latest film, *Hold the Dark* (2018), point to the continued relevance of *Green Room* amid this sociocultural violence and its rather prophetic narrative:

> When I first promoted the film, it was 'it's not a political film, I don't want to talk about them . . .' I did a lot of research for *Green Room* and at that point the White Nationalist movement was mostly available in chat rooms and on the Internet. It was this terrible side of our culture which I had to mine for research purposes . . . hearing the *exact* same jargon and talking points at an executive level in our country, the exact same talking points about White victimhood, and vilifying others is disgraceful, and I wish the film wasn't so relevant . . . it's truly disturbing.[57]

Alongside films like *BlacKkKlansman* and *Get Out* (Jordan Peele, 2017), Saulnier's *Green Room* is part of a much wider narrative concerning culturally ingrained systemic and structural violence, a narrative that exposes the tenuousness of whiteness and a false need to preserve a sense of its hegemonic centrality.

Perhaps the most troubling place to end this chapter is to draw upon one of the contemporaneous critical reviews of the film from the ideological perspective of the alt-right itself:

> The Nazi Skinhead . . . is not a made-up monster, it's something all too real, and it's no joke. These aren't your cartoonishly portrayed Nazis spitting cookie crumbs everywhere, these are exactly the kind of skinheads that Negros and Jews might meet on the Day of the Rope . . . *Green Room* is only a horror movie if you're a shill, a race traitor, a Negro, a Jew or a cowardly lemming. To a National Socialist this is a very comfy movie to watch that sends you very nice vibes . . . the skinheads in red laces have become the first ever portrayal of what early Right-Wing Death Squads might look like in the coming Race War.[58]

With such a vehement level of rhetoric in response to the film, the position of the neo-Nazi in recent horror fiction presents an interesting form of narrative tension. This figure can tell us a lot about the contemporary political climate characterised by forms of extremism, and also what can be done to combat such systemic violence as it continues to preside over contemporary American culture.

Notes

1. The title of the current chapter stands as an amalgamation of The Who's 1965 single 'The Kids are Alright' and the introductory chapter to Henry A. Giroux's 1996 book *Fugitive Cultures: Race, Violence and Youth*. Moreover, during the writing of the current chapter, US punk band Bad Religion released the stand-alone song 'The Kids are Alt-Right' (2018), referencing a cultural climate of 'fake news', violent protests, populism and iconography associated with the Trump presidency (the lyrics 'red hats gathered at the liquor store' being indicative of the sentiment expressed within this particular song). As such, the relationship between punk subcultures, hardcore music and contentious political discourse is further evidenced. The beginnings of this chapter were first presented at the 'Fear 2000: Horror Media Now' conference at Sheffield Hallam University, UK (April 2018) as part of the panel 'Make America Hate Again: Horror and US Politics'.
2. R. Futrell and P. Simi, 'The [Un]Surprising Alt-Right', *Contexts*, 16/2 (2017), 76.
3. Kirsten Dyck, *Reichsrock: The International Web of White-Power and Neo-Nazi Hate Music* (New Brunswick, NJ: Rutgers University Press, 2016), p. 107.
4. This is documented in the report *Charlottesville: Race and Terror – VICE News Tonight on HBO* (2017).
5. The films that comprised this screening programme were *12 Angry Men* (Sidney Lumet, 1957), *The Battle of Algiers* (Gillo Pontecorvo, 1966), *Blazing Saddles* (Mel Brooks, 1974), *Cabaret* (Bob Fosse, 1972), *Do the Right Thing* (Spike Lee, 1989), *Hairspray* (John Waters, 1988), *In the Heat of the Night* (Norman Jewison, 1967), *Putney Swope* (Robert Downey Sr., 1969) and *Selma* (Ava DuVernay, 2014).
6. J. Ring, 'Watching Green Room after Charlottesville', *Things We Watch* (27 August 2017), http://www.thingswewatch.com/2017/08/27/watching-green-room-charlottesville (accessed 11 December 2019).
7. J. Bailey, '"Green Room" Is a Horror Movie for Trump's America', *Flavorwire* (13 April 2016), http://flavorwire.com/571081/green-room-is-a-horror-movie-for-trumps-america (accessed 11 December 2019).
8. Adam Lowenstein, *Shocking Representation: Historical Trauma, National Cinema, and the Modern Horror Film* (New York, NY: Columbia University Press, 2005), p. 2.
9. For example, Lowenstein's analysis of *Eyes Without a Face* (Georges Franju, 1960), *Deathdream* (Bob Clark, 1974) and *Last House on the Left* (Wes Craven, 1972) locates these films in the wake of the Holocaust and Vietnam

respectively, pointing to the ways these films *can* represent the traumas of the unrepresentable.
10. Lowenstein, *Shocking Representation*, p. 9.
11. For studies into these concerns beyond a US-centric focus, see S. Duncombe and M. Tremblay (eds), *White Riot: Punk Rock and the Politics of Race* (London: Verso, 2011); N. Copsey and M. Worley (eds), *'Tomorrow Belongs to Us': The British Far Right since 1967* (London: Routledge, 2018); A. Raposo and R. Sabin, 'New visual identities for British neo-fascist rock (1982–1987): White Noise, "Vikings" and the cult of Skrewdriver', in N. Copsey and M. Worley (eds), *'Tomorrow Belongs to Us': The British Far Right since 1967* (London: Routledge, 2018), pp. 132–49.
12. Petra Rau, *Our Nazis: Representations of Fascism in Contemporary Literature and Film* (Edinburgh: Edinburgh University Press, 2013), pp. 3–4.
13. J. Marmysz, 'The Lure of the Mob: Contemporary Cinematic Depictions of Skinhead Authenticity', *Journal of Popular Culture*, 46/3 (2013), 626.
14. Kevin Borgeson and Robin Maria Valeri, *Skinhead History, Identity, and Culture* (London: Routledge, 2018), p. 3.
15. Borgeson and Valeri, *Skinhead History*, p. 10.
16. R. A. Winkler, 'Was John Wayne a Nazi? The racial politics of taste in 1980s US hardcore punk', *Punk & Post-Punk*, 5/2 (2016), 132.
17. Winkler, 'Was John Wayne a Nazi?', 133.
18. James Ridgeway, *Blood in the Face: The Ku Klux Klan, Aryan Nations, Nazi Skinheads, and the Rise of New White Culture* (New York, NY: T. Thunders Mouth Press, 1995), p. 93.
19. Winkler, 'Was John Wayne a Nazi?', 132.
20. Winkler, 'Was John Wayne a Nazi?', 137.
21. S. Duncombe and M. Tremblay, 'White Power', in S. Duncombe and M. Tremblay (eds), *White Riot: Punk Rock and the Politics of Race* (London: Verso, 2011), pp. 114–15.
22. D. S. Traber, 'L.A.'s "White Minority": Punk and the Contradictions of Self-Marginalization', *Cultural Critique*, 48/0 (2014), 30.
23. Kevin Dunn, *Global Punk: Resistance and Rebellion in Everyday Life* (London: Bloomsbury, 2016), p. 21.
24. Dunn, *Global Punk*, p. 21.
25. Dunn, *Global Punk*, pp. 54–5.
26. Dunn, *Global Punk*, p. 55.
27. M. Worley and N. Copsey, 'White Youth: The far right, punk and British youth culture, 1977–87', in N. Copsey and M. Worley (eds), *'Tomorrow Belongs to Us': The British Far Right since 1967* (London: Routledge, 2018), pp. 114–15.

28. Worley and Copsey, 'White Youth', pp. 114–15.
29. J. M. Cotter, 'Sounds of hate: White power rock and roll and the neo-Nazi skinhead subculture', *Terrorism and Political Violence*, 11/2 (1999), 111.
30. See A. Nagle, *Kill All Normies: Online Culture Wars from 4chan and Tumblr to Trump and the Alt-right* (London: Zero Books, 2017).
31. Dyck, *Reichsrock*, p. 108.
32. Sarah Thornton, *Club Cultures: Music, Media and Subcultural Capital* (Cambridge: Polity, 1995), p. 10.
33. Thornton, *Club Cultures*, p. 11.
34. Thornton, *Club Cultures*, p. 26; emphasis in the original.
35. DMs skinheads are typically associated with the punk/hardcore scene, DMs referring to the common attire of Doctor Marten boots. SHARPs is an acronym for Skinheads Against Racial Prejudice, a counter ideology to the racist leanings of skinheads within the White Power movement.
36. The green room also contains numerous swastikas, Celtic sun crosses and depictions of the number 88 (88 is commonly seen in the White Power movement and refers to the chant 'Heil Hitler', 'H' being the eighth letter of the alphabet).
37. The sense of subcultural authenticity and embodied experience noted previously in relation to live performance is mirrored at this point within these extremely violent contexts. In a conversation with Pat, the murderous 'skinhead' Werm (Brent Werzner) compliments the bass player as follows: 'Your set was pretty good . . . what was the second to last song?' Pat replies with the hesitant '. . . Toxic Evolution . . .' to which Werm retorts '. . . Fucking hard man, that's the one I did her to'. The live experience so coveted by Pat in the earlier stages of the film is therefore flipped violently in relation to this very live and brutally authentic murder.
38. M. Foucault, 'The Subject and Power', *Critical Enquiry*, 8/0 (1982), 777–95.
39. Sabine Hake, *Screen Nazis: Cinema, History, and Democracy* (Madison, WI: University of Wisconsin Press, 2013), p. 21.
40. The wearing of red laces means that those in possession have shed blood for the skinhead movement, Darcy's references to 'boot parties' (the group killing of a perceived threat) making this image all the more poignant.
41. Hake, *Screen Nazis*, p. 21.
42. T. Robinson, 'Green Room director Jeremy Saulnier on recreating his teen years through horror films', *The Verge* (14 April 2016), *https://www.theverge.com/2016/4/14/11432110/green-room-director-jeremy-saulnier-interview* (accessed 29 August 2019).
43. D. Jenkins, 'Film Review: Green Room', *Little White Lies* (10 May 2016), *https://lwlies.com/reviews/green-room/* (accessed 29 August 2019).

44. T. Johnston, 'Band on the Run', *Sight & Sound*, 26/6 (2016), 34.
45. Robinson, 'Green Room director Jeremy Saulnier'.
46. Leighton Grist, *Fascism and Millennial American Cinema* (Basingstoke: Palgrave Macmillan, 2018), p. 36.
47. Foucault, 'The Subject and Power', 786–7.
48. See C. Bowen, 'Is it time for a horror movie about the evils of Donald Trump?', *The Guardian* (5 July 2016), https://www.theguardian.com/film/2016/jul/05/donald-trump-horror-movie-they-live-john-carpenter (accessed 11 December 2019); A. Romano, 'Horror movies reflect cultural fears. In 2016, Americans feared invasion.', *Vox* (21 December 2016), https://www.vox.com/culture/2016/12/21/13737476/horror-movies-2016-invasion (accessed 11 December 2019); M. Lakin, 'Why Horror Movies Will be the Most Exciting Art Form of the Donald Trump Era', *W Magazine* (17 March 2017), https://www.wmagazine.com/story/horror-movies-social-thrillers-get-out-the-purge/ (accessed 11 December 2019); J. Chang, 'Has horror become the movie genre of the Trump era?', *Los Angeles Times* (13 October 2016), https://www.latimes.com/entertainment/movies/la-ca-mn-horror-movies-trump-20171013-story.html (accessed 11 December 2019); J. Patterson, 'Get Out: the first great paranoia movie of the Trump era', *The Guardian* (6 March 2017), https://www.theguardian.com/film/2017/mar/06/get-out-movie-jordan-peele-trump (accessed 11 December 2019); A. Godfrey, 'Making America Gory Again: how the Purge films troll Trumpism', *The Guardian* (4 July 2018), https://www.theguardian.com/film/2018/jul/04/how-the-purge-trolls-trumps-america-jason-blum-first-purge (accessed 11 December 2019).
49. K. Newman, 'The Year in . . . Horror', *Sight & Sound*, 27/1 (2017), 54–5.
50. Newman, 'The Year in . . . Horror', 54–5.
51. Johnston, 'Band on the Run', 34.
52. See Robinson, 'Green Room director Jeremy Saulnier'; A. Page, 'Jeremy Saulnier's *Green Room* & the Anarchy of Punk Violence', *MPAA* (26 April 2016), https://www.motionpictures.org/2016/04/jeremy-saulniers-green-room-anarchy-punk-violence/ (accessed 11 December 2019); G. Lodge, 'Cannes Film Review: "Green Room"', *Variety* (17 May 2015), https://variety.com/2015/film/festivals/green-room-review-1201498852/ (accessed 11 December 2019).
53. L. Kern, 'Scare Tactics: The Pleasures of Cinematic Horror', *Film Comment*, 54/5 (2018), 22–3.
54. Duncombe and Tremblay, 'White Power', p. 115.
55. K. Aftab, 'Deep Cover', *Sight & Sound*, 28/9 (2018), 22–7.
56. Commenting on the film, and this transition in particular, director Martin Scorsese offered the following assessment: 'The picture takes you to a safe

place – we're watching a movie, it's up on a screen – and suddenly we're catapulted into now. Right next to you. Because it's not only real, what you're seeing up there on the screen – it's happening. It is happening. And it's sanctioned by government' (cited in Aftab, 'Deep Cover', 22–7).

57. R. Camilleri, 'Jeremy Saulnier On How The Neo-Nazi Language of "Green Room" Has Been Echoed By The President', *Build Series* (26 September 2018), *https://www.youtube.com/watch?v=Xj52OQxGJ78* (accessed 11 December 2019).

58. A. Slavros, 'Nazi Movie Review: Green Room (2016)', *Daily Stormer* (5 July 2016), *https://dailystormer.su/nazi-movie-review-green-room-2016/* (accessed 11 December 2019).

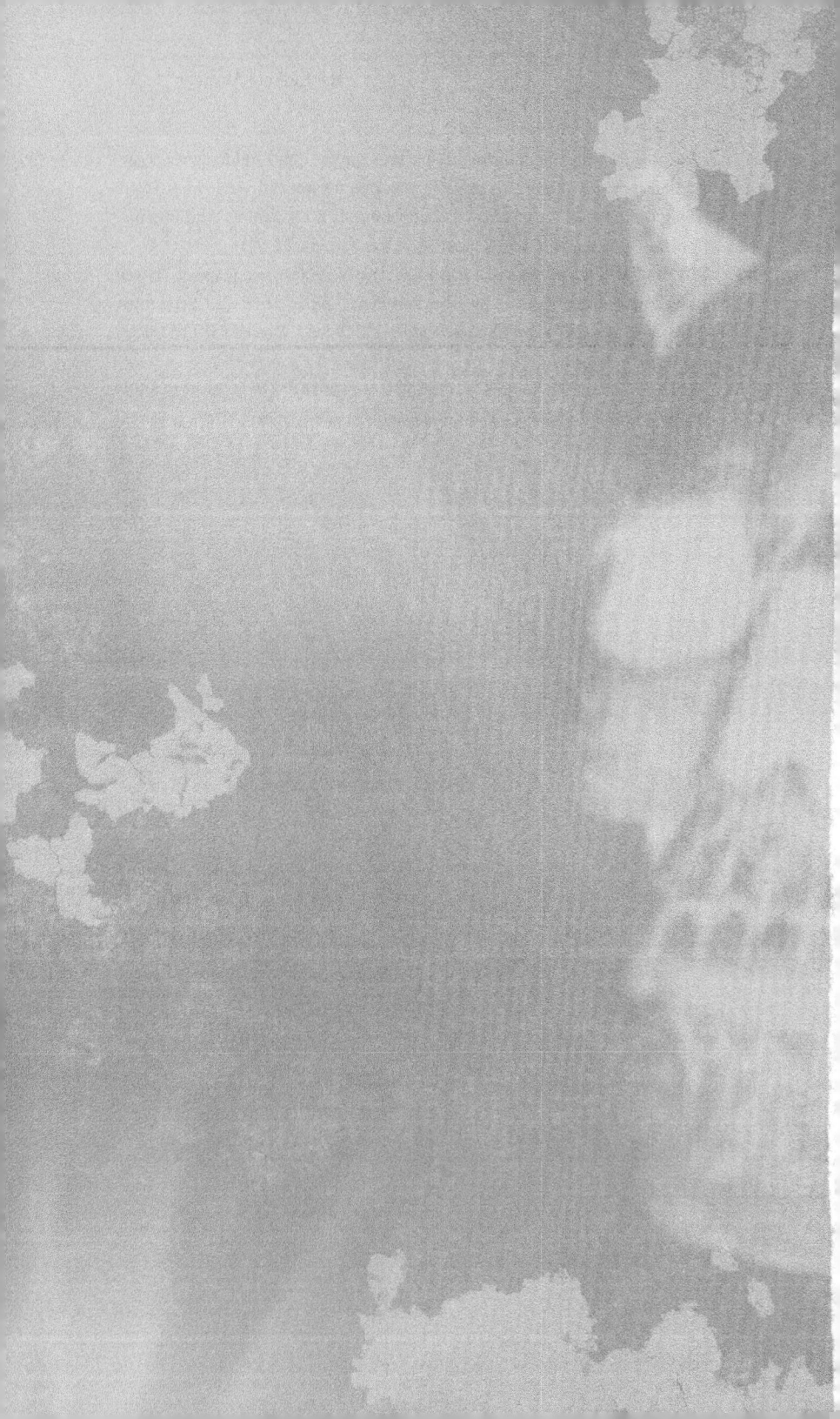

12

Twenty-first-century Euro-snuff

A Serbian Film for the Family

Neil Jackson

WHENEVER IT HAS BEEN afforded any such privilege, even sensible discussion of *A Serbian Film* (Srđan Spasojević, 2010) has prioritised its transgressive features. Its global censorship has shaped an identity compounded by an often outraged reception by critics and audiences alike, locating it firmly beyond the pale even for many seasoned genre critics and aficionados. Consequently, its status as a twenty-first-century pop cultural *bête noire* has positioned it securely under the banner of Euro-cinema 'extremity', but moral opprobrium has plagued its proper evaluation and placement as a genre film.[1] Debates around gruesome spectacle are unavoidable, yet such deliberate provocation tends to clutter the hermeneutic path with gory detritus to the point where subtextual depths are transformed into rhetorical swamp. Therefore, sober judgement is best achieved by extracting it from those dominant discourses to foreground other fundamental aspects of its internal and external dynamics. To address this, the ensuing analysis offers a brief overview of debates that have been generated by the film; however, its major objective is to assess key textual detail to identify its primary thematic focus. Crucially, this analysis locates *A Serbian Film* amid a global strain of fictional films that have dealt with the salacious mythology of the so-called snuff movie,[2] an ongoing sub-cycle to which it effectively serves as an indexical summary.

This snuff movie sub-cycle reaches back to *Peeping Tom* (Michael Powell, 1960), in which a proto-snuff film-maker's activities unfold against the backdrop of an under-the-counter pornography racket in post-war London, prefiguring controversies over snuff that developed across the Atlantic a decade later. I have argued elsewhere that a disparate range of films that followed *Peeping Tom* envisioned snuff variously as: 'a perverse and murderous auteurist vision . . . the consequence of corporate cultural or political conspiracy . . . a violent, pornographic sensory exciter . . . and a catalyst for conservative recuperation'.[3] *A Serbian Film* absorbs and refines all of these themes, which have developed over five decades since the release of *Peeping Tom*: the figure of the monstrous snuff film director has encompassed the embittered class avenger of *The Last House on Dead End Street* (Victor Janos, 1977) and the venal opportunists of *Effects* (Dusty Nelson, 1980), *Special Effects* (Larry Cohen, 1984) and *8mm* (Joel Schumacher, 1999); a snuff-related conspiracy of social control is at the centre of *Videodrome* (David Cronenberg, 1983), its protagonist deploying the body-morphing tools of his own (possibly hallucinated) oppression against those seeking control of his very consciousness; and the pivotal quest of *A Serbian Film*'s protagonist to protect and avenge the cultural institution of the family is central to the narrative and thematic trajectory of both *Hardcore* (Paul Schrader, 1979) and *8mm*. After these films, technological developments were instrumental in situating the mythology of snuff firmly in the digital epoch of the twenty-first century. The most resonant modern moving images of actual murder have been online documents of hostages bound, shot, beheaded, burnt and exploded by ideologically motivated captors upon a shifting geopolitical stage, and *A Serbian Film* entered into a world in which fictional horror had partly collapsed under the epistemological weight of these stark, brutal and politicised visual renditions.

A brief synopsis reveals *A Serbian Film*'s narrative simplicity. In the film, retired porn star Miloš (Srđan Todorović) is lured from his happy but financially testing family life to take up a lucrative film offer from a mysterious director, Vukmir (Sergej Trifunović). Soon, Miloš realises that the director's intentions go beyond artistic flamboyance and pretension into the violent abuse and murder of his cast. Outlining the preparation, enactment and aftermath of the snuff film, the narrative is conveyed through an increasingly fragmented subjectivity, utilising a combination of video replays and memory flashes experienced by the beleaguered protagonist.

The film is partly representative of what Cynthia A. Freeland somewhat loosely calls 'realist horror':

> the fascination of the realistic monster [and] gruesome spectacle over plot . . . [monsters] are typically men who exercise hideous violence against women, [but] do not participate in the traditional patriarchal order (law, politics, the working world, medicine, religion, morality).[5]

Freeland's argument foregrounds 'violence in general as it relates to social class, race and urban alienation', stressing the relationship between human monsters and their immediate social formations.[6] Accordingly, snuff has become the most extreme expression of interpersonal and sociocultural exploitation that has figured regularly in a whole range of realist horror fictions. Founded upon this interrelationship of masculinity, misogyny and violence, *A Serbian Film*'s monstrous male is a tripartite construction: Miloš, the disenfranchised but prodigiously endowed porn star; Vukmir, the pseudo-creative capitalist and snuff film-maker; and an unidentified patriarch silently dictating the snuff film's shadowy purpose.

Miloš emerges as both monster *and* victim, his participation placing him in collusion with the film-makers/paymasters exploiting and controlling his fate. His sexual potency is repeatedly emphasised (frequently by other men), but despite his education – his wife, Marija (Jelena Gavrilović), comments that he is probably the only Serbian porn star with a college degree – his agency is restricted by his low hierarchal status. Until his grisly demise, Vukmir is seemingly in control of this whole narrative. However, a grimly ironic coda renders his death moot as the snuff film continues regardless of the fate of both its director and primary participants, revealing an oppressive hegemonic order exploiting its subjects beyond death. A wry joke on the expendability of 'creative' figures in the pursuit of ultra-conservative socio-economic imperatives underpins the entire film, the structural tension of the family/porn underworld straining at the 'legitimate' existence that Miloš is struggling to uphold from the outset.

The film's very title invokes national specificity, reflecting recent sociopolitical transformations strewn in armed conflict and genocide. As Michael Brooke argues, 'not since *The Texas Chain Saw Massacre* has a title's geographical location proved so potent: *A Swiss Film*, *A Norwegian Film* or even (tellingly) *A Croatian Film* would have far less impact'.[7] Mark

Featherstone has asserted that it must be viewed through dual concepts of 'wound culture' and 'Balkan Hardcore', embodying

> the sexualized nature of everyday culture [that is] militaristic, aggressive, and concerned with the objectification of the other . . . [it] isn't simply a critique of the Serbian death drive [but also how] . . . the idea of globalization, and particularly global capitalism [enables us] to contextualize the notion of the Serbian death drive.[8]

In particular, the film defines sexual violence as culturally embedded, a sentiment articulated repeatedly by Vukmir through his dementedly personal cinematic vision. While this point affirms radical tenets of feminist theory, it also expresses the pervading national despair present in the self-reflexive commentary upon modern horror's international nuances and peculiarities. This refusal of positive cultural projection is evident in the very first frames as a folksy accordion score, warm crimson backdrop and decorative title font are jarringly obliterated by the crashing imposition of an alternative graphic, fracturing the image to the accompaniment of bass-heavy electronic music and serving as an immediate statement of stylistic intent.

The use of metaphor or allegory offers tacit reassurance that anything so relentlessly unpleasant is not merely trading upon the film's affective charge. Co-writer/director Srđan Spasojević protested that *A Serbian Film* 'express[es] our deepest and most sincere inner feelings about how strongly we in Serbia feel violated'[9] and that it was 'a hard-hitting diary of our own molestation by the Serbian government'.[10] Such comments insist upon a serious purpose distinct from mindless corporeal spectacle, but lending *A Serbian Film* a sympathetic critical ear is not to argue necessarily for its status as art. It is doubtlessly crude, abrasive and hysterical, its principal ideas in constant tension with its brutalising surface effects. Its nature becomes particularly pronounced in the second half, where its 'excess' tends to obscure the intuitive intelligence evident elsewhere. Notable amid critical brickbats was the frequent refusal to accept a synergy of explicit horror imagery with utilities of allegory and metaphor, as if these modes were somehow critically incompatible. Peter Bradshaw's dismissal was typical: 'a migraine-inducing "controversy" . . . [a] badly acted and directed porn-horror nightmare that aspires to be a satire'.[11] Here, suspicion of pretension, contrivance and stylistic bombast are underpinned by queasy resistance to a 'porn-horror' hybridity. While the 'controversy' is implied as superficial, the critique of its acting and direction suggests artistic failure inversely correlative to misguided satirical aspirations.

Even Mark Kermode, a critic often enthused by horror's outrageous potentiality,[12] was cynically dismissive:

> The director says that it is allegorical . . . [but the message] just gets lost amidst the increasingly stupid splatter. The high watermark of this genre film-making would be something like Pasolini's *Salo* . . . this is more like *A Cat in the Brain* . . . less Pasolini than a Lucio Fulci movie. Some of the extreme gore resembles Hong Kong Category III stuff . . . some have likened it to Gaspar Noé [but] actually the thing it is closest to is Jörg Buttgereit [and Ruggero Deodato] . . . it fails [but] it is technically well done . . . torture porn is one thing. Pompous, pretentious torture porn is kind of something else . . . it's a piece of exploitation trash.[13]

While condemning the violence as merely 'stupid', Kermode's dismissal is more complex, incorporating broader allusions to specific cinematic movements and personalities. Technical achievements are deemed insufficient to counter ethical shortcomings: it is 'well done' on one level but 'fails' on a largely undefined other. However, the generic and authorial alignment supporting this assessment is somewhat dubious. Setting *A Serbian Film* alongside *Salò, or the 120 Days of Sodom* (Pier Paolo Pasolini, 1975), *Cannibal Holocaust* (Ruggero Deodato, 1980), *A Cat in the Brain* (Lucio Fulci, 1990) and *Nekromantik* (Jörg Buttgereit, 1987) locates it amid a loosely defined European tradition but clouds distinctions between specific cultural movements and creative practices. Ignoring variations in tone, treatment and local contextualisation, the aggregate result is the conflation of wildly disparate 'extreme' works, congregating *A Serbian Film*'s creative team with Italian art and exploitation film-makers and a German director rooted in the independent underground. Category III films are even thrown into the mix – films placed in Hong Kong's highest censorship bracket due to their outlandish violence and erotic content. Alongside 'torture porn' and the conclusively pejorative 'exploitation trash', these references broaden the generic base, yet also widen the fissure between notions of artistic responsibility and wilful obnoxiousness.

In a fit of unintentional self-irony, negative hyperbole surrounding *A Serbian Film* was startlingly reminiscent of that generated by the British critical establishment around *Peeping Tom* half a century earlier,[14] but some horror specialist critics did offer measured, contrary assessments. Kim Newman called it 'a remorseless, well made, horrifying descent into personal Hell . . . [with a] distinctive widescreen look, and an impressive, slightly stylised use of dim lighting and art direction'. Eric Somer commented that while 'regarded as one of the most morally repugnant and egregiously gruesome of all narrative films . . . [it is] an absolutely riveting film of bold, undeniable power, imaginatively staged, and nicely accented by credible casting and convincing performances'.[15] While technical proficiency and formal invention might be noted as signifiers of particular qualities, they were more often decried as masking for offending standards of cultural and aesthetic refinement. This is characteristic of what Steve Jones, in this collection and in other work, sees as a meaningless critical insistence that such films must be patently 'about something' in order to justify their affective surfaces.[16] However, the sociopolitical context of *A Serbian Film* could only be, as Kermode contests, 'lost' through wilful suspension of critical observance, so insistent is its verbal and visual expression. For example: Marija observes that the name 'Vukmir' 'sounds like one of our guys at the Hague tribunal'; Marko (Slobodan Beštić) comments that 'you can't check friends in Serbia enough'; Vukmir proclaims that 'this whole country is one big, shitty kindergarten, a bunch of kids discarded by their parents'. These are crude but deliberate articulations of political cynicism, paranoia and fears of state control, each bearing relevance to the snuff film Vukmir will develop. The infamous 'newborn porn' segment (in which Vukmir screens the rape of a baby fresh from the womb) is merely a metaphorical adjunct to those verbal assertions, an obscenely poetic evocation of a newly independent state at the hands of its ruling elites. This layer of articulation exists on the very surface of the film, defining a social hierarchy for which pornography serves as a viable metaphor. Despite this, there is a deep-seated conservatism at its ideological base, with the moral certainties of a traditional family unit (embodied by father/mother/son) positioned against extreme pornography and its practitioners.

This simple dialectic is in place from the very first sequence: the camera slowly tracks forward into an alleyway strewn with signifiers of machismo (a motorcycle, beer kegs), hard, grey concrete walls tinged intermittently in steam and red neon. To an insistent electro-percussive beat, a male–female couple emerge from 'Le Club Filth' already engaged in rough sex. He enters her from behind, uttering aggressive obscenities, using the motorcycle as a makeshift platform. The editing emphasises the jerks and thrusts of their upper and lower bodies, immediately defining sex in terms of violent (but consensual) domination, the controlling gaze and physicality of the male satisfying the predominant tendencies of pornography.

A sudden cut to a young boy, Petar (Luka Mijatović), watching this activity on a television transports the film from porno-fantasy space into the familial realm, revealing the opening as a piece of fiction in which the male performer is actually the boy's father, Miloš. Pornography is seen immediately to contaminate domestic space – a theme that the film will pursue to its logical terminus – while uninhibited, animalistic sex conflicts with the mundane intimacies of parenthood. The sleazy ambience of the alleyway contrasts the cluttered, muted earth tones of the family home, exhibiting a cold depersonalisation that imbues the habitats of the porn community throughout the rest of the film.

Miloš's porn-fantasy persona is offset by the revelation of his current circumstances, with his wife, Marija, exasperated by their son's exposure to his father's former profession. Nevertheless, the films have financed a modest domestic arrangement, with the career-spanning video collection adorning their home concealing the now dwindling cash that Miloš has accumulated. The maternal authority of Marija counters Miloš's evident fascination with, and partial nostalgia for, the material (and carnal) fruits of his former profession, ruefully gazing at his own porn image on the television screen. Uncememoniously switched off, it is replaced momentarily by the screen's reflection of his current, tangible circumstances: mother protectively caressing child amid Miloš's protestations that he saw his first pornographic film at the same age. As Marija – herself educated and earning money as a translator, indicating the current labour division within their home – asks Miloš for money to pay for Petar's music lessons, a mournful piano chord, used repeatedly to accentuate the impending desperation of Miloš's family life, diverges from the electronic thud of the earlier alleyway tryst.

While drawing sustenance from the porn industry's sensational allure, the film insistently defines its personnel as a loathsome community of crass exploiters. Meanwhile, marital domesticity, childhood innocence and sibling resentment and rivalry are the focal point of the film's melodrama, occasionally sentimental thematic layers at odds with images of decapitation, genital mutilation and baby rape. But amid this, the gradual destruction and grotesque parody of the family becomes the primary foundation upon which the snuff film's outrages are constructed. Tony Williams sees the family as a consistent thematic motif from early literary incarnations of horror (such as those by Edgar Allan Poe and H. P. Lovecraft) through to its cinematic incarnations in the contemporary era.[17] Family members have often manifested as psychologically disturbed, sexually deviant or physically deformed human monsters, vividly present in the 1970s in *The Last House on the Left* (Wes Craven, 1972), *The Texas Chain Saw Massacre* (Tobe Hooper, 1974) and *The Hills Have Eyes* (Wes Craven, 1977). In these examples, the family could constitute either the source or the subject of sustained onslaught, with Craven's films offering scenarios in which contrasting social embodiments of the family unit came into unrelenting and violent conflict with each other.

This utilisation of family-centred horror has not been exclusively American, but its influence has been global, with Williams arguing that the genre has often failed as a radical assessment of 'the ideologically imposed version [of the family] that denies any alternatives to its rule in human society'.[18] Given the local and transcultural borrowings openly admitted by its film-makers, the pervasive presence of the family motif in *A Serbian Film* is hardly surprising. Yet, it does not offer a critique that would satisfy Williams's privileging of films offering progressive responses to the 'symbolic alarm bell of our era's internal and external problems'.[19] Miloš's socially and economically fragile family unit is indeed mired in moral and existential threat, and they can ultimately offer nothing much beyond a despairing submission to the forces that exploit its range of vulnerabilities.

It is clear then that focus upon the tropes of 'extreme cinema' tends to obscure other varied layers of critical interest and that conflating the film with a vague corpus of transgression serves little practical use beyond the identification of exceptionally general trends. Tanya Horeck and Tina Kendall identify a broader 'new European extremism' that has utilised 'provocation as a mode of address' since the late 1990s, citing the work of film-makers such as Catherine Breillat, Gaspar Noé, Bruno Dumont, Philippe Grandrieux, Michael Haneke, Lukas Moodysson, Lars von Trier and Ulrich Seidl as central.[20] Their emphasis is still upon culturally enshrined auteur cinema, but the infiltrations of contemporaneous global trends of 'torture porn', 'new brutality' and 'Asia extreme cinema' point to inherent critical and conceptual shortcomings in assuming comfortable equivalence.[21] They write that:

> there is a clear need to differentiate the films of Michael Haneke, which, despite their reputation for brutality, are characterized more by visual restraint than by excessive violence or horror, and the 'self-consciously trashy', in-your-face sex and violence of a film like *Baise-moi* [Virginie Despentes and Coralie Trinh Thi, 2000].[22]

Mattias Frey is mindful, too, that 'critical discourse on extreme cinema generally hinges on one key distinction: art or exploitation?', a somewhat limiting dialectic that supports either an 'aesthetic embrace' of artistic ambition or 'cynicism criticism' that dismisses exploitation altogether.[23] *A Serbian Film* sits uncomfortably amid auteurist readings, the signature of its first-time director rendered vague by the lack of a larger body of work and the circulation of critical characterisations of him as an attention-seeking upstart. Lacking auteur privilege, its reception through a lens of provocation befitted its placement in the exploitation sector. Promotional strategies actively discouraged art-cinema-oriented readings, and its reputation was established instead at horror-themed festivals, in magazines and online.

Shaun Kimber assesses this international reception in light of these dominant discourses, offering an account of the film's place in Serbian film culture and an overview of its formal and stylistic strategies in its capacity for 'transgressive edge play'.[24] In this context, 'extremity' is in constant negotiation with spectator engagement; rather than being merely aberrant, the film is seen to lie at the edges of cultural norms across various global territories. Its controversy thus 'resides in its ability, depending upon context and audience, to impinge, contravene, and ultimately restore the fraying ends of what is held to be tolerable within contemporary horror films'. Kimber contests that this is a work steeped in recent historical trauma and also highly conversant in multiple historical developments of the horror film. His claims are supported by the film's co-writer, Aleksandar Radivojević, who stated, '[W]e were big genre fans, especially of American 1970s cinema', indicating an at least implicit awareness of the extent to which historical trauma, domestic unrest and divisive international conflict impacted upon American genre motifs of that period.[25]

Underlying cultural anxieties are channelled in *A Serbian Film* through Miloš, conveyed casually at first through his frequent reliance upon whisky and cigarettes, vices that have supplanted the sensory but mechanical pleasures of pornographic performance. Petar questions his parents about his arousal while viewing the porn film (implying an inherent violence in the young male's sexual drives). Marija also queries why Miloš has never 'performed' aggressively with her. Despite her seemingly amused detachment from his former career, he can only offer clichéd responses professing to separate feelings of love and professionally engaged lust. Their ensuing rough-sex scenario, founded in performed gestures implying violence, satisfies this curiosity, with Marija's goading of Miloš again underscored by discordant electronic music and intercut with pornographic images on the TV screen in their bedroom. Marija's natural physical beauty and casual attire are offset by the make-up, latex, high heels, dog collar and fishnet apparel of Lejla (Katarina Žutić), an 'early starter' porn veteran and bestiality specialist deployed to seduce Miloš back to his former life. Brandishing a penis-shaped cigarette lighter, Lejla expresses contempt and suspicion of Miloš's family aspirations, complimenting him on his sexual skills ('you were an artist!') and outlining new high-quality pornography, international in its reach. Her views are at odds with Miloš's negative self-critique of his career, an assessment supported by periodic glimpses of porno clichés including troilism, mechanically rutting bodies and gurning in settings anywhere from an industrial workshop to a luxury swimming pool. Later, Lejla tests Miloš's marital fidelity, with his rebuke prompting her suggestion that marriage and copious amounts of alcohol has blunted his prowess. The very notion of pornography as an art form is cynically dismissed, defined instead through both ideological assertion and monetary gain for those controlling the snuff project.

Miloš's brother, Marko, is a police officer also fascinated by the lure of the porn industry. His ostensible power is state-sanctioned, but he suffers from a sexual impotence ameliorated initially only by an unrequited desire for Marija, a longing he can only express as he masturbates in their bathroom during a social visit. Introduced as he discreetly observes the first meeting of Miloš and Lejla, Marko is a professional yet impotent voyeur, whose own links to the porn underground remain obscure even beyond the film's conclusion. As he is later fellated by a prostitute, he views a video recording of Petar's birthday party; in the video, the image of a deflating balloon and the vocal encouragement of the doting parents to 'blow harder' on the birthday cake's candles mock his sexual affliction. This domestic home video is suddenly interrupted by footage from another porn film featuring Miloš, with Marko channelling his emasculation through visual possession and failed physical emulation of his brother's image. Their fragile bond is severed when both participate in the ultimate act of familial violation during the film's latter stages.

Making claim to an exclusive international clientele, Vukmir voices banal proclamations on pornography's artistic potential ('truth!', 'reality!', 'minimal editing!'), patronising assessments of conventional pornographers ('butchers') and misogynistic disdain for Miloš's former female co-stars. His documentation and monetisation of victimhood for an overseas market is redolent of what Alexandra Kapka perceives as 'dated tropes of self-Balkanization', which, in this instance, build upon generic conventions absorbed from other nations.[26] The snuff metaphor thus becomes more than just an expression of interpersonal abuse and objectification: it also articulates a global exchange value of creative impulses mired in self-loathing and victimhood repackaged for global consumption. Describing Miloš as an 'artist of fuck', Vukmir's insincere flattery colours his stated ambitions for international impact that will satisfy his creative and economic drives. His empowered gaze feeds vicariously upon this 'artistry', authoring Miloš's sexual capacities through scenarios founded in the debasement of values the latter is so longingly nurturing. In desperate parody of the auteur/actor collaboration, Vukmir's expressions of greater political purpose dismiss standard conventions of pornography, supplanted by images of torture, rape, evisceration and murder that refute traditional family ideals founded in a broader nationalistic zest.

These aesthetic ideals of authenticity support a narrative of abuse and degradation, an explicitly Sadean creative principle founded jointly in class and gender contempt. Vukmir's attire and art-furnished living space suggest material fruits of porno-capitalism, a stark visual contrast to the casual clothing and bland functional interiors of Miloš's home. In short, he embodies what Georges Bataille labelled de Sade's 'sovereign man', for whom social status and moral privilege often denied reason, absolved responsibility and celebrated excess.[27] Bataille's caricature aspires to a 'transcendent pleasure no longer confined to the senses', consuming those less empowered on the sociocultural scale.[28] Seeing family ambitions restricted by economic options, Vukmir's financial offer is merely capitalist exploitation, which also pre-empts Miloš's wholesale dehumanisation and demise. Revealed as a former child psychologist embroiled in state-governed television and security, Vukmir is embedded in institutional social control, which seems responsible for the mysterious inaccessibility of his pornographic output. His skills in child psychology transfer quite readily to his cinematic manipulations, which violate the sanctities of childhood, and the family members within his snuff scenario are fragile emblems of all he wishes to mock and destroy. Nourishing sadistic rather than artistic appetites, this power appears to extend as far as the presence of a mysterious, briefly glimpsed elder figure and his armed associates, one of whom bears a tattoo of a reel of celluloid film on his neck. Cinema itself, or at least signifiers of its historical-material properties, are implicated directly in the organisational process of this social system.

Many previous fictional incarnations of snuff have stressed a primitive artlessness. Here, it has theme and structure, predetermined dramatic scenarios and is shot over several days utilising hidden cameras, multiple set-ups and lighting arrangements, playback screens, exterior and interior locations and specifically designed sets. Vukmir directs Miloš through a concealed earpiece in 'real-time' action, shot by cameramen in paramilitary attire. While this technology suggests a temporal integrity in line with Vukmir's earlier aesthetic proclamations, it allows for editorial control that will enhance their manipulation. The interiors of these sets are dark, hard and sparse, pools of light illuminating focal spaces where the sex-murders will occur. Drawing upon another iconographical trope of snuff fiction, its climactic space is an industrial interior, with Vukmir's description of it as a 'warm family home' expressing his ironic, impersonal detachment from any such ideal.

Vukmir's initially remote, disembodied direction compounds the sense of pure objectification in his film, each participant/victim representative of a process of familial or maternal breakdown. They are comprised of: the war-widowed 'whore' mother (Ana Sakić) and teenage daughter Jeca (Anđela Nenadović); the newborn baby raped upon delivery; the unnamed female 'doctor' (Lena Bogdanović); Lejla, whose recognition of Vukmir's intentions marks her own end; and ultimately Miloš and his family, their fate forming the centrepiece to a final refutation of the protagonist's domestic aspirations.

Accordingly, the first sequences of the snuff film are shot in a 'home for abandoned and orphaned children', wherein Jeca sits solitary and silent at the foot of a staircase as she is admonished by her anxious and abusive mother. This scenario reveals that Jeca's father is a deceased war veteran sexually betrayed by the mother, but its veracity remains unclear. Therefore, a possible 'performance' of loss and abuse blurs perceptions of an already corrupted porn fantasy, Miloš serving as an initially silent observer, seduced and fellated by an unidentified woman as TV screens transmit fetishised images of the girl. Later in the film, Vukmir positions Miloš as the replacement father of Jeca, beckoned to abuse her by her grandmother, who in turn discloses that her own father visited the same treatment upon her. This context defines the whole process as an intra-familial generational rite endorsed and encouraged by its former victims. Accentuating the drab domestic layout of the interior, a sepia-filter effect evokes the tainted nostalgia of bygone ideals being systematically dismantled, with Vukmir no longer a disembodied presence but wholly immersed on the set of his unfolding scenario.

Eventually drugged and brutalised by his paymaster after his refusal of child pornography, Miloš's fragmented subjectivity is conveyed through subliminal images, flashbacks and hallucinatory abstractions, undermining his already fragile narrative agency and offering subliminal glimpses of events only gradually revealed in their entirety. Vukmir's admonishment to complete the snuff film with 'me and this wonderful family you are so anxious to leave' is facilitated by this disorientation and confusion. The primary signifiers of Miloš's personal and professional realms collide as the film itself becomes less rooted in its linear foundations. Snuff porn is shown to encroach further upon domestic space as flash-cuts of an eyeball and vagina are intercut with Petar playfully beating his weary father's head with a phallic balloon, transforming this playful gesture into a pre-emptive evocation of the atrocities Miloš will perform. The balloon reappears later in Miloš's dreamed reconstruction, brandished by a production assistant and then by his own son, whose mocking chant of 'hit it dad, tear it dad, Uncle Vukmir is shooting' over a battered female body emphasises the insidiously paternal role of the film-maker.

Combined with these memory fragments, Vukmir's footage allows for a brief, final reclamation of Miloš's lost narrative moments. Revealed through camera viewfinders and TV screens, such self-reflexivity reaches back to the recurring tropes of *Peeping Tom* and *Cannibal Holocaust*, as Miloš subjectively 'edits' the snuff film temporarily obliterated by his drug-addled memory. While revealing the grotesque extent of his acts, the tapes also expose the stark mechanics of on-set preparation that lie beneath Vukmir's artistic pretensions. Miloš's porno-stud image is dismantled as he is sodomised by one of the camera crew, his consciousness – and conscience – removed while his sexual prowess is artificially enhanced by the animal aphrodisiac with which he has been injected. Vukmir repeatedly identifies Miloš as a 'bull' or a 'he-goat', alternately taunting that his child will become a 'dog-fucker's bitch'. Such obscene but evocative phrases of bestiality refer back to the earlier revelation of Lejla's pornographic speciality, yet they are counterpointed in the lullaby sung by Marija to coax Petar to sleep in the early and latter sequences of the film. This song, sentimentalising the life of a rabbit, recalls the stuffed toy presented earlier to Miloš by Lejla and placed as an adornment on the rear-view mirror of his car. In their final violated state, Marija's tortured recital of the song to her catatonic son is stripped of its previous reassurances, becoming the final verbal communication of the family in the aftermath of the snuff film.

As the snuff film progresses to its end scenario, Miloš's resistance to Vukmir's increasingly hysterical directions precipitates their ultimate destruction of each other. The director incorporates the sibling frictions of Miloš and Marko, orchestrated by Vukmir as a grotesque assault upon Marija and Petar by the two brothers, extending the assault to Miloš's broader familial attachments. Stripped of his own tenuous authority, Marko is initially hooded and seemingly under the influence of the same drug, violently fulfilling his barely concealed desire for his brother's wife. The possibility that Marko himself has been complicit in his brother's manipulation broadens the network of corruption and oppression into the realm of law enforcement. His earlier playful antagonism with Lejla (in which she resists his flirtation by biting his lip) is thus rhymed by his violation of her in the snuff film, his impotence overcome as his erect penis is forced into her mouth after it has been bloodily relieved of its teeth. In turn, Miloš's final, unwitting sexual assault upon his own infant son mirrors the earlier invitation by the grandmother to visit abuse upon her grandchild. His vengeance is therefore less than cathartic, mired instead in knowledge that his idealised family vision has been rigorously managed by a system of patriarchal control in which he forms the very weakest link. While Vukmir gasps his final breath (somewhat ludicrously still voicing the cinematic integrity of his vision), Miloš's final gesture of defiance emerges as a blackly comic metaphor: his oversized erection penetrates the eye of one of the camera crew, the bearer of the pornographic gaze literally destroyed by the phallus wielded as a weapon.

The family unit is terminated through an act of self-administered annihilation. Conjoined on their marital bed, Miloš and Marija silently agree to a single gunshot that will kill both them and their child. However, the final act of an authority seemingly founded in yet another level of institutional power renders the gesture meaningless, the tacit reassurances of familial solidarity merely folded into the film's blank nihilism. Literally and figuratively fucked beyond death, the shadowy orchestrator of the whole enterprise violates the family further in pursuance of an appropriate climax to the snuff film that has already desecrated their bond. By way of casual instruction that multiple acts of necrophilia be performed for the camera, Vukmir's mode of oppressive masculine dominance is merely overridden by an even more rigidly and impersonally applied system of control.

Clearly, *A Serbian Film* goes far beyond its manifest ability to run the somewhat limited gamut of shock, disgust and revulsion. It does not achieve this elegantly, but contrary to its most negative dismissals, it sustains an interest beyond the merely symptomatic, its thematic centralisation of the family intensifying its common genre function as an object of destabilisation. Initially, Miloš's aspiration is posited as a viable and potentially progressive alternative to exploitative processes of porno-capitalism, but the film rejects coherent expression of this ideal as a radical alternative. As its doomed protagonist despairingly seeks his place in a patriarchal order, the film can only surrender him to the grim inevitability of utter abjection. This blunt nihilism verges on self-loathing and one cannot be surprised that many critics would rebut the film for pretentious overreach beyond the horror ghetto in which they would prefer it to reside. Although it is certainly a *succès de scandale*, it has generated no sequels or spin-offs, its self-containment articulating the sense of a terminal statement, offering a limit to which irreverence or even irresponsibility might coalesce with overtly 'serious' subject matter. By the film's conclusion, progressive discourse is immutably crushed, its negative energies begetting a descent into the genre maelstrom from which there is no upward reversal. In 2018, the allegorical, socially alert modes of *Get Out* (Jordan Peele, 2017) were sufficient to propel the horror genre to an uncommon success at the Academy Awards. While this was partly a symptom of its appeal to liberal race consciousness, its sense of disturbance is tempered by a climactic reassurance and uplift. *A Serbian Film* offers no such concession. While entrenched in its own historical context, its uncomfortable cultural percolation is the natural consequence of the unpalatable things it is compelled to show and say – things which the lens of the snuff movie motif throws into sharp and horrifying focus.

Notes

1. See T. Horeck and T. Kendall (eds), *The New Extremism in Cinema: From France to Europe* (Edinburgh: Edinburgh University Press, 2011); Mattias Frey, *Extreme Cinema: The Transgressive Rhetoric of Today's Art Film Culture* (New Brunswick, NJ: Rutgers University Press, 2016); Aaron Kerner and Jonathan L. Knapp, *Extreme Cinema: Affective Strategies in Transnational Media* (Edinburgh: Edinburgh University Press, 2016).
2. See David Kerekes and David Slater, *Killing for Culture: Death on Film and the Enigma of Snuff* (London: Headpress, 2015); and N. Jackson, S. Kimber, J. Walker and T. J. Watson (eds), *Snuff: Real Death and Screen Media* (London: Bloomsbury, 2016).

3. N. Jackson, 'Shot, Cut, and Slaughtered', in N. Jackson, S. Kimber, J. Walker and T. J. Watson (eds), *Snuff: Real Death and Screen Media* (London: Bloomsbury, 2016), p. 14.
4. See N. Jackson, 'Wild Eyes, Dead Ladies: The Snuff Filmmaker in Realist Horror', in N. Jackson, S. Kimber, J. Walker and T. J. Watson (eds), *Snuff: Real Death and Screen Media* (London: Bloomsbury, 2016), pp. 189–209.
5. C. A. Freeland, 'Realist Horror', in C. A. Freeland and T. E. Wartenberg (eds), *Philosophy and Film* (London: Routledge, 1995), pp. 133–9.
6. Freeland, 'Realist Horror', p. 135.
7. M. Brooke, '*A Serbian Film*', *Sight & Sound*, 21/2 (2011), 74.
8. M. Featherstone, 'Coito Ergo Sum: Serbian Sadism and Global Capitalism in *A Serbian Film*', *Horror Studies*, 4/1 (2013), 127–41.
9. Srđan Spasojević quoted in J. Slater, 'A Serbian Film to Disturb You', *Fangoria*, 295 (2010), 67.
10. Spasojević quoted in A. Jones, 'The Nightmare of Truth', Liner notes for *A Serbian Film*, Blu-ray release (Revolver Entertainment, 2011), 2.
11. P. Bradshaw, 'A Serbian Film', *The Guardian* (9 December 2010), https://www.theguardian.com/film/2010/dec/09/a-serbian-film-review (accessed 29 August 2019).
12. See M. Kermode, 'I was a teenage horror fan, or "How I learned to stop worrying and love Linda Blair"', in M. Barker and J. Petley (eds), *Ill Effects: The Media Violence Debate* (London: Routledge, 2001), pp. 126–34.
13. M. Kermode, 'A Serbian Film', *BBC Radio 5 Live* (10 December 2010), https:// www.youtube.com/watch?v=KLiwki7-dSE (accessed 29 August 2019).
14. For a concise account, see J. Patterson, 'Peeping Tom may have been nasty but it didn't deserve critics' cold shoulder', *The Guardian* (13 November 2010), https://www.theguardian.com/film/2010/nov/13/peeping-tom-john-patterson (accessed 29 August 2019).
15. See K. Newman, '*A Serbian Film*', *Empire*, 259 (2011), 53; E. Somer, '*A Serbian Film*', *Video Watchdog*, 167 (2012), 61–4.
16. Steve Jones, *Torture Porn: Popular Horror after Saw* (Basingstoke: Palgrave Macmillan, 2013), pp. 22–6.
17. See Tony Williams, *Hearths of Darkness: The Family in the American Horror Film* (Jackson, MS: University Press of Mississippi, 2014).
18. Williams, *Hearths of Darkness*, p. 3.
19. Williams, *Hearths of Darkness*, p. 9.
20. T. Horeck and T. Kendall, 'Introduction', in T. Horeck and T. Kendall (eds), *The New Extremism in Cinema: From France to Europe* (Edinburgh: Edinburgh University Press, 2011), p. 2.

21. Horeck and Kendall, 'Introduction', p. 1.
22. Horeck and Kendall, 'Introduction', p. 5.
23. Frey, *Extreme Cinema*, pp. 34–45.
24. S. Kimber, 'Transgressive Edge Play and *Srpski Film/A Serbian Film*', *Horror Studies*, 5/1 (2014), 107–25.
25. Aleksandar Radivojević quoted in Jones, 'The Nightmare of Truth', p. 6.
26. A. Kapka, 'Understanding *A Serbian Film*: The Effects of Censorship and File Sharing on Critical Reception and Perceptions of Serbian National Identity in the UK', *Frames Cinema Journal*, 6 (2014), http://framescinemajournal.com/article/understanding-a-serbian-film-the-effects-of-censorship-and-file-sharing-on-critical-reception-and-perceptions-of-serbian-national-identity-in-the-uk/ (accessed 29 August 2019).
27. See Georges Bataille, *Erotism: Death and Sensuality* (San Francisco, CA: City Lights Publishers, 1986), pp. 164–76.
28. Bataille, *Erotism: Death and Sensuality*, p. 173.

Bibliography

Abbott, Stacey, 'High Concept Thrills and Chills: The Horror Blockbuster', in Ian Conrich (ed.), *Horror Zone: The Cultural Experience of Contemporary Horror Cinema* (London: I. B. Tauris, 2009), pp. 27–44.

'About', *Graham Humphreys Limited*, http://www.grahamhumphreys.com/about.html (accessed 29 August 2019).

'About – Bleeding Skull!', *Bleeding Skull!*, http://bleedingskull.com/about/ (accessed 29 August 2019).

'About – Untold Horror', *Untold Horror*, http://www.untoldhorror.ca/about/ (accessed 29 August 2019).

Aftab, Kaleem, 'Director Julia Ducournau on her cannibal film Raw: "I asked my actor, what do you think in principle about shoving your hand up a cow's arse?"', *The Independent* (15 April 2017), https://www.independent.co.uk/arts-entertainment/films/features/julia-ducournau-raw-a7666871.html (accessed 29 August 2019).

——, 'Deep Cover', *Sight & Sound*, 28/9 (2018), 22–7.

Aldana Reyes, Xavier, *Body Gothic: Corporeal Transgression in Contemporary Literature and Horror Film* (Cardiff: University of Wales Press, 2014).

Alexander, Chris, 'TIFF 2016 Review: I Am the Pretty Thing That Lives in the House', *ComingSoon.net* (12 September 2016), http://www.comingsoon.net/horror/reviews/766113-tiff-2016-review-i-am-the-pretty-thing-that-lives-in-the-house (accessed 29 August 2019).

Altman, Rick, *Film/Genre* (London: BFI Publishing, 1999).
Ashley, Britt, 'In horror film "The Witch", terror stems from patriarchal control of women', *Bitch* (3 March 2016), *https://www.bitchmedia.org/article/horror-film-witch-terror-stems-puritanical-control-women* (accessed 29 August 2019).
Aston, James, '"A Malignant, Seething Hatework": An Introduction to US 21st Century Hardcore Horror', *Senses of Cinema*, 80/1 (2016).
——, *Hardcore Horror Cinema in the 21st Century: Production, Marketing and Consumption* (Jefferson, NC: McFarland, 2018).
Atkinson, Sarah, *Beyond the Screen: Emerging Cinema and Engaging Audiences* (London: Bloomsbury, 2014).
'Audio Commentary', *Flowers*, DVD release (Unearthed Films, 2015).
Austin, Bruce A., 'Portrait of a Cult Film Audience: *The Rocky Horror Picture Show*', in Ernest Mathijs and Xavier Mendik (eds), *The Cult Film Reader* (Berkshire: McGraw-Hill, 2008), pp. 392–403.
Bailey, Jason, '"Green Room" Is a Horror Movie for Trump's America', *Flavorwire* (13 April 2016), *http://flavorwire.com/571081/green-room-is-a-horror-movie-for-trumps-america* (accessed 29 August 2019).
Balanzategui, Jessica, 'Creepypasta, "Candle Cove", and the Digital Aesthetics of Uncanny Analogue Nostalgia', *The Journal of Visual Culture*, 18/2 (2019), 187–208.
—— and Naja Later, '"Dark and Wicked Things": The Slenderman, Tween Girlhood and Deadly Liminalities', in Markus Bohlmann (ed.), *Misfit Children: An Inquiry into Childhood Belongings* (Lanham, MD: Lexington Books, 2016), pp. 71–88.
'Banned: Self-Censored', *Melon Farmers*, *http://melonfarmers.co.uk/banned.htm* (accessed 29 August 2019).
Barker, Martin, '"Knowledge–U–Like": The British Board of Film Classification and its Research', *Journal of British Cinema and Television*, 13/1 (2016), 121–40.
Baron, Zach, 'How A24 is disrupting Hollywood', *GQ* (9 May 2017), *http://www.gq.com/story/a24-studio-oral-history* (accessed 29 August 2019).
Basinger, Jeanine, *The World War II Combat Film: Anatomy of a Genre* (Middletown, CT: Wesleyan University Press, 2003).
Bataille, Georges, *Erotism: Death and Sensuality* (San Francisco, CA: City Lights Publishers, 1986).
Beer, David, *Popular Culture and New Media: The Politics of Circulation* (Basingstoke: Palgrave Macmillan, 2013).
Bekmambetov, Timur, 'Rules of the Screenmovie: The *Unfriended* Manifesto for the Digital Age', *MovieMaker* (22 April 2015), *https://www.moviemaker.com/*

archives/moviemaking/directing/unfriended-rules-of-the-screenmovie-a-manifesto-for-the-digital-age/ (accessed 29 August 2019).

Belau, Linda and Kimberly Jackson, 'Introduction: Binging on Horror', in Linda Belau and Kimberly Jackson (eds), *Horror Television in the Age of Consumption: Binging on Fear* (London: Routledge, 2018), pp. 1–15.

Bennett, James, 'Public Service Algorithms', in Des Freedman and Vana Goblot (eds), *A Future for Public Service Television* (London: Goldsmiths Press, 2018), pp. 111–19.

Benshoff, Harry M., 'The Monster and the Homosexual', in Harry M. Benshoff and Sean Griffin (eds), *Queer Cinema: The Film Reader* (London: Routledge, 2004), pp. 63–74.

——, *Monsters in the Closet: Homosexuality and the Horror Film* (Manchester: Manchester University Press, 2004).

Berenstein, Rhona J., *Attack of the Leading Ladies: Gender, Sexuality, and Spectatorship in Classic Horror Cinema* (New York, NY: Columbia University Press, 1996).

Bernard, Mark, *Selling the Splat Pack: The DVD Revolution and the American Horror Film* (Edinburgh: Edinburgh University Press, 2014).

Berriman, Ian, 'Charlie Brooker Talks the Twilight Zone and Technology', *GamesRadar* (1 February 2013), *http://www.gamesradar.com/charlie-brooker-talks-the-twilight-zone-and-technology/* (accessed 29 August 2019).

Bettinson, Gary, *The Sensuous Cinema of Wong Kar-wai: Film Poetics and the Aesthetic of Disturbance* (Hong Kong: Hong Kong University Press, 2015).

—— and Daniel Martin (eds), *Hong Kong Horror Cinema* (Edinburgh: Edinburgh University Press, 2018).

Betz, Mark, 'High and Low and in Between', *Screen*, 54/4 (2013), 495–513.

Bickel, Christopher, 'The Criterion of Shit Movies: Arrow Video's Lionization of Lowbrow', *Dangerous Minds* (22 April 2016), *http://dangerousminds.net/comments/the_criterion_of_shit_movies_arrow_videos_lionization_of_lowbrow* (accessed 29 August 2019).

Billson, Anne, 'Cheap thrills: The frightful rise of low-budget horror', *The Telegraph* (6 May 2015), *http://www.telegraph.co.uk/film/it-follows/rise-of-low-budget-horror-movies-babadook/* (accessed 29 August 2019).

Birks, Chelsea, 'Body Problems: New Extremism, Descartes and Jean-Luc Nancy', *New Review of Film and Television Studies*, 13/2 (2015), 131–46.

Birnbaum, Laura, '*The Blackcoat's Daughter*: The film you aren't ready to see (but should)', *Film Inquiry* (1 July 2016), *https://www.filminquiry.com/blackcoats-daughter-2015-review/* (accessed 29 August 2019).

Bishop, Kyle William, *American Zombie Gothic: The Rise and Fall (and Rise) of the Walking Dead in Popular Culture* (Jefferson, NC: McFarland, 2011).

—, 'Nazi Zombies', in June Pulliam and Anthony J. Fonseca (eds), *Encyclopedia of the Zombie: The Walking Dead in Popular Culture and Myth* (Santa Barbara, CA: Greenwood, 2014), pp. 180–3.

Blacktooth, 'Flowers (review)', *Horror Society* (15 January 2015), https://www.horrorsociety.com/2015/01/14/flowers-review/ (accessed 29 August 2019).

Blank, Trevor, *Folklore and the Internet: Vernacular Expression in a Digital World* (Logan, UT: Utah State University Press, 2009).

Blichert, Frederick, 'What's next for the indie horror movie wave', *Vice* (9 June 2017), https://www.vice.com/en_us/article/kzq7kz/heres-what-to-watch-next-if-youre-riding-the-prestige-horror-wave (accessed 29 August 2019).

Booth, Paul, 'Fans' list-making: memory, influence, and argument in the "event" of fandom', *MATRIZes*, 9/2 (2015), 85–107.

Bordun, Troy, *Genre Trouble and Extreme Cinema: Film Theory at the Fringes of Contemporary Art Cinema* (Basingstoke: Palgrave Macmillan, 2017).

Bordwell, David, 'The art cinema as a mode of film practice', in Timothy Corrigan, Patricia White and Meta Mazaj (eds), *Critical Visions in Film Theory: Classic and Contemporary Readings* (Boston, MA: Bedford/St. Martin's, 2011), pp. 558–73.

—— and Kristin Thompson, *Minding Movies: Observations on the Art, Craft, and Business of Filmmaking* (Chicago, IL: University of Chicago Press, 2011).

Borgeson, Kevin and Robin Maria Valeri, *Skinhead History, Identity, and Culture* (London: Routledge, 2018).

Bourdieu, Pierre, *Distinction: A Social Critique of the Judgement of Taste* (London: Routledge, 2010).

Bowen, Chuck, 'Is it time for a horror movie about the evils of Donald Trump?', *The Guardian* (5 July 2016), https://www.theguardian.com/film/2016/jul/05/donald-trump-horror-movie-they-live-john-carpenter (accessed 29 August 2019).

Bradshaw, Peter, 'Audition', *The Guardian* (16 March 2001), http://www.guardian.co.uk/film/2001/mar/16/1 (accessed 29 August 2019).

—, 'Ichi the Killer', *The Guardian* (30 May 2003), http://www.guardian.co.uk/culture/2003/may/30/artsfeatures1 (accessed 29 August 2019).

—, 'Enter the Void', *The Guardian* (23 September 2010), https://www.theguardian.com/film/2010/sep/23/enter-the-void-review (accessed 29 August 2019).

—, 'A Serbian Film', *The Guardian* (9 December 2010), https://www.theguardian.com/film/2010/dec/09/a-serbian-film-review (accessed 29 August 2019).

Brinkema, Eugenie, 'Violence and the Diagram; Or, *The Human Centipede*', *Qui Parle*, 24/2 (2016), 75–108.

Broe, Dennis, *Birth of the Binge: Serial TV and the End of Leisure* (Detroit, MI: Wayne State University Press, 2019).

Brooke, Michael, 'A Serbian Film', Sight & Sound, 21/2 (2011), 74–5.
Brooker, Charlie and Annabel Jones with Jason Arnopp, Inside Black Mirror (London: Ebury Press, 2018).
Brophy, Philip, 'Horrality – the Textuality of Contemporary Horror Films', Screen, 27/1 (1986), 2–13.
Brottman, Mikita and David Sterritt, 'Irreversible', Film Quarterly, 57 (2004), 37–42.
Brown, Don, 'Report: Japan Premiere of Miike Takashi's Big Bang Love, Juvenile A', Ryuganji (22 May 2006), http://www.ryuganji.net/news/index.php?entry= entry060523-104118 (accessed 29 August 2019).
Brown, Todd, 'TIFF Review: Martyrs', Screen Anarchy (7 September 2008), https://screenanarchy.com/2008/09/martyrs-review.html (accessed 29 August 2019).
Brown, William, 'Violence in Extreme Cinema and the Ethics of Spectatorship', Projections, 7/1 (2013), 25–42.
Burgess, Jean, 'Hearing Ordinary Voices: Cultural Studies, Vernacular Creativity and Digital Storytelling', Continuum: Journal of Media & Cultural Studies, 20/2 (2006), 201–14.
Butler, Andrea, 'Sacrificing the Real: Early 20th Century Theatrics and the New Extremism in Cinema', Cinephile, 8/9 (2012), 27–31.
Butler, Judith, '"Subjects of Sex/Gender/Desire" (1990)', in Imre Szeman and Timothy Kaposy (eds), Cultural Theory: An Anthology (Chichester: Wiley-Blackwell, 2011), pp. 472–91.
Butler, Rose, 'The Eaten-for-Breakfast Club: Teenage Nightmares in Stranger Things', in Kevin J. Wetmore, Jr. (ed.), Uncovering Stranger Things: Essays on Eighties Nostalgia, Cynicism and Innocence in the Series (Jefferson, NC: McFarland, 2018), pp. 72–83.
Campbell, Peter Oder, 'Intersectionality Bites: Metaphors of Race and Sexuality in HBO's True Blood', in Marina Levina and Diem-My T. Bui (eds), Monster Culture in the 21st Century: A Reader (London: Bloomsbury, 2013), pp. 99–114.
'Candle Cove – does it exist?', TV Forum (2009), https://tvforum.uk/tvhome/candle-cove-does-exist-30175/ (accessed 29 August 2019).
Carlsson, Ronny, 'Maskhead review', Film Bizarro, http://www.filmbizarro.com/view_review.php?review=maskhead.php (accessed 24 March 2020).
Carroll, Noël, The Philosophy of Horror or Paradoxes of the Heart (London: Routledge, 1990).
Chandrashekar, Ashok, Fernando Amat, Justin Basilico and Tony Jebara, 'Artwork Personalization at Netflix', The Netflix Tech Blog (7 December 2017), https://

medium.com/netflix-techblog/artwork-personalization-c589f074ad76 (accessed 29 August 2019).

Chang, Justin, 'Has horror become the movie genre of the Trump era?', *Los Angeles Times* (13 October 2016), *https://www.latimes.com/entertainment/movies/la-ca-mn-horror-movies-trump-20171013-story.html* (accessed 11 December 2019).

Cheney-Lippold, John, *We Are Data: Algorithms and the Making of Our Digital Selves* (New York, NY: New York University Press, 2017).

Cherry, Brigid, *Horror* (London: Routledge, 2009).

——, 'Stalking the Web: Celebration, Chat and Horror Film Marketing on the Internet', in Ian Conrich (ed.), *Horror Zone: The Cultural Experience of Contemporary Horror Cinema* (London: I. B. Tauris, 2009), pp. 67–85.

Chess, Shira, 'Open-Sourcing Horror: The Slender Man, Marble Hornets, and Genre Negotiations', *Information, Communication & Society*, 15/3 (2012), 374–93.

Choi, Jinhee, 'Sentimentality and the Cinema of the Extreme', *Jump Cut*, 50/1 (2008).

Church, David, 'Queer Ethics, Urban Spaces, and the Horrors of Monogamy in *It Follows*', *Cinema Journal*, 57/3 (2018), 3–28.

Clover, Carol J., *Men, Women, and Chain Saws: Gender in the Modern Horror Film* (Princeton, NJ: Princeton University Press, 1992).

Cochrane, Kira, 'For your entertainment', *The Guardian* (1 May 2007), *https://www.theguardian.com/film/2007/may/01/gender.world* (accessed 29 August 2019).

Cohn, Jonathan, *The Burden of Choice: Recommendations, Subversion, and Algorithmic Culture* (New Brunswick, NJ: Rutgers University Press, 2019).

Condit, Jon, 'Roth, Eli (Hostel)', *Dread Central* (2 January 2005), *https://www.dreadcentral.com/news/3349/roth-eli-hostel/* (accessed 29 August 2019).

Conrich, Ian (ed.), *Horror Zone: The Cultural Experience of Contemporary Horror Cinema* (London: I. B. Tauris, 2010).

Cook, Tommy, 'Director Takashi Miike Discusses the Bizarre Absurdity of "Yakuza Apocalypse"', *Collider* (10 October 2015), *http://collider.com/takashi-miike-yakuza-apocalypse-interview/* (accessed 29 August 2019).

Cook-Wilson, Winston, 'It's been 10 years since the last major VHS release. Is there a future for the format?', *Inverse* (26 March 2016), *https://www.inverse.com/article/13482-it-s-been-10-years-since-the-last-major-vhs-release-is-there-a-future-for-the-format* (accessed 29 August 2019).

Cooley, Patrick, '"Mother!" is so controversial Paramount had to defend its decision to release the movie', *Cleveland* (18 September 2017), *http://www.*

cleveland.com/entertainment/index.ssf/2017/09/why_is_mother_so_controversial.html (accessed 29 August 2019).

Copsey, Nigel and Matthew Worley (eds), 'Tomorrow Belongs to Us': The British Far Right since 1967 (London: Routledge, 2018).

Corrigan, Timothy, 'The Commerce of Auteurism', in Virginia Wright Wexman (ed.), *Film and Authorship* (New Brunswick, NJ: Rutgers University Press, 2003), pp. 96–111.

Cotter, John M., 'Sounds of hate: White power rock and roll and the neo-Nazi skinhead subculture', *Terrorism and Political Violence*, 11/2 (1999), 111–40.

Coulthard, Lisa, 'The Violence of Silence: Vocal Provocation in the Cinema of Michael Haneke', *Studies in European Cinema*, 9/2–3 (2012), 87–97.

'Cover Exclusive: Jennifer Lawrence Calls Photo Hacking a "Sex Crime"', *Vanity Fair* (7 October 2014), https://www.vanityfair.com/hollywood/2014/10/jennifer-lawrence-cover (accessed 29 August 2019).

Creed, Barbara, *The Monstrous-Feminine: Film, Feminism, Psychoanalysis* (London: Routledge, 1993).

Crucchiola, Jordan, 'Let's Talk About the Ending of *The Blackcoat's Daughter*', *Vulture* (31 March 2017), http://www.vulture.com/2017/03/blackcoats-daughter-ending.html (accessed 29 August 2019).

——, 'Why Do Prestige-Horror Trailers Keep Lying to Us?', *Vulture* (13 June 2017), http://www.vulture.com/2017/06/it-comes-at-night-why-are-horror-trailers- lying-to-us.html (accessed 29 August 2019).

Cruz, Ronald Allan Lopez, 'Mutations and Metamorphoses: Body Horror is Biological Horror', *Journal of Popular Film and Television*, 40/4 (2012), 160–8.

Davis, Blair and Kial Natale, '"The pound of flesh which I demand": American horror cinema, gore, and the box office, 1998–2007', in Steffen Hantke (ed.), *American Horror Film: The Genre at the Turn of the Millennium* (Jackson, MS: University Press of Mississippi, 2010), pp. 35–57.

de Valk, Mark (ed.), *Screening the Tortured Body: Cinema as Scaffold* (Basingstoke: Palgrave Macmillan, 2016).

Debruge, Peter, 'Film Review: "Unfriended"', *Variety* (3 August 2014), http://variety.com/2014/film/festivals/film-review-cybernatural-1201274261/ (accessed 29 August 2019).

Del Rio, Elena, *The Grace of Destruction: A Vital Ethology of Extreme Cinemas* (London: Bloomsbury, 2016).

Dew, Oliver, '"Asia Extreme": Japanese Cinema and British Hype', *New Cinemas: Journal of Contemporary Film*, 5/1 (2007), 53–73.

Dinello, Daniel, *Technophobia! Science Fiction Visions of Posthuman Technology* (Austin, TX: University of Texas Press, 2005).
Dixon, Simon, 'The Figure in the Background: Stardom and Filmic Space', in Kylo-Patrick R. Hart (ed.), *Film and Television Stardom* (Newcastle upon Tyne: Cambridge Scholars Publishing, 2008), pp. 280–307.
Dowd, A. A., 'The Blackcoat's Daughter finally rises from release-date purgatory to give everyone the creeps', *AV Club* (30 March 2017), *http://www.avclub.com/review/blackcoats-daughter-rises-release-date-purgatory-g-252881* (accessed 29 August 2019).
Driscoll, Paul, *Stranger Things – Season 1* (Edinburgh: Obverse Books, 2019).
Duncan, Heather, 'Human "ish": Voices from Beyond the Grave in Contemporary Narratives', *English Language Overseas Perspectives and Enquiries*, 15/1 (2018), 83–97.
Duncombe, Steven and Maxwell Tremblay (eds), *White Riot: Punk Rock and the Politics of Race* (London: Verso, 2011).
——, 'White Power', in Steven Duncombe and Maxwell Tremblay (eds), *White Riot: Punk Rock and the Politics of Race* (London: Verso, 2011), pp. 114–15.
Dunleavy, Trisha, *Complex Serial Drama and Multiplatform Television* (London: Routledge, 2018).
Dunn, Kevin, *Global Punk: Resistance and Rebellion in Everyday Life* (London: Bloomsbury, 2016).
Dupont, Jane, 'Takashi Miike's Heartrending Samurai Tale, Told in 3-D', *The New York Times* (20 May 2011), *http://www.nytimes.com/2011/05/21/arts/21iht-DUPONT21.html?_r=0*> (accessed 29 August 2019).
Dworkin, Andrea, *Intercourse* (New York, NY: Free Press, 1987).
Dyck, Kirsten, *Reichsrock: The International Web of White-Power and Neo-Nazi Hate Music* (New Brunswick, NJ: Rutgers University Press, 2016).
Dyer, Richard, *The Culture of Queers* (London: Routledge, 2002).
Edelstein, David, 'Now Playing at Your Local Multiplex: Torture Porn', *New York Magazine* (28 January 2006), *http://nymag.com/movies/features/15622/* (accessed 29 August 2019).
——, 'In *Green Inferno*, Eli Roth Honors the Cannibal-Gore Tradition With Bravura', *Vulture* (25 September 2015), *https://www.vulture.com/2015/09/movie-review-green-inferno-goes-for-the-kills.html* (accessed 29 August 2019).
Edwards, Kyle, '"House of horrors": Corporate strategy at Universal Pictures in the 1930s', in Richard Nowell (ed.), *Merchants of Menace: The Business of Horror Cinema* (London: Bloomsbury, 2014), pp. 13–29.
Egan, Kate, *Trash or Treasure? Censorship and the Changing Meanings of the Video Nasties* (Manchester: Manchester University Press, 2007).

——, 'The Criterion Collection, cult-art films and Japanese horror: DVD labels as transnational mediators?', *Transnational Cinemas*, 8/1 (2017), 65–79.

Eisner, Ken, 'Review: "Audition"', *Variety* (31 October 1999), *http://variety.com/1999/film/reviews/audition-1200459973/* (accessed 29 August 2019).

Elsaesser, Thomas, 'Truth or Dare: Reality Checks on Indexicality, or the Future of Illusionism', in Anu Koivunnen and Astrid Soderbergh Widding (eds), *Cinema Studies into Visual Theory?* (Turku, Finland: D-Vision, 1998), pp. 31–50.

Enk, Bryan, 'Hostel: Where Did Eli Roth Come From?', *Heavy* (15 October 2010), *http://heavy.com/movies/get-your-gore-on/2010/10/hostel-where-did-eli-roth-come-from/* (accessed 29 August 2019).

Ettinger, Art, Liner notes for *Flowers*, DVD release (Unearthed Films, 2015).

Featherstone, Mark, 'Coito Ergo Sum: Serbian Sadism and Global Capitalism in *A Serbian Film*', *Horror Studies*, 4/1 (2013), 127–41.

—— and Beth Johnson, '"Ovo Je Srbija": The Horror of the National Thing in *A Serbian Film*', *Journal for Cultural Research*, 16/1 (2012), 63–79.

'Films – Bloody Muscle Body Builder in Hell', *Terracotta Distribution*, *http://terracottadistribution.com/films/bloody-muscle-body-builder-in-hell* (accessed 29 August 2019).

Fiske, John, 'The cultural economy of fandom', in Lisa Lewis (ed.), *The Adoring Audience* (London: Routledge, 1992), pp. 30–49.

Fleming, David H., *Unbecoming Cinema: Unsettling Encounters with Ethical Event Films* (Bristol: Intellect, 2017).

'Flight of the Living Dead: Outbreak on a Plane', *BBFC* (2007), *http://www.bbfc.co.uk/releases/flight-living-dead-outbreak-plane-2007-1* (accessed 29 August 2019).

Follows, Stephen, *The Horror Report*, StephenFollows.com (2017), *https://stephenfollows.com/horrorreport/* (accessed 29 August 2019).

Foucault, Michel, 'The Subject and Power', *Critical Enquiry*, 8/0 (1982), 777–95.

——, 'Of Other Spaces: Utopias and Heterotopias', *Architecture/Mouvement/Continuité* (1984), 1–9.

Frank, David A. and Caroline Joan Picart, *Frames of Evil: The Holocaust as Horror in American Film* (Carbondale, IL: Southern Illinois University Press, 2006).

Frank, Russell, 'Caveat Lector: Fake News as Folklore', *The Journal of American Folklore*, 128/509 (2015), 315–32.

Freeland, Cynthia A., 'Realist Horror', in Cynthia A. Freeland and Thomas E. Wartenberg (eds), *Philosophy and Film* (London: Routledge, 1995), pp. 133–9.

Frey, Mattias, *Extreme Cinema: The Transgressive Rhetoric of Today's Art Film Culture* (New Brunswick, NJ: Rutgers University Press, 2016).

Friel, Jenny, 'Warning as horror film shocks public', *The Mirror* (21 May 2001), 12.

Futrell, Robert and Pete Simi, 'The [Un]Surprising Alt-Right', *Contexts*, 16/2 (2017), 76.
Galluzo, Rob and Mike Cucinotta, 'Fright Exclusive Interview: Mick Garris', *Icons of Fright* (8 September 2008), *http://www.iconsoffright.com/IV_Mick.htm* (accessed 29 August 2019).
Garber, Megan, 'Justice for Sansa Stark', *The Atlantic* (20 June 2016), *https://www.theatlantic.com/entertainment/archive/2016/06/justice-for-sansa-stark/487814/* (accessed 29 August 2019).
Gerrard, Steven, 'Introduction', in Steven Gerrard, Samantha Holland and Robert Shail (eds), *Gender and Contemporary Horror in Television* (Bingley: Emerald Publishing, 2019), pp. 1–7.
Gilson, Che, 'Misogynist Review', *UK Horror Scene*, *http://www.ukhorrorscene.com/tag/horror-review/page/20/* (accessed 29 August 2019).
Giroux, Henry A., *Fugitive Cultures: Race, Violence and Youth* (London: Routledge, 1996).
Godfrey, Alex, 'Making America Gory Again: how the Purge films troll Trumpism', *The Guardian* (4 July 2018), *https://www.theguardian.com/film/2018/jul/04/how-the-purge-trolls-trumps-america-jason-blum-first-purge* (accessed 11 December 2019).
Grant, Barry Keith, *Film Genre: From Iconography to Ideology* (London: Wallflower Press, 2007).
——, (ed.), *The Dread of Difference: Gender and the Horror Film* (Austin, TX: University of Texas Press, 2015).
Grant, Catherine, 'On Desktop Documentary (Or, Kevin B. Lee Goes Meta!)', *Film Studies for Free* (6 April 2015), *http://filmstudiesforfree.blogspot.co.uk/2015/04/on-desktop-documentary-or-kevin-b-lee.html* (accessed 29 August 2019).
Grisham, Therese, Julia Leyda, Nicholas Rombes and Steven Shaviro, 'Roundtable Discussion on the Post-Cinematic in *Paranormal Activity* and *Paranormal Activity 2*', *La Furia Umana*, 11 (2011).
Grist, Leighton, *Fascism and Millennial American Cinema* (Basingstoke: Palgrave Macmillan, 2018).
'Grotesque', *BBFC* (2009), *http://www.bbfc.co.uk/releases/grotesque-video* (accessed 29 August 2019).
Grusin, Richard, 'DVDs, Video Games, and the Cinema of Interactions', in Shane Denson and Julia Leyda (eds), *Post-Cinema: Theorizing 21st-Century Film* (Falmer: REFRAME, 2016), pp. 65–87.
Guins, Raiford, 'Blood and Black Gloves on Shiny Discs: New Media, Old Tastes, and the Remediation of Italian Horror Films in the United States', in

Steven Jay Schneider and Tony Williams (eds), *Horror International* (Detroit, MI: Wayne State University Press, 2005), pp. 15–32.

Haflidason, Almar, 'Review: Ichi the Killer', *BBC* (28 May 2003), http://www.bbc.co.uk/films/2003/05/28/ichi_the_killer_2003_review.shtml (accessed 29 August 2019).

Hainge, Greg, 'A full face bright red money shot: Incision, wounding and film spectatorship in Marina de Van's *Dans ma peau*', *Continuum: Journal of Media & Cultural Studies*, 26/4 (2012), 565–77.

Hake, Sabine, *Screen Nazis: Cinema, History, and Democracy* (Madison, WI: University of Wisconsin Press, 2013).

Hallam, Lindsay, 'Genre Cinema as Trauma Cinema: Post 9/11 Trauma and the Rise of "Torture Porn" in Recent Horror Films', in Mick Broderick and Antonio Traverso (eds), *Trauma, Media, Art: New Perspectives* (Newcastle upon Tyne: Cambridge Scholars Publishing, 2010), pp. 228–36.

Hanich, Julian, *Cinematic Emotion in Horror Films and Thrillers: The Aesthetic Paradox of Pleasurable Fear* (London: Routledge, 2010).

Hantke, Steffen (ed.), *Horror Film: Creating and Marketing Fear* (Jackson, MS: University Press of Mississippi, 2004).

—, 'Japanese Horror Under Western Eyes: Social Class and Global Culture in Miike Takashi's *Audition*', in Jay McRoy (ed.), *Japanese Horror Cinema* (Edinburgh: Edinburgh University Press, 2005), pp. 54–65.

—, (ed.), *American Horror Film: The Genre at the Turn of the Millennium* (Jackson, MS: University Press of Mississippi, 2010).

Harries, Dan, 'Watching the Internet', in Dan Harries (ed.), *The New Media Book* (London: BFI Publishing, 2002), pp. 171–82.

Haslop, Craig, '"Do you wanna come with me?" The role of the star image as brand for the commodification of cult in mainstream telefantasy', *Celebrity Studies* (2019), 1–15.

'Hate Crime', *BBFC* (2015), http://www.bbfc.co.uk/releases/hate-crime-vod (accessed 29 August 2019).

Hawkins, Joan, *Cutting Edge: Art-horror and the Horrific Avant-garde* (Minneapolis, MN: University of Minnesota Press, 2000).

—, '"It fixates": indie quiets and the new Gothics', *Palgrave Communications*, 3 (2017), https://doi.org/10.1057/palcomms.2017.88 (accessed 29 August 2019).

Hayward, Joni, 'No Safe Space: Economic Anxiety and Post-recession Spaces in Horror Films', *Frames Cinema Journal*, 11 (2017), http://framescinemajournal.com/article/no-safe-space-economic-anxiety-and-post-recession-spaces-in-horror-films/ (accessed 29 August 2019).

Heffernan, Kevin, *Ghouls, Gimmicks, and Gold: Horror Films and the American Movie Business, 1953–1968* (Durham, NC: Duke University Press, 2004).

Heller-Nicholas, Alexandra, *Rape-Revenge Films: A Critical Study* (Jefferson, NC: McFarland, 2011).

Hicks, Jess, 'Everybody be cool: How to rise above genre-fan backlash', *Blumhouse.com* (5 July 2017), *http://www.blumhouse.com/2017/07/05/everybody-be-cool-how-to-rise-above-genre-fan-backlash/* (accessed 29 August 2019).

Hills, Matt, 'An event-based definition of art-horror', in Steven Jay Schneider and Daniel Shaw (eds), *Dark Thoughts: Philosophic Reflections on Cinematic Horror* (Lanham, MD: Scarecrow Press, 2003), pp. 138–57.

——, *The Pleasures of Horror* (London: Continuum, 2005).

——, 'Attending Horror Film Festivals and Conventions: Liveness, Subcultural Capital and "Flesh-and-Blood Genre Communities"', in Ian Conrich (ed.), *Horror Zone: The Cultural Experience of Contemporary Horror Cinema* (London: I. B. Tauris, 2009), pp. 87–103.

——, '*Black Mirror*: "Bandersnatch" and "The Affair" of Re-Narration in (Gendered TV) Taste Cultures', *CST Online* (18 January 2019), *https://cstonline.net/black-mirror-bandersnatch-and-the-affair-of-re-narration-in-gendered-tv-taste-cultures-by-matt-hills/* (accessed 29 August 2019).

——, '*Black Mirror* as a Netflix Original: Program Brand "Overflow" and the Multidiscursive Forms of Transatlantic TV Fandom', in Matt Hills, Michele Hilmes and Roberta Pearson (eds), *Transatlantic Television Drama: Industries, Programs, & Fans* (Oxford: Oxford University Press, 2019), pp. 213–38.

Hintz, Arne, Lina Dencik and Karin Wahl-Jorgensen, *Digital Citizenship in a Datafied Society* (Cambridge: Polity, 2019).

Hitchcock, Peter, 'Niche Cinema, or *Kill Bill* with *Shaolin Soccer*', in Gina Marchetti and Tan See Kam (eds), *Hong Kong Film, Hollywood and the New Global Cinema: No Film is an Island* (London: Routledge, 2007), pp. 219–32.

Hobbs, Simon, '*Salò, Or the 120 Days of Sodom*: The Contemporary Distribution of Sexual Extremity', *Cine-Excess*, 2 (2016).

Hoffman, Jordan, 'February review – Pseudo-intellectual horror of the dullest kind', *The Guardian* (14 September 2015), *https://www.theguardian.com/film/2015/sep/14/february-film-review-kiernan-shipka-osgood-perkins-horror* (accessed 29 August 2019).

Holden, Stephen, '"Bliss": Cultures and Sexes Clash in the Aftermath of a Rape in Turkey', *The New York Times* (7 August 2009), *https://www.nytimes.com/2009/08/07/movies/07bliss.html* (accessed 29 August 2019).

Horeck, Tanya, *Justice on Demand: True Crime in the Digital Streaming Era* (Detroit, MI: Wayne State University Press, 2019).

—— and Mareike Jenner and Tina Kendall, 'On binge-watching: Nine critical propositions', *Critical Studies in Television: The International Journal of Television Studies*, 13/4 (2018), 499–504.

—— and Tina Kendall, 'Introduction', in Tanya Horeck and Tina Kendall (eds), *The New Extremism in Cinema: From France to Europe* (Edinburgh: Edinburgh University Press, 2011), pp. 1–17.

—— and Tina Kendall (eds), *The New Extremism in Cinema: From France to Europe* (Edinburgh: Edinburgh University Press, 2011).

Howell, Peter, 'Stranger Danger', *The Toronto Star* (15 September 2017).

Hughes, Jessica, 'The Festival Collective: Cult Audiences and Japanese Extreme Cinema', in CarrieLynn D. Reinhard and Christopher J. Olson (eds), *Making Sense of Cinema: Empirical Studies into Film Spectators and Spectatorship* (London: Bloomsbury, 2016), pp. 37–56.

Hunt, Leon, 'A Sadistic Night at the Opera: Notes on the Italian Horror Film', in Ken Gelder (ed.), *The Horror Film Reader* (London: Routledge, 2000), pp. 324–36.

Hutchings, Peter, 'Monster Legacies: Memory, Technology and Horror History', in Lincoln Geraghty and Mark Jancovich (eds), *The Shifting Definitions of Genre: Essays on Labelling Films, Television Shows and Media* (Jefferson, NC: McFarland, 2008), pp. 216–28.

——, 'Northern Darkness: The Curious Case of the Swedish Vampire', in Leon Hunt and Sharon Lockyer (eds), *Screening the Undead: Vampires and Zombies in Film and Television* (London: I. B. Tauris, 2013), pp. 54–70.

——, *The Horror Film* (London: Routledge, 2014).

Hyland, Robert, 'A Politics of Excess: Violence and Violation in Miike Takashi's *Audition*', in Jinhee Choi and Mitsuyo Wada-Marciano (eds), *Horror to the Extreme: Changing Boundaries in Asian Cinema* (Hong Kong: Hong Kong University Press, 2009), pp. 119–218.

Ide, Wendy, 'The Life Before Her Eyes', *The Times* (26 March 2009), https://www.thetimes.co.uk/article/the-life-before-her-eyes-zxgwlhtw9ch (accessed 29 August 2019).

Isaacson, Johanna, '"Unfriended" Unpacks Cyber-Sociality', *Blind Field: A Journal of Cultural Inquiry* (18 February 2016), https://blindfieldjournal.com/2016/02/16/unfriended-unpacks-cyber-sociality/ (accessed 29 August 2019).

Itzkoff, Dave, 'Surgery Helps Lift British Ban on *Human Centipede 2* Film', *The New York Times* (7 October 2011), https://archive.nytimes.com/query.nytimes.com/gst/fullpage-950CEEDF1130F934A35753C1A9679D8B63.html (accessed 29 August 2019).

Jackson, Neil, 'Shot, Cut, and Slaughtered', in Neil Jackson, Shaun Kimber, Johnny Walker and Thomas Joseph Watson (eds), *Snuff: Real Death and Screen Media* (London: Bloomsbury, 2016), pp. 1–19.

——, 'Wild Eyes, Dead Ladies: The Snuff Filmmaker in Realist Horror', in Neil Jackson, Shaun Kimber, Johnny Walker and Thomas Joseph Watson (eds), *Snuff: Real Death and Screen Media* (London: Bloomsbury, 2016), pp. 189–209.
——, and Shaun Kimber, Johnny Walker and Thomas Joseph Watson (eds), *Snuff: Real Death and Screen Media* (London: Bloomsbury, 2016).
James, Nick, 'You have 15 minutes to crawl from the cinema', *Sight & Sound*, 10/3 (2000), 10.
Jancovich, Mark, 'Genre and the Audience: Genre Classifications and Cultural Distinctions in the Mediation of *The Silence of the Lambs*', in Richard Maltby and Melvyn Stokes (eds), *Hollywood Spectatorship: Changing Perceptions of Cinema Audiences* (London: BFI Publishing, 2001), pp. 33–44.
——, 'Relocating Lewton: Cultural Distinctions, Critical Reception, and the Val Lewton Horror Films', *Journal of Film and Video*, 64/3 (2012), 21–37.
——, 'Beyond Hammer: The first run market and the prestige horror film in the early 1960s', *Palgrave Communications*, 3 (2017), https://doi.org/10.1057/palcomms.2017.28 (accessed 29 August 2019).
——, 'Horror in the 1940s', in Harry M. Benshoff (ed.), *A Companion to the Horror Film* (Chichester: Wiley-Blackwell, 2017), pp. 237–54.
Jelfs, Tim, *The Argument about Things in the 1980s: Goods and Garbage in an Age of Neoliberalism* (Morgantown, WV: West Virginia University Press, 2018).
Jenkins, David, 'Film Review: Green Room', *Little White Lies* (10 May 2016), https://lwlies.com/reviews/green-room/ (accessed 29 August 2019).
Jenner, Mareike, 'Is this TVIV? On Netflix, TVIII and binge-watching', *New Media & Society*, 18/2 (2016), 257–73.
——, *Netflix and the Re-invention of Television* (Basingstoke: Palgrave Macmillan, 2018).
Jiménez-Morales, Manel and Marta Lopera-Mármol, 'Why *Black Mirror* Was Really Written by Jean Baudrillard: A Philosophical Interpretation of Charlie Brooker's Series', in Angela M. Cirucci and Barry Vacker (eds), *Black Mirror and Critical Media Theory* (Lanham, MD: Lexington Books, 2018), pp. 103–13.
Johnson, Catherine, *Online TV* (London: Routledge, 2019).
Johnson, Jennifer, 'The End of an Era: Last VHS Tape Shipped', *Hot Hardware* (24 December 2008), https://hothardware.com/news/the-end-of-an-era-last-vhs-tape-shipped (accessed 29 August 2019).
Johnston, Trevor, 'Band on the Run', *Sight & Sound*, 26/6 (2016), 34–5.
Jokinen, Rain, 'Bleak "It Comes at Night" is a thoroughly unpleasant experience', *SFist* (9 June 2017), http://sfist.com/2017/06/09/bleak_it_comes_at_night_a_thoroughl.php (accessed 29 August 2019).

Jones, Alan, 'The Nightmare of Truth', Liner notes for *A Serbian Film*, Blu-ray release (Revolver Entertainment, 2011).

Jones, Steve, 'The Lexicon of Offence: The Meanings of Torture, Porn, and "Torture Porn"', in Feona Attwood, Vincent Campbell, I. Q. Hunter and Sharon Lockyer (eds), *Controversial Images: Media Representations on the Edge* (Basingstoke: Palgrave Macmillan, 2012), pp. 186–200.

——, *Torture Porn: Popular Horror after Saw* (Basingstoke: Palgrave Macmillan, 2013).

——, 'Sex and Horror', in Feona Attwood and Clarissa Smith with Brian McNair (eds), *The Routledge Companion to Media, Sex and Sexuality* (London: Routledge, 2018), pp. 290–9.

Jordan, Randolph (ed.), 'Twenty Years of Takashi Miike at the Fantasia International Film Festival' [special issue], *Off Screen*, 21/3 (2017), https://offscreen.com/issues/view/volume-21-issue-3 (accessed 29 August 2019).

Jowett, Lorna and Stacey Abbott, *TV Horror: Investigating the Dark Side of the Small Screen* (London: I. B. Tauris, 2013).

Jüngerkes, Sven and Christiane Wienand, 'A Past that Refuses to Die: Nazi Zombie Film and the Legacy of Occupation', in Daniel H. Magilow, Elizabeth Bridges and Kristin T. Vander Lugt (eds), *Nazisploitation! The Nazi Image in Low-Brow Cinema and Culture* (London: Continuum, 2012), pp. 238–57.

Kapka, Alexandra, 'Understanding *A Serbian Film*: The Effects of Censorship and File Sharing on Critical Reception and Perceptions of Serbian National Identity in the UK', *Frames Cinema Journal*, 6 (2014), http://framescinemajournal.com/article/understanding-a-serbian-film-the-effects-of-censorship-and-file-sharing-on-critical-reception-and-perceptions-of-serbian-national-identity-in-the-uk/ (accessed 29 August 2019).

Kattelman, Beth, 'Carnographic Culture', in Mikko Canini (ed.), *The Domination of Fear* (New York, NY: Rodopi, 2010), pp. 3–16.

Kawin, Bruce, *Horror and the Horror Film* (London: Anthem Press, 2012).

Keesey, Douglas, 'Split Identification: Representations of Rape in Gaspar Noé's *Irréversible* and Catherine Breillat's *A ma soeur!/Fat Girl*', *Studies in European Cinema*, 7/2 (2010), 95–107.

Kehr, Dave, 'Horror Film Made for Showtime Will Not Be Shown', *The New York Times* (19 January 2006), http://www.nytimes.com/2006/01/19/arts/television/19horr.html?_r=2&oref=slogin& (accessed 29 August 2019).

Kelso, Tony, 'And now no word from our sponsor: How HBO put the risk back into television', in Marc Leverette, Brian L. Ott and Cara Louise Buckley (eds), *It's Not TV: Watching HBO in the Post-Television Era* (London: Routledge, 2008), pp. 46–64.

Kendrick, James, 'A return to the graveyard: Notes on the spiritual horror film', in Steffen Hantke (ed.), *American Horror Film: The Genre at the Turn of the Millennium* (Jackson, MS: University Press of Mississippi, 2010), pp. 142–58.

Kerekes, David and David Slater, *See No Evil: Banned Films and Video Controversy* (Manchester: Critical Vision, 2001).

——, *Killing for Culture: Death on Film and the Enigma of Snuff* (London: Headpress, 2015).

Kermode, Mark, 'I was a teenage horror fan, or "How I learned to stop worrying and love Linda Blair"', in Martin Barker and Julian Petley (eds), *Ill Effects: The Media Violence Debate* (London: Routledge, 2001), pp. 126–34.

——, 'A Serbian Film', *BBC Radio 5 Live* (10 December 2010), *https://www.youtube.com/watch?v=KLiwki7-dSE* (accessed 29 August 2019).

Kern, Laura, 'Scare Tactics: The Pleasures of Cinematic Horror', *Film Comment*, 54/5 (2018), 22–3.

Kerner, Aaron, *Film and the Holocaust: New Perspectives on Dramas, Documentaries, and Experimental Films* (London: Continuum, 2011).

—— and Jonathan L. Knapp, *Extreme Cinema: Affective Strategies in Transnational Media* (Edinburgh: Edinburgh University Press, 2016).

Kimber, Shaun, 'Transgressive Edge Play and *Srpski Film/A Serbian Film*', *Horror Studies*, 5/1 (2014), 107–25.

Klinger, Barbara, 'Digressions at the Cinema: Reception and Mass Culture', *Cinema Journal*, 28/4 (1989), 3–19.

——, 'Film history terminable and interminable: recovering the past in reception studies', *Screen*, 38/2 (1997), 107–28.

——, *Beyond the Multiplex: Cinema, New Technologies and the Home* (Berkeley, CA: University of California Press, 2006).

——, 'The DVD Cinephile: Viewing Heritages and Home Film Cultures', in James Bennett and Tom Brown (eds), *Film and Television after DVD* (London: Routledge, 2008), pp. 19–44.

Knopf, Christina M., 'Zany Zombies, Grinning Ghosts, Silly Scientists and Nasty Nazis', in Cynthia J. Miller and A. Bowdoin van Riper (eds), *The Laughing Dead: The Horror-Comedy Film from Bride of Frankenstein to Zombieland* (Lanham, MD: Rowman and Littlefield, 2016), pp. 25–38.

Kooyman, Ben, 'Snow Nazis Must Die', in Steffen Hantke and Agnieszka Soltysik Monnet (eds), *War Gothic in Literature and Culture* (London: Routledge, 2015), pp. 117–35.

Koven, Mikel J., *La Dolce Morte: Vernacular Cinema and the Italian Giallo Film* (Lanham, MD: Scarecrow Press, 2006).

Kraszewski, Jon, 'Recontextualizing the Historical Reception of Blaxploitation: Articulations of Class, Black Nationalism, and Anxiety in the Genre's Advertisements', *The Velvet Light Trap*, 50 (2002), 48–62.

Lakin, Max, 'Why Horror Movies Will be the Most Exciting Art Form of the Donald Trump Era', *W Magazine* (17 March 2017), *https://www.wmagazine.com/story/horror-movies-social-thrillers-get-out-the-purge/* (accessed 11 December 2019).

Lawson, Richard, '*It Comes at Night* is a pretty but pointless downer', *Vanity Fair* (6 June 2017), *http://www.vanityfair.com/hollywood/2017/06/it-comes-at-night-review* (accessed 29 August 2019).

Lee, Nikki J. Y., 'Salute to Mr. Vengeance! The Making of a Transnational Auteur Park Chan-wook', in Leon Hunt and Leung Wing-Fai (eds), *East Asian Cinemas: Exploring Transnational Connections on Film* (London: I. B. Tauris, 2008), pp. 203–19.

—— and Julian Stringer, 'Counter-programming and the Udine Far East Film Festival', *Screen*, 52/2 (2011), 301–9.

Leeder, Murray, 'Introduction', in Murray Leeder (ed.), *Cinematic Ghosts: Haunting and Spectrality from Silent Cinema to the Digital Era* (London: Bloomsbury, 2015), pp. 1–14.

Leitch, Will, '*The Witch*: Suffer the Little Children', *The New Republic* (19 February 2016), *https://newrepublic.com/article/130182/witch-suffer-little-children* (accessed 29 August 2019).

Lindsey, Shelley Stamp, 'Horror, Femininity, and Carrie's Monstrous Puberty', in Barry Keith Grant (ed.), *The Dread of Difference: Gender and the Horror Film* (Austin, TX: University of Texas Press, 2015), pp. 279–95.

Lobato, Ramon, *Netflix Nations: The Geography of Digital Distribution* (New York, NY: New York University Press, 2019).

Lockwood, Dean, 'All Stripped Down: The Spectacle of "Torture Porn"', *Popular Communication*, 7/1 (2008), 40–8.

Lodge, Guy, 'Cannes Film Review: "Green Room"', *Variety* (17 May 2015), *https://variety.com/2015/film/festivals/green-room-review-1201498852/* (accessed 11 December 2019).

Lowenstein, Adam, *Shocking Representation: Historical Trauma, National Cinema, and the Modern Horror Film* (New York, NY: Columbia University Press, 2005).

McGill, Hannah, 'Film festivals: a view from the inside', *Screen*, 52/2 (2011), 280–5.

McIntyre, Gina, *Stranger Things: Worlds Turned Upside Down* (London: Century, 2018).

McKenna, Mark, 'Constructing the Economic Canon: Technological Capability and Perceptions of Value in DVD and Blu-ray Distribution', in Jonathan

Wroot and Andy Willis (eds), *Cult Media: Re-packaged, Re-released and Restored* (Basingstoke: Palgrave Macmillan, 2017), pp. 31–47.

Mackie, Rob, 'Video releases: "Audition"', *The Guardian* (28 September 2001), http://www.guardian.co.uk/lifeandstyle/2001/sep/28/shopping.artsfeatures (accessed 29 August 2019).

McLarty, Lianne, '"Beyond the Veil of the Flesh": Cronenberg and the Disembodiment of Horror', in Barry Keith Grant (ed.), *The Dread of Difference: Gender and the Horror Film* (Austin, TX: University of Texas Press, 2015), pp. 259–80.

McLoone, Kieran, '*It Comes at Night* and the power of the unseen horror', *Cultured Vultures* (12 July 2017), https://cultured-vultures.com/it-comes-at-night-horror/ (accessed 29 August 2019).

McRoy, Jay, '"Parts is Parts": Pornography, Splatter Films and the Politics of Corporeal Disintergration', in Ian Conrich (ed.), *Horror Zone: The Cultural Experience of Contemporary Horror Cinema* (London: I. B. Tauris, 2009), pp. 191–204.

Manovich, Lev, 'Database as Symbolic Form', *Convergence: The International Journal of Research into New Media Technologies*, 5/2 (1999), 80–99.

Marks, Laura, *The Skin of the Film: Intercultural Cinema, Embodiment and the Senses* (Durham, NC: Duke University Press, 2000).

Marmysz, John, 'The Lure of the Mob: Contemporary Cinematic Depictions of Skinhead Authenticity', *Journal of Popular Culture*, 46/3 (2013), 626–46.

Marso, Lori J., 'Must We Burn Lars von Trier? Simone de Beauvoir's Body Politics in *Antichrist*', *Theory & Event*, 18/2 (2015).

Martin, Daniel, 'Japan's *Blair Witch*: Restraint, Maturity, and Generic Canons in the British Critical Reception of *Ring*', *Cinema Journal*, 48/3 (2009), 35–51.

——, 'Body of Action, Face of Authenticity: Symbolic Stars in Transnational Marketing and Reception of East Asian Cinemas', in Leung Wing-Fai and Andy Willis (eds), *East Asian Film Stars* (Basingstoke: Palgrave Macmillan, 2014), pp. 19–34.

——, *Extreme Asia: The Rise of Cult Cinema from the Far East* (Edinburgh: Edinburgh University Press, 2015).

Massumi, Brian, 'Notes on the Translation and Acknowledgements', in Gilles Deleuze and Félix Guattari, *A Thousand Plateaus* (Minneapolis, MN: University of Minnesota Press, 1987).

Masters, Tim, '"Video nasty" director Deodato debates censorship', *BBC News* (26 May 2011), https://www.bbc.co.uk/news/entertainment-arts-13550879 (accessed 29 August 2019).

'*Masters of Horror: Imprint*', DVD release (Anchor Bay, 2006).

'*Masters of Horror: Season 1*', DVD release (Anchor Bay, 2007).

Mathijs, Ernest and Jamie Sexton, *Cult Cinema: An Introduction* (Chichester: Wiley-Blackwell, 2011).

Mendik, Xavier, 'The Fantastisk Film Festival: An overview and interview with Magnus Paulsson', in Ernest Mathijs and Xavier Mendik (eds), *Alternative Europe: Eurotrash and Exploitation Cinema Since 1945* (London: Wallflower Press, 2004), pp. 232–7.

——, *Bodies of Desire and Bodies in Distress: The Golden Age of Italian Cult Cinema 1970–1985* (Newcastle upon Tyne: Cambridge Scholars Publishing, 2015).

Miller, Cynthia J., 'The Rise and Fall – and Rise – of the Nazi Zombie in Film', in Christopher M. Moreman and Cory James Rushton (eds), *Race, Oppression and the Zombie: Essays on Cross-Cultural Appropriations of the Caribbean Tradition* (Jefferson, NC: McFarland, 2011), pp. 139–48.

Mitchell, Elvis, 'Film Review; Wife Hunting Sure Is a Sick and Frightful Business', *The New York Times* (8 August 2001), http://www.nytimes.com/movie/review?res=9B0CEEDB1F3CF93BA3575BC0A9679C8B63 (accessed 29 August 2019).

Mollet, Tracey, 'Looking through the upside down: Hyper-postmodernism and transmediality in the Duffer Brothers' *Stranger Things*', *Journal of Popular Television*, 7/1 (2019), 57–77.

Morrow, Brendan, '"It Follows" is Not About STDs. It's About Life As a Sexual Assault Survivor.', *Bloody Disgusting* (27 April 2016), https://bloody-disgusting.com/editorials/3387893/follows-not-stds-life-sexual-assault-survivor (accessed 29 August 2019).

Murphy, Mekado, 'In "Unfriended," Horror Unfolds on a Desktop Screen', *The New York Times* (12 April 2015), http://www.nytimes.com/2015/04/12/movies/in-unfriended-horror-unfolds-on-a-desktop-screen.html (accessed 29 August 2019).

Musetto, Vincent, 'Super "Hostel" – Asian Horror Master is Scared by New Film', *New York Post* (1 January 2006), http://nypost.com/2006/01/01/super-hostel-asian-horror-master-is-scared-by-new-film/ (accessed 29 August 2019).

Nagle, Angela, *Kill All Normies: Online Culture Wars from 4chan and Tumblr to Trump and the Alt-right* (London: Zero Books, 2017).

Nayar, Pramod K., *The Extreme in Contemporary Culture* (Lanham, MD: Rowman and Littlefield, 2017).

Ndalianis, Angela, *The Horror Sensorium: Media and the Senses* (Jefferson, NC: McFarland, 2012).

Neale, Steve, 'Art Cinema as Institution', *Screen*, 22/1 (1981), 11–39.

——, *Genre and Hollywood* (London: Routledge, 2000).

Nealon, Jeffrey T., *I'm Not Like Everybody Else: Biopolitics, Neoliberalism and American Popular Music* (Lincoln, NE: University of Nebraska Press, 2018).

Needham, Gary, 'Playing with genre: An introduction to the Italian *giallo*', *Kino-eye: New Perspectives on European Film*, 2/11 (2002), 1–7.

——, 'Japanese Cinema and Orientalism', in Dimitris Eleftheriotis and Gary Needham (eds), *Asian Cinemas: A Reader and Guide* (Edinburgh: Edinburgh University Press, 2006), pp. 8–16.

Newman, Kim, '*A Serbian Film*', *Empire*, 259 (2011), 53.

——, 'The Year in . . . Horror', *Sight & Sound*, 27/1 (2017), 54–5.

Nissenbaum, Asaf and Limor Shifman, 'Internet memes as contested cultural capital: The case of 4chan's /b/ board', *New Media & Society*, 19/4 (2017), 483–501.

Noble, Cody, 'Vagina Dentata: Re-examining Teeth (2007)', *Diabolique Magazine* (29 January 2017), *https://diaboliquemagazine.com/vagina-dentata-re-examining-teeth-2007/* (accessed 29 August 2019).

Noblett, K., 'Successful Excess', *Cinema Business*, 34 (2007).

Och, Dana and Kirsten Strayer (eds), *Transnational Horror Across Visual Media* (London: Routledge, 2014).

O'Hara, Helen, 'Is VHS making a comeback?', *The Telegraph* (23 April 2015), *http://www.telegraph.co.uk/culture/film/film-news/11555663/Is-VHS-making-a-comeback.html* (accessed 29 August 2019).

Orange, Michelle, 'Taking Back the Knife', *The New York Times* (6 September 2009), *https://www.nytimes.com/2009/09/06/movies/06oran.html* (accessed 29 August 2019).

Page, Aubrey, 'Jeremy Saulnier's *Green Room* & the Anarchy of Punk Violence', *MPAA* (26 April 2016), *https://www.motionpictures.org/2016/04/jeremy-saulniers-green-room-anarchy-punk-violence/* (accessed 11 December 2019).

Pariser, Eli, *The Filter Bubble* (London: Penguin, 2012).

Patterson, John, 'Peeping Tom may have been nasty but it didn't deserve critics' cold shoulder', *The Guardian* (13 November 2010), *https://www.theguardian.com/film/2010/nov/13/peeping-tom-john-patterson* (accessed 29 August 2019).

——, 'Get Out: the first great paranoia movie of the Trump era', *The Guardian* (6 March 2017), *https://www.theguardian.com/film/2017/mar/06/get-out-movie-jordan-peele-trump* (accessed 11 December 2019).

Peck, Andrew, 'Tall, Dark and Loathsome: The Emergence of a Legend Cycle in the Digital Age', *The Journal of American Folklore*, 128/509 (2015), 333–48.

Peirse, Alison and Daniel Martin (eds), *Korean Horror Cinema* (Edinburgh: Edinburgh University Press, 2013).

Perks, Lisa Glebatis, *Media Marathoning: Immersions in Morality* (Lanham, MD: Lexington Books, 2015).

Petley, Julian, 'Nazi Horrors: History, Myth, Sexploitation', in Ian Conrich (ed.), *Horror Zone: The Cultural Experience of Contemporary Horror Cinema* (London: I. B. Tauris, 2009), pp. 205–26.

Pett, Emma, 'A New Media Landscape? The BBFC, Extreme Cinema as Cult, and Technological Change', *New Review of Film and Television Studies*, 13/1 (2015), 83–99.

——, 'Transnational cult paratexts: exploring audience readings of Tartan's Asia Extreme brand', *Transnational Cinemas*, 8/1 (2017), 35–48.

Pheasant-Kelly, Frances, *Abject Spaces in American Cinema: Institutional Settings, Identity and Psychoanalysis in Film* (London: I. B. Tauris, 2013).

'Pig Hunt', *BBFC* (2008), https://www.bbfc.co.uk/releases/pighunt-2008 (accessed 29 August 2019).

Pittman, Matthew and Kim Sheehan, 'Sprinting a media marathon: Uses and gratifications of binge-watching television through Netflix', *First Monday* (5 October 2015), https://firstmonday.org/ojs/index.php/fm/article/view/6138 (accessed 29 August 2019).

'Press Note regarding charges against Ángel Sala, Festival Director, for the screening of *A Serbian Film* in 2010', *Sitges Film Festival* (9 March 2011), https://sitgesfilmfestival.com/eng/noticies?id=1003040 (accessed 29 August 2019).

Price, Brian, 'Pain and the Limits of Representation', *Framework: The Journal of Cinema and Media*, 47/2 (2006), 22–9.

Pye, Doug, 'Movies and tone', in John Gibbs and Douglas Pye (eds), *Close-Up 02* (London: Wallflower Press, 2007), pp. 4–80.

Queenan, Joe, 'Bring on the creepy girls', *The Guardian* (22 February 2008), http://www.theguardian.com/film/2008/feb/22/worldcinema (accessed 29 August 2019).

'r/TheoryOfReddit', *Reddit* (2010), https://www.reddit.com/r/TheoryOfReddit/comments/88disb/did_reddit_change_the_front_page_algorithm_again/ (accessed 29 August 2019).

Raposo, Ana and Roger Sabin, 'New visual identities for British neo-fascist rock (1982–1987): White Noise, "Vikings" and the cult of Skrewdriver', in Nigel Copsey and Matthew Worley (eds), *'Tomorrow Belongs To Us': The British Far Right since 1967* (London: Routledge, 2018), pp. 132–49.

Rau, Petra, *Our Nazis: Representations of Fascism in Contemporary Literature and Film* (Edinburgh: Edinburgh University Press, 2013).

Rawle, Steven, 'From *The Black Society* to *The Isle*: Miike Takashi and Kim Ki-Duk at the intersection of Asia Extreme', *Journal of Japanese and Korean Cinema*, 1/2 (2009), 167–84.

——, 'Ringing *One Missed Call*: Franchising, Transnational Flows and Genre Production', *East Asian Journal of Popular Culture*, 1/1 (2015), 97–112.

Rees, Emma, *The Vagina: A Literary and Cultural History* (London: Bloomsbury, 2013).

Ridgeway, James, *Blood in the Face: The Ku Klux Klan, Aryan Nations, Nazi Skinheads, and the Rise of New White Culture* (New York, NY: T. Thunders Mouth Press, 1995).

Rife, Katie, 'Horror is a Trojan horse for *The Blackcoat's Daughter* director Oz Perkins', *AV Club* (30 March 2017), http://www.avclub.com/article/horror-trojan-horse-blackcoats-daughter-director-o-252538 (accessed 29 August 2019).

Ring, Johnny, 'Watching Green Room after Charlottesville', *Things We Watch* (27 August 2017), http://www.thingswewatch.com/2017/08/27/watching-green-room-charlottesville (accessed 29 August 2019).

Riskala, Tuomas, 'The Espoo Ciné International Film Festival', in Ernest Mathijs and Xavier Mendik (eds), *Alternative Europe: Eurotrash and Exploitation Cinema Since 1945* (London: Wallflower Press, 2004), pp. 228–31.

Ritzer, George and Nathan Jurgenson, 'Production, Consumption, Prosumption: The nature of capitalism in the age of the digital "prosumer"', *Journal of Consumer Culture*, 10/1 (2010), 13–36.

Robinson, Tasha, 'Green Room director Jeremy Saulnier on recreating his teen years through horror films', *The Verge* (14 April 2016), https://www.theverge.com/2016/4/14/11432110/green-room-director-jeremy-saulnier-interview (accessed 29 August 2019).

Romano, Aja, 'Horror movies reflect cultural fears. In 2016, Americans feared invasion.', *Vox* (21 December 2016), https://www.vox.com/culture/2016/12/21/13737476/horror-movies-2016-invasion (accessed 11 December 2019).

Romney, Jonathan, 'Dutch treat', *The Guardian* (9 February 2000), http://www.guardian.co.uk/film/2000/feb/09/artsfeatures.rotterdamfilmfestival (accessed 29 August 2019).

Rose, Steve, 'Blood isn't that scary', *The Guardian* (2 June 2003), http://www.theguardian.com/film/2003/jun/02/artsfeatures.dvdreviews2 (accessed 29 August 2019).

——, 'How post-horror movies are taking over cinema', *The Guardian* (6 July 2017), https://www.theguardian.com/film/2017/jul/06/post-horror-films-scary-movies-ghost-story-it-comes-at-night (accessed 29 August 2019).

Rougeau, Michael, 'Horror Anthology *Channel Zero* and the Challenge of Hunting Down Creepypastas', *GameSpot* (20 September 2017), https://www.gamespot.com/articles/horror-anthology-channel-zero-and-the-challenge-of/1100-6453480/ (accessed 29 August 2019).

Rowan-Legg, Shelagh, 'Charges against Sitges Festival & director Ángel Scala dropped', *Screen Anarchy* (22 February 2012), https://screenanarchy.

com/2012/02/charges-against-sitges-festival-director-angel-sala-dropped.html (accessed 29 August 2019).

Rucka, Nicholas, 'Review: Imprint', *Midnight Eye* (15 September 2006), http://www.midnighteye.com/reviews/imprint/ (accessed 29 August 2019).

Russell, Jamie, *Book of the Dead: The Complete History of Zombie Cinema* (Guildford: FAB Press, 2005).

Sacks, Ethan, '"The Witch" casts a spell on critics even though it's not very good', *New York Daily News* (17 February 2016), http://www.nydailynews.com/entertainment/movies/witch-casts-spell-critics-not-good-article-1.2529738 (accessed 29 August 2019).

'Salo', BBFC (2008), http://www.bbfc.co.uk/case-studies/salo120-days-sodom (accessed 29 August 2019).

Sandvoss, Cornel, *Fans: The Mirror of Consumption* (Cambridge: Polity, 2005).

Schaefer, Eric, *"Bold! Daring! Shocking! True!" A History of Exploitation Films, 1919–1959* (Durham, NC: Duke University Press, 1999).

Schiesel, Seth, 'No Mercy and Ample Ways to Die', *The New York Times* (12 October 2009), https://www.nytimes.com/2009/10/12/arts/television/12saw.html (accessed 29 August 2019).

Schilling, Mark, 'Takashi Miike Makes His Mark', *The Japan Times* (23 June 2006), http://www.japantimes.co.jp/culture/2006/06/23/culture/takashi-miike-makes-his-mark/#.Vxjh0HErLC0 (accessed 29 August 2019).

Schneider, Steven Jay and Tony Williams (eds), *Horror International* (Detroit, MI: Wayne State University Press, 2005).

Schrey, Dominik, 'Analogue Nostalgia and the Aesthetics of Digital Remediation', in Katharina Niemeyer (ed.), *Media and Nostalgia: Yearning for the Past, Present and Future* (Basingstoke: Palgrave Macmillan, 2014), pp. 28–38.

Sconce, Jeffrey, 'Irony, Nihilism, and the New American "Smart" Film', *Screen*, 43/4 (2002), 349–69.

——, 'Trashing the Academy: Taste, Excess and an Emerging Politics of Cinematic Style', in Ernest Mathijs and Xavier Mendik (eds), *The Cult Film Reader* (Berkshire: McGraw-Hill, 2008), pp. 100–19.

Sexton, Jamie, 'US "Indie-Horror": Critical Reception, Genre Construction, and Suspect Hybridity', *Cinema Journal*, 51/2 (2012), 67–86.

——, 'The allure of otherness: transnational cult film fandom and the exoticist assumption', *Transnational Cinemas*, 8/1 (2017), 5–19.

Shalit, Wendy, *Girls Gone Mild* (New York, NY: Random House, 2007).

Shaviro, Steven, '*Teeth*', *The Pinocchio Theory* (3 May 2008), http://www.shaviro.com/Blog/?p=632 (accessed 29 August 2019).

—, 'Post-Cinematic Affect: On Grace Jones, *Boarding Gate* and *Southland Tales*', *Film-Philosophy*, 14/1 (2010), 1–102.

Shifman, Limor, 'The Cultural Logic of Photo-Based Meme Genres', *The Journal of Visual Culture*, 13/3 (2014), 340–58.

Shin, Chi-Yun, 'The Art of Branding: Tartan "Asia Extreme" Films', in Jinhee Choi and Mitsuyo Wada-Marciano (eds), *Horror to the Extreme: Changing Boundaries in Asian Cinema* (Hong Kong: Hong Kong University Press, 2009), pp. 85–100.

Shortall, Eithne, '"Torture Porn" Horror Film Sequel Seeks Irish Release', *The Sunday Times* (16 October 2011), https://www.thetimes.co.uk/article/torture-porn-horror-film-sequel-seeks-irish-release-after-cuts-jrzbkq67cn8 (accessed 29 August 2019).

Shouse, Eric, 'Feeling, Emotion, Affect', *M/C Journal*, 8/6 (2005), http://journal.media-culture.org.au/0512/03-shouse.php (accessed 29 August 2019).

Sibielski, Rosalind, 'Gendering the Monster Within: Biological Essentialism, Sexual Difference, and Changing Symbolic Functions of the Monster in Popular Werewolf Texts', in Marina Levina and Diem-My T. Bui (eds), *Monster Culture in the 21st Century: A Reader* (London: Bloomsbury, 2013).

Sims, David, '*Black Mirror* Is the Perfect Show for Netflix', *The Atlantic* (8 September 2015), https://www.theatlantic.com/entertainment/archive/2015/09/netflix-and-black-mirror-a-match-made-in-digital-heaven/404275/ (accessed 29 August 2019).

Skal, David J., *The Monster Show: A Cultural History of Horror* (London: Plexus, 1993).

Skenazy, Lenore, 'It's Torture! It's Porn! What's Not to Like? Plenty, Actually', *AdAge* (28 May 2007), https://adage.com/article/lenore-skenazy/torture-porn-plenty/116897 (accessed 29 August 2019).

Slater, Jay, 'A Serbian Film to Disturb You', *Fangoria*, 295 (2010), 66–8.

Slavros, Alexander, 'Nazi Movie Review: Green Room (2016)', *Daily Stormer* (5 July 2016), https://dailystormer.su/nazi-movie-review-green-room-2016/ (accessed 11 December 2019).

Smith, Justine, 'The Blackcoat's Daughter', *RogerEbert.com* (29 March 2017), http://www.rogerebert.com/reviews/the-blackcoats-daughter-2017 (accessed 29 August 2019).

Smith, Martin, 'Revulsion and Derision: *Antichrist*, *The Human Centipede II* and the British Press', *Film International*, 13 (2015).

Snelson, Tim, '"From Grade B Thrillers to Deluxe Chillers": Prestige Horror, Female Audiences, and Allegories of Spectatorship in *The Spiral Staircase* (1946)', *New Review of Film and Television Studies*, 7/2 (2009), 173–88.

Sobchack, Vivian, *Carnal Thoughts: Embodiment and Moving Image Culture* (Berkeley, CA: University of California Press, 2004).

Somer, Eric, 'A Serbian Film', *Video Watchdog*, 167 (2012), 61–4.

Soukup, Charles, '*I Love the 80s*: The Pleasures of a Postmodern History', *Southern Communication Journal*, 75/1 (2010), 76–93.

Spadoni, Robert, 'Carl Dreyer's Corpse: Horror Film Atmosphere and Narrative', in Harry M. Benshoff (ed.), *A Companion to the Horror Film* (Chichester: Wiley-Blackwell, 2014), pp. 151–67.

——, 'Horror Film Atmosphere as Anti-narrative (and Vice Versa)', in Richard Nowell (ed.), *Merchants of Menace: The Business of Horror Cinema* (London: Bloomsbury, 2014), pp. 109–28.

Squires, John, 'What Was the Final Horror Film Officially Released On VHS?', *Bloody Disgusting* (4 May 2017), http://bloody-disgusting.com/news/3435649/last-horror-film-officially-released-vhs/ (accessed 29 August 2019).

——, 'UK Store HMV Releasing "The Thing" Blu-ray in Exclusive VHS Packaging!', *Bloody Disgusting* (18 June 2018), https://bloody-disgusting.com/home-video/3504836/uk-store-hmv-releasing-thing-Blu-ray-exclusive-vhs-packaging/ (accessed 30 January 2020).

Stam, Robert and Roberta Pearson, 'Hitchcock's *Rear Window*: Reflexivity and the Critique of Voyeurism', in Marshall Deutelbaum and Leland A. Poague (eds), *A Hitchcock Reader* (Chichester: Wiley-Blackwell, 2009), pp. 193–206.

Stiglegger, Marcus, 'Cinema beyond Good and Evil? Nazi Exploitation in the Cinema of the 1970s and its Heritage', in Daniel H. Magilow, Elizabeth Bridges and Kristin T. Vander Lugt (eds), *Nazisploitation! The Nazi Image in Low-Brow Cinema and Culture* (London: Continuum, 2012), pp. 21–37.

Straub, Kris, 'Candle Cove', *IchorFalls* (2009), http://ichorfalls.chainsawsuit.com/ (accessed 29 August 2019).

Striphas, Ted, 'Algorithmic culture', *European Journal of Cultural Studies*, 18/4–5 (2015), 395–412.

Stubblefield, Thomas, 'Disassembling the Cinema: The Poster, the Film and In-Between', *Thresholds*, 34 (2007), 84–8.

Taylor, Alison, *Troubled Everyday: The Aesthetics of Violence and the Everyday in European Art Cinema* (Edinburgh: Edinburgh University Press, 2017).

Telotte, J. P., '*The Blair Witch Project* Project', *Film Quarterly*, 54/3 (2001), 32–9.

Terrell, Lacey, 'The Brutal and the Banal Become Us', *The Star-Ledger* (8 March 2009).

Thomas, Kevin, '"Audition": Gruesome but Skillful', *The Los Angeles Times* (16 November 2001), http://articles.latimes.com/2001/nov/16/entertainment/et-kevin16 (accessed 29 August 2019).

Thomson, Desson, 'If these Walls Could Talk, They'd Scream', *The Washington Post* (4 January 2008).
Thornton, Sarah, *Club Cultures: Music, Media and Subcultural Capital* (Cambridge: Polity, 1995).
'Three collapse at Swiss horror premiere', *The Guardian* (10 January 2002), http://www.guardian.co.uk/film/2002/jan/10/news2 (accessed 29 August 2019).
Tobias, Scott, 'Of thee I scream: How horror films reflect politics', *The Washington Post* (2 July 2016), https://digitaledition.chicagotribune.com/tribune/article_popover.aspx?guid=18309593-fff7-4bdc-895a-e59d1b5e448f (accessed 29 August 2019).
Tompkins, Joe, 'Bids for Distinction: The Critical-Industrial Function of the Horror Auteur', in Richard Nowell (ed.), *Merchants of Menace: The Business of Horror Cinema* (London: Bloomsbury, 2014), pp. 203–14.
——, '"Re-imagining" the canon: examining the discourse of contemporary horror film reboots', *New Review of Film and Television Studies*, 12/4 (2014), 380–99.
Tookey, Chris, 'Antichrist: The man who made this horrible, misogynistic film needs to see a shrink', *Daily Mail* (24 July 2009), https://www.dailymail.co.uk/tvshowbiz/reviews/article-1201803/ANTICHRIST-The-man-horrible-misogynistic-film-needs-shrink.html (accessed 29 August 2019).
Traber, Daniel S., 'L.A.'s "White Minority": Punk and the Contradictions of Self-Marginalization', *Cultural Critique*, 48/0 (2014), 30–64.
Tyron, Chuck, *Reinventing Cinema: Movies in the Age of Media Convergence* (New Brunswick, NJ: Rutgers University Press, 2009).
Tzioumakis, Yannis, '"Independent", "Indie", and "Indiewood": Towards a periodisation of contemporary (post-1980) American independent cinema', in Geoff King, Claire Molloy and Yannis Tzioumakis (eds), *American Independent Cinema: Indie, Indiewood, and Beyond* (London: Routledge, 2013), pp. 28–40.
Van Extergem, Dirk, 'A Report on the Brussels International Festival of Fantastic Film', in Ernest Mathijs and Xavier Mendik (eds), *Alternative Europe: Eurotrash and Exploitation Cinema Since 1945* (London: Wallflower Press, 2004), pp. 216–28.
'VHS Special Features That Have Yet to Be Released on DVD or Blu ray', *DVD Talk Forum* (2012), http://forum.dvdtalk.com/hd-talk/603442-vhs-special-features-have-yet-released-dvd-Blu-ray.html (accessed 29 August 2019).
Vijn, Ard, 'IFFR 2012 Interview: Miike Takashi Talks Ace Attorney', *Screen Anarchy* (11 February 2012), http://screenanarchy.com/2012/02/iffr-2012-interview-miike-takashi-talks-ace-attorney.html (accessed 29 August 2019).

Vivar, Rosana, 'A film bacchanal: Playfulness and audience sovereignty in San Sebastian Horror and Fantasy Film Festival', *Participations: Journal of Audience & Reception Studies*, 13/1 (2016), 234–51.

Walker, Johnny, 'A Wilderness of Horrors? British Horror Cinema in the New Millennium', *Journal of British Cinema and Television*, 9/3 (2012), 436–56.

Walton, Brian, 'Fantastic Fest Review: *Open Windows* with Elijah Wood and Sasha Grey', *Nerdist* (6 October 2014), *http://nerdist.com/fantastic-fest-review-open-windows-with-elijah-wood-sasha-grey/* (accessed 29 August 2019).

Ward, James J., 'Utterly Without Redeeming Social Value? "Nazi Science" Beyond Exploitation Cinema in Nazisploitation', in Daniel H. Magilow, Elizabeth Bridges and Kristin T. Vander Lugt (eds), *Nazisploitation! The Nazi Image in Low-Brow Cinema and Culture* (London: Continuum, 2012), pp. 92–112.

Ward, Sam, 'Box Sets on the Set-Top Box: The Promotion of on Demand Television in Britain', in Jonathan Wroot and Andy Willis (eds), *DVD, Blu-ray and Beyond: Navigating Formats and Platforms within Media Consumption* (Basingstoke: Palgrave Macmillan, 2017), pp. 177–96.

Wee, Valerie, 'The *Scream* Trilogy, "Hyperpostmodernism", and the Late-Nineties Teen Slasher Film', *Journal of Film and Video*, 57/3 (2005), 44–61.

Weir, Kenneth and Stephen Dunne, 'The Connoisseurship of the Condemned: *A Serbian Film*, *The Human Centipede 2* and the Appreciation of the Abhorrent', *Participations: Journal of Audience & Reception Studies*, 11 (2014), 78–99.

West, Alexandra, *Films of the New French Extremity: Visceral Horror and National Identity* (Jefferson, NC: McFarland, 2016).

Wetmore, Jr., Kevin J., *Post-9/11 Horror in American Cinema* (London: Continuum, 2012).

Wheatley, Catherine, *Michael Haneke's Cinema: The Ethic of the Image* (New York, NY: Berghan, 2009).

Wheatley, Helen, *Gothic Television* (Manchester: Manchester University Press, 2006).

White, Michele, *The Body and the Screen: Theories of Internet Spectatorship* (Cambridge, MA: MIT Press, 2009).

Whitney, Erin, '24 Easter Eggs from All Three Seasons of "Black Mirror," Plus a Timeline Connecting Every Episode', *Screen Crush* (26 October 2016), *http://screencrush.com/black-mirror-easter-eggs-theory/* (accessed 29 August 2019).

Williams, Linda, 'Film Bodies: Gender, Genre, and Excess', in Barry Keith Grant (ed.), *Film Genre Reader III* (Austin, TX: University of Texas Press, 2003), pp. 141–59.

—, 'When the Woman Looks', in Barry Keith Grant (ed.), *The Dread of Difference: Gender and the Horror Film* (Austin, TX: University of Texas Press, 2015), pp. 15–34.

Williams, Tony, *Hearths of Darkness: The Family in the American Horror Film* (Jackson, MS: University Press of Mississippi, 2014).

Winkler, Robert A., 'Was John Wayne a Nazi? The racial politics of taste in 1980s US hardcore punk', *Punk & Post-Punk*, 5/2 (2016), 131–46.

Wood, Robin, 'The American Nightmare: Horror in the 70s', in Mark Jancovich (ed.), *Horror, the Film Reader* (London: Routledge, 2001).

Worley, Matthew and Nigel Copsey, 'White Youth: The far right, punk and British youth culture, 1977–87', in Nigel Copsey and Matthew Worley (eds), *'Tomorrow Belongs to Us': The British Far Right since 1967* (London: Routledge, 2018), pp. 113–31.

Wright, Benjamin, 'Canada's Great Shame: Tax Shelters, Nationalism, and Popular Taste in Canadian Cinema', *Spectator*, 32/2 (2012), 20–5.

Wroot, Jonathan, 'The Stories of Arrow Video, as told by Trailers for their DVDs', *Watching the Trailer* (29 April 2015), *http://www.watchingthetrailer.com/trailers-blog/the-stories-of-arrow-video-as-told-by-trailers-for-their-dvds* (accessed 29 August 2019).

—, 'Distributing Asian Cinema, Past and Present: Definitions from DVD Labels', in Aaron Han Joon Magnan-Park, Gina Marchetti and Tan See Kam (eds), *The Palgrave Handbook of Asian Cinema* (Basingstoke: Palgrave Macmillan, 2018), pp. 201–19.

— and Andy Willis (eds), *Cult Media: Re-packaged, Re-released and Restored* (Basingstoke: Palgrave Macmillan, 2017).

— and Andy Willis, 'Introduction', in Jonathan Wroot and Andy Willis (eds), *DVD, Blu-ray and Beyond: Navigating Formats and Platforms within Media Consumption* (Basingstoke: Palgrave Macmillan, 2017).

Wynne, Ken, 'An Interview with Director Shinichi Fukazawa – Bloody Muscle Body Builder in Hell', *Attack From Planet B* (4 January 2017), *https://www.attackfromplanetb.com/2017/04/an-interview-with-director-shinichi-fukazawa/* (accessed 29 August 2019).

Young, Liam Cole, *List Cultures: Knowledge and Poetics from Mesopotamia to BuzzFeed* (Amsterdam: Amsterdam University Press, 2017).

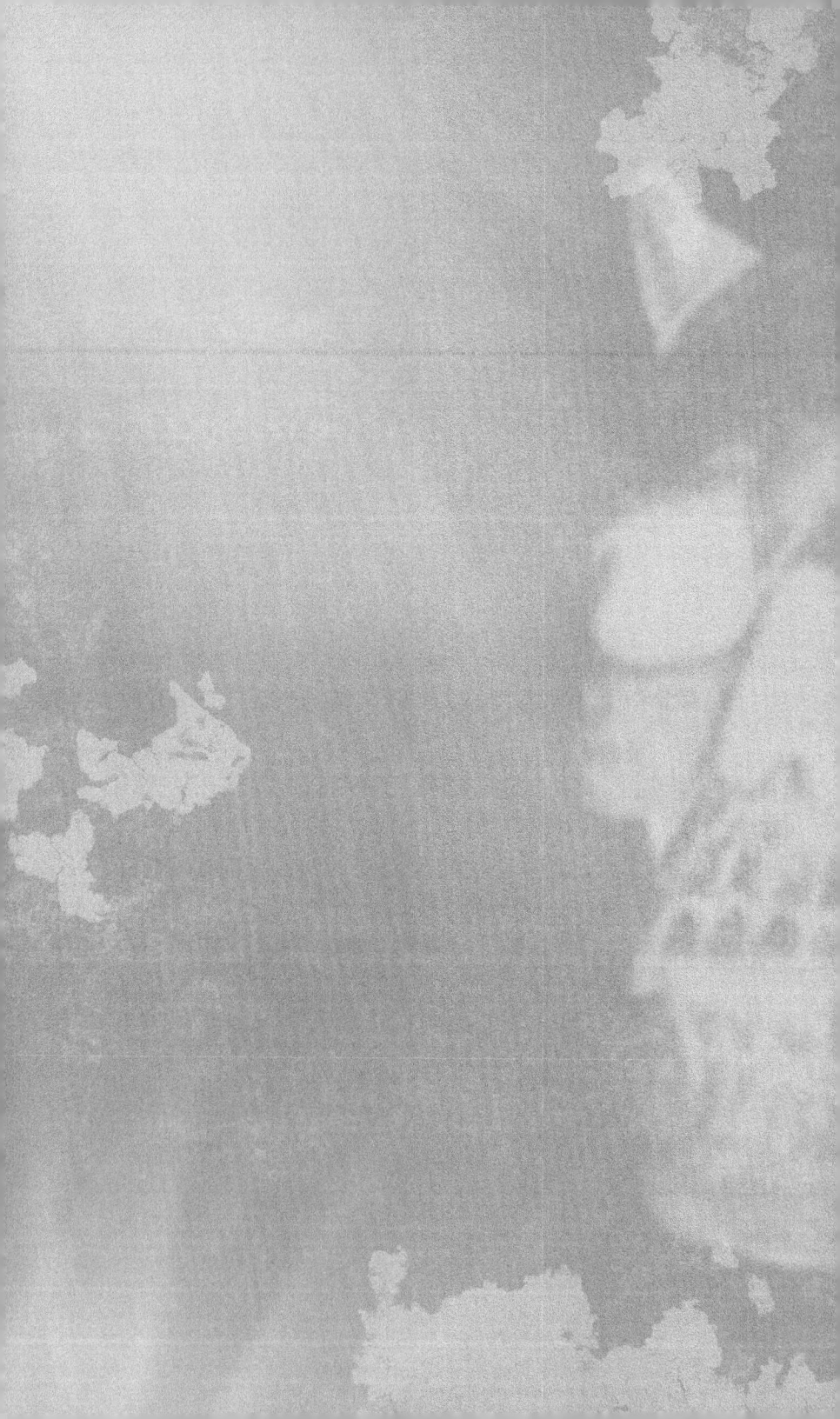

Index

8mm (1999) 248
10 Cloverfield Lane (2016) 238
28 Days Later (2002) 4, 171

A24 (studio) 6, 25, 27, 32
Abbott, Stacey 30, 125–6, 130, 138
Age of Innocence, The (1993) 135
All Girls Weekend (2016) 73
Alt-right (political movement) 225–46
Always Watching: A Marble Hornets Story (2015) 148
American History X (1998) 228
American horror 6, 22, 38, 168, 225, 227, 229, 236, 238, 241, 244
 see also USA
American Horror Story (2011–) 7
American Mary (2012) 5, 6
American Werewolf in London (1981) 65
Amsterdamned (1988) 75
…And Then I Helped (2010) 45
Andromedia (1998) 98

Annabelle (2014) 26
Annabelle: Creation (2017) 28
Antichrist (2009) 45
Apostle (2018) 7
Apt Pupil (1998) 167
Arrow Video (distributor) 7, 99, 115, 117, 119–20, 123
Art/Crime (2011) 45
As the Gods Will (2014) 98
Asia Extreme 44, 83–104, 107–23, 254
Atroz (2015) 45
Audiences
 cult 8, 25, 47, 49, 53–78, 96, 99, 100–1, 108, 111, 115, 117, 119, 121–2, 129, 135, 138, 141, 179, 217, 233
 fans 2, 6–9, 16, 27–9, 32, 33, 40, 41, 50, 58, 59, 61–5, 67, 70, 71, 73, 96, 97, 107–10, 113, 115, 118, 120, 130, 131–8, 140, 142, 154, 186, 187, 193, 230, 255, 262

general 18, 27–8, 57–9, 61–3, 73, 76, 85–8, 90, 91, 93, 96–7, 113, 121, 126–8, 130–1, 133, 135–8, 187–8, 190, 195, 196, 211–12, 230, 237, 255
horror capital 7, 9, 25–9, 37, 57–9, 61, 90, 93, 96, 99, 100, 112, 115, 120, 126, 127, 134–8, 141, 163, 177, 232, 238, 242
Audition (1999) 8, 85–7, 89, 90, 92, 96–9, 101–2, 107, 115, 119
Austin, Bruce A. 57–8, 60, 76
Auteur 2, 16, 27, 84–5, 87, 89, 92–5, 98–100, 104, 254–5, 257
Authorship 8, 85, 108, 148–51, 158, 160–2

Babadook, The (2014) 6, 20
Bad Batch, The (2016) 6
Baise-moi (2000) 254
Bates Motel (2013–17) 7
Battle Royale (2000) 107, 119
Bay, The (2012) 185
BBFC 38–9, 47, 49, 70, 116
   see also Censorship
Believer, The (2001) 228
Benshoff, Harry M. 32, 179, 207–8, 218, 220–1, 223
Beset by Demons: The Lou Perryman Story (2017) 72
Beware the Slenderman (2016) 148
Binging horror 126–7, 130–3, 137, 139–40, 142
Bird with the Crystal Plumage, The (1970) 97
Birds, The (1963) 134
Black Mirror (2011–) 7, 125–9, 132–41

Black Society, The (film trilogy) (1995–9) 99
Black Summer (2019–) 127
Blackcoat's Daughter, The (2015) 16, 20–3, 27, 30–1, 33
BlacKkKlansman (2018) 6, 239–40
Blade of the Immortal (2017) 83, 98–9
Blair Witch (2016) 25
Blair Witch Project, The (1999) 23, 25, 110, 121, 184–8, 198
Blood Creek (2009) 170
BloodRayne: The Third Reich (2011) 175, 181
Bloody Muscle Body Builder in Hell (2012) 8, 107–20
Blumhouse (studio) 6, 25, 33
Body horror 5, 8, 28–9, 36, 48, 50–5, 84, 107, 112, 122, 176, 196, 203–22, 234, 248, 255, 259
Bordwell, David 19, 30, 47
Bourdieu, Pierre 57, 232
Bradshaw, Peter 42, 87, 88, 101, 102, 262
Brain Dead (1992) 111
Bram Stoker's Dracula (1992) 16
Britain 116, 140, 228
   see also United Kingdom
Buffy the Vampire Slayer (1997–2003) 149
Bunny Games, The (2011) 38
Butcher Boys (2012) 72
Butler, Judith 207, 221

Cabin Fever (2002) 92
Cabin in the Woods, The (2012) 20
Cam (2018) 192
Candle Cove (Creepypasta story) 153–60, 162–3

Cannibal Holocaust (1980) 70, 75, 251, 259
Capitalism 9, 19, 50, 127, 162, 188, 190, 249, 250, 257, 261, 262
Captain America: The First Avenger (2011) 168
Carrie (1976) 214–16
Carroll, Noël 22, 23, 31, 169, 178, 219
Castle Rock (2018–) 7
Cat in the Brain, A (1990) 251
Cat People (1942) 16, 170
Cave, The (2005) 118
Censorship 35–41, 43–5, 47, 49, 70, 71, 94, 115, 116, 120, 121, 247, 251, 263
Chambers (2019) 127
Channel Zero (2016–18) 148, 153–5, 157–61, 163
Cherry, Brigid 169, 178, 187, 197
Childhood of a Leader, The (2015) 238
Choi, Jinhee 49, 51, 100–1, 121
Cine-Excess 2, 8, 49, 53–78
Closed Circuit Extreme (2012) 72
Clover, Carol J. 11, 195, 199, 220
Cloverfield (2008) 185–6, 188–9
Collar (2014) 45
Collingswood Story, The (2002) 185, 198
Conjuring, The (2013) 2, 26–7
Conrich, Ian 10, 30, 76, 179, 197, 220
Contracted (2013) 204, 208, 211–13, 216, 218, 219, 222
Controversy 38, 45, 47, 77, 85, 87, 88, 96, 112, 250, 255
Corrigan, Timothy 30, 93
Crash (1996) 59
Crazies, The (1973) 2
Crazies, The (2010) 2
Creed, Barbara 11, 204, 219
Creep (2014) 185

Creep 2 (2017) 185
Creepypasta 147–9, 151–4, 156, 157, 162, 163
Crimson Peak (2015) 4, 26
Criterion (distributor) 108, 117, 119, 121, 123
Cronenberg, David 59, 60, 65, 77, 99, 117, 196, 204, 207, 220, 248
Crows Zero (2007) 98
Crows Zero 2 (2009) 98
Cruelty 70, 90, 96, 174
Cult *see* Audiences
Curses 21, 24, 98, 107, 117, 147, 213, 214

Dark Water (2002) 119
Dead or Alive (film trilogy) (1999–2002) 99
Dead Snow (2009) 168, 169, 172, 177–80
Death Ship (1980) 167
Death Weekend (1976) 71
Deep Red (1975) 97, 112
Den, The (2013) 186, 192
Desktop horror 9, 183–5, 190–2, 197, 198
Devil's Rock, The (2011) 168, 170
Dew, Oliver 49, 88, 100, 102, 108, 121
Diary of the Dead (2007) 185
Digital horror 9, 11, 15, 35, 36, 39, 40, 74, 115, 118, 125, 138, 139, 141, 147–63, 183–7, 189–91, 196–8, 248
Distribution (horror) 1, 16, 24–5, 35, 36, 40–1, 49, 72, 84–5, 94, 96, 100, 108–11, 113, 115–17, 119–20, 122, 130, 138, 148–9, 152–3, 157–8, 161, 231

Distributor (horror) 7, 25, 33, 40, 43, 74, 75, 84, 85, 88, 89, 96, 98, 99, 107, 109, 110, 112, 115, 118–20, 188
Documentary 10, 45, 55, 72, 75, 100, 148, 187, 188, 191, 198, 239
Don't Breathe (2016) 21, 238
Doom (2005) 118
Dracula (novel) (1897) 206–7
Dracula (1931) 16
Driller Killer, The (1979) 112
DVD (home media) 7, 36–40, 47, 55, 59, 71, 74, 75, 95–7, 101, 103, 109–11, 113, 115, 117–23, 131, 140, 170, 186, 187, 189, 197

Eden Lake (2008) 136
Effects (1980) 248
Egan, Kate 108–10, 112, 116–17, 119, 121–3
Evil Dead (2013) 2, 5
Evil Dead, The (1981) 2, 108–13, 115
Excess 42–3, 55, 58, 60, 73, 76, 78, 101, 158, 205, 215, 217, 220, 250, 254, 257
Exorcist, The (1973) 18
Exploitation 7, 9, 48, 57, 77, 84, 89, 93, 96, 99, 115–6, 119, 136, 170, 178–9, 181, 195, 196, 203–4, 227, 238, 249, 251, 253–5, 257, 261
Extremity 8, 11, 22, 35–8, 40–7, 49–51, 53, 67, 70, 72, 85–92, 96, 97, 100–2, 107, 108, 110, 112, 113, 116, 118–21, 192, 205, 207, 210, 218, 226, 227, 231, 237, 243, 249, 251, 252, 254, 255, 261, 263

see also Hardcore horror; Torture porn
Eyes of My Mother, The (2016) 26

Faces of Snuff (2016) 39
Fandom 113, 115, 121, 130, 131, 133, 135, 136, 138, 140, 142
Fantacide (2007) 170, 177–8
Fantasy 18, 22, 24, 25, 74–7, 83, 87, 100, 127, 134, 137, 141, 150, 168, 199, 206, 209, 215, 225, 253, 258
Fascism 171, 174, 175, 227, 228, 230, 231, 233, 238, 239, 242, 243
Fear 3, 10, 19, 21–3, 28, 30, 49, 75, 130, 138, 149, 150, 153, 159, 161, 168, 171, 173, 174, 176–8, 183–5, 188, 197, 205, 210, 217, 219, 241, 244, 252
Fear the Walking Dead (2015–) 7
Featherstone, Mark 50, 250, 262
Festival (horror) 8, 25, 33, 54, 55, 58–68, 70–8, 83, 86–8, 100, 101
Fifty Shades (novels) (2011–12) 206
Final Girl (2015) 5
Final Girls, The (2015) 5, 20
Flight of the Living Dead (2007) 37
Flowers (2015) 39, 42
Fog, The (1980) 97, 112
Fog, The (2015) 118
Folk horror 9, 147–9, 151, 156, 162, 163, 250
Folklore 148, 162, 163
Follows, Stephen 4, 11
For Love's Sake (2012) 98
Foucault, Michel 216–17, 223, 234–5, 237, 243
Found footage 25, 72, 183–5, 187, 189–93, 195, 197

Frankenstein (1931) 16
Frankenstein's Army (2016) 168, 172, 176, 177
Frostbite (2006) 75, 167, 170, 175, 177
Frozen Dead, The (1966) 167

Game of Thrones (2010–19) 213
Gender 5, 11, 30, 138, 140, 199, 205–10, 212, 216, 219–21, 223, 230, 257
Genre 1–6, 8–10, 15–16, 18–29, 32–3, 36, 42–4, 46, 51, 54, 58, 60–2, 64, 70–3, 76, 78, 84, 86, 88–92, 94–5, 97–9, 102, 115, 117, 121–2, 125–6, 128–30, 133–8, 147–8, 150–1, 157, 162, 190, 203–8, 210, 219–20, 222, 237, 238, 244, 247, 251, 254–5, 261
  hybridity 32, 54, 65, 73, 75, 126, 133, 160, 172, 174–6, 178, 250
  subgenre 21, 55, 97, 111, 167–72, 174–80, 183, 185, 204, 206, 207
Gerald's Game (2017) 7
Get Out (2017) 1, 2, 6, 20, 240, 244, 261
Ghost Story, A (2017) 6, 21–2
Ghosts 4, 6, 10, 11, 21–2, 25, 31, 89, 97, 98, 112, 147, 172, 181, 222
Ginger Snaps (2000) 5, 214, 215
Girl Walks Home Alone at Night, A (2014) 4, 6
Global horror 2, 3, 5, 35, 50, 63–4, 71, 92, 94, 98, 101, 108, 128, 148, 173, 180, 242, 247, 250, 254–5, 257, 262

Godzilla (2014) 2, 4
Gore 5, 19, 26, 29, 32, 35, 39, 41, 42, 60, 87, 91, 111, 244, 247, 251
Gothic 9, 26, 32, 72, 130, 140, 147–63, 179, 220
Grant, Barry Keith 179, 219, 220, 223
Great Yokai War, The (2005) 98
Green Room (2016) 2, 9, 225–44
Grotesque (2009) 38
Grudge, The (2004) 89

Haeckel's Tale (2006) 95
Halloween (1978) 97, 195
Halloween (2018) 1, 2, 4, 5, 99
Hannibal (2013–15) 7
Hantke, Steffen 3, 10, 32, 101, 179
Happiness of the Katakuris, The (2001) 98
Happy Death Day (2017) 5, 6
Happy Death Day 2 U (2019) 5, 6
Hardcore (1979) 248
Hardcore horror 8, 10, 35–51, 226–30, 233, 238, 241–3, 248, 250
  see also Extremity; Torture porn
Hate Crime (2012) 38–9
Haunting, The (1963) 16, 23
Haunting of Hill House, The (2018–) 7, 127
Hawkins, Joan 18, 20, 26, 30, 32
Heathers (1989) 135
Hellboy (2004) 167, 170
Hemlock Grove (2013–15) 127, 138
Hereditary (2018) 2, 4, 6, 16, 21, 22, 26, 27
Hills Have Eyes, The (1977) 254
Hills, Matt 23, 28, 31, 54, 58, 59, 74, 76, 140

History of Violence, A (2005) 117–18
Hitchcock, Alfred 16, 87, 134, 193–5, 199
Hold the Dark (2018) 239
Home media 2, 3, 7, 9, 37, 41, 74, 75, 88, 96, 98, 109, 110, 113, 115, 117, 122, 127, 130–2, 194, 256 *see also* DVD (home media)
Hong Kong 3, 11, 49, 88–9, 100–1, 121, 251
Horeck, Tanya 49, 137, 139, 142, 254, 261, 263
Horrors of War (2006) 171, 174
Hostel (2005) 25, 35, 41, 44, 90–4
House of the Devil (2009) 21
Human Centipede II (Full Sequence), The (2011) 38, 44
Hunter, I. Q. 46, 102
Hutchings, Peter 115, 116, 120, 122, 169, 170, 175, 179, 180

I Am the Pretty Thing That Lives in the House (2016) 16, 20–2, 31
I Spit on Your Grave (1978) 36, 37
Ichi the Killer (2001) 85–90, 92, 96–8, 102
Identity 28, 29, 50–1, 57, 67, 129–31, 133–4, 149–50, 152, 155–6, 158, 160–1, 169–70, 174, 180, 184, 192–3, 203–7, 212, 216–19, 223, 227, 230, 235–6, 242, 247, 254, 263
Ideology 57, 171, 174, 175, 179, 207, 213, 226–8, 231–2, 234–8, 240, 243, 248, 252, 254, 256
Ilsa, She Wolf of the SS (1975) 167, 177
Imperium (2016) 228
Imprint (2006) 94–8, 103

Industry (horror) 1, 3, 4, 8, 9, 16, 38, 41, 46, 54, 58, 62, 64, 73, 74, 99, 104, 126–30, 136, 140, 148, 156, 157, 161, 177, 179, 196, 253, 256, 258
market 3, 4, 7, 8, 10, 16, 18, 24, 26, 28, 30, 35–41, 43, 46, 49, 62, 70, 71, 74, 76, 84, 86, 88–90, 93, 95, 96, 98–100, 108–13, 115–20, 131, 133, 185–8, 197, 257
Inside (2007) 5
Inside (2011) 186, 189–90
Insidious (2011) 6, 26
Invitation, The (2015) 21
Iron Wolf (2013) 168, 175, 177
Irreversible (2002) 42, 44–5
It (2017) 1, 2
It Comes at Night (2017) 6, 10, 16, 21–3, 27, 28, 31, 33
It Follows (2014) 2, 6, 16, 19–24, 28, 31, 204, 208, 211, 213, 214, 216, 218, 219, 222
Italy 40, 65, 67, 72, 75, 78, 97, 122, 195, 251

Jancovich, Mark 30, 122, 170, 179, 210, 220, 222
Japan 3, 5, 49, 55, 73, 83–6, 89, 91–3, 95–6, 98, 100–3, 107, 108, 111, 112, 117, 121, 189
Jessabelle (2014) 26
Jones, Steve 46, 51, 92, 102, 206, 220, 252, 262
Jump scares 6, 19, 21, 24, 26, 27, 32
Ju-on: The Grudge (2002) 4, 89

Keep, The (1983) 167
Kendall, Tina 49, 142, 254, 261, 263

Kermode, Mark 142, 251, 252, 262
Kill or Be Killed (2015) 72
King of the Zombies (1941) 171
Klinger, Barbara 108, 113, 115, 121, 122
Kolchak: The Night Strangler (1973) 125

Last Broadcast, The (1998) 190
Last Exorcism, The (2010) 185
Last House in the Woods, The (2006) 72
Last House on Dead End Street, The (1977) 248
Last House on the Left, The (1972) 241, 254
Lowenstein, Adam 10, 227, 241

Made in Britain (1982) 228
Mainstream horror 9, 19, 20, 25, 26, 28, 29, 35, 36, 39, 41, 42, 53–5, 57–64, 67, 71, 74, 76, 87, 91, 96, 97, 108, 128, 134–6, 138, 141, 147–9, 153, 157, 161, 162, 231, 236
Martyrs (2008) 5, 42
Maskhead (2009) 42
Masque of the Red Death, The (1964) 65
Mass media 122, 130, 134, 149, 151, 232
Masters of Horror (2005–7) 7, 94–100
Mathijs, Ernest 53, 54, 59–61, 64, 67, 72, 74, 76, 170, 179
Memory 3, 4, 21, 70, 108, 110, 115, 116, 120, 122, 137, 142, 153–5, 157, 172, 177, 178, 188, 248, 259
Midnight movies 25, 57–60, 63, 64, 74, 75, 88

Miike, Takashi 8, 83–103, 107
Misogynist (2013) 42
Mole Song: Hong Kong Capriccio, The (2016) 98
Mole Song: Undercover Agent Reiji, The (2013) 98
Monsters 4, 5, 19, 22–3, 27, 55, 115, 122, 134, 138, 150, 151, 159–61, 167, 169, 171–5, 178, 180, 189, 203–9, 211, 218–21, 223, 234, 240, 249, 254
monstrosity 5, 6, 9, 11, 15, 18, 160, 168, 172, 203–5, 207–11, 214, 215, 217–19, 223, 238, 248, 249
Moonlight (2016) 25
mother! (2017) 21, 41–2, 99
Movie Orgy, The (1968) 67
Mummy, The (2017) 4
Murder Collection V.1 (2009) 39
Murder-Set-Pieces (2004) 38
Music (general) 15, 20, 23, 30, 57, 84, 98, 139, 141, 230–2, 239, 241, 242, 250, 252, 253, 256
score 15, 18, 20, 23, 27, 193, 194, 223, 250

Nazi horror 9, 10, 167–81, 226–31, 233–7, 239–44
Neale, Steve 93, 169, 179
Needham, Gary 78, 100
Nekromantik (1987) 251
Netflix (studio/distributor) 7, 9, 125–41, 191–2, 198
Newman, Kim 237, 238, 244, 251, 262
Night of the Living Dead (1968) 111, 112, 171
Nightmare on Elm Street, A (1984) 113

Ninja Kids!!! (2011) 98
Norway 169, 249
Nostalgia 4, 8, 110, 115–17, 119, 120, 139, 147, 153–5, 162, 163, 226, 228, 253, 258
Nowell, Richard 30, 32, 104

Occult 22, 177
Oldboy (2003) 90
One Missed Call (2003) 89–90, 97–8
Open Windows (2014) 186, 192–7
Oppression 5, 28, 174, 179–80, 207–8, 210–12, 216, 218–19, 237, 248, 249, 260
Otherness 5, 24, 38, 108, 121, 203–4, 206–8, 210, 217, 223, 237–8, 250–1
Others, The (2001) 25
Outer Limits, The (1963–5) 125
Outpost (2008) 167, 169, 172–7
Overlord (2018) 9, 168, 170

Paracinema 55, 57, 61
Paranormal Activity (2007) 4, 6, 185–8, 191, 197, 198
Pariah (1998) 228
Peanuts (1996) 98
Peeping Tom (1960) 18, 248, 251, 259
Penny Dreadful (2014–16) 7
Phantasm (1979) 149
Pig Hunt (2008) 37
Politics 9, 10, 22, 43, 46, 51, 55, 57, 70, 72, 76, 92, 101, 128, 139, 141, 170–1, 177, 203–4, 208, 214, 218–20, 225–44, 248–9, 252, 257
Poor Pretty Eddie (1975) 71
Post-horror 8, 10, 16, 21, 31, 214, 222
  see also Prestige horror

Post-modern 126–30, 137, 139, 203, 214
Power 4, 9, 25, 33, 99–100, 116, 131–3, 150, 156, 172, 188, 193, 205–11, 214, 216, 218–19, 227–31, 233–5, 237, 239, 241–4, 252, 256–7, 260
Prestige horror 8, 16, 18–21, 23–33, 116
  see also Post-horror
Prison of Hell: K3 (2009) 39
Profile (2018) 186, 192
Promotion 3, 25, 36, 40, 54, 58–61, 67, 72–6, 83, 88, 89, 93, 96, 98, 100, 107–11, 113, 115–17, 119, 120, 126, 131, 137–8, 140, 209, 212, 222, 229, 231–3, 239–40, 255
Psycho (1960) 16
Punk 55, 63, 226–44
Purge, The (2013) 6
Purge: Election Year, The (2016) 238

Quiet Place in the Country, A (1968) 67

Rabid (1977) 196
Racism 20, 71, 176, 179, 184, 220, 225–31, 233, 234, 238–43, 249, 258, 261
Raiders of the Lost Ark (1981) 168
Rain, The (2018–) 127
Ratline (2011) 168
Ratter (2015) 185
Raw (2016) 2, 6, 9, 214–19
Rawle, Steven 86, 89, 100–2
Reality Bites (2004) 135
Re-Animator (1985) xii, 65
Rear Window (1954) 193
[Rec] (2007) 185

Reception (horror) 1, 8–10, 18, 27, 29–30, 32, 58, 65, 75, 76, 84–6, 88, 90, 93–5, 99, 100, 108–11, 113, 120–2, 130, 168, 210–13, 222, 247, 255, 263
Red Eye (2005) 118
Reddit 28, 33, 132, 137, 152, 155–6, 163, 209
Revenge 71, 87, 167, 176, 178, 209, 212, 213, 222, 238
Revenge of the Zombies (1943) 167, 176, 178
Ring, The (2002) 89
Ringu (1998) 4, 89, 102, 107, 110, 121
Rocky Horror Picture Show, The (1975) 57–8
Romper Stomper (1992) 228
Rope (1948) 193
Rosemary's Baby (1968) 16
Roth, Eli 25, 35, 43, 90–4
Russia 88 (2009) 228

Safe (1995) 20
Salaryman Kintaro (1999) 97–8
Salò, or the 120 Days of Sodom (1975) 43, 251
Saw (2004) 2, 4, 25–6, 35
Saw II (2005) 118
Saw III (2006) 37
Saw VI (2009) 47
Schneider, Steven Jay 3, 11, 31, 122
Science 20, 22, 83, 133, 134, 168, 175–7, 181
scientist 134, 167, 174–6, 178, 181
Sconce, Jeffrey 19, 31, 55, 57, 59–61, 76
Scream (1996) 5, 20, 25
Scream Queens (2015–16) 5

Searching (2018) 186, 190, 192
Sensoria (2015) 75
Serbia 249, 250, 252, 255, 262, 263
Serbian Film, A (2010) 10, 35, 42, 44, 45, 50, 70, 247–63
Sex 5, 7, 9, 22, 30, 38, 39, 46, 48, 49–51, 63, 70, 75, 87, 91, 111, 175, 179, 181, 196, 199, 203–23, 249–60
sexual violence 42, 48, 51, 71, 95, 207, 210–13, 222, 252–3, 257, 258
Sexton, Jamie 24, 32, 53–4, 59–61, 64, 67, 72, 74, 76, 108, 121, 170, 179
Shangri-la (2002) 98
Shape of Water, The (2018) 6
Shaviro, Steven 183–4, 190–1, 193, 197, 208–9, 221
Shin, Chi-Yun 49, 100, 108, 121
Shining, The (1980) 16
Shivers (1974) 65
Shock Waves (1977) 167, 170, 171
Sickhouse (2016) 186, 192
Silence of the Lambs, The (1991) 16
Sinister (2012) 6, 26
Sixth Sense, The (1999) 16
Skinheads: The Second Coming of Hate (1989) 228
Slasher 5, 25, 72, 97, 127, 129, 195, 214
Slender Man (2018) 148
Slender Man (Creepypasta story) 148–53, 156, 160, 162
Slow Torture Puke Chamber (2010) 42
Snuff 10, 39, 248–63
Sobchack, Vivian 44, 220
Social media 40, 147, 186, 188, 189, 197

Sontag, Susan 44
Sound 15, 23, 30, 111, 160, 184, 193, 242, 252
Special Effects (1984) 248
Spiral Staircase, The (1946) 16
Stardom (horror) 5, 16, 67, 93–5, 103, 117, 135, 141, 190, 193, 196, 248, 249, 256
Strain, The (2014–17) 7
Stranger Things (2016–) 7, 125–42
Subculture 5, 7, 9, 28, 29, 50, 54, 55, 57–9, 62, 72–3, 76, 116, 118, 120, 126, 134–8, 141, 216–17, 227–8, 230–4, 237–9, 241–3
Supernatural (2005–20) 7
Supernatural horror 19, 21–3, 25, 26, 28, 75, 150, 157, 159, 169, 172, 173, 191, 214, 215
Survival 21, 23, 24, 192, 222, 234, 236, 237
Suspiria (1977) 2, 56, 65, 75, 97
Suspiria (2018) 2, 7, 99

Tarantino, Quentin 91–3
Tartan (distributor) 49, 87, 100, 107–8, 110, 113, 115, 119, 121
Taste cultures 1, 3, 16, 18–19, 42–3, 46–7, 55, 57, 59, 73, 76–7, 87, 92, 119–20, 122, 130, 133, 137, 140, 177, 212, 214, 232, 242
Tax Shelter Terrors (2016) 75
Technology 9, 39, 47, 73, 74, 89, 98, 122, 128, 129, 138, 139, 147, 150, 154, 155, 157, 158, 161, 176, 181, 183, 184, 190, 191, 193, 195, 248, 258
Teeth (2007) 5, 9, 204, 208–19
Television 6, 7, 30, 47, 50, 94–100, 103, 108, 122, 125–42, 147, 148, 153–60, 180, 195, 221, 253, 257
Terminator 2: Judgement Day (1991) 5
Terra Formars (2016) 98
Terracotta (distributor) 107–22
Texas Chain Saw Massacre, The (1974) 72, 249, 254
That's La Morte: Italian Cult Cinema and the Years of Lead (2018) 75
Thing, The (1982) 97, 118, 134
This is England (2008) 228
Thornton, Sarah 134, 141, 232, 242
Three (2017) 73
Three... Extremes (2004) 89
Tokyo Gore Police (2008) 5
Tompkins, Joe 99, 104, 136, 141
Torture 46, 86, 91, 92, 95, 96, 98, 167, 172, 183, 203, 220, 238, 257, 259
Torture porn 25, 26, 42, 46, 48, 49, 91, 92, 102, 183, 206, 220, 251, 254, 262
see also Extremity; Hardcore horror
Train to Busan (2016) 4
Transmedia 9, 139, 184–9, 192
Transnational horror 3, 11, 49, 54, 61, 74, 75, 92, 102, 108, 121, 126, 129, 133, 138, 261
Trash 55, 57, 72, 76, 109, 112, 121, 251, 254
Trauma 3, 4, 9–10, 22, 89, 150, 203–5, 208, 211, 213–14, 216–19, 227, 241, 255
True Blood (2008–14) 7, 125, 206
Trump, Donald 209, 225–7, 230, 237–9, 241, 243, 244
Tulpa (2013) 72
Twilight (novels) (2005–8) 206

Twilight (2008) 4
Twilight Zone, The (1959–64) 125, 129, 139

Uncanny 22, 94, 136, 138, 147, 150, 151, 154–6, 160–2
Under the Shadow (2016) 22
Under the Skin (2013) 20, 22
Unfriended (2014) 186, 192
Unfriended: Dark Web (2018) 186, 192
Unholy (2007) 167
United Kingdom 7, 11, 35, 36, 37, 38, 49, 51, 54, 64, 65, 70, 71, 72, 73, 75, 87, 88, 92, 102, 107, 108, 109, 110, 111, 113, 115, 118, 119, 120, 121, 126, 130, 131, 228, 262, 263
see also Britain
USA 7, 61, 108, 118, 122, 225, 230
see also American horror

Vampires 4, 60, 75, 149, 174, 175, 180, 206, 207
VHS (home media) 8, 10, 11, 39, 108–23
see also Home media
V/H/S (2012) 118, 185–6, 191
V/H/S 2 (2013) 118
Video games 151, 168, 187, 194, 195, 197, 199
Videodrome (1983) 248
Violence 10, 19, 26, 38–9, 42, 45–6, 49, 50, 62, 70, 85–8, 90–3, 96, 98, 101, 112, 116–18, 128, 160, 168, 173, 195, 203, 205–7, 209–12, 215, 218–19, 225–9, 231–44, 248–55, 260, 262
Viva (2007) 75
Walking Dead, The (2010–) 7

War of the Dead (2011) 173, 175
Webcam 185, 189, 190, 195, 198
Werewolves 5, 65, 174–5, 205–6, 220
Wes Craven's New Nightmare (1994) 20
What We Do in the Shadows (2014) 4
White Zombie (1932) 171
Wildman of the Navidad, The (2008) 72
Williams, Linda 44, 205, 220
Williams, Tony 3, 11, 122, 253–4, 262
Window 184, 192, 193–7, 199
Witch, The (2015) 2, 6, 15–16, 19, 20–5, 27–8, 31, 33
Witches 22, 24, 27, 187
Witchfinder General (1968) 67
Wolf Man, The (1941) 174–5
Wolfman, The (2010) 4
Woman in Black 2: Angel of Death, The (2014) 26
Women's Flesh: My Red Guts (1999) 39
Women's horror 5, 6, 9, 16, 20, 22, 30, 73, 88, 98, 203–19, 236, 252, 256, 258–9
World horror *see* Global horror
World War Z (2013) 2, 4

X-Files, The (1993–2002) 125

Yatterman (2009) 98

Zebraman (2004) 98
Zebraman 2: Attack on Zebra City (2010) 98
Zombi 2 (1979) 111
Zombie Lake (1981) 167
Zombies 4, 112, 167–81

also in series

Sandra Becker, Megen de Bruin-Molé and Sara Polak (eds), *Embodying Contagion: The Viropolitics of Horror and Desire in Contemporary Discourse* (2021)

Lindsey Decker, *Transnationalism and Genre Hybridity in New British Horror Cinema* (2021)

Stacey Abbott and Lorna Jowett (eds), *Global TV Horror* (2021)

Michael J. Blouin, *Stephen King and American Politics* (2021)

Eddie Falvey, Joe Hickinbottom and Jonathan Wroot (eds), *New Blood: Critical Approaches to Contemporary Horror* (2020)

Darren Elliott-Smith and John Edgar Browning (eds), *New Queer Horror Film and Television* (2020)

Jonathan Newell, *A Century of Weird Fiction, 1832–1937: Disgust, Metaphysics and the Aesthetics of Cosmic Horror* (2020)

Alexandra Heller-Nicholas, *Masks in Horror Cinema: Eyes Without Faces* (2019)

Eleanor Beal and Jonathan Greenaway (eds), *Horror and Religion: New Literary Approaches to Theology, Race and Sexuality* (2019)

Dawn Stobbart, *Videogames and Horror: From Amnesia to Zombies, Run!* (2019)

David Annwn Jones, *Re-envisaging the First Age of Cinematic Horror, 1896–1934: Quanta of Fear* (2018)